Twice Upon a Time

LALI SERNA CASTILLO

Christel,
our memories are one
of God's greatest gifts. May
you be blessed with many.
Always,
Lali

Printed in the United States of America
First Printing, December 2017

ISBN-13: 978-1981226726

This is a work of fiction. Names, characters, businesses,
places, events and incidents are either the products of the
author's imagination or used in a fictitious manner. Any
resemblance to actual persons, living or dead, or actual
events is purely coincidental.

Cover design by SelfPubBookCovers.com/ FrinaArt
Editing by Lisa Marie Curtner
Author's photograph by Adrian Castillo

DEDICATIONS

For my mom.
She was more than my moral compass. Even now she's my true north.

For my dad.
He was my Jiminy Cricket. Every moment was a teaching moment.

For Ed and our entire family - Lisa, Leanne, Adrian, Jay Daniel, Ryan, Jacob, Josh and Jay Daniel Jr. They are my greatest blessings from God.

ACKNOWLEDGEMENTS

Armando Weaver, Adrienne Simoneaux Merrell, Robert Garza, Maria Mooney, Lucy Jimenez Elizarde, and Ramona Diaz. I am grateful to each of you for reading my manuscript and providing your feedback which kept me going; Stefne Miller, for the valuable lessons; Greg Jordan, for your invitation to do a book signing while this book was still just a manuscript; Lisa Curtner, for making the time to help me when I needed it most; Leanne Mazoch, for the unlimited use of your beach house. It was my favorite place to write; Adrian Castillo, my muse until the very end.

1

1971 – Gabriel Marquez

Some people drink for refreshment. Others drink for courage. Right now, I need both. When I see Ella walk in from the kitchen, I take a long sip of my rum and Coke keeping my gaze on her. She pauses and leans against the doorframe twirling her wedding rings and biting down on the corner of her lip. Those are definite clues my baby's preoccupied. Probably still mulling over the surprise I planned for our anniversary, so my guess is she's still antsy about it.

I had everything all laid out for a lake house getaway, down to the details, when I hit a bump in the road. Ella said *no.* I'd rather not get into one of our *discussions,* but I need to change her mind. This may be my last chance.

Come on courage.

What I'd rather do right now, is take her in my arms and hold that beautiful body right up against mine before taking off to join our old friend, Anthony Bartelli, for dinner. Ella looks amazing in her white short shorts with that sun-kissed tan. She wears her shoulder-length hair parted on the left, just as she did in high school and has the same coquettish way of dealing with her hair when it falls along the right side of her face. A toss of her head bounces it back into place, or she brushes it away with her fingers and a sensual tilt of her head.

Stay focused, Marquez, last chance here. Go on, say it.

"Hey baby, I told Dad I was driving into Houston to have dinner with Anthony this evening. Dad suggested I drop by after dinner and maybe stay the night with him and Mom."

"Your mom would be thrilled. Do it, Gabe."

"Figured you'd agree, so I packed a change of clothes. Umm...Dad also said I can get the keys to the lake house while I'm there...*if* we're still interested."

"Oh gosh, babe," Ella says, twirling her rings. "I just don't know. I guess I'm still nervous about this place. There's something eerie about a cabin hidden deep in the woods, you know? Especially one that does vanishing acts with little children."

"Come *on*, Ella. It happened over a year ago. When I talked to Dad this morning, he mentioned the caretaker who goes to the lake house twice a month said there's been no one lurking around the whole time he's been taking care of the place. Hasn't seen a soul."

She rests her hands on her hips and nibbles on her lower lip as I explain once more.

"Consider this, Ella. The girls could've wandered off on their own and were abducted somewhere down the road. Nobody knows what happened; it's all mere speculation."

I know what she needs. A smile tugs at her lips as I walk over to her. She knows I'm about to put my arms around her, I can see it in her face. Hand-holding and hugs always make Ella feel better. She thrives on both.

"Ella, we need this," I say, wrapping my arms around her. She lays her head on my chest, and I hold her for a moment breathing in the sweet blend of her shampoo and wild musk perfume. "Please say *yes,* baby."

Ella pulls away as she runs her hands through her hair taking a deep breath and exhaling a soft audible sigh.

"Well?" I look at her, my eyes wide pleading for a *yes.*

Her eyes hold my gaze as she moistens her lips. "You honestly believe a week at this mysterious lake house will do it." She lifts her brows at me, nodding her head as if in agreement. Little nods, but still a good sign. Presented with the facts Ella can be pretty reasonable...usually. I hope the facts are sinking in and leaning in my favor.

"I do. There's nothing wrong with the cabin. Two kids wandered off. That's all. Plus, it happened over a year ago."

She hangs her head with a sigh. "I know I've been such a baby. You do make a lot of sense. No one knows the circumstances of what happened."

I smile, relieved she's giving our getaway a chance.

"Besides," I say, "we'll only be there for a week. What could possibly happen in seven days?"

Ella wraps her arms around me and gives me a kiss, pulling gently on my lower lip. She smiles as she traces her fingertip across my mouth. "We are sooo hot together, aren't we?"

I give her a couple of eyebrow raises. I get a mischievous grin.

"Yeah, you know we are. Come on baby, let's do it." I take her hands in mine. "Imagine this, you and me alone for a whole week. It can't get any hotter than that."

I place my arms around her waist and pull her toward me for an embrace. I love how she's able to totally melt herself into me at every point our bodies meet. It feels like heaven holding her this way.

I lift a few strands of hair away from her forehead and kiss her there. "I'll stay the night with my folks, spend time with Mom and get the keys to the lake house."

"Gabriel, you *always* know what's best for us."

I pull back, take in those beautiful dark brown eyes. "So…it's a yes?"

Her eyes are on mine for a long moment, and then she nods. "Okay, let's do it."

I cup her face in my hands. "I promise you won't regret it. We're going to love this place. It will be magical."

The cabin my parents purchased earlier this year is tucked away on forty acres of wooded land in Northeast Texas. It came with a lake, so they call it the lake house. Dad said there's a small boat, fishing rods and plenty of fish. A couple of creepy stories are also attached to it. Well, one of them is creepy, the other one is just plain mysterious.

About a year ago, four-year-old twin girls disappeared in broad daylight while playing in a shed which sits a few yards away from the main house. Those poor little girls are still missing.

Then there's the creepy. The house, which is a converted log cabin church, was built in the early 1800s by a community of settlers. Historical documents state an entire village inhabited the forty acres and the area surrounding it, noting there were actual hangings from large trees on the land adjoining the church. My parents love their new place and aren't bothered by its history at all. Mom says it's a piece of heaven. Since the closest neighbor is over four miles away, Dad thinks it's the most peaceful place ever.

When they first told me about it, I made plans for Ella and me to spend a week at the cabin to celebrate our first wedding anniversary. I knew we needed this getaway. I thought our marriage needed it too. However, when I told Ella about the plans I'd made, she wanted no part of it. So this morning when I woke up I decided I would give it one last try. If it doesn't work, I'm ready to throw in the towel – on the lake house, not the marriage. No, I'll never give up on Ella. That girl is peaches and cream, sugar and spice and *salsa*, lots of fiery *salsa*.

"Are you sure you don't want to come along for the ride? Listen to good music, talk about the old days? I know how much you love to reminisce. Plus you can sit real close, and I can reach over and—"

She laughs. "Why you little tease. Tell me you haven't forgotten about my meeting with the benefactor's assistant."

"No, I haven't. I guess that's important."

"You bet it is. That's one hefty grant."

Yes, it's a biggie. It allows Ella to offer free ballet lessons to underprivileged children. This benefactor's gift was a big surprise. Ella couldn't believe it, insisted there must be a mistake. It's an amazing gift. The children selected will get their tuition paid for as well as leotards, shoes, and recital costumes.

"Oh, I forgot to tell you. I found the perfect instructor for those extra classes." She takes a piece of paper off the dining room table and hands it to me. "Here's her resumé."

I glance over it. "For the Saturday morning classes?"

"Uh-huh."

"Great." I hand it back. "Looks good."

"I was afraid I'd have to teach the classes myself. Didn't want to cut into our weekends. I know how much you enjoy our impromptu outings."

"Hey, I would've understood, you've got a dance school to run. Besides, it's temporary."

"Temporary?" She places the resumé on the table. "It's for five years."

There's a hint of irritation in her voice. I know I'm going to hear it, *I half-listen to anything she says.*

"Five years is hardly temporary, and I wish he didn't want to remain anonymous. I'd love to thank him personally."

"If it is a *he*," I say. "Possibly a *she* or even a company. But I thought it was for one year."

"You see there, you always half-listen, and it's a guy, I'm sure of it. Mrs. Hernandez referred to him as *he* at least three times when we spoke. Regardless of who it is, I'm thankful he chose my dance studio to rain his blessings on." A smug smile appears on her face.

"My question is, why did he pick *your* studio? Why you? There are plenty of bigger, more established studios than yours."

She stuffs the resumé into her briefcase. Her frown tells me she's not at all happy with my observation.

"Now don't give me that look, baby. Your school merits this generous donation. We know it does, but how would this person know? Aren't you a little bit curious, Ella?"

"Yes, I am. Flat out asked for a name, but Mrs. Hernandez said the benefactor wants to remain anonymous. It's kinda strange."

Kinda? Try very strange.

A little over a year ago Ella and I moved to Clear Lake, a planned community southeast of Houston in the Bay Area after I graduated from college and landed my first job. Once we settled in, Dad gave us a start-up loan, so Ella could open a dance studio. I was engrossed in my new career which turned out to be demanding, and Ella immersed herself into learning the ins and outs of running a business and a dance studio which was a success right from the start. It was perfect timing when the tenant next door to her vacated. She negotiated with the building owner and was able to expand.

I'm proud of her accomplishments and how she single-handedly achieved them. But compared to the more established studios in the Houston area, hers is small and has been in operation less than a year. I would like to know what made this benefactor select Ella's dance studio. There must've been a criteria, but what was it?

"Okay, so you can't come along. But I want you to know it wasn't a tease. Checked you out in your snug little shorts and the thought just popped into my head." I give her the smile I know she loves.

She kisses my cheek. "No surprise there. But forget it lover boy, your adorable smirk isn't going to change my mind." She takes the glass I left on the coffee table and heads to the kitchen.

"I figured...just thought I'd give it a try," I say, raising my voice to make sure she can hear me.

She returns to the living room smiling. "I would've been disappointed if you hadn't. I do wish I could come along to visit with everyone and for the, *you know,*" she says with a wink.

I smile, move in close, and we share one long passionate kiss. Ella's hands roam to where they shouldn't. Well, not now. Not when I'm about to leave and not when it's daylight.

I pull away and smile. "*Now* who's being a tease?"

"I know, I'm as bad as you are."

Yes, Ella's as bad and quickly gets caught up in the feeling. I would love to let her continue with those wandering hands of hers. I want to. I would enjoy a bit of grabbing myself. But I can't. Ella's got a few sexual issues. She wants it, she needs it, but making love in daylight is risky. When we least expect it, a memory from her past kicks in and can take her from pleasure to mental anguish and sometimes physical pain in a matter of minutes. The past still torments my baby, and the horrible memories can surface without any warning. So to avoid putting her through unnecessary trauma, I need to have self-control. It's hard, but I do it for Ella, I do it for us.

I stroke my thumb along her cheek. "Baby, I hate to stop, but I've gotta go, Anthony will be waiting. How about we pick up where we've left off when we get to the cabin?"

"Promise?"

I kiss her forehead. "Promise."

She takes my hand, walks me to the door. "Give my love to Anthony and your folks."

As I walk toward the car, I look over my shoulder and see Ella standing there with her hands shoved deep into the pockets of her shorts. A gentle breeze plays with strands of her long brown hair, while rays of sunshine send streaks of auburn through it. She smiles when our eyes meet. I kiss my fingertips and wave. She tries to yank a hand out, but it's stuck in her pocket against her tight shorts. She struggles, laughs, tugs again and finally, manages to pull her hand out with one last jerk. She kisses her fingertips and sends the kiss to me with a wave and a giggle. *God, I love that girl.*

2

1971 – Ella Marquez

The first thing I notice about Mrs. Hernandez is the way her eyes crinkle when she smiles. I sense so much kindness in them. Her demeanor is professional, but there's softness in her expression. I'll bet she's much warmer and more cordial than her navy-blue suit and white starched blouse portray her to be. The brooch pinned to her lapel catches my attention. I glance at it long enough to notice it's an incredible piece of jewelry. I'm guessing the smaller dark blue stones are sapphires. But the larger ones, those are definitely diamonds. I know rhinestones, and those are *not* rhinestones.

"May I offer you something to drink? Iced tea or water?"

"No, thank you, dear, we'll be done here in no time."

Once we're seated at the table, she removes a manila folder from her briefcase. "There are a few initials and signatures which are required," she says as she takes several sheets of paper from the folder.

To my surprise, the requirements and the verbiage are simple and straightforward. No legal mumbo jumbo anywhere. What touches me are the benefactor's words in a letter addressed to me. I smile as I read it. He states his goal is to help introduce the beauty and benefits of ballet to children. He hopes it will also improve communication and social skills in children who are shy, withdrawn, or find it difficult to socialize with others. He requests I give them special consideration in the selection process. Interestingly, this was the same reason my parents introduced me to ballet. I was shy and withdrawn. Although I'm touched by his kindness, there's still the unsettling question.

Why did he select my dance studio?

I consider asking Mrs. Hernandez if I'll ever be given the benefactor's name but decide I might appear suspicious of his motives, which I am, and unappreciative. *Don't look a gift-horse in the mouth, Ella.*

Fifteen minutes later we are done. Mrs. Hernandez places the paperwork in her briefcase and hands me a copy. She shakes my hand with both of hers, patting the top of my right hand with her left. This handshake is friendlier than the one I got when we first said hello. She looks at me, and her expression radiates warmth. I return her smile.

As I walk Mrs. Hernandez toward the door, I turn and look at her. "It would be wonderful to meet this kind benefactor someday."

She nods and smiles. "Have a good evening, Mrs. Marquez."

Guess that's a no. "Thanks, you too."

I look at her one last time, my heart filled with emotion. "Would you please extend my gratitude to our kind benefactor? Let him know I am touched by his generosity."

Her eyes look misty. Maybe she's as moved by his kindness as I am. She nods and walks away.

Back inside I slide the chain into the door guard. As I put away the paperwork Mrs. Hernandez gave me, I recall Gabe's questions earlier about who the benefactor might be. I wanted to discuss my concerns with him but didn't want to worry him. Who knows, he may just say I'm paranoid. I've been stalked once before, and it turned out badly. So he'd be right, I *am* paranoid. I'll mention it later when we return. Don't want Gabe focusing on this while we're at the lake house.

Holy cow! The realization that we're going to the lake house kicks in. I told Gabe we could spend a whole week at this creepy cabin, which I instantly regretted. It made him so happy. I didn't have it in my heart to take it back. *What was I thinking?* I know exactly what I was thinking. We need this, and I'll pretty much do anything to make *us* work, even if it means staying at this freaky little place in the woods. Not sure what worries me more, the missing children or knowing once upon a time thieves and murderers hung from nearby trees by a noose as punishment. *Horrors!* I know, it's silly of me, it was ages ago. Besides, we'll only be there for a week.

What could possibly happen in seven days?

I check my watch realizing Nancy will be here any minute. I put away the paperwork I was given and make a quick bathroom visit. While changing back into the shorts I was wearing earlier, I hear several knocks. That's got to be Nancy. I zip and snap as I hurry through the living room and open the door as far as the chain allows and peer out.

"Hey, you," I say then quickly close the door to undo the chain.

"You are so paranoid," she yells through the closed door.

"You never know if it's the boogieman," I say, waving her in.

She walks in fanning her face. "It's hotter 'n hell out there!"

Nancy lives at the far end of our large apartment complex. In this heat, a short walk can leave one drenched. The perspiration on her skin glistens, and her cheeks are blushed. She spends a lot of time poolside so her summer tan rivals mine. Nancy's a cute, perky brunette, with dark brown eyes. For a petite girl, she is well-endowed; she looks like Gidget with a cleavage.

"A glass of ice cold lemonade will cool you off. With or without rum?"

She laughs. "Like you have to ask?"

"Rum it is."

She tosses her purse on the sofa and follows me into the kitchen pausing when she notices a picture of Gabe and me. We're on a sailboat, the Golden Gate Bridge and a magnificent sunset in the background. She takes it off the shelf. "Fabulous picture. Honeymoon? Don't recall seeing it before."

"Yes, it was. We loved San Francisco. Since tomorrow's our anniversary, I thought we'd enjoy a visual memory, so I took it from our album and stuck it in a frame a week ago. Come to think of it, I don't think Gabe noticed it."

"What a lovely memory," she says, placing it on the shelf. "Men aren't as perceptive as we are. The sooner you accept this fact, the happier your marriage will be."

"Great, I already know Gabe catches only half of what I say."

"Same thing with Carl. They're guys, darlin', get over it."

Although Carl and Nancy graduated from the same high school as Gabe and I, we didn't meet until about six months ago while playing tennis at the courts in our complex. That's when we found out they graduated four years before Gabe and I did and had lived in

Brownsville all their lives. We hit it off immediately and consider them good friends.

Nancy leans against the counter and watches as I pull out a couple of tall glasses and a bottle of rum from the cabinet. "How'd your meeting go?"

"Great. It's all set, and we're ready to rock-n-roll."

"Did you find out the benefactor's name?"

"Nope, and I probably never will. Maybe he doesn't want others calling on him for donations." I take ice cubes from the freezer, the pitcher of lemonade from the fridge and kick the door closed with my foot. "I don't think I've told you we're going away for the week. It's an anniversary celebration," I say as I add the rum.

"Fantastic. Where?" Nancy takes a lemon from a bowl I have sitting on the counter, breathes in its fragrance then puts it back.

"A lakeside cabin somewhere in Northeast Texas. Gabe's parents recently purchased it and thought we would enjoy the outing." I decide not to mention the lake house mysteries. Afraid it wouldn't take much for her to change my mind about going. I'm actually still arguing with myself about it. So not saying a word.

I take our extra door key from a drawer. "I'd like to leave you a key to our apartment in case there's an emergency." I hold it up in front of her.

"Sure," she says, taking it from me. She holds the key chain tag in her hand to read it. "*Brownsville, Texas - On the Border, By the Sea.*"

"Yep, that's our hometown," I say.

Nancy fills the glasses I've set out with ice. It crackles as I fill them to the brim with our spiked lemonade. I hand her one. "Let's go sit in the living room."

I close the mesh curtains to cut the glare coming in through the sliding glass door. As I do, I notice several teenagers frolicking in the pool below, having fun and enjoying life without a care in the world. I remember that feeling well. I sigh thinking how life can take a turn in a matter of seconds.

We get comfortable on the cushioned rattan furniture, but then Nancy notices a magazine I have on the coffee table. She leans over to pick it up. It's a 1964 issue of *The Saturday Evening Post* featuring The Beatles.

She takes a sip of her drink. "Mmm, delicious, so fresh. I love the lemony fragrance." She squints as she reads the date on the magazine. "Nineteen sixty-four? Wow, this is a keeper."

"I bought it at a resale shop a few weeks ago."

"John was my favorite Beatle," she says all dreamy. "Who was yours?"

"Paul, the cute one. His adorable face still gives me a twinge," I say with a giggle. I kick off my sandals and sit cross-legged in my chair.

"Wow, look at these pictures, seven years ago. I've never seen them in concert, did you?"

"Nope. A friend saw them when they came to Houston. I was glad her favorite was Ringo. Figured she'd be staring at him and not my Paul."

"Funny how tastes differ, my sister adored George."

"I know! I've never been able to understand how my friends could love anyone other than Paul. Who can look past that face?" I ask with a shake of my head.

"Goes to show you, there's no accountin' for taste, Ella."

I take a long sip of my drink while Nancy flips through the magazine. I think her smile is there to stay.

"Geez, seems like forever-ago," I say. "Back then all I ever wanted was to get married and live happily ever after." I take another long sip. "I was sixteen. Hadn't started dating yet. Then came Michael Damon, my first boyfriend, my first kiss. Stupid jerk cheated on me."

Her eyebrows arch. "Caught him in the act?"

"I wish! I found out after the fact. But listen to this, the night it happened I almost caught him. Do you remember The Drive Inn, the upscale restaurant across the border?"

"Yes," she says, "it was so elegant with a big brass dance band and a dance floor."

"Yes, that's the one. We only went there on special occasions. One evening Dad took us there for dinner to celebrate the completion of a big project. Would you believe it's the same one Michael took this girl to? We were there having dinner at the exact same time."

"Expensive for teenagers, huh?"

"No kidding. Bridget had a reputation for putting out. I'm sure Michael was counting on getting a return on his investment." I laugh.

Nancy puts the magazine on the table, takes a cigarette and a lighter from her purse. She stretches her legs out and props her feet on the coffee table.

"Wait a second." Nancy scrunches her brow, tilts her head looking at me all puzzled. "I thought you said you *didn't* catch him in the—"

"I didn't. Never saw them."

"How's that? You were there at the same time as they were, right?" I nod. "Right."

She lights her cigarette, inhales until the tip turns a bright orange then leans her head back and exhales a cloud of smoke that begins to settle and invade my space. "How'd you miss seeing them?"

"We sat at the back of the restaurant. Dad likes to sit away from all the activity, you know, waiters zipping by and couples weaving their way to and from the dance floor. Months later I was told Michael and his date sat in a cozy candle lit area on the other side. There was no way I could've spotted them from where we were sitting."

"Wow, that's crazy." Nancy places her feet on the floor, reaches for the ashtray, flicks the cigarette and ashes fall off the end.

"The funny thing is, I almost asked my dad if we could sit near the dance floor. If I had only sat by the dance floor, I would've seen him."

"No shit! You would have caught him."

"Uh-huh."

"So you found out via the grapevine?"

"Yeah. Just as well, not sure how I would've reacted if I'd caught Michael cheating on me. Who knows, though, by then I already knew it wasn't working out for us. All Michael wanted was sex. I knew the last thing I wanted was to lose *it* to someone who wanted to make love for the *sex* of it."

"So," she says with a shrug, "why not dump him?"

I wince. "I didn't want to be alone. Plus, there was the prom, had to have a date."

Close my eyes for a moment thinking how stupid and insecure I must sound then look at her, brows arched. "Kinda pathetic, huh?" I ask with no amusement in my laugh. "It always bothered me that I felt so needy I would actually hold on to someone who I no longer cared to be with just so that I'd have a date for the prom. Well, not like I did when we first met. Back then he was sweet, wasn't a jerk and smelled like soap and not cigarettes, no offense."

She waves off my comment with a flip of her hand. "None taken. Hey, as for hanging on till a better guy comes along, I've heard girls say it many times." She holds her hand over the ashtray and flicks her cigarette.

"Damn, when you put it that way, I feel worse. Thanks a bunch."

"Don't be silly, Ella, it happens all the time. Girls hang on for the wrong reasons. We'll never dump a guy around prom time. Like you just said, a girl's gotta have a date."

"You make a good point there," I say, a little relieved that I'm not the only pathetic one.

Nancy smiles when she notices mine. "What? What's that smile about?"

"Gabriel Marquez," I say. "Although I was with Michael, I had Gabe on my cute-guy radar. He didn't have a clue who I was, well, that's what I thought at the time. Yet when Michael cheated on me, I was furious. I should have dumped him before he had a chance to pull it off. Does that make sense?"

Nancy takes a long puff of her cigarette then presses it into the ashtray to extinguish it, exhaling the last cloud of smoke I'll have to endure.

"Oh yeah, you're not gonna leave me, I'm gonna leave *you*," she responds.

"Exactly! I was furious at the time, so I don't know why it hurt so much." As I twirl the ice in my drink, I realize I've pretty much guzzled it down.

"It sucks, huh?"

"Yeah, but then one day I finally met Gabe. He was my happy ending. He was so handsome, and I was crazy about his smile."

Nancy nods her head. "You hooked yourself a good one, Ella."

"I sure did. Gabe was different than most guys I knew. He was quiet, had a strong Christian upbringing. Didn't drink, although he does now. Didn't smoke either, nor do drugs. Wait a minute, he did do drugs."

"Uh-oh, we got a wild one here, let's hear about that bad boy."

"Sorry, not much to tell. Anthony, our best friend, got him on a technicality, insisted the Bible states nothing about smoking pot. For all we know, it grew in abundance in the Garden of Eden. Gabe gave in. He still thinks it's funny."

"So Gabe was a follow God's word to a T kind of guy?"

"He tried, he still tries, but he had his weaknesses." I wink.

Nancy stops me with her hand. "Let me guess. Sex?"

"Oh yeah, big time. Gabe wanted it badly. Still does." I laugh. "Boy, did he struggle. What made things worse was I wanted it as much as he did."

"One hot momma!"

"Well, not at first." I give her a half smile.

"What? Sex drive took a while to kick in?"

"It wasn't that. Long story...don't ask." I look away for a moment then back at Nancy and smile. "But later in our relationship? Hell, yeah!" I giggle. "*Aye*, the visions I see."

"I take it those aren't sugar plums you're picturing," she says, wiggling an eyebrow.

"Not even close."

Nancy rattles her empty glass at me. I nod and head to the kitchen.

"Hurry up, I wanna hear more."

I return with the pitcher and fill our glasses. "Nope, your turn, spill it."

"Okay, how about this?" A mischievous grin creeps across her face.

I rub my palms together in anticipation. "Oh boy, something tells me this is going to be fun." I sit reclined into a pillow and place my feet on the coffee table. "Come on, come on. I'm waiting."

"My first boyfriend, Frankie and I did it—" She giggles. "Okay let's see if I can say this without laughing. We did *it* in...the high school auditorium."

My jaw drops. "You're kidding! You lost it *there*? In the auditorium?"

She nods. "Yes, on stage."

"Our auditorium? Brownsville High School auditorium?"

I get another nod.

"On stage?"

"Yes, yes and yes," she says through laughter.

I laugh right along with her. Can't stop, although I try, neither can Nancy.

"Well, the curtains *were* closed. Plus we hid behind an old upright piano. Besides, it was over *really* quick, it was Frankie's first time too."

We crack up, and we're doubled over laughing, clutching our stomachs.

"I can't imagine what you two did for an encore," I say, trying to regain my composure.

We laugh louder, and harder. It takes a while to calm down. When we manage to stop laughing, we look at each other and burst into giggles again. We finally stop and wipe our tears. I can't remember the last time I laughed so hard.

"Okay, enough said about my rollicking," she says still breathless. Let's hear about your first time? Was it Gabe? Huh? Huh?" she asks, leaning toward me, poking me in the ribs like a silly school girl.

The lifted corners of my smile straighten. I swirl the glass in my hand and watch the ice spin around.

"Well? Uh-oh, don't tell me, there was someone else! Who? Tell me, tell me!"

The ice swirls longer than I think it should. It spins round and round and round as a swell of emotions overcomes me. I'm being pulled under into a glass of swirling deep waters.

God help me, I don't want to drown.

I look up at Nancy. Her smile has abandoned her, too.

Ella?"

3

1971 – Gabriel Marquez

One of the first things you learn when you move from a small town to a big metropolitan area is you gotta plan for traffic delays. I would've enjoyed an afternoon romp with Ella, but if I had given in to her sweet seduction, I might've ended up in a terrible mess - Houston's going-home traffic.

I've Just Seen a Face by The Beatles comes on and my fingers immediately start thumping to the lively rhythm. Think about Ella every time I hear it. Definitely a favorite.

Traffic? What traffic? I got Ella on my mind…

I fell hard the first time I laid eyes on Ella Galvez. I'd say it was love at first sight. It happened the fall of sixty-five, our senior year at Brownsville High. Ella was a vision in pink as she entered the hallway from the school's main entrance. She had the sweetest smile and those eyes, they had a sparkle to them. This was the moment I decided I had to make that little darlin' mine. In my mind, I knew we'd be a perfect fit. Oh man, the things I imagined. Had she read my mind, I'm sure she would've blushed, and I probably would've gotten slapped.

My eyes were on Ella when they should've been on where I was going. I bumped into someone and dropped my books. She must've heard the clatter when they hit the floor because she looked in my direction as I stooped to pick them up.

That perfect moment was rudely interrupted when Michael Damon walked up to her and planted a kiss on the side of her neck. Ella's hand went right to the spot he kissed. She rubbed on it as if to wipe it off and gave him a disapproving look. She moved strands of hair away from her face with a brush of her hand and walked off. He called out to her, but Ella didn't bother turning back. He stood there with a frown on his face. I was left with a smile on mine. *Ah, satisfaction.*

I snap back to the present when I realize Anthony's just around the corner. As I pull up to his apartment, I see his living room curtains being drawn to one side. Anthony's face appears in the window with Champ, his dog below his. They look right at me. By the time I close the car door, Anthony's front door's wide open, and they're standing there waiting for me.

"Hey," he says, "you're prompt."

I glance at my watch. "Guess I am."

Champ does his usual *hello* sniff and stays by my side until I pet him. I'm happy to oblige.

"Hey old fella," I say as I scratch Champ behind the ears. He gives me his happy dog smile, wagging his tail, then rolls over for the obligatory tummy rub. Anthony adopted Champ when his owners moved and left him behind. By then they were already best friends since it was Anthony who made sure Champ had water in his dish during those hot Brownsville summers. Champ was probably glad he got left behind.

I grin at Anthony. "I love this guy."

"Yeah, it's hard not to," Anthony says, patting Champ on the head.

Anthony takes his keys from the coffee table. "Come on, I'm ready for a cold one. I'll drive."

We get into his jeep. "How about Mexican?" he asks.

"Mexican food, cold beer, I'm in."

"Great." He starts the engine then checks his rearview mirror.

"Ella and I talked about getting together with you and Doreen. It's been a long time since we've done a double date," I say as he pulls out of the complex.

He turns to look to the left, then speeds up to merge with traffic. "Those were fun times. We were falling in love with our babes, and we were hot." He chuckles. "We made the girls drool."

"We had a lot of tall, dark and handsome going on," I say, laughing. Anthony and I are similar in looks and height, we both have dark brown hair, trimmed clean and neat on the sides and back, but with a little extra length on the top. At six feet tall, he's one inch taller than I am. We were both athletic, and as far as teenage guys go, we thought we were hot stuff.

El Patio's parking lot is packed, but we manage to find a spot up front. While we wait for our table, we check over the menu and give the waiter our order as soon as we're seated.

"Just like old times." I laugh, "We gotta have those enchiladas."

"We'll never outgrow those damn things," he says.

The waiter returns with our beer, chips and salsa.

I lift my beer. "To our babes and enchiladas."

Anthony laughs. "Here, here."

We munch on chips and take long sips of our icy cold beers. Anthony checks his bottle to see how much he guzzled down and smiles. "How's Ella doing?"

"She's great. Excited about the studio's expansion."

"Doreen said something about Ella getting an investor."

"A benefactor. He's paying tuition for underprivileged children."

"Fantastic! I'm proud of her. Did she have to apply for it? How does that work?"

"Nope, didn't apply for it. That's what's so weird."

As I sip my beer, my thoughts jump to the day Ella learned about the grant. She was so excited. We celebrated with champagne, but it didn't take long for me to wonder, why Ella's studio? The question's been stuck there ever since.

"It doesn't make sense." My jaws clench, and I take a slow deep breath. Anthony's frown tells me he notices the tightness in my voice and the tension of my facial muscles. He knows I have a quick temper, so I'm sure he's ready to calm me down and defuse whatever might be brewing beneath the surface.

His eyes narrow. "Okay, what's up?"

Our dinner arrives, and Anthony orders a couple more beers. When the server's gone, Anthony leans into me. "Come on, Gabe, what's going on?"

"Not sure. I've had an uneasy feeling about it."

"Which part?"

"Well, it's an anonymous grant, for one. Plus, Ella's studio has only been in operation eight months. Why would this benefactor choose hers when there are plenty of dance studios in the surrounding area which have been in business a lot longer than Ella's?"

"Hey, don't knock it, money in the bank." He raises his beer for another clink of the bottles.

I oblige, raising mine. "I'm serious, man, I checked the yellow pages. The list of dance studios is impressive, so many to choose from, larger, well-established ones."

"Okay, I get it," he says.

Enchiladas are my weakness, Anthony's too, and we dig into them; once we start, we can't stop. After a long sip of his beer, Anthony looks at me through narrowed eyes.

He leans in. "You think it's all about Ella and not her studio, don't you?" He turns his head to either side as if afraid someone might overhear us.

I nod. "Yes," I say as chills run through me.

Settle down. Just because you thought it doesn't make it true.

"What does Ella have to say?"

"Well, she *was* curious and asked the benefactor's assistant for a name, but Ella was told the grant is anonymous and the name can't be disclosed. Following benefactor's instructions, I guess. Ella doesn't seem too concerned about it, and I haven't mentioned how uneasy I feel. Ella's dealt with one crazy stalker in her life, so I don't want to worry her."

"I hate to say it, Gabe, but you need to hear this. Remember Ella's next-door neighbor back in Brownsville?"

"Prada?"

"Yes, Sebastian Prada. Dad once mentioned the guy had deep pockets. The house next to Ella's wasn't his primary residence. Turns out he lived in one of the most expensive homes in Rio Viejo. From what I gathered, he's a philanthropist and world traveler. The guy's never been found guilty of anything, so he's still out there."

"Right, you can't arrest a man for peering out his window to watch young girls at all hours of the day…and night."

"Oh, one more thing, his full name is Sebastian Prada Garcia. Garcia is his mom's maiden name. Not that it will help much since the name Garcia is so common. I'll ask my dad if there's a way to find out where he's living."

I place my beer down on the table a little harder than I had intended. "Son of a bitch," I say under my breath.

"Whoa, sorry, didn't mean to upset you," he says.

"Don't be, I need to get riled up. Hearing Prada's name validates my concerns about Mr. Money Bags and his eagerness to throw unsolicited funds at my wife. I'm not ready to say anything to Ella about it yet, but when we return from the lake house, I'm on it. Thanks for the info. It might come in handy."

"Good. Let me know if Dad or I can help."

I open my wallet. "I've got the number for the lake house in here somewhere." I pull out a couple of receipts and movie stubs and toss them off to the side. "If you hear anything, give me a call."

"Are you sure? Maybe you shouldn't think about this while you and Ella are at the lake house."

I shake my head. "Trust me it's stuck in my head. Any new information will help me get all my ducks in a row." I find the piece of paper with the number and hand it to Anthony. "Call me, okay?"

He places it in his wallet. "Okay, if it's what you want." He looks up at me with eyebrows raised.

"I do. Thanks, buddy."

"Buddy. You haven't called me that since, shit, who knows how long."

"Yeah, I guess it's been a while."

A grin spreads across Anthony's face as he points at my plate with his fork. "Liked the enchiladas, huh?"

"Yep, all gone."

"Mine too," he says.

We finish up our beers talking about sports and music. We used to have a great time jamming with friends back in our hometown. The chicks seemed to know when we'd be playing because they'd show up and watch us. We thought that was cool. Anthony played the drums, and a couple of us guys played guitar. We would jam in our garage, and we had a blast.

Back at Anthony's apartment, we agree once more to make plans to get together. Before I take off, Anthony leans into my window. "Give my girl a kiss for me. I hope you and Ella have a great time at the lake house," he says, giving me a thumbs up as I drive away.

On the way to my parent's house, I think about my concerns. Prada's name coming up after all these years really put me on edge. It's been five years since this man's name came into Ella's life. It changed everything. I begin to recall what happened.

This is what still tortures Ella, and this is what still tears at my heart:

Ella was raped and brutally beaten the summer after high school graduation. There was absolutely nothing I could do to comfort her. I couldn't hold her, and I couldn't tell her that I loved her. I wanted to let her know I would be there for her, no matter what. But I couldn't do that either. I couldn't do any of these things because Ella Galvez didn't even know I existed.

Her rape occurred several months before we met. Anthony gave me the bad news and his words rocked my world.

Late one evening Anthony dropped by the house unexpectedly. As soon as I opened the door I knew something was terribly wrong. His clenched jaw turned into a forced smile as he stepped in and looked around, firmly rubbing the tendon that runs from the top of his neck to his shoulder.

"Parent's home?"

I nodded. "They're in bed, though. Marc's at a friend's house."

"Can we go up to your room and talk?"

"Sure, but what's up? You look like shit, buddy."

"Right. Can we just go upstairs, please?" His voice strained at the end of his plea.

I waved him in with a tilt of my head and bolted up the stairs, Anthony right behind me. My parent's room was downstairs, so he knew we'd have some privacy. When I closed the door to my room, I turned and looked at him. He just stood there. Didn't say a word. He bit down on his lip, and looked at me, eyes narrowed. I placed a hand on his shoulder and squeezed it.

"Buddy, what's wrong? Tell me."

He rubbed his hand across his mouth, trying to control a quiver, took a deep breath, and tears pooled in his eyes.

"It's Ella," he said.

I shook his shoulder. "*What* about Ella?"

He took another deep breath, and as he exhaled, his face showed a grimace of pain, and his tears spilled.

"She was raped, Gabe. The son-of-a-bitch raped her!"

My knees grew weak, and my heart sank.

"Who did?" I ask, shaking his shoulder again. For some reason my first thought was Michael.

He turned around, shoved my arm aside and punched his fist into the door. When he turned to face me, I could see the anger radiate from his eyes.

"I don't know!" He shrugged his shoulders, glanced down at his hands. "She didn't see his face. He really messed her up, Gabe," he said, his voice breaking as he wiped away the blood which had surfaced on his knuckles.

I couldn't speak. I dropped to a stoop against my bed. The shock and the grief took over. I cried right there in front of Anthony. Felt no shame.

He sat on the floor next to me, wrapped his arm around my shoulder and pulled me in close. I breathed in a few long breaths, wiped my eyes and my face with the sleeve of my shirt. The feel of Anthony's strong hold on me somehow comforted me, but it also made me feel even more helpless. All I wanted to do was hold *her* and comfort *her*, but I couldn't; she was still with Michael. She didn't even know I existed.

Damn! I pull over into a gas station to wipe my eyes and get a grip. This is one memory that will mess me up forever. I hadn't thought about it in a while, but today, with Mr. Prada's name coming up, it just surfaced. Sebastian Prada was a suspect in Ella's rape. He managed to come up with an alibi and was able to explain away the evidence held against him. They believed him, and that was that.

Ella and I are well matched sexually, and while our sex life is fulfilling and most often incredible, there are problems. Ella has blocked most of what happened to her as if it had never occurred. But sometimes when we're making love, something can unexpectedly cause a sensation or a memory to kick in. It's a downward spiral from there. What saddens me is Ella blames herself for ruining the moment.

This is why so much is riding on our week at the cabin. I'm not sure why we expect this week to help except that we'll be alone without the pressures from work. Who knows with God's help maybe we can get through this.

Anthony's right, I need to focus on Ella, not Sebastian Prada. I'll deal with him later. Hearing his name again felt like I'd been kicked in the gut, but that's okay, I'm on guard now. I'm not letting him anywhere near my Ella.

4

1971 – Ella Marquez

My first? Who was my first?

No! This can't be! A rapist was my first. I never thought of it that way before, he being my first. It was bad enough that he raped me, but I'm now reminded he also took my precious passage into womanhood and tainted it. He took something from Gabe and me that was supposed to be special and beautiful, and he ruined it. And it didn't end there. He continues to intrude in our lives during the most intimate moments that a husband and wife can share.

I notice the movement of the ice in my glass has finally stopped. I take a deep breath before speaking. *I can do this.*

My eyes meet Nancy's. "A rapist was my first."

I say it nonchalantly, showing no emotion. I've always had trouble saying or even thinking the words. But I say them, probably for the first time since it happened.

The words reverberate in my head as they swirl around until they find a place to settle. I moisten my lips and swallow a bit of courage.

"I was raped...I was raped on my eighteenth birthday."

These words pass my lips just as easily. I don't know what's come over me. I've kept my rape hidden, even from me, for such a long time. Why bring it up now? I never, ever, and I mean *never* talk about it. I don't ever *think* about it, yet here I am telling Nancy *I lost it* to a rapist.

Did I just tell her I lost it to a rapist?

Maybe not...maybe I just imagined saying it. No, the look on Nancy's face says it plainly. It mirrors exactly what I'm feeling. Shock. I *did* say it.

"Oh, Ella! I am so sorry, I had no idea. I never would've asked. I hope they put that bastard away."

I give Nancy a fraction of a smile and shrug my shoulders hoping to convince her I'm okay, which I'm not. But how does one pull off a *never mind* after blurting out a shocker like this? *Go on, Ella. You can't backtrack now.*

"They didn't...put him away."

Nancy's eyes go wide. She turns in her seat to face me. "Why the hell not?" she asks, placing her drink on the table.

She leans toward me resting her elbows on her knees and waits. She's going to think I'm an idiot for letting this animal get away.

"It was the questioning." I moisten my lips. "The questioning at the police station." I moisten them again. "They were so brutal."

"Who cares? The son of a bitch deserved it!"

"No," I say with a quick shake of my head. "They were brutal with me. You should've heard them."

"Wait a minute...you?"

"Yes." I breathe in deeply before continuing. This is part of a story I've kept locked away for so long.

I notice the magazine which is now face down on the table. *Things go better with Coke,* the Coca-Cola advertisement states.

Hell no! With rum, things go so much better with rum. Coke could never have pulled out all this crap that I've kept buried inside for so long out of me!

I can't seem to pull my eyes away. They're locked on the advertisement. I sit there staring at it twirling my wedding rings around my finger. I can't stop now. I *want* to keep going. I do.

"They shot their questions at me…one right after another…after another. Do you wear short shorts? Do you lay out in a bikini?"

"Hold it. Are you saying they—"

"Do you undress in front of open windows? Do you make out with your boyfriend where others can see you?" I keep rattling them off.

"Ella, are you kidding me?"

"No, I'm not."

"This is crazy," she says under her breath, shaking her head.

"Nancy, I couldn't believe what I was hearing. They made it sound like I enticed this man to rape me. I was the perpetrator." I wipe the tears away. "It was my damn fault!"

I bite down on my quivering lip and turn to Nancy, my eyes welling up with fresh tears. Nancy moves closer and holds me.

"Ella, I'm so sorry. What they put you through was horrible. How could they get away with it?"

Nancy pulls tissues from the box sitting on the table, wipes away my tears with one and hands me the rest. I take a long breath and straighten up as if doing so could possibly give me the strength I need to finish this emotional disclosure. I know I need to continue. I *have* to.

"Well, they got away with it," I say, sniffling and wiping away tears, "and so did the rapist. To protect me from being assaulted again my parents refused to allow the questioning to continue. It may have been verbal, but the sting was just as hard to bear."

"I can't begin to imagine, Ella, the rape, the questioning, that was so wrong. And you were so young."

I set my glass down, then place my palms flat on the table trying to steady my breathing. My chest rises and falls as I try to hold in the anger building up inside of me, the hate that has suddenly reared its ugly head. I slide one hand across the surface of the table sending the magazine along with the box of tissues flying against the sliding glass door. Nancy jumps back, her hands clutching her chest. Her face goes pale. It startles me too. It's been five years since I was raped, and this is the first show of emotion I've had. It's also the first time I've said the word *rape* since it happened. *Why now?*

I hold up my hands motioning Nancy not to get up. "I'm okay. I'm all right," I say as I walk to the corner of the room where the magazine landed. I stoop to pick it up and notice an earring buried inside the shag carpet. As I reach for it, I recall how it ended up there. It happened Saturday when Gabe and I were sitting on the floor with our backs against the sofa watching television. Gabe got a little frisky, so we made love right here. I was laying on my back, and just as he began to enter me, I reached up to hold on to his shoulders pulling myself upward, so he could feel my breasts against his chest. My hands slipped, I lost my grip, and I fell back onto the carpet. It didn't hurt, but the combination of penetration and sudden movement sent me reeling. Frightened, I beat against Gabe's chest to get him away. *I couldn't breathe!*

Wow, I didn't realize it when it happened, but it hits me now. The reason I was pounding on Gabe's chest was that it felt like I was being suffocated...someone or something was keeping me from breathing.

When this happened on Saturday, I had no idea what made me respond the way I did. But I do now.

I feel a tingle surge through me as I realize that I just now recalled something that happened during my rape. I jerk my head toward Nancy. My eyes are wide in disbelief.

"What's the matter?" Nancy asks, her voice bringing me back to the present.

"What?"

"You seemed so far away. I spoke to you, but you didn't respond. And now you look like you've seen a ghost. Are you okay?"

I'm shaken, but I give her a couple of nods. "I'm fine. I recalled something unsettling, but I'm fine now." *Like hell I am.*

I get up, place the mangled magazine and the box of tissue back on the table. Laughter coming from the pool below distracts me. I push the curtain aside once again. Those kids are still out there splashing around, having fun, and enjoying life.

"What was I saying?" I ask, hoping I can get past this intrusive unveiling of a part of my suppressed memory. As troubling as this revelation was, it may be just what I needed. *But now what?*

"You had finished telling me about the horrible questioning session."

"Yes, yes. Well, it gets worse, a whole lot worse."

I force myself to stop staring down at all the frolicking and turn around to face Nancy, my arms folded at my chest.

"Ella, you don't have to continue."

I nod. "Yes, I do. I do need to."

"Okay," she whispers.

I go on to tell Nancy how with the charges dropped, my rapist was free to live his *sick*, pathetic life, rape another girl and get away with that one too. That it was Anthony's fourteen-year-old sister and how he got off with another flimsy alibi.

"I had to deal with so much hate, anger, fear and self-pity. That's what his filthy act left me infected with. Not just for what he did to me, but what he did to sweet little Sophia."

"I'm so sorry, Ella."

"Look at me," I say, holding out my shaking hands. "It's been five damn long years! No matter how many times I hear the word rape, it still has the same resonating sound of a double-edged sword whittling away at my soul. Boy, do I need another drink! Can we please change the subject?"

"Yes. Yes, we can," she says, reaching out to hug me.

I welcome Nancy's arm around me and lean against her shoulder. I sit there for a while, the words that I spoke now replaying inside my head as well as the memory that slipped out of its hiding place of someone suffocating me. This may be the beginning, the first trickle allowed to penetrate the wall I'd built around this horrific day in my life. The eyes of my soul have been opened, and now I'm afraid of what else I might see.

I begin to calm; my breath becomes slow and steady. Maybe I *can* do this a trickle at a time. I take a tissue, wipe my eyes, my nose and look at Nancy.

"Do you have any idea how difficult it is to forgive someone who isn't even sorry?" I ask.

"No," she whispers.

We sit there holding hands in silence for a while longer.

"So how about one last glass of that lemony concoction?" I ask, hoping she'll agree.

"Yeah, why not. I'm walking home, not driving. Don't even have to cross the parking lot. I'll follow the same path I took getting here. I'm sure I can handle one very long lighted sidewalk and a few stepping stones till I'm home, don't you?"

"It's those stepping stones that will be tricky." I laugh, sounding like I'm suffering from a major head cold.

I flip on the radio, and we enjoy a third glass of rum lemonade. I tell Nancy about the anniversary gifts I bought for Gabriel, the location of the lake house, and where we can be reached if necessary. I still don't offer any information about our mysterious destination.

"Ella, I know how hard it must've been to share this. You know you can talk to me anytime. I'm here for you."

I give her a genuine smile, or maybe it's a hopeful one. Yes, hopeful. That's exactly what it is. I walk Nancy out, she pecks my cheek with a kiss and gives me a hug.

Why did this morsel which was buried way deep inside for such a long time surface now? Maybe it's time to deal with what happened. As an adult, I dealt with a lot of the pain and most of the anger with God's help. However, when I was eighteen, the healing didn't come easy. I just didn't have God in my life at that age, although I believed He was there. I just didn't know how to connect with God...I didn't get it.

Everyone told me the same thing. It will all be over soon, and you'll get back to living your life. What I couldn't bring myself to tell them was I didn't want to. I didn't want to go on living. So I crawled into a deep dark tunnel. No one could pull me out. Michael, the guy who used to always tell me how much he loved me hardly came around. He got himself a girlfriend on the side, and I dumped him when I found out.

Then one day I caved in completely. I remember when it happened. It was the day I wished I could just will myself to die. I think that's when I must've tucked it all away for safekeeping, so I wouldn't have to feel any more pain. Well, except when something triggers a memory and ruins a perfectly beautiful moment between Gabriel and me.

Everything changed when I met Gabriel. This was when the healing began. By then I was so broken, and in such despair, so the process was slow. It took months for me to open up to him, believe his words and feel safe. He never gave up. Even now he's still waiting, still not giving up. *It sure is amazing how one person can change your life.*

I take the pitcher and our glasses back to the kitchen, clean up and gather what I'll need for the week at the cabin. Gabe's ready. He packed before I even agreed to go. Yes, he's one determined and very optimistic guy. Has been since the day we first saw each other in our high school hallway.

I double-check the door chain, then get a hot shower running. I want to bathe early, so I don't risk missing Gabe's call later tonight. I won't mention what happened here, not yet.

I'm positive we need to get away now. For whatever reason, memories about my rape have surfaced along with pent up emotions. It just might be the right time to work through my long-suppressed memories. Well, not all of them are suppressed, I remembered something: "I was struggling to breathe. He held a glove over my face." I sigh knowing this was so painful, but it was healing too.

I removed a small splinter from my soul today, and it feels good. It feels very good.

5

1971 – Gabriel Marquez

I love the expression on Mom's face as she waves goodbye. Her mood improved in the short time we were together. Glad I came. She enjoyed the stories I shared about Marc and me when we were kids and the things we did when they weren't watching. By the look on Dad's face, I think he got a kick out of them too.

Since the day Nixon announced he would begin the removal of 150 thousand troops from Vietnam, we've been anxiously waiting for one of those soldiers to be my brother, Marc. With the casualties still mounting, Mom has become increasingly distressed. I'm glad Dad suggested I spend time with her.

When I pull up in front of our apartment, I notice the living room lights are on. Ella must be up. I unlock the front door pushing it in as far as the chain allows.

"Yay! You made it!" She smiles at me through the gap. "Hold on." She shuts the door and slides off the guard.

I'm actually surprised she's up this early. It's not even six o'clock. I give her a kiss then the hug I know she's been waiting for. "Boy, have I missed you, baby."

"Missed you too. How was your drive home?"

"Fine, traffic was light." I take her hand and walk to the sofa. I sit and pat the spot next to me.

"Sumtin for Ella," I say. *Sumtin for Ella* was what her dad would say when he'd show up with his hands behind his back, holding little Ella's newest surprise. The gifts were inexpensive dime-store trinkets, sometimes a lollypop, but what held the most value for Ella was the time spent exchanging gifts for hugs. Ella still misses her dad very much, so these memories are her treasures.

"For me?" she asks, her eyes smiling.

"Yes," I nod. "You *do* remember what today is, don't you?"

"Hmm, let me think." Ella stands there, one hand on her cocked hip, while the fingertips of her other hand rub her forehead as if in deep thought. "Nope," she says with a shrug. "Can't think of anything remotely special about today."

I shove my hand in my pocket. "Well, maybe I need to return these special—"

"Wait, wait, I remember now. Come on, let me see what you've got in there. Pretty please."

When Ella's hand reaches for my pocket, I playfully swat it away.

"Come on, I love you to the moon and back, and happy anniversary, love of my life!" She laughs as she makes another attempt to get into my pocket.

I grab her hand and pull her close to me. I love Ella's silly moods. She's smart and often smart-alecky, but there's a part of her which will always be a little girl, and it totally entertains me.

She plants a kiss on my forehead, scoots a tissue box and a mangled magazine which has seen better days to one side and sits on the coffee table facing me. "Thanks for the sweet memory of my daddy."

She picks up a bottle of root beer which she'd left on the coffee table and takes a long sip, all the while keeping her eyes on me. Her attention turns to my hand and follows it as it goes into my pocket. As she places her drink on the table, a smile spreads across her face.

Oh yeah, my baby's anxious.

I'm anxious too. I love the necklace I bought her. It's a gold pendant with *Bella Ella* engraved in the center. Around the raised edge, I had the jeweler inscribe, *Here, There and Everywhere.* It's one of our favorite Beatles songs.

"Happy anniversary, baby."

I place the box in her hands and wait. Her gaze stays on me rather than on the gift she's holding. She bites down on the corner of her lip as she opens it. In a matter of seconds, a tear trickles down her cheek.

Ah, waterworks! It's a winner.

"Gabriel, it's beautiful!"

"Flip it over."

She turns the medallion and places it in her hand. A smile spreads across her face as she reads it. "I'll never leave you, Gabriel." She strokes her finger across the words. "You say that all the time."

"I mean it all the time."

"How did you come up with something so beautiful, so perfect?"

"Easy, thought of you. Here, let me put it on you."

Once it's hooked on, she turns to me and leans in close. "I'm loving you so much right now, Gabriel Marquez. This is beautiful."

"Got one more," I tell her. I reach into my pocket and extend a closed fist, palm up. She lifts two of my fingers and peeks into my cupped hand. Her face lights up when she sees the Eiffel Tower. Are we going to Paris?"

"Yep, how about late August before your classes begin which is also the same time my current project will be complete. I already put in for vacation time."

"Yes, I would love to! Just don't tell me we'll be staying at some old hotel haunted by soldiers from the French Revolution."

"Damn," I say with a laugh, "my vacation planning has already gotten a bad reputation."

"Just teasing, babe. I'd love to go to Paris, *The City of Lights*."

Ella gets up and kisses my forehead again. "You, stay right there," she says. She returns with a perfectly gift-wrapped package. White wrapping paper tied with a red satin ribbon. She places it on the table right in front of me with a smug look on her face.

"See, I told ya I didn't forget. Open it." She scoots it closer to me.

I give the ribbon a gentle tug, and the bow comes undone.

"Your gifts are always a cinch to undo."

"It's a Tiffany bow. All it needs is a gentle pull and *voilà*. Go ahead, rip it open."

I tear off the wrapping and open the carton. Inside is a mahogany jewelry box with a picture-frame top. Ella inserted a beautiful photograph of us taken on the bay at South Padre Island. The backdrop is the most amazing sunset. Ella loves sunsets and is always in search of one. She plans walks, picnics, and dinners around them.

"Wow, Ella, this is great. Love the picture you stuck in here."

I lift the lid and find a silver key chain inside the blue velvet lined box. It has a shiny flat outer silver ring, and the center is an opaque silver medallion suspended on its axis which is attached to the outer ring. I flick the disk with my finger, and it spins freely on its axis. The inscription on one side reads, *Here, There and Everywhere.*

I wink. "Catchy little phrase."

I turn the disk over to read the flipside. *"I'm yours forever, Ella.* I love it. I love them both!"

Our life is filled with coincidences. We seem to always be in sync, and we have so much in common. We love music, tennis and baseball. We enjoy Padre Island and Boca Chica Beach and walking along the surf looking for sand dollars. Ella also picks up the broken pieces and keeps them in a jar labeled *Spare Change.* Her silly quirks amuse me.

Ella leans over and gives me the sweetest smile. "I've missed you, babe. It's no fun when you're not around. I hate sleeping alone."

I lift a few strands of hair that lay across her cheek. "Trouble falling asleep?"

"At first I did. I needed to feel your warm body next to the coolness of mine. No one to scoot up to and wrap my leg around. You know how much it helps me drift off to sleep. But I survived. Wrapped my leg around your pillow, hugged it tight. But I longed to feel your kisses."

Ella tilts her head to one side, closes her eyes and strokes a finger down the length of her neck, all the way to the tip of her shoulder. I place kisses following the trail her fingertip made.

"Mmm...that's exactly what I needed," she moans softly. She hugs me and presses her face against the opening of my shirt taking in a deep breath. "And I needed to smell you, to taste you...every part of you."

"Oh baby, hold that thought," I say, my voice suddenly husky and at least two octaves lower than it was moments ago. "Come on, I want to be at that cabin now."

"Hey, I'm ready." She points to an overnight case and a suitcase sitting by the entrance. "You'll never guess what I remembered to pack," she says, putting her bracelet inside a compartment of her case. She drops her new charm inside the box the necklace came in and places it on the table. She smiles at me when I shrug my shoulder. "I packed the top layer of our wedding cake."

"Atta girl, glad you remembered."

"Me too. Now let's go before I change my mind."

"You're on. *Vamonos.*"

"Gabe, are you sure we don't have to take any food, paper plates or utensils?"

"Yes, I'm sure. Mom and Dad were there earlier this week to stock the kitchen for us."

"Perfect. I did pack us some bacon and egg tacos for the road and a thermos of hot coffee."

"Nice! From the list Mom rattled off, it sounds like she thought of everything," I say, picking up a couple of bags to carry out. "Stuff like this keeps her mind occupied, less time to worry about Marc." I look back and give Ella a wink. "We may want to make another trip to the cabin and give Mom something to focus on. She needs all the distractions we can give her."

"Another trip? We haven't survived the first one yet."

I drop the bag I'd picked up and take her in my arms. "Don't you worry; I won't let anyone steal you away." A smirk creeps onto my face. "In fact, I should tie your hand to the bed post so they can't snatch you. And to be on the safe side, I'll tie the other one up too."

Ella lifts an eyebrow at me. "Every night?"

I give her a mischievous grin.

She giggles. "Oh babe, time to put the pedal to the metal!"

6

1971 – Gabriel Marquez

As we drive off, Ella slips a cassette into the player then cocks her head in my direction. Without saying a word returns her gaze back toward the road ahead and sighs. A moment later she props her sunglasses on her head and clears her throat.

"What is it?" I ask Ella, wondering what could possibly be on her mind. She's not good at hiding her emotions, too honest for that. I can usually figure out when something's up, and I can tell something is. Her eyes search my face, and I'm thinking she's trying to guess how I'll respond to whatever she's about to ask or say.

"Gabriel, we're going to work this all out. I'm so sure of it. I think I'm on the cusp of something big."

She shoves a strand of hair behind her ear, scrunches up her forehead. I gather she's still playing around with whatever idea she's got going on in there.

"Something big?" I ask.

"I'll tell you in a bit," she says, handing me a cup of coffee and placing some tacos on a napkin between us. "I want to talk about my visit with Mom, first."

"Wait a minute, Ella, you were about to share what sounded like some kind of revelation and—"

"I know, I know, bear with me," she says and takes a sip of her coffee. I do the same.

Why does she do that? So typical. We'll be in the middle of a conversation about whatever and then she steers the conversation to something entirely unrelated. But I know Ella, and I know exactly why she's doing it. She needs to stay focused, and obviously, the story about her mom will be a distraction unless she gets it out of the way.

She locks her door then scoots around in her seat to face me, stretching her legs out on the seat, her bare feet up against my thighs. Her toes immediately begin tapping to the beat of Chicago's *Make Me Smile.*

"Mom looked incredible today, and she seemed so happy."

"Seemed? You didn't buy it?" I reach over and turn the volume down and take another bite of food and several sips of coffee.

"Oh no, she's definitely happy, no doubt about it. In fact, I think it's the happiest I've ever seen her. I've grown up watching Mom's practiced smile which she has perfected throughout the years. Her face was radiant, and the smile I saw was genuine. I have a feeling it has something to do with the note she received."

I look at Ella. "What note?"

When I got there, Mom was sitting on the porch reading a notecard. Said she'd just come from picking up her mail. We sat and talked there for a while. Later, when we went inside, she placed the card on her coffee table before heading to the bathroom. I noticed the opened envelope on top, so I looked at it."

"You snooped?"

"No, I just looked at it to see...okay, I snooped. But I'm glad I did. Listen to this, the sender was S. Prada."

"Prada?"

Why am I hearing that name again?

"Are you sure? That's the name of the—"

"Yes, the guy who lived next door, whose pastime was peeping out of his second story window at me!" She nibbles on a fingernail and gives me a sideways glance.

"And may have been the one who..." I stop myself. I can't believe I was just about to mention her rape. *What an idiot.*

"Yes, the guy who could have been my stalker...and, my rapist," she says then takes small sips from her cup.

My head snaps in her direction. *Rapist? My rapist?* Ella hasn't spoken about her rape since it happened. Hell, she hasn't even said the word rape. I decide not to question it. Maybe she isn't aware of what she said. I keep my eye on the road and continue as if nothing out of the ordinary just occurred.

"Well, it could be another guy or girl named Prada whose first name also begins with the letter *S,*" I say.

"Hmm, a female? It's not a common name. My first thought was he's harassing Mom, maybe intimidating her. But that's impossible. How would he know where Mom lives? She's only lived there three months."

I shake my head. "Nah, no way he would know."

"But listen to this, Mom told me about her lunch plans with an out-of-town friend. When I asked who it was, she pulled her change-the-subject routine and talked about the beautiful pastel flowers in her flowerbed. Showed me her freshly planted periwinkles.

"That's strange, why wouldn't she want to tell you who her lunch date was? You think it's a guy?"

She shrugs. "Don't know. That was my first guess, though, the way she changed the subject and all."

"Where's this Prada person from?"

"It had a Houston postmark."

"Then S. Prada couldn't possibly be her date. Clear Lake's in Houston. She said out-of-town friend, right?"

"Yes, but to Mom, Clear Lake is separate from Houston. So it could be him."

"Well, if it is, it's got to be someone else with the same last name. That other scenario makes absolutely no sense."

She nods. "You're right, you're absolutely right."

Or not.

That's the second time in two days that Mr. Prada's name has popped up. I'm trying hard not to get myself all worked up over a mere coincidence, not now. We've got plenty of stuff to keep our mind occupied without adding this dilemma on top of it. And I still can't believe Ella talked about her attack or the upstairs window. After her rape, she said the window seemed to take on a life of its own. It taunted her is what she said. Mr. Galvez had to build a patio cover in their backyard to block its view. Ella's bedroom blinds remained closed at all times since, as did the shades in her dance room. It's not only that she mentioned the rape and the window, but how casual she was about it as if it was an everyday topic of conversation.

"Okay, Ella, I've waited long enough. Back to what you said about being on the cusp of something. What's that all about?"

"Okay, I'll tell you, but don't freak out."

"Freak out? What the hell!"

"You're already freaking out. I told you *not* to."

"Sorry, sweetie, but when someone says, *don't freak* out, one automatically does exactly that – freaks out. But okay, go on." I turn off the radio and lower the A/C fan. Don't want any kind of distraction here.

God, I hope I'm not gonna freak out.

"Gabe, you know how I've been tormented with flashbacks since I was attacked. Right?"

"Yes, it's been rough for you."

"Well, I may be on the verge of something which could be a turning point of sorts."

"A turning point? What exactly are you saying, Ella?"

I consider pulling over, but I don't. Traffic is light, it's a long straight highway for now and feel I can keep my attention on both the road and Ella.

"Alright, here it is. Nancy and I sat around chatting while we drank our rum lemonade."

"Ahh, rum. There was liquor involved, this should be interesting."

"*Interesting* is not even close, you are not going to believe—"

I flick a finger against her leg. "There you go again."

"Ouch, sorry. No need to get brutal," she says with a giggle. "We got to talking about our teen years. The subject of old boyfriends came up. Who our first kiss was and who we lost our virginity to, you know, those kinds of things."

"Do girls usually discuss *that* sort of stuff or does it require massive amounts of alcohol?"

"If three glasses is massive, yes."

"Oh, to be a fly on that wall," I say, stroking her leg where I'd just flicked.

"When it was my turn to share…"

"Go on," I say still rubbing her silky-smooth leg.

"I blurted out a rapist was my first." She spewed out those words so fast as if they were poison in her mouth.

My jaw drops, I look at her. Her eyebrows arch, and she bites down on her lower lip. There it is again, she said *rapist*.

She scoots over and wraps her arm around mine and snuggles up close. "It's okay, babe. I'm fine." She nods her head a couple of times. "Well, *now* I am. But what's important is for the first time in five years, I was able to speak about my rape. Do you know I have never said that word since the day it happened?"

"Yes, I do. Well, until just a moment ago, when you said Mr. Prada could have been the one who raped you. You were so blasé. Played it cool, but I was shocked."

She turns and looks at me. "Gosh, I'm sorry, I didn't realize I'd said it twice. I *know* I said it but didn't put any importance to it. That *is* odd. Gabe, this is what I meant about being onto something big."

I'm still in shock. Definitely not sure I understood correctly.

"You shared this with Nancy? Told her you were raped?"

"I did. Told Nancy all about it, the difficulties I had in dealing with it and about how Michael treated me like shit instead of trying to help me. And about how he cheated on me and about what happened to Sophia."

I flip my blinker and move over onto the shoulder. "Come here," I say, reaching out for Ella's hand. "I should've been there, could've held you, made you feel safe."

"I kind of felt you were. I felt a strength which couldn't have been my own. I mean, I was scared, hell I was in shock, but kept on going."

"Maybe it was God holding you," I say, squeezing her hand.

Ella glances off to the side, eyes narrowed as if processing what I just said. She looks back at me with a smile and nods.

"So you remembered the whole incident?"

"No, just one thing, something about not being able to breathe, someone holding a glove over my mouth kept me from breathing."

I wrap my arms completely around Ella. She burrows into me like a little kitten.

"I also told Nancy how everything changed after you came into my life," she says, stroking my chest. "That part of my story I enjoyed. But recalling everything else made me so angry…and it scared me. These were emotions I've kept locked away for so long. But this may be a new beginning for me…for us." She pulls away and looks at me. "What do you think? Could this be a turning point? Maybe now it might be possible for me to work through all the issues I've had…we've had?"

"Baby, this is a significant step for you. Being able to say the word is a biggie, but talking about the whole incident is unbelievable."

"I think so too, Gabe." She pops out the cassette and starts punching buttons looking for music on the radio.

"Plus, all this is still fresh in your mind, yet you're so calm."

"Wow, you're right. I was calm, I *am* calm," she says, nodding. I see hope in her eyes.

"This couldn't have come at a better time," I say. "We have a week to talk through it all, slow and easy. No need to rush."

"We shall see. Like Mom always says, *que sera, sera.*"

I lean over, give her a kiss, and squeeze her hand lightly. "It's going to be alright."

"Well, then let's giddy up," she says, rocking her body as if riding a horse.

I turn up the radio when *Let it Be* by The Beatles comes on.

"How about that? Even Paul McCartney's mother, Mary, agrees, let it be."

"Ha! Let it be, que sera, sera. Same idea. There you go, mothers and their wisdom."

Ella scoots back to her spot. I glance over at her and watch as she puts her seat belt back on. She sighs, and I catch the sweetest look on her face.

"Penny for your thoughts," I say.

She turns to me. "I'm feeling good," she says, then looks back at the road in front of us with that same sweet expression on her face. Then with another sigh, she grabs a taco, takes a big bite and bobs her head to the music. She looks over at me and smiles. I finish the other one she'd placed there for me.

I deliberately do not mention the lake house, don't want Ella to get apprehensive. She's in a quiet and peaceful mood, and that's where I want her to stay. If the lake house is half as beautiful as Mom and Dad said it was she'll be taken in, the moment we drive up. I steer the conversation to her dance studio, ask Ella what her expectations are for her first year working with underprivileged children. That's all it takes, we are totally entertained with her dreams for the coming year.

"So how often do you have to provide reports or updates on how the kids are progressing?"

"None, he didn't request any updates. It was more like *here's your money; you and the kids have fun.*"

"Sounds like Mr. Moneybags can't get rid of his dough fast enough. Nice of him to throw it at you and your students." I try not to give much importance to what she just said, but it just doesn't sit right with me.

Who the hell is this person?

Ella yawns. "I'm getting sleepy, but I hate to abandon you. I'll try to stay awake."

"Go ahead, get your rest. I'll take in the view and listen to the music."

"Thanks." She unbuckles her seatbelt again and leans against the window with her legs stretched out along the seat. A few minutes later she's out. Ella must've had more trouble falling asleep than she realized. I glance over and watch her sleeping so peacefully.

That's what my baby needs, peace. Besides dealing with the scars from her rape, Ella continues to be preoccupied with the threat of eminent danger and is apprehensive around strangers, especially if she's alone. She seems to always be on high alert. Maybe we're on the right track here. I just hope we can approach this without causing her any pain. If we need to go slow, we will. I don't care if it takes forever.

I've waited on Ella before. I waited patiently for her and Michael to split. Anthony would hold me over with his stories. He told me she used to be such a tomboy but also loved ballet. Said it would crack him up to watch her go indoors after a game of baseball with skinned knees and smudged face, then reappear all fresh and prissy in her pink tutu and ballet slippers hanging over her shoulder headed to her dance class. This totally blew my mind, and from that point on she was my tomboy in a tutu.

I'm realizing just how deep in the middle of nowhere this cabin is. Kind of glad Ella isn't awake to notice we're still cruising through so many long, curving roads that take us deeper into the woods and closer to that secluded little lake house which I'm praying is a place of hope and healing…and fun.

Ella stirs, but her eyes are still closed and appears to be asleep. Her legs are sprawled across the seat. One foot rests on my thigh, the other on the floorboard. Being the mischievous guy that I am, I lift up her sundress and peek at her white satin panties.

Oh, if she could see the smile on my face now.

I think it's time to wake Ella up…gently. When I come to a stop sign, I reach under Ella's sundress knowing darn well I'm about to get my hand slapped. I lightly touch the silkiness of her panties with my fingertips. The sweetest smirk slowly creeps onto her face. She looks at me through halfway opened eyes.

"You naughty, naughty little boy," she says, lightly slapping my hand.

Someone behind us honks the horn letting me know the stop sign isn't ever going to turn green. I swear I hadn't seen anyone behind us. I go to pull my hand away, but she grabs it and holds it down.

"Hey, I can't do *that* and drive."

Ella giggles and lets my hand go. I shift into first gear and drive off. When he honks the horn again, I look back at him in my rearview mirror. The jerk gives me the finger.

"Up yours, buddy."

"Let me guess." Ella sits up and turns to look back at the guy. "He gave you the bird. Sorry, my fault."

I wink. "My pleasure."

She smiles. "Mine too."

Ella looks around, takes in the view. "Wow, it's beautiful, I've never seen so many trees. Are we almost there?"

"Just about. Glad you woke up; the fun is about to begin."

7

1971 – Ella Marquez

I've been so apprehensive about this place, yet I'm excited about spending time out here in this little cabin nestled deep in the woods. I'm ready to pull out all the stops and gently tread through the memories I've held captive for so long. Yes, I'm going to face my fears head-on. But slowly. I must do it slowly. Who knows, the next seven days might be the beginning of our happily ever after.

Gabriel flips on the blinker for his turn. "This is it."

All I see is a gravel road and wooded land on either side of it. "Where's the house?"

"It's further back, but the property starts here. The road and what you see on either side belong to my folks, and this road leads directly to it. Think of it as a very, *very* long driveway," Gabe says.

"Long and winding?"

He turns to look at me and laughs. "Only you, Bella Ella, would ask that. But yeah, it's definitely long and winding. Whoa, check it out, this is looking good, huh?"

"It sure is. Doesn't get any more secluded than this. I love it."

Just like Gabe said, the road comes to an end directly in front of the cabin, and what a sight it is. Up until this point, all we saw was the gravel road, trees, and brush. Rabbits, I saw two rabbits. Finally, the lake house is right there before us.

"Gabriel, this is perfect!"

I stand there in awe, all my senses absorbing the beauty around us. A glance at Gabe and I know he's experiencing pretty much the same thing. He takes in a deep breath and looks around. "Baby, this whole place is damn near perfect."

I nod in agreement as I scan the dense woods that run along at least three-quarters of the lake's perimeter.

"Dad wasn't kidding; this place is incredible."

"Gabe, look at that old church bell!"

The church bell sits on a brick tower over three feet tall. The brick's edges are worn and smooth, a visual reminder of just how long it's been sitting out here.

"I think it's so cool they decided to bring the bell down and display it like this," I say, walking around it, running my hand along the brick's time-worn edges. "What a treasure and a wonderful reminder of the history this place holds."

Gabe raps his hand along the bottom edge of the bell, feeling its thickness. "This thing's got to be very heavy. It must've been difficult to bring it down without breaking it."

There are two weathered lounge chairs surrounded by wild flowers of various colors at the front of the cabin. I immediately imagine us sitting there with a glass of wine, watching butterflies flit about, or birds feeding at one of the three feeders and splashing in the birdbath located right where the garden ends. A light breeze caresses my face and swirls the scent of freshly mowed grass around us. It brings the scene I'd imagined to life. The caretaker must've been here today. For a place that hasn't been lived in for a long while, it looks incredible.

Gabe takes my hand, pulls me toward the entrance. "Come on, ready to peek inside?"

"No, not yet, let's walk around. I want to take it all in. I never imagined it would be this beautiful. I want to stay here a month."

"Listen to you. I had to halfway drag your pretty little butt out here, missy."

"I know, isn't it crazy?"

Gabe fixes his attention on the lake that surrounds a good portion of the property.

The house sits at the top of a slope which leads down to the lake. I walk up the incline toward the cabin.

"Holy Moly! Holy...Moly!"

Gabe hollers. "Was that a good *holy moly* or a bad *holy moly*?"

"Good, come see." I wave him over. "It's identical to Mom's arbor swing in our old backyard."

"Hell, it sure is. Aren't those the same statues you had?"

"Well, one of them. We only had the little girl with the basket of daisies and a birdbath like this one. We didn't have the boy."

"Yeah, you...forget it, don't know what I was thinking."

"Do you remember the climbing yellow roses which grew up along either side? They cascaded over the top."

"I remember a big ol' bunch of tiny yellow flowers."

"Yes, they were miniature roses. It looked amazing when they were in bloom. Mom and I hated leaving it behind when we moved. I've dreamed of one day having one in my own backyard."

Gabe places his arm around my shoulder. "I'm glad you're enjoying all of this."

"I am. But now I'm left with a deep desire to see Mom's old swing. Oh, how I wish I could be there at our old house.

 Not as beautiful as Mom's, although it could be with lots of care. Unlike the wild flowers we've seen, these leaves are kind of puckered."

Gabe grabs ahold of one of the posts supporting the structure and gives it a shake. "Sturdy."

"You know, I can almost picture it with healthy vines and flowers. I think it's a Jasmine. It'll be fragrant and will look amazing climbing over the arbor."

I step back to get a better perspective. "It's going to be—" I gasp. My arms and my body work together to keep me from falling.

Gabe reaches out to steady me. "Whoa, are you okay?"

"Holy cow!"

Gabe's expression tells me he's waiting for an explanation. I don't have one. "What just happened?"

"You tell me! It was swirling...I couldn't get it into focus...it's...it's hard to explain."

"Maybe we should go inside," Gabe says, taking my hand.

I pull my hand away and point to the swing. "Wait, look! Isn't this crazy? This is...not possible!"

"Look at what?"

"This!" I point again. "Don't you see it? It isn't the same arbor swing. The colors. So vivid! I've never seen anything this breathtaking!"

"Are you imagining it or actually seeing it?"

"Seeing. It's Mom's arbor swing. Right here, right now." I point to the swing again. "See, the yellow roses are tumbling over the sides in the most vibrant colors. And for a short moment, I saw sparkly lights that flickered then fizzled." I turn to Gabe. "Wow! I'll bet this is how Dorothy felt when her world went all Technicolor in the Land of Oz."

"What's going on? Are you saying you—"

"A ViewMaster!" I exclaim, thrilled I can finally describe what I see.

"Okay, you're not making any sense here. A ViewMaster?"

"Yes. You know the toy which comes with pictures on a circular disk. You look through it like binoculars. It's 3-D. I want to touch the fronds with my fingertips, they're spilling over and sparkling."

"Ella, look at me."

I shake my head. "It's gone. It went away right when it was starting to feel weird... well, weirder."

Gabe places his hands on my shoulders, turns me toward him. "Okay Ella, run it by me again. What happened?"

"Well, what I saw was *not* this." I shake my pointed finger at an arbor that's once again covered with shriveled up vines. Gabe stops me, turns me so I'm facing him, and my eyes are in line with his.

"Don't look over there, Ella. Look here," he says, pointing two fingers toward his eyes. There's concern in his voice. "And speak slowly. I want to understand what happened."

Hell, I don't even know what happened!

"I saw Mom's old arbor swing." I say it slow and in a low, calm tone. Slow for his benefit, calm for mine. "It was three-dimensional and absolutely beautiful."

"What was the weird part?"

"The little boy." I shudder. "It gave me some strange vibes. I got this ominous sensation, yes, that's it - a foreboding." I rub my hands along my arms. "It left me with chills." Gabe holds me close, rubs along the length of my arms and my back. His body feels warm against mine.

I've got chills in the middle of July?

"Gabe, he stood right there." I point to where I'd just seen the boy statue. "Right there beside the girl. Mom had one exactly like her. The boy did *not* belong there, we never had one in our backyard." I frown recalling the feeling I had. "He seemed to mock me. So unsettling."

I stop, see the expression on Gabe's face. "You didn't see any of what I just saw, did you?"

Gabe's eyes dart from one side to the other. He's more confused than I am. He shakes his head. "No, baby, I didn't."

His response sends a new wave of chills over me causing me to shudder. How could he not see it? He turns to look in the direction of the swing then back at me. He's probably trying to filter out just how much of what I saw was an exaggeration on my part. None of it was, it was all right there. And now how can I explain the unexplainable?

"I knew something weird was happening," he says, rubbing my arms again. "You reached out, fluttering your fingertips. What were you reaching for?"

"The fronds of flowers spilling over. I thought I could touch them. It was so strange, a Twilight Zone-ish kind of weird. I shake my head, wave both hands in front of my face as if I could actually rid myself of the visions which linger there. "I'm okay now...it's gone...I think."

Gabe keeps his eyes on mine, delving deeper looking for an answer I know he won't find. It's just not there. "Let's sit here. In a while we can go inside and decide what we'll have for lunch."

We sit on weathered, yet sturdy, lawn chairs under the shade of the covered porch which has two empty hummingbird feeders hanging from its cross beams. Three large pecan trees a couple of yards beyond the porch provide lots of shade for the picnic table. As I close my eyes, I push aside those crazy visions as quickly as they appear. I focus instead on the sweetness of Gabe's touch as he lightly strokes his fingers back and forth along the top of my bare foot which I've propped on his knee. Then I giggle when he begins to sing.

"Gotcha! I knew it was only a matter of time before you'd start singing *The Long and Winding Road.*"

"Yeah, it's been in my head since you said *long and winding.*"

"Mine too."

"How do you feel?" I still hear concern in his voice.

"Fine, babe. I'm fine. Maybe it was the heat, or lack of sleep or a combination of the two. *Or perhaps I'm going crazy?*

Why wouldn't he be concerned? Probably thought I'd gone bonkers. Damn me for starting our week here this way. But it's not like I purposely tilted my antenna to pick up whatever freak show was playing. *It just happened.* I make a decision to banish any thoughts of what occurred. I let myself sit back and relax. From this point on it will only be Gabe, me, and this beautiful lake house.

We have a view of the whole lake from where we're sitting. Stepping stones lead to a weathered grey pier. There's a small rowboat laying upside down on the grass beside it.

"Wow," Gabe says, pointing to a fish jumping through the air. I haven't gone fishing in a long time. You want to try it? I can teach you."

"Gabe, if I recall correctly, the one time you took me fishing my rod ended up in the water the first time I tried to cast."

He laughs. "Yeah, I remember. Guess I can tie your hand to the rod."

"What is it with you and tying up my hands?"

"Ha! Thanks for reminding me," he says, wiggling his eyebrows.

"You're incorrigible, Gabe."

"Sorry, I'm a lost cause. So are you interested?"

"In what? Fishing or my hands getting tied up?"

"Both."

"Can I use fake bait?"

Gabe chuckles. "Yes, you can use a lure." Dad's tackle box is in the shed. Got plenty of lures to pick from."

Gabe gets up, offers me his hand. "Come on, baby, let's go check out our little sugar shack."

As Gabe reaches for the doorknob, I glance back at the swing. *Good, nothing weird going on there.*

We walk into the screened porch. A washer, dryer, and storage cabinets stand along one side, a footlocker on another. There are four folding chairs and a folding table leaning against the wall, a croquet set and badminton rackets alongside them. I see garden tools, lady's garden gloves and a few badminton birdies inside a basket which sits on a table. Gabe shoves open the door which leads into the house.

We enter a combination kitchen/living area divided by a kitchen counter with four barstools. I expected a musty smell, but there's the slight smell of Mr. Clean and the unmistakable smell of Johnson's Wax, a scent which is forever imbedded in my memory.

"Smells like your mom did some housecleaning."

"Yeah, I can smell cleaning stuff."

There's a rustic feel to the spacious living room with its vaulted ceiling and exposed beams. A sofa which sits against one wall has big plush cushions which I could easily get lost in, plus there are two over-stuffed chairs on either side of a wood-burning fireplace which is made of stacked boulders and reaches to the top of the pointed ceiling.

A coffee table sits in the center of the room on a braided rug with two child-sized wooden chairs pushed up against it. The wood floors are stained a dark shade of brown. French doors to the left lead to a room which faces the lake, another door leads to the bedroom.

"I love it, Gabe. So rustic."

Gabe opens the French doors. "Check out this wall of windows facing the lake."

I follow him into a room with the most unbelievable view. The room has three twin beds evenly spaced across the room and a sofa at one end with a small bookshelf beside it. *Little Golden Books* line the bottom shelf. The next two shelves hold an array of adult books.

I point to them. "These people left in a hurry. Probably too painful for them. Left the books and the girl's chairs. They walked away...didn't look back."

Gabe nods. "Yeah, it's sad."

Old linen covered books with worn edges line the top shelf. I pull one out. *How to be Personally Efficient in Business. Hmm, copyrighted 1912.*

"War and Peace," Gabe says, flipping through the pages. *"Revised translation copyright, 1949."*

I pull out a small one with frayed edges. "What about this. *The Book of Life,* by Robert Collier. Listen to this. *Yours is the world and everything that's in it.*" I flip a few pages. "It's the first volume of seven. Wow, a signed copy and the copyright date is 1925. Didn't bother to take these either."

Gabe shrugs. "They'd lost their little girls. Nothing else mattered."

How horrible to have to walk away without your little girls. Compared to losing your children, these books mean nothing. It makes sense to me how they were able to leave it all behind.

The three beds are covered with patchwork quilts. A cedar chest sits at the foot of each one. I open a chest, Gabe another, they're both lined with cedar. One has toys, the other has blankets. The third one has board games and various children's toys.

We move on to the master bedroom. There's a double bed centered between two windows and a chest of drawers on the wall to the right. On the opposite side, they've placed two upholstered wingback chairs by a double window which overlooks the garden. It's the one we saw when we arrived. Between the chairs is a table with a reading lamp. Two books sit on the table top and a stack of *Reader's Digest* magazines on the lower shelf.

"I love everything about this place. So glad your dad bought it. I hope we'll get to use it often."

"Just listen to you. *I don't know, Gabe, it's such a creepy little place,*" he says in a girly voice.

"I know, I know," I say, then giggle recalling the silly voice he just used. "Can you do your prissy girl voice again for me?"

"No! I have no idea where I pulled her from. But she's gone. And we must never speak of her again," he says, trying to suppress a smile, but then there it is. I'm sure the smirk on his face is to buy my silence. I twist an invisible key at the corner of my tightly closed lips.

"Mums the word...Gabriella," I say with a wink which makes Gabe laugh. He reaches out to flick a finger against my arm, which I manage to dodge.

Back in the kitchen area, we decide this is going to be the perfect setting for us to try to work through some tough issues.

"Gabe, this place and my unexpected spill-your-guts-session with Nancy has left me optimistic. Maybe the time has come to go back to my past. Time to make things right."

"What? Go back in time?"

"Oh gosh, back in time? I wish. But no, I didn't mean physically. I'd like to mentally go back, make peace with the bad memories and enjoy reliving the good ones. This has got to be the perfect place to do it."

Gabe takes me into his arms. Oh, how I love his hugs. Already my words and his arms around me radiate a warmth which moves right through me. I'm left with a tremendous sense of hope believing we can accomplish what we came here to do.

"I'll get our bags so we can get settled then maybe get started on lunch. Dad says there are steaks in the fridge we can grill."

"Dad was right, not much of a kitchen. Small sink, small refrigerator, and a microwave oven. He said we'd find an electric skillet and a toaster in there somewhere."

A cursory glance in one open cabinet tells me this small kitchen has plenty to offer. Included in the heap of small kitchen appliances is a waffle iron. I see a yummy breakfast in our future. Now if I can find us some syrup and bacon. Knowing Gabe's mom, she bought both.

"Yes, it's small," I say, "but it's fine, after all, it's just the two of us."

I check to see what we might have for an appetizer to have with our wine while our steaks are grilling. I take out the Swiss cheese and check the cabinet for crackers. Find a box of Ritz. I also find paper plates and plastic wrap.

I slice up the cheese and arrange it on a paper plate, cover it with plastic wrap and set it back in the refrigerator. I put away the wedding cake, which Gabe placed on the counter; it will be our dessert. I read the label on the bottle of wine Gabe brought in. Wow, he bought this while on our honeymoon in San Francisco to help us celebrate our first anniversary. It was Gabe's idea. I love that he's romantic like that, and I'm impressed he remembered to bring it.

I'm washing my hands at the kitchen sink when Gabe walks in. "Guess what, no charcoal. We'll need to go to the Horton's farm. It's about four miles away."

"Think Mr. Horton will have some?"

"He told Dad there was plenty and we can help ourselves."

"Maybe you should go alone," I say, grabbing a dish towel to dry my hands. "I'll stay here and work on lunch."

"Are you sure, you're not—"

"Afraid I'll get snatched away?"

"Just checking."

"I'll be fine. This place is so isolated; I'm not worried. I'm good, really."

Gabe stands there with his thinking face on. "No, I've decided I want you to come with me. We said we'd be together for a *whole* week, so let's be together for the *whole* week."

"Okay, your call."

Gabe pats his shirt pocket. "Good."

"What are you looking for?"

"Dad gave me Mr. Horton's phone number, I took it out of my pocket and stuffed it inside the glove compartment."

"So go get it."

"Dad said he left a copy in the phonebook, let me check. Gabe opens it, takes out a slip of paper and glances at it. He looks back at the phonebook and pulls a newspaper clipping from between the pages. He unfolds it and scans it.

"Hey, baby, check this out. It's an article about the disappearances."

"You mean, the twins? From here?"

"Yep. Are you ready to hear what happened?"

8

1971 – Gabriel Marquez

The realization kicks in. It really happened. I hope Ella can handle this. Hell, I'm not so sure that *I* can.

Ella reaches for my hand. Her other hand goes to her stomach. "Gabe, my heart spun into overdrive, and my stomach turned into a knot."

"Know what you mean."

"You too? The title...it jumped off the page at me, *Four-year-old Twins Missing from Their Home.* Not just any home...this home. I'm not ready to hear it." Her hand goes to her mouth, she closes her eyes, and the color drains from her face.

"Let me get you some water." I fold the article in half and set it down on the counter.

"Thanks. I got all queasy when I thought about what might have happened to them. And it all started right here."

"It gave me a strange feeling too," I say, opening a cabinet.

Ella points to the cabinet beside the refrigerator. "Glasses are right there."

I give Ella her water, pick up the clipping and step away to read it.

"It reads okay," I say. "The article's not shocking or sensationalized. There's a picture of the girls."

"Yes, I caught a glimpse." She sits there rubbing her arms.

"Are you cold? I can adjust the air conditioner."

Ella nods. I go to the window unit, turn it up a couple of notches. "I know what else will warm you up."

"Hmm, I haven't seen that smirk since you threatened to tie me to the bed post."

Smiling, I ask, "You keep a smirk log?"

"Would you believe me if I said *yes?*"

"Yes, I would. Close your eyes and don't move," I say as I head to the bedroom.

"Tell me you didn't go in there to fetch a rope," she says, raising her voice so that I'll hear her. "And how is it you can make me laugh when I'm feeling glum?"

"Me? You're the one saying all the funny stuff."

"No, you said *smirk log.* That was funny."

I return to the living room, and she's still sitting there with her eyes closed, hands sweetly folded in her lap, her bare feet propped on the stool rung. When I strum my guitar, a smile brightens her face and she opens her eyes.

"You brought your guitar?"

I walk up to Ella, and she places her hands on my shoulders then strokes the back of my neck. The tips of her fingers run through my hair, and the light touch of her fingernails against my scalp sends goosebumps all over me, and it feels so good.

"When did you put it in the car?"

I place a kiss on her forehead. "Snuck it in before I left for dinner with Anthony. I hid it behind the front seat."

I take a stool from the bar and place it facing Ella, sit down and strum four cords on my guitar.

"Good Day Sunshine?"

I smile. "Yep."

She pulls me forward and kisses the corner of my mouth. *She loves that smirk.* I love watching her smile and her eyes sparkle as I sing the song for her. I knew I'd picked the perfect song, one that would lift her spirits.

"You are so wonderful," she says through tears. "I know, I know, I'm such a cry baby. It's just that I was so touched. The guitar was a surprise, and you couldn't have picked a better song. Thank you."

"Glad you liked it."

"I did, and it really helped." She takes a deep breath. "It actually calmed me. I think I'm ready to hear the story now. Let's get it over with so we can put it behind us, and the rest of the week will be ours."

"Good idea."

I take the clipping and lay it on the counter for us to read. It's a half-page story with photos of the twins and a smaller one of the shed they were last seen entering. I look at Ella before beginning just to make sure.

"Go ahead, read it."

She stands next to me leaning in to follow along, looping her arm snuggly around mine.

"Oh, Gabe, look at those adorable faces. Those beautiful curls. Those smiles. Look at those crinkly eyes. I think they're giggling in this picture. Gabriel this is so sad."

I clear my throat and look at Ella, again wanting to make sure she's ready for this. "Go on," she says, nodding her head.

"Here's a quote from the mother.

I'd read to them from their favorite book, Madeline's Rescue, *while we enjoyed our lunch outdoors on the picnic table. I've read it to them several times this year. When I finished reading, they went off to play in the shed. One side of it is set up as a play area; it's their favorite place to be. I gathered everything we'd brought out for lunch and went inside to put it away. When I came back outside to work on the flowerbeds, I heard the girls laughing and counting to five over and over again. They were enjoying themselves. About fifteen minutes or so later they came running out giggling, said they were counting fireflies. I told them they were silly. There are no fireflies in the daytime. They ran back into the shed, giggling all the way.*

"Fireflies?" I ask.

Ella shakes her head. "Not during the day."

I go back to reading the article. *"I continued to work in the flowerbeds for maybe another fifteen minutes when I realized I hadn't heard a peep out of them since they'd gone back inside the shed. I don't know when I stopped hearing them count. I called for Elizabeth and then Amelia, neither answered. I went to look for them, and they weren't there. Searched everywhere. They were nowhere to be found. I couldn't understand. I never saw them come out."*

Ella wipes her hand across her eyes. "How horrible to find your children missing. Their parents haven't seen those beautiful little faces in over a year."

"Baby, this doesn't sound right to me," I say, shaking the article in my hand. "Their mom was so close to the shed. There's no way anyone could have taken them without her noticing something. How could she not have heard the girls call out?"

Ella nods. "Right, those girls were definitely not taken. They had to have left quietly on their own when the mom wasn't looking, exactly as you said."

I reach to take her hand, but she pulls it away, stares at her palm, fingers spread apart. I wait. Ella's about to count off points of logic.

"First," she says, ticking it off on her little finger, "is it possible the mom went back inside and didn't remember? I doubt it. Think about it, who wouldn't remember even the tiniest detail of the day their children disappeared? Second, can a four-year-old walk fast enough to get beyond the bend in the road in fifteen or twenty minutes? Don't think so. Third, if a car or truck took them away how could she not hear it come up the private road or when they drove away? A car scenario doesn't work. This is so *out of this world* crazy, Gabe."

Ella rolls her shoulders then bends her head from side to side. I place my hands on her shoulders and give her a gentle massage. My fingers feel the tightness there. I continue to rub until she gives in to my touch and allows herself to relax. She takes a deep chest raising breath then slowly releases it.

"Ah, thank you, babe. I needed that."

I kiss Ella on the side of her neck, and she responds with a sigh. "There's more where that came from."

"Have you been inside the shed?" She asks as she spins around on her stool to face me.

"Yes, when I was out looking for wood."

"What's in there?"

"A cabinet chock full of all kinds of tools and fishing rods resting across brackets on the wall. You'd appreciate how organized everything is in there. You'll like the shelving and baskets attached to the walls used to hold an array of gadgets."

"Did you see a play area?"

"Uh...yes. It's a separate small room to the right side. There's a rug, a couple of dolls, and doll clothes laying on it. One doll was halfway wrapped in a blanket; another blanket was thrown off to one side. I also noticed a shelf with toys."

"Oh, Gabe, the girls were playing there before they disappeared. Those poor parents left all that stuff behind too. That's how painful it was."

"Yeah, the hairs on the back of my neck stood on end when I saw the toys, knowing those were the last things they'd probably touched. I found an empty box, put the toys inside and stuck it against the wall on the other side of the shed."

"Sorry. So glad I didn't see it."

"I figured. That's why I didn't mention it before."

Ella finishes the rest of her water and scoots herself off the stool. While she takes her glass to the kitchen, I call Mr. Horton.

"Come on," I say, taking her hand. "Mr. Horton said we could come by. Think of a good excuse we can use to leave. According to Mom, they'll talk forever."

"How about we say we're starved?"

"That should work, it's past lunchtime. You can give me a nod when you're ready to go, I'll do the same."

Once outside, we're greeted by a gentle breeze, and with the sun shining brightly on the rippling water, it gives us a brilliant display of dancing diamonds on its surface. I take a deep breath, Ella does too. "Gotta love this country air," I say.

"Yeah. And listen to the sound of the trees swaying to the rhythm of the song the birds are singing," Ella says. "You know, those big ol' trees have witnessed so much. They stood right there where they're standing now when those girls disappeared, but they aren't talking. So many stories they could tell about what's gone on within these forty acres. If only trees could talk."

As we drive down the private drive leading out to the main road, I realize how long it takes to reach the bend from the cabin, and this is by car. I can't imagine how those short legs could possibly make the hike to the point where the road turns in a matter of twenty minutes. If the mom checked down the road, she would've seen them. Nope, they couldn't have walked off on their own.

"Babe, there's no way they could've walked to this point in twenty minutes or even an hour," Ella says.

"Yeah, was just thinking the same thing."

"So what happened to them, Gabe? Where'd they go? None of it makes sense. The sheriff's office must still be scratching their heads."

Soon after arriving at the Horton's farm, I realize mom was right, it isn't going to be easy to wrap up a conversation with folks who love to tell stories. They treat us like old friends and insist we call them Tom and Tina. Tom's a tall, stocky old man, with a scruffy beard and grey hair that's slicked back.

They take pride showing us around the place, pointing out what's growing *here and yonder,* while their golden lab, Mrs. Beasley, follows behind. They talk about each of their four children and grandkids. We're patient, let them enjoy their chance to visit.

Tina is also tall with hair as grey as his and has striking blue eyes that contrast her dark sun-leathered skin. "Move along, Darla," Tina says to a calico cat sitting on a bench, then picks up a large basket filled to the brim with yellow onions. "Have a seat, Ella." Tina carries the onions to the other side of the porch.

I'll bet Tina does her share around this farm.

Tina runs her hands through her short curly hair. "Guess you've heard about the missing Carlton girls,"

I nod. "Yes, found a news article."

Tina shakes her head. "They were so sweet. They spoke with an adorable British accent. The mother's British, the father's American. But one look at those rosy red cheeks you'd swear they were Brits."

"We found a newspaper article with a picture of the twins. It gives the mother's account of what happened," Ella says.

"Bless their hearts, Martha had finished reading to them from *Madeline's Rescue.* They would beg her for a puppy like the ones in the story, but Martha's allergic to dogs and would tell them there weren't any puppies available rather than explain her illness to them."

Ella turns to Tina. "Has there been more information on the twins?"

"We haven't heard a thing," Tina says, shaking her head. "Nothing at all. The last time we spoke to the Carlton's was a couple of months after it happened. Martha said Frank, the girls' father, accepted a job in Dallas and they planned to move that week. I never heard from her again. She was still so distraught when we spoke."

Ella looks at me, gives me the nod.

"Well, we need to get going. It was nice meeting you both," I say.

"Yes, it was," Ella quickly adds.

"Must you rush off?" Tina asks.

"I wish we could stay longer," Ella says, "but we have a couple of steaks waiting to be put on the grill. I'm starved."

Larry pats my back. "Let's get that wood loaded in the trunk before it starts raining. You're welcome to come back for more."

"Thanks, appreciate it," I say.

We load up, get in the car, and wave goodbye. As we take off, a misty drizzle begins to cover the windshield. Ella lowers her window, takes a deep breath. "Don't you just love the smell of rain as it hits the ground?"

"Yes," I say, lowering my window. "And you know what, I think it smells even sweeter out here. Probably the combination of rain on the ground and all these trees."

The rain stops when we're about a mile away from the cabin. It's dry out here. We begin unloading the wood laying it down along the side of the shed. When we head back with our last batch laughter catches our attention.

"Who's that?"

Ella shrugs.

As we make our way up to the top of the slope, two curly haired little girls come walking out of the shed toward us. One has brown hair, the other red. They're in long nightgowns, little bare feet poking out from under them. They stop, look at each other, and giggle. They return their gaze back to us and smile. My jaw drops. Ella turns back in my direction, eyes wide.

"It's them," Ella whispers.

9

1971 – Gabriel Marquez

A look of disbelief quickly turns into one of amazement. Ella stoops and places the wood on the ground. The girls look at us, eyes wide and unblinking. The redhead reaches for the brunette's hand. They look at each other. The brunette shrugs and smiles at her sister.

The redhead turns back to look at Ella. "*Bon matin.*"

"*Bon matin,*" I respond.

Ella's head snaps back at me, eyebrows raised.

"She said good morning in French," I say.

"With a British accent," Ella whispers. "It's them."

I nod, turn back to the girls. "Comment tu t'appelles?" I ask.

"Elizabeth," says the redhead. She turns to her sister, tugs at her hand.

"Amelia," the brunette responds.

Ella stays where she is, resting her hands on her knees. "Ella," she says, placing a hand to her chest.

I place my hand on mine. "Gabe."

"Where do you live?" Ella asks.

Amelia shrugs, Elizabeth points to the cabin.

Ella turns and says, "I think Elizabeth understood me. Can you ask again in French?"

"That French class in college was so long ago...let me think." Not sure this is right, but what the heck I'll give it a shot. "*Habitez*? No, wait. *Habites-tu*?"

"Paris en France," Amelia says. Elizabeth points to the cabin again.

"France?" I ask.

They nod.

Ella's eyes grow wide. I'm as puzzled as she is. These are the children we saw in the newspaper article. Maybe a little older, but same faces, same hair, same names. No one said anything about them speaking French, though. French with a British accent. This is crazy, and today of all days, they return. And their reappearance is as strange as their disappearance. Elizabeth remembers the cabin. Maybe Amelia doesn't recognize where she is.

"*Nous avons vu lucioles.*" Elizabeth points to the shed, smiling.

"Oui!" Amelia exclaims.

"They saw fireflies," I tell Ella.

"Fireflies? In broad daylight? Again."

"That's what they said."

"And you just happen to know how to say fireflies in French?"

"We translated a poem about fireflies by Robert Frost in French class. I guess the word *lucioles* stuck with me."

Ella turns to look at me. "I'm impressed." She gives me a half-smile, nodding her head.

"Yeah, I'm a lot smarter then I look." I laugh.

"Gabe, we need to find their mommy and daddy."

"Mommy! Daddy!" both girls exclaim at once.

"Oh, you sweethearts, you want to see your mommy and daddy."

They nod, but one of them says *oui* and the other *yes*.

"They're bilingual," Ella says in amazement.

"I don't know what to think, I better go make phone calls," I say.

"Okay, I'll get them something to eat. They might be hungry."

Ella waves at them to follow her into the house and takes them to the bathroom sink to wash their hands. When they're done, I pick up Amelia and place her on a stool, then Elizabeth. Ella begins washing peaches as the twins sit there watching and rattling on in French with a little bit of English thrown in and giggling between sentences. Ella slices some peaches and places them on plates then motions to the girls to join her. She helps them off their stools, and they follow her into the dayroom.

I stand there and watch.

"Hey you, make that phone call," Ella says, shutting the paneled glass doors.

I'm still in disbelief, and I'm stuck standing here wondering what the heck I'm going to say, and who the hell am I going to say it to. I take the sheet of paper Dad gave me with important numbers and find the sheriff's office listed. I begin dialing the number then decide I should call the Horton's first. Have no idea how long it will take for the girls' parents to show up so it would be helpful to have someone around who actually knows them.

Tina answers. "Hello?"

"Hello, Tina, this is Gabe Marquez. You are *not* going to believe what I'm about to tell you."

"Oh dear," she chuckles." What is it?"

"The twins, Elizabeth and Amelia Carlton, they're here." There's a pause. I wait. "Tina, did you hear me?"

"Could you repeat that, please?"

"The Carlton girls, they're here with us at the cabin."

"Oh my stars! Are you sure it's them?"

"They look just like the twins we saw in the article, both have curly hair. One is a brunette, and the other's a redhead, and—"

"Did they actually say they were Elizabeth and Amelia?"

"Yes, ma'am, they did."

"Glory be! Thank you, God!"

"I thought it would be a good idea if you and Tom would come here since they know you."

"Yes, we'll be right over."

As I put the receiver down, I hear Tina yell out. "Tom, get over here!"

Good luck explaining that one, Tina.

I pop my head into the dayroom and motion for Ella to come with me.

"I don't want to leave them alone," she says through a partially opened door.

"We can keep an eye on them from here."

They're sitting on the couch enjoying their peaches. It's still hard to believe this is happening. As soon as the Horton's show up and can say they are the Carlton kids, I'll call the sheriff's office.

Ella puts her arms around my waist. I hug her back, then give her a kiss. She tastes and smells like peaches.

"What if I hadn't agreed to come? What would have happened to these poor little girls if we hadn't been here?"

"It's a scary thought."

"Very. They would be miles from the closest house. Poor kids running around barefoot and in long flannel nightgowns." She hugs me again then pulls away, a crease forming between her brows. "Flannel? It's July."

She turns to watch the girls enjoying their peaches, giggling between bites.

"You know what I thought was strange," Ella says. "In her statement, Mrs. Carlton said the girls were laughing about seeing fireflies, and—"

"It's exactly what they were doing when we found them. Coincidence?" I ask.

"Who knows? So were you able to talk to someone?"

"I spoke to Tina instead. Wanted to make sure it's really them first. They're on their way."

"Good idea." Ella shakes her head. "I don't get this. Could someone have dropped them off while we were gone?"

"They must've. But who? Obviously, someone who speaks French, unless their father's French."

"Nope, Tina said the dad is American. Maybe French-American?" Ella asks.

"Carlton doesn't sound French to me. We'll find out soon enough."

We hear a vehicle coming up the road. "See there," I say, "the truck isn't even here yet, and we can hear it from inside the cabin."

"Right, we definitely can rule out any idea that they were taken by truck or car."

When the Horton's pull up, I walk out to greet them. They quickly run in my direction.

"Where are they?" Tina asks, her eyes filled with tears.

"Inside eating peaches."

We walk in, Ella points toward the dayroom with a huge smile on her face and tears in her eyes. Tina leans in to take a peek.

"Dear God in heaven, it's them, it's Amelia and Elizabeth."

"Auntie Tina?" Amelia asks with a big smile.

The twins quickly get up and come to the door. Amelia goes to Tina and Elizabeth to Tom.

They speak to Tina and Tom in French too fast for me to follow.

"Are they speaking in French?" Tina is apparently surprised by this.

I point to Tina and Tom and tell the girls, "*Ne parle pas français.*"

Hearing that, Elizabeth immediately switches to English, which she speaks a little slower than she does her French. "Eat some, Auntie Tina," she says, handing her a slice of peach.

"Thank you," Tina says.

Amelia pats Tina's knee wanting her attention. "Where's Mommy?" she asks.

Tina presses her hands to her cheek, her eyes shiny with new tears. "Oh, honey, mommy and daddy aren't here right now. They'll be here soon," she says then takes a deep breath.

Amelia hugs Tina, and Elizabeth joins them. No telling what these girls have been through. They appear to be fine on the outside, but how are they doing emotionally. What's going on in their little heads?

Tina runs a hand through each of the girl's curly locks. "Who brought you here?"

"Fireflies," Elizabeth says.

"Oui," Amelia giggles.

Ella whispers into my ear. "What is it with those dang fireflies?"

I shrug. "Beats me, but this time Elizabeth says the fireflies brought them here, not that they saw fireflies."

Ella rolls her eyes. "Kids and their crazy imaginations, I guess."

Tom leans in. "I've got to make an important phone call. Can't wait to tell the sheriff's office we've found the Carlton twins."

Tom carries the phone as far as the line will allow, which is all the way into the screened porch. He closes the door behind him.

Ella pulls me toward the kitchen. "This is unbelievable. I'm so glad Tom and Tina know them. Hope someone can reach their parents right away," she whispers. She takes out a plate of assorted cheese from the refrigerator and sets it on the counter.

"I'd hate for them to be placed in a strange home until the parents show up," I say, grabbing a cube of cheese. "I forgot that I was hungry."

"I know, me too." Ella picks up a slice of Swiss. "Do you think they might let the Horton's take them home with them? They seem as close as family." She takes a box of crackers and places them in a bowl. "I hope so."

I notice a serving tray on the top of the refrigerator. "Need this?"

"Yes, let me wipe it off first." She runs a wet sponge over the surface, grabs a dish towel to dry it as she watches me munch on crackers.

"Poor baby, I bet you're starved," she says, placing a cracker with cheese in my mouth.

"Gabe, bring the bowl of peaches, will ya?" Ella carries the tray to the coffee table, and then goes to the dayroom and peeks in. "Would anyone like a glass of juice with cheese and crackers? I've got more peaches too."

The twins immediately get up. "Yes, please," Elizabeth says.

"I've got tea if you'd prefer, Tina, or wine."

"Thank you, Ella, but I'm fine, we had just finished eating when Gabe called."

I pour Ella and me a glass of wine. I know my nerves need settling, I'm sure hers do too. I'm helping myself to more of the cheese and crackers when Tom walks in with the phone in hand. He sets it down on the table and turns to us, his eyes are moist, and his face is flushed.

"Why don't we step into the porch, we can watch the girls from there," I say

When we're all gathered, Tina asks, "So what did they say?"

"Well, for starters, they were as shocked as we were," he says with a huge grin on his face. "The more excited the deputy got, the louder he got."

"This is a biggie for them. It turns out the sheriff's a good friend of the Carlton's. He and his wife are the children's God parents. How 'bout that?"

"Do they know where the Carlton's are living?" Tina asks.

"Said they live in the Dallas area, less than two hours away. The Sheriff was already on the phone with them when we hung up."

"Wow," I say, "I didn't expect things to move so quickly."

"So is someone from the sheriff's department coming out?" Tina asks, glancing over at the twins. "Shhhh, they're coming this way," she whispers.

Tom lowers his voice. "Sheriff's gonna wait for Martha and Frank to show up and drive out here with them. Should be three hours or so. I told them we would take the girls to the house to get them fed," Tom says, smiling at Tina.

"We've got clothes that belonged to our grandkids they can change into. They've got to be warm in those nightgowns. Who puts flannel on kids in the middle of summer?" Tina asks, then breathes a sigh. "What an unbelievable day this turned out to be."

We go back inside, and Tina goes to the twins. "Your mommy and daddy will be here soon, but first let's go to my house and get you out of those pajamas, okay?"

The girls clap their hands and smile at each other. "We get to see Darla and Mrs. Beasley!" Amelia says, and they clap their hands again.

We walk Tom, Tina, and the girls out to the truck. Before they climb in, Elizabeth and Amelia give Ella and me hugs. They wave as they drive away.

I turn to Ella. "I still can't believe that happened."

Ella shrugs. "Whatever *that* was! Kids showing up after being gone for a year, speaking a language they didn't learn at home, wearing flannels...in July. Do hope the girls will be able to provide some clues."

"I'm glad those poor little girls will be back with their parents soon," I say.

Ella nods. "But two hours can seem like a long time for little kids. I wish I would've thought to send the dolls and a few toys with them to keep them busy. Those girls were so excited to be home they didn't even think about their toys either."

I stop as I go to open the door to the screened porch. "Why don't I get the box of toys and run them down to the Horton's. It'll help keep them entertained."

We go to the shed to get the box of toys I'd gathered earlier. Back inside, we add a few books off the shelf. I take my keys out of my pocket. "You want to come along?"

"No, I'll stay, it'll give you a good reason to leave. You can tell them you don't want to keep me waiting."

"Ella, do you realize that we've been here over half a day and we haven't even begun to get our first wedding anniversary in motion?"

"Yes, the thought just crossed my mind. That's quite a distraction we've had."

"Come here, baby." I take her in my arms and hold her for just a moment. Ella looks up at me, and I kiss her lips. Then again, a bit more passionately. My kisses move to her neck then run along her sweet shoulder. She moans. It's barely audible, but it has a major affect on me, none the less. "You are so easy," I whisper.

"Hey, come on, you know how those kisses on my neck turn me on."

"Uh-huh, you want more?" I give her a few more kisses, making it hard for her to resist. Her head tilts back allowing me to place more of those kisses she loves from the tip of her chin down the front of her neck then toward her breast. But then she wiggles out from under me. "Oh, baby, you have no idea what you're doing to me," I moan.

"Umm, actually, I can *feel* what I'm doing to you," she says, giving me a couple of eye brow raises.

"You are such a tease," I say and give her another passionate kiss on the lips which she readily responds to, and then I feel her tense up.

I pull away. "You need me to stop, don't you?"

She nods. "Yeah. I'm sorry, but just for a little while. A glass of wine will help."

"Don't be sorry. I understand. Besides, I have a box of toys to deliver, remember? We can pick up where we left off after dinner."

As we walk to the car with the toys, Ella snaps her head toward the arbor swing and gasps. I turn and look at her. *Not again*

"I could've sworn I saw two fireflies, but they fizzled away."

"In broad daylight, Ella? You've heard way too many stories about *lucioles*."

"Right," she says, looking back at the arbor swing again as we walk toward the car.

10

1971 – Ella Marquez

While Gabe is off delivering toys, I work on getting our sides ready for dinner. As I chop, cook and stir, my mind is not on what I'm doing, rather on the fireflies, the ones I saw as we walked past the swing. A bright, sunshiny day and I saw fireflies. What is it with lightning bugs around here?

"You mean, *lucioles*, Ella," I say with a giggle.

This place holds so much wonder, what will we encounter next?

It occurs to me that it's been almost a half hour since Gabe left. I'm guessing he'll be coming around any moment. As I put away the skillet, I notice a tea kettle and decide a cup of tea is just what I need. I get the water boiling and find mint tea in the cupboard. After everything I've been through today, I could use something herbal. First, there was the unexplainable ViewMaster experience, then the twins reappeared, and later I saw two fireflies. It was the middle of the afternoon, but there they were. I really did see them, and then they fizzled away.

But fireflies don't fizzle away.

I add the boiling water to the tea, and as it steeps, I watch the steam rise from my cup. I'm totally captivated by it billowing upward. I stare at it and inhale the sweet, warm minty aroma. What's going on here? I'm sharing a *moment* with my tea? I laugh feeling like a spaced out hippy tripping on mint tea. All I need is a flowing white gauzy gown and flowers in my hair. But hippies didn't snort stuff, they only smoked funky grass...I think.

What is it with this cabin? It's a mind bending, mind opening, kinda place.

I take my tea with me out to the swing and check my watch. Gabe's been gone over an hour. Well, I think I know what happened, he got caught in all the excitement of the twins showing up. Tom and Tina probably had more stories to share, and I'm not there to nod my head and tell him it's time to split.

I check around before taking a seat on the swing. No *lucioles.* None above me either just dried up twisted vines resting on the arbor. I place my cup on the table beside the swing to cool and then take several long deep breaths. *It's been one crazy day.*

As I take my first sip of my tea, I hear the faint sound of a car coming up the road. My shoulders slump in relief. *Finally.*

I head toward the driveway to wait for Gabe, carefully sipping my tea as I walk along the path. But it's not him making his way around the final curve, it's a police car. He must've gotten his wires crossed.

When his car finally comes to a stop on the crunchy gravel, I wave hello. "I'm afraid you've come to the wrong place," I tell him as he walks toward me. "The twins are—"

"Mrs. Marquez?"

"Yes, that's me, but the twins aren't here."

He reaches his hand out. "Hello," he says, shaking my hand with a firm grip. "I'm from the county sheriff's department, I'm Officer Collins."

Not sure he heard what I said, so I repeat myself.

"Ma'am, I'm sorry, this isn't about the Carlton twins. It's about Mr. Marquez."

"What about him?" I ask, my breath catching in my throat. "Where's Gabe?" Suddenly I'm afraid to hear his answer. I take a deep inhalation of the minty fragrance from my cup as if it would help absorb the brunt of what I'm about to hear.

"Mrs. Marquez there's been an accident."

I look up at him. "An accident? Gabe?" I ask wrapping my hands around my mug. It feels warm against my hands, yet there's a cold chill running through me. *But it can't be,* I tell myself. *He just went down the road to drop off some toys.*

"He's been taken to a nearby hospital."

My breath comes in quick shallow breaths. I try to inhale deeply, but I can't. To stop my hands from shaking, I grip them tighter around my mug.

"What happened? He's okay, right?" I ask, trying to read his face.

"I reached your husband shortly after the accident. He was more coherent by the time they put him in the ambulance."

"What do you mean *more* coherent?"

"He was unconscious when we got to him."

"Lost consciousness?" Goosebumps surface all over my arms as I picture Gabe being taken away unconscious. My body trembles, my knees buckle, and I fall forward against the officer, splashing some of my tea on his shirt. "Oh, I'm so sorry."

"It's okay, ma'am. I got you."

"I'm fine now." I straighten my shoulders, broaden my stance. *I need to be strong.* "So he opened his eyes, and he's okay now?"

He nods. "My partner and I happened to be in the area. We heard the accident as it was happening, the screeching of tires, crashing of metal. I immediately called it in. An ambulance was dispatched right away. Your husband was lucky we were nearby."

"So *is* he okay now? Tell me!"

"He was disoriented. His speech was slurred."

"Thank God, he was talking. Did he tell you if he was hurting? How he felt?"

"He said *Ella* and smiled. Then I think he said, *Hey Bartelli,* or something like that. And he smiled again. For a guy who was just broadsided, he sure seemed happy. Oh, he also said the name Fishers, a Mr. Fishers maybe? He was able to tell us you were here. Held on to my arm until I assured him I knew exactly what cabin he was talking about. I asked if it was the Carlton cabin. He nodded and let go of my arm."

I'm stunned, and I'm scared beyond belief. But If Gabe's smiling, he must be okay. Funny thing is I wanted to go back in time, but it sounds like Gabe's mentally there now.

"So there weren't any bad injuries?" I ask.

"From what I could see, there was a scrape along one side of his face from the edge of his eye to his jaw. He was unconscious for a moment, so it's possible he may have sustained a head injury."

"So they took him to the hospital for observation? Is that what you're saying? What hospital?"

"Yes, they did. Mrs. Marquez, but I haven't been told which one yet. When I find out I can drive you there if you'd like."

"Yes, please, but I need to get my purse."

"Take your time. I need to radio back to let the dispatcher know I've contacted you. And I'll see if I can get more information on Mr. Marquez's status."

"Thank you, I'll wait at the swing behind the cabin, if that's okay," I say, pointing toward the swing."

He nods and heads toward his car. I take in a big breath and exhale it long and slow as I head back inside. I grab my purse and go back outside to wait, damning myself the whole time for not going with Gabriel. Maybe it wouldn't have happened if I'd been there and saw the other car coming before it hit.

I place my mug on the table beside the swing and sit there, my head recalling everything the officer said. Leave it to Anthony to be there for his buddy, his best friend, and his best man. He also stood in for my father who wasn't there to give me away. Anthony waited at the front of the church with Gabe. When I took my place where the white satin aisle runner began, Anthony walked down the aisle to join me. He then took my hand in his, told me I looked beautiful and kissed me on the forehead. When Anthony and I reached Gabriel, the love of my life, who stood there waiting for me to join him, to become his wife, Gabe stepped forward and took my hand and smiled. I breathed in a little gasp. Anthony looked at Gabe and said, "I told you all you had to do was smile."

I look at my watch. Darn, I wish the officer would hurry. I need to be with Gabriel.

I whisper a prayer. "God, please be there with him, hold him for me, and please let him feel your presence."

I hold the pendant Gabe gave me in my hand. So much has happened since he placed it around my neck this morning. As I run my thumb over his name I picture Gabe's face, feel him so close. I love that he said something about Fisher's. Anthony introduced us there. Seems like Gabe's making a mental trip back in time. We had our whole life ahead of us then. How foolish it was to assume life would be perfect. It wasn't.

Now I'm wishing I could *really* go back in time. I'd go back to the summer of sixty-six and would spend my time figuring out how to fix everything that went wrong. I'd make it right, undo everything that caused us sadness, remove all the pain, all the tears. Wish I could be sitting on mom's old swing instead of this one. *But I can't.*

The flickering fireflies appear again, but this time they seem to multiply and then a shimmer appears. I look around. It surrounds me and the arbor swing. It has an iridescent sheen, and the firefly lights flicker within and around it. And as before their glow doesn't last, it dissipates as quickly as it lights up again.

Fireflies?

I playfully twirl my necklace around my finger, as my eyes try to make sense of it all. As I bring the pendant up to my lips to kiss it, I feel a weird sensation, something pulling me toward the shimmer. I see the visions of the home I grew up in, and Mom's arbor swing again as colorful as I saw it before. There's a feeling of weightlessness, and there's an incredible desire to reach up and let myself be lifted into it. If I'd allow myself to fly with the fireflies, I know I could. I'm filled with this longing to reach out to them, but thoughts of Gabe hold me back. I'm so torn. Then I feel a sting along the back of my neck. I grip the arm of the swing with one hand, my other hand still holding on to my necklace. It upsets me when I see the broken chain hanging over my fist. As I open my hand to check it, it slips away, I fall forward trying to catch it, and then…

11

1966 – Ella Galvez

I can't believe I'm sitting here hoping Michael won't answer the phone when I'm the one who dialed his stupid number in the first place. *Hang up, now!*

"Hello."

Dadgummit, he answered! "H-hey, Michael."

"Hey, it's you sugar pie," he says.

Somebody sounds all perky.

"How'd your party go?"

"That's what I'm calling about. I wanna know why you couldn't make it, and I want the truth."

"Baby, I already told you the honest truth."

I turn the picture I have of us on my bedside table face down. *Liar.*

"Yeah, right, but you stuttered through your whole excuse."

"I don't stutter."

"Exactly! That's why I know you're lying. The whole thing was a stutter. Remember? *I c-can't make it to your p-party.* Do I need to give you a playback of the entire conversation?"

"So," he says with a laugh, "sweet little Ella is making fun of people who stutter now."

"No! I would never do that! What I'm saying is people sometimes stutter when they lie, and that's exactly what you did!"

"Come on, don't be that way. I really had to work. I promise."

I hate it when he uses his whiny voice. And lately, he uses it a lot.

"You gotta believe me," he whines again. "I would never lie to you. Come on, we're going to the movies day after tomorrow, I'll show you you're the only girl for me. Okay?"

"Okay, whatever. Gotta go."

"Bye, sugar."

It takes a lot of effort not to slam the phone, but only because I haven't any proof. Not yet.

"Agh!"

Welcome to my not-so-happy life. My dad's *never* home, my mom's harboring a deep secret...or *something* and my boyfriend brandished the ultimate insult. He stood me up last night. Well, maybe I'll save *ultimate insult* for what he was doing while he stood me up. *I will find out.*

Mom and I have entirely different opinions as to whether Michael's excuse for his sudden no-show is good enough. She says he had an excellent reason – volunteered for a last-minute opening in the work schedule, or so he says. Me? I'm not buying it; I *know* he's lying.

Enough of Michael! I want him out of my head. I grab my book, transistor radio and head downstairs. I find Mom at her favorite spot, the kitchen table where she can gaze out the window while enjoying a cup of coffee or leafing through a magazine. Her eyes peek over the top of the Ladies' Home Journal, shakes her head.

"You're still moping, I see."

"I'm not moping. I'm indulging in my misery. There *is* a difference."

She sets her magazine on the table and places her reading glasses on top. "Ella, surely you don't blame Michael?"

"But I *do* blame him, Mom." *Great, now he has* me *whining.*

I push myself up to sit on the counter. Mom gives me *the* look, so I ease myself down and lean against it instead.

"He was only trying to earn extra money for college," she says with a little shake of her head. "You should admire him for working to earn his tuition."

Her words *are* a bit slanted. Michael has charmed my mom, so she adores him. He makes it a point to comment on her beautiful garden, her cooking, and he always treats me like a princess...when she's around. Plus, he always gives her compliments about how beautiful she is. I'm not knocking it. She is an attractive woman. Striking, when she's all made up and wears her black shoulder-length hair in an elegant French twist.

Mom places her cup and saucer in the sink and then pulls two ice cream cups from the freezer. "How about some ice cream," she says over her shoulder. "It will make you feel better."

"So ice cream's been declared the new cure-all?"

Mom laughs as she hands me one. "Oh Ella," she says as she pulls the cardboard tab on the lid of her cup, "why don't you give Michael a chance to show you that he does care and has been hard at work. Give him a little credit, I'm sure you won't regret it."

I already regret it.

"You'll see. You and Michael will continue to enjoy each other's company just as you have this past year."

That's my mom, only positive, uplifting words ever escape her lips, and are spoken with a lilt in her voice as if they were God's own truth, given to her to dispense to those in need. *My mom, the prophetess.*

I roll my eyes. I'm caught.

"Tsk, tsk," she says, shaking her head at me.

I give her my, *whatever* look, tuck my book under my arm, grab my radio and head out the door to the swing, with my own cup of life-changing vanilla ice cream, or so I'm told.

"Come on, shorty." Cooper's little paws hurry along beside me.

Once I set my book and ice cream down, I get myself comfortable. I adjust the dial on my radio and find The Beatles' *Twist and Shout* playing. As I reach to turn up the volume, I'm jolted forward and stumble out of the swing. My arms reach out to help me keep my balance, and I'm somehow able to keep from falling. Cooper and my radio land in the grass a couple of feet in front of me.

"Holy cow, what was that?"

Cooper jumps back on his feet, cocks his head at me. My radio's still playing, so no harm done. There's no way the swing jerked like that on its own. I turn around expecting to see Rita and Anna, my close and very mischievous friends, standing there and grinning ear to ear.

They're not there, but I'm totally convinced it was them. "Give it up. I know you're here. Come out, time to fess up."

I giggle as I walk toward the area behind the garage, thinking I'll find them crouching there, but I don't. Huh, where'd they go? Check around the shrubs, still nothing.

"This is so juvenile, y'all."

Still convinced it was them, I continue to look around. When I turn back toward the house, I gasp, and my breath catches in my throat. There's an incredible display of shimmering lights. It envelopes the arbor swing, the little girl statue, the bird bath and part of the rose garden. The shimmer falls on everything like a sparkling mist. It's mirage-like, the way the roadway looks when the heat beats down on it on a super-hot summer's day. That's how it appears, but iridescent. And there are tiny flickering lights. Fireflies? Can't be. Fireflies don't fizzle out the way these do. Plus, it's daylight.

I reach my hand out, try to wave the shimmer aside. Wow, my arm feels so light, not weightless, but almost there. My heartbeat kicks into double time as I realize this can't possibly be Rita and Anna's doing. Something else is going on. I think my heart is either going to bounce out of my chest or come to a complete stop. A nervous laugh escapes me as I slowly turn, taking it all in, trying to make sense of what's happening here. The shimmer, the weightlessness – definitely not normal.

Jeepers! Now the ground doesn't feel firm beneath my feet, and I can't even feel the grass between my toes. I've often wondered what it would feel like to walk on water, this might be it. I take a few more tentative steps.

"Whoa, wait a minute."

A statue of a little boy holding a floppy eared puppy stands there next to the little girl, and the sight of him sends shivers down my spine. Where the heck did he come from? He's gotta be new. I stare at him. He stands there as if he belongs there. But no, he doesn't.

As I reach to pick up my radio, I find a gold chain hanging from my hand. It's a necklace, partially looped around my middle finger, hanging there with a medallion swinging at the end. What the heck! Where'd this come from? There's an inscription. *Bella Ella* is etched in the center, and circling the edge are the words, *Here, There and*

Everywhere. Who could this belong to? Rita calls me Ella Bella, but the name engraved here is Bella Ella.

Nice try Ella. The necklace isn't yours.

Okay, so it's not mine, I get it, but what bothers me most is the necklace wasn't in my hand a moment ago. How did it get there? And when? I know I didn't have it when I came outside – my hands were full of stuff. I think back. I held a radio in my left hand, ice cream in my right. It wasn't there when I took my book from under my arm and placed it on the table, or I would have seen it and felt it dangling as I did just now. I reached out to the shimmering light with my left hand, but I found the necklace in my right. It could have been in my right hand since then. But how did it get there?

This is crazy!

I rub my eyes trying to remove all the bewilderment they've seen. As I open them I feel the weight return to my body, I'm walking on firm ground, and the shimmer slowly lifts like a stage curtain. I watch it rise until it's completely out of sight.

That did not just happen!

Close my eyes and just stand there, afraid of what else I might see. I take a deep breath of fresh air, and as I slowly exhale, I stop shivering, and my skin no longer feels clammy from perspiration. Looking around, I run my eyes across the length and depth of the yard, and I'm relieved to find everything the way it was before. Except for the menacing boy and his dog. He's sticking around. Poor Cooper is trembling. I stoop down and give him a reassuring pat on his head.

I could use a reassuring pat on my head right about now.

"Agh! Somebody tell me what's going on!" I look up, cast my eyes beyond the fluffy white clouds. "Will someone please tell me I'm not going crazy?"

A part of me wishes I'd find an answer scrawled across the sky in angelic handwriting. After all the crazy stuff I've seen today, why can't there be angels? All bets are off. Anything is possible here in my backyard. I feel like I fell through a rabbit hole into my own fantasy world.

"Ella in Wonderland, yeah, that's what this is."

Okay, I get it now. This whole thing is way too bizarre. Gotta be another one of my kooky convoluted dreams. I pinch my forearm, digging my nails into the skin. Yes, I felt that.

Ohmygosh! This is real.

Okay. First, I've gotta calm down. I take deep breaths. Now if this is real, there's got to be a logical explanation for everything that happened. That's just how things work. There's always a reasonable answer for every question. So let's see, what actually happened here.

For starters, I was jerked off my swing, saw a shimmering curtain, and a little boy statue that doesn't belong here. Oh, and those crazy fireflies that fizzled. Don't think I've seen fireflies do that before in my whole life, and I've never seen them in broad daylight. Like if that's not weird enough, a necklace appeared out of nowhere.

I scan my surroundings, again, look for anything I might've missed. There's no way to explain what happened here to anyone. Nope, not saying a word to Mom unless I absolutely must. The last thing she needs is to think I've flipped my lid. After all, there is that aunt on my dad's side whom my family speaks of in hushed voices. All I know is that she ended up in some institution in San Antonio.

Yep, Mom is liable to think I've gone nuts, so I can't speak of this to her or anyone. Not yet...maybe not ever! What I need to do is clear my head. I'll sneak up to my room and find somewhere safe to keep the necklace. I'll tell Mom about it once I can make some sense of things. *Make sense of things? Ha!*

I wipe the perspiration on my face and neck with the bottom edge of my dress then head inside. Oh my gosh! What if everything's gone all crazy inside too? *Please don't let me find the Queen of Hearts in there instead of Mom.*

I pause, take a deep breath, open the door slowly and peek in.

"Back so soon, Ella?"

Darn, she heard me. Dad needs to fix this squeaky door already.

"Enjoy your ice cream?"

"Haven't finished it yet." *I didn't even get started!* "I'm going back out, forgot something," I lie.

I'm relieved when Mom gets back to mopping rather than interrogating me as to why it's taking me so long to finish my ice cream and asking me if my concerns about Michael are giving me a queasy stomach. Then she'll rehash why I shouldn't be worrying. Don't need that.

On my way upstairs, I decide the perfect place for the necklace is in my jewelry box. I place it in its own velvet covered compartment. "Here, There and Everywhere," I whisper to myself as I place it there.

It has a nice ring to it. I'll bet it means something very special to somebody – somebody named Bella Ella. A different Ella, an Ella who is happy and is loved and not cheated on by her lying boyfriend. I run my finger across her name. "I want to be *that* Ella."

When I head downstairs, Mom's mopping the hallway, so I go out the front door. My eyes are drawn to our neighbor's upstairs window which faces our house. How weird, something made me look at it. A tingle runs down my spine, and it makes me shiver. I wiggle my shoulders and run my hands along my arms.

Shivers? In this heat? What the heck was that all about?

Funny, I've never noticed that window. I'm sure it's been there all along, but I can't recall ever looking at it, being drawn to it. I swear it *made* me look. Our homes are separated by a driveway, and large patches of lawn between them, so it's a good distance away. Guess that's why I never noticed it before. If anyone had asked me this morning if the neighbor's house had an upstairs window facing mine, I would've answered *don't know.* But there it is.

Just as I'm turning away, a shadow moves, then the curtain closes. I quickly walk away. Why the uneasy feeling? It's only a window...and a shadow that ducked back behind the curtain before closing it. That *is* creepy. I shake my shoulders wanting to remove the feeling I'd just felt then head back to the swing not giving the window another glance. The chills are gone, but still, a picture of it lingers. I try to scoot it away, but it's kinda stuck there.

I pat the spot beside me on the swing. "Come on, Cooper." He seems hesitant. "Come on," I say again. He finally joins me.

I look at the little boy and girl, then over my shoulder. Just checking. Part of me wants to get up and go back inside, the stupid part of me, the, I'll-be-damned part, decides to stick around. So here I sit, canvassing my backyard until I finally feel comfortable. But I swear, if it happens again, I'm yelling out for Mom. I need someone else to see it, so I'll know I haven't gone bananas.

I open my little Dixie cup and let Cooper lick the layer of ice cream left on the lid. Strange, I expected it to be softened, it's been sitting out here for a while, but it's not. Still hard, still cold.

The first spoonful is always the coldest.

Love how the coldness turns into sweet warmth as it melts. The flavor spreads all over my mouth, and it tastes so yummy as it slips down my throat. I focus on every spoonful, each time gently sucking on the wooden spoon. I slowly savor each and every single spoonful. Eating ice cream never felt so good. My gears must've switched into slow motion. I'll have to remember to do it this way again, left me with such a good feeling. *Holy moly. Mom was right, I do feel better.*

I laugh as I set the empty cup and spoon on the table, and then my head bounces back to what I just witnessed. Déjà vu hits me. I've seen this whole crazy scene before – the lights, the shimmer, fireflies. But where? When? Fourth of July? A carnival sideshow during *Charro Days* festivities? Possible clues, maybe. The little boy statue bugs me the most, I definitely need to ask Mom about him.

Once inside, the smell of Johnson's wax hits me as I walk back into the house. There she goes again. Mom's a fanatic about her floors, labors over them tirelessly. Her evening ritual is to take her fluffy Stanley dust mop and glide it over all the wood floors in the house, as well as the linoleum in the kitchen. You can hear the clickity-click the dust mop makes as it moves side to side, from room to room.

Every night at bedtime the sound of the mop comforts me. Makes me feel safe, that all is right with the world and my home-sweet-home. The smell of freshly cut grass and the sound of my dad's prized possession, his gasoline lawnmower, give me warm fuzzy feelings too.

The sweet fragrance of fresh baked cookies blends in with the smell of floor wax. The combination screams *a happy homemaker lives here*. But I don't think she is, not really.

"Thanks for the ice cream, Mom, it hit the spot."

"You're welcome, sweetie." She turns her cheek leaning it toward me. I give it a kiss.

"Uh, Mom, about the boy statue in the garden," I say, tossing my Dixie cup and wooden spoon into the wastebasket. The cup makes it, but the spoon doesn't. Mom raises one eyebrow sharply at me. Roll my eyes and pick it up. "When did we get it?"

She turns to me and smiles. "Don't you remember?" Her look and that sparkle in her eyes tells me she's about to reminisce, one of her favorite things to do. "Your father bought those two little darlings after our visit to *Abuelita's*. You were about twelve, same time he surprised me with the arbor swing. You fell in love with those two cuties. Remember how you insisted we name the dog Daisy?"

"Oh yeah, I remember now." *I lie...again.*

I fell in love with those two cuties? I named the puppy Daisy? What the heck! I don't remember the boy statue at all.

Now what, Ella?

Maybe I *have* totally cracked. Well, decision made, don't bring up the boy statue nor anything else, or it's the funny farm for me. I'm on my own here. Here's something more to add to my journal along with all the stuff that happened out there: *Why does the little boy give me the creeps?* I shiver at the memory of him.

12

1966 – Ella Galvez

I'm usually facing the wall toward the left side of my bed when I wake up each morning, and Paul McCartney's dreamy face is the first thing I see. There's a poster of him tacked there, and he greets me with his sweet, good morning smile. But not today. Instead, I'm facing my window, and my eyes flutter and squint as they meet the bright sunlight shining through.

Mom would have a hissy fit if she knew I fell asleep with the blinds wide open...again. Left my lamp on too. *The Moonstone Castle Mystery* lays on my bed. I remember kissing Mom goodnight then coming upstairs. I crawled into bed hoping I could finish my book which is due at the library in a couple of days. I put it down when I couldn't keep my eyes open any longer. How could I? Yesterday was exhausting. Freak shows in your own backyard have a way of doing that, draining your energy. I laid there, eyes closed, making a mental list. Recalled every unexplainable event, spinning each one around in my head over and over until I couldn't stay awake any longer. The last thing I remember is the sound of Mom's dust mop clicking in the hallway.

Come on, Ella, time to get up and enjoy a new day.

Hopefully, it will be a different kind of day. One which doesn't involve shimmering lights, fireflies, nor that concrete kid with his dog. I'm sure there must be some reasonable explanation why I can't remember him and for everything else that happened in my backyard yesterday. What I need to do is carefully analyze each event which took place until I can make sense of them all. Otherwise, it will be the looney bin for me.

Before getting out of bed, I go through my morning whole body stretch. It energizes me from head to toe motivating me to finally get up. I'm pulling my pajama top off, but then I stop when I realize my blinds are still open. I quickly yank my top down and reach for the cord, my eyes go wide when I look out past the open slats.

What was that?

I tilt my head, trying to figure out what it was I saw. I gasp, drop the cord and stagger backwards.

It's him. The shadow.

There he is...again. Before yesterday, I'd never noticed that upstairs window. And now I wonder if that person's been watching me all along. Why does that window which I didn't realize was there before suddenly feel like its inches away? I take sideways steps until I'm sure I'm out of view. Reach for the blind cords again and shut them.

Geez, less than five minutes into my so-called *new day* and my stomach's already queasy. Not ready for this. I grab my radio and scoot myself back underneath my cover. Life feels good right here in my room, in my bed. Forget the rest of the world. It's totally overrated. I'm staying here in my room.

My room, my pink world. One thing not pink, my baby blue teddy bear. We've been friends a long time. I named him Teddy Bear Blue, but call him Blue for short.

As a kid, I was obsessed with *monsters* in my dreams and under my bed. Mom would try to sooth me, but reciting *now I lay me down to sleep,* only went so far. Kinda got stuck on *if I should die before I wake.* It made my worries seem all the more real. Not only were monsters under my bed, there was also a possibility I could be dead by morning.

So she bought me Blue. I squished the heck out of him, but he made me feel better. He still does. With Blue around, I always have someone to talk to. *Oh boy, the things I've told Teddy Bear Blue.*

I love spending time alone in here. Well, not entirely alone, I have Blue, my Beatles' music, and my books. I surround myself with what I love, my treasures. I keep a few special keepsakes in my bookcase. On one shelf I have a few of my favorite books, *The Call of the Wild, Black Beauty,* and *Alice in Wonderland.*

"Alice in Wonderland. Ha! That was all make-believe, it wasn't real. But *Ella* in Wonderland, that's a whole different thing."

On another shelf sits a tin box which holds my jacks, a ball, and a tube of pick up sticks. I still play with them when I'm bored. My roller skate key with the same old pink satin ribbon still attached to it is also there.

I loved the incredible sense of freedom that would come over me when I would glide along the street. My skate key hung from the ribbon around my neck swaying from side to side. Everything was synchronized: my skate key, my legs, and arms. My mind was transfixed by the sound of the skates' ball-bearing wheels, combined with the sound they made rolling along the pavement.

My first pointe ballet shoes are on the next shelf, along with a framed picture of Teddy Bear Blue and me. Surprisingly, I like how I look in this picture. Blue, of course, is a babe. On another shelf, I keep my baseball mitt, a baseball, a softball, a cigar box filled with marbles. Oh, one more little treasure, a sling shot. Anthony, my best friend, showed me how to make it. I whittled it myself out of a thick twig. Yes, I was a tomboy who happened to love ballet.

Not much of a tomboy now. Playing with the guys gave way to fashion the summer Mom taught me how to sew. *Simplicity* patterns, fabrics, and embellishments became my new pastimes. It was also the summer Anthony moved away. It was a sad time for me. Sure, I had my girlfriends, but none were like Anthony.

Daily life was different after he moved. I missed our long walks through the wooded areas. We were adventurers. We'd follow the canal down to the railroad tracks, or sneak into spooky old abandoned houses. Miss all the stuff we weren't allowed to do but did anyway. I never worried about anything bad happening. I knew Anthony would protect me. He always did.

My tomboy days slowly slipped away, I guess you could say I've outgrown them. But if I find myself under a big ol' tree, barefoot, *not* wearing a dress and my mom's not watching, I'm climbing it.

I swing my legs off the bed, take my journal out of the drawer and begin my own account of my backyard adventure. I replay each freakish scene in my head twice to make sure I capture every single detail. Add another entry about the window, the shadow, and the shivers it gave me. I put my journal away then quickly take it out again. I write another entry. *Why does the little boy statue give me the willies?* I shudder as I picture him standing there with his puppy in his arms. *Good grief, Ella, get a grip.*

I place the journal in the drawer then slam it shut. I throw on some shorts and a top then grab my hairbrush and run it through my hair in long strokes in front of my mirror, stopping to admire how soft and shiny it is.

The necklace I'm wearing catches my eye. It's a simple silver rectangle which hangs horizontally, a delicate chain attached at each end. It's inscribed with *Que Sera, Sera on the front.* The words are the title of a song which held a special meaning for me. I've always been a worrier, and I would share those worries with Mom. She gave me this necklace to remind me we can't ever know what our future holds, so rather than worry, enjoy life. Mom bought it for my seventeenth birthday, but the jeweler failed to engrave the back of it with *Love, Mom,* as she had requested. She wrapped it up and gave it to me anyway. She said we could take it back and have him engrave it, but I've never wanted to take it off, so it's still blank. I really should get it done.

"Oh my gosh, oh my gosh, oh...my...*gosh*!" I never looked!

I rush to my jewelry box and open it. Then I just stand there as my mind runs through words and phrases I might find engraved on the back of the medallion. It could be Bella Ella's boyfriend's name, or her husband's, or maybe it'll be a date, or *Happy Birthday,* or *Happy Anniversary.* I lift the velvet cover and take the necklace by the pendant and slowly flip it over.

"Forever yours, Gabriel."

My eyes are locked on the name. Gabriel. That's his name, the guy who's in love with Bella Ella. I know two, there's the grody one who seems to always have a wad of gum in his mouth, and the other one is Gabriel Marquez, the handsome one, with an adorable smile.

The one who doesn't even know you exist, Ella.

Well, it doesn't matter who this Gabriel is, the necklace doesn't belong to me. I'm Ella Bella, not Bella Ella. So why was it in *my* hand, why does it have *my* name on it or at least a name kind of like mine?

As I put the necklace in its safe place, I wonder how many times Gabriel has whispered these words in Bella Ella's ear. I can't explain the warm connection I feel between me and this necklace with Gabriel's name on it, laying in its own little velvet compartment. Hmm, butterflies.

Stop it. What's all this ooh Gabriel stuff? Geez, I'm no different than Michael.

It's not like I make those fluttery feelings dance around in my tummy on my own. They show up with no encouragement from me. When I saw Gabriel at the movies, he smiled, well, I think he *might* have since I didn't actually look directly at him. Well, I did, but only for a split second which was long enough to make me melt inside.

The feeling was so new, so sweet, but nowhere close to my tummy. It was much lower. Such a sweet sensation. I run my fingers across my lips, wonder what it would be like to touch them to his.

There I go again. I *am* just like Michael. He calls me his girl while cheating on me. Well, I think he's cheating on me. I call him my guy, yet I'm all dreamy about Gabriel Marquez. But there's nothing I can do about it. It happens without any help from me. Every day I tell myself not to think about Gabriel, but every day I do...a lot.

The heart wants what it wants, loves who it loves.

I pick my hairbrush up again and stroke along the length of my hair. I wince when I feel the bristles scratch against my neck and touch where it smarted right under the chain I'm wearing. I remember feeling a sting when I took my shower last night. I completely forgot to ask mom to take a look at it.

I remove my necklace and place it on the dresser, then lean in against the mirror to, take a closer look. I can see the beginning of the welt on either side of my neck, each one running toward the back. The phone rings, but I ignore it and take a closer look at my scratch. It looks kinda fresh, but heck if I can remember when it happened.

My finger lightly traces the thin welt as I go to answer the phone which is now on its fourth ring.

"Hey, glad I caught you at home."

"What's up, Michael?"

I glance over at our picture which is still face down on the table.

"Please don't have a cow, but...but I'm gonna have to fink out on our movie date tomorrow night."

"Don't tell me. You have to work again." I hope he noticed the irritation in my voice.

"I'm so sorry, you know I really want to go, right? But I gotta be at a meeting, a family kind of meeting."

"What's with these last-minute cancellations?"

"Hey, I know, I'm upset too. It just came up, this meeting. It's gonna be boring, but I gotta be there. It's a family meeting, you know, with the whole family for a family meeting."

I'm not buying it.

Okay, Ella? Uh, baby?"

"Okay, fine." I hang up without saying goodbye.

Uh, baby? What the heck was that? Now I'm totally not buying it. Smart guy, he was careful not to stutter, but I noticed he kept repeating himself. How many times did he say the words meeting and family? Oh brother! I'm not *that* stupid!

Damn you, Michael.

I reach for Blue and sit on the floor. I can't believe he would do something like this to me...again. Not sure what's going on with Michael, but I've had enough. Time to break it off. Why wait around for him to dump me? Why do I even care when I'm all gaga over smiley guy. The sad and pathetic truth is I'd rather have Michael than have no one. I don't want to be alone, period. This is not okay. I have gotta pull myself together. Then I need to break up with Michael. That's what I need to do.

I think my life is about to go from awful to worse.

I have a quick breakfast of cinnamon toast and chocolate milk. Mom joins me with her cup of coffee and a crossword puzzle. She puts her pen down a few times to ask about how things are going with Michael.

I'm surprised at how many times I'm able to say *fine* without her questioning me further. Mom is usually more inquisitive. It's times like this that I know her mind's preoccupied with something she obviously can't share with me.

When I'm done with breakfast, I take a basket of towels out of the washer and haul it outside to hang on the clothesline. As I hang each towel my eyes move from one side of the yard to the other, recalling yesterday's unbelievable exhibition. I'm amazed how calm I've been able to remain since it happened. Haven't really been overly preoccupied with it, well, except for the number of times I walked down the hall to take a peek out here. I guess it didn't totally spook me since it was quite beautiful. Except for the little boy. *He* spooked me.

That's the craziest part. I had an out of this world experience in my backyard, and it's a little boy made out of stupid concrete that's unnerving me. If it would just happen again I'd ask Mom to come watch with me. It happened once, who says it can't happen twice.

I spend the rest of the morning reorganizing my closet. I take the time to stick mementos in my scrapbook along with photographs. When I'm done, I spend time looking at all my keepsakes from the past few months. I notice something very interesting. Why hadn't I seen it before? The trend is right there before my eyes.

Michael *has* changed. It happened a little at a time. He was so different, so caring and sweet. Yes, Michael's personality changed, and I don't like it. As I put the scrapbook away in its new spot on the shelf, I realize how much I miss the way things used to be.

I grab the tray Mom brought in for me with lunch and head downstairs. Mom's on the phone when I walk into the kitchen. She looks at her wristwatch then shoots a sideways glance at me when she notices I'm there. I put my dishes in the sink filled with soapy water, place the tray on top of the refrigerator.

"Well, I have to go now, so nice talking with you, goodbye."

She hangs up, grabs her apron, and pulls a dish out of the soapy water, as she hums *Young at Heart.* I grab a kitchen towel and stand by her, rinse each dish as she hands it to me, then place it on the dish rack. I couldn't help but notice how quickly she dismissed whoever it was she was talking to - a little too abrupt. Mom's all about manners. *What's up, Mom?*

She clears her throat. "How was your bacon sandwich?"

"Just the way I like it, thanks, lots of mayonnaise."

I feel the welt on my neck again. "Mom, can you look at what's on my neck, please?" I ask, lifting the hair so she can check.

She dries her hands and leans in close. "I think it's a scratch. No, it's a thin welt. Looks fresh. What happened?"

"Don't know." I look at my nails, checking for rough edges. "I felt it yesterday in the shower, and just now while I was brushing my hair. I ran the bristles over it, and it hurt."

She looks at me, forehead scrunched. "Hmm, strange you don't remember."

"Well, I don't," I snap. *Cool it, Ella.*

I finish rinsing the cup I've been holding in my hand. "It must've not hurt," I say with a shrug. *Or I was distracted by an iridescent glow.*

"Where's your necklace. Could it have been yanked off? That's what it looks like."

"Nope," I say, letting my hair fall back into place. "I took it off just now. It's on my dresser."

"Put some ointment on it," she says, taking another look. "Don't want it to get infected."

The phone rings and I hurry to answer. If it's Michael, I've got a few more questions for him. "Hi, Daddy!"

"Hello, baby. I'm in a hurry, please put your mother on."

"Okay, Daddy. Mom, its Dad."

She takes the phone, I begin drying the dishes and putting them away. She says something about The Drive Inn and seven o'clock, tomorrow night. Guess we have a dinner date. Dad mentioned he was finishing up a construction job, he must've gotten paid.

Hmm, I would've had to cancel my movie date with Michael anyway. Glad he cancelled first, though. Otherwise, I wouldn't have found out he's up to something again...or somebody. When Mom hangs up she tells me about our dinner plans for tomorrow then runs upstairs to work in her sewing room. I go back to putting dishes away.

"If I had only sat by the dance floor, I would've seen him."

I stop, look over my shoulder. "What? Who said that?"

I place the last dish in the cupboard then look around. I'm positive I heard Mom go upstairs. I hang up the dish towel then press my fingers hard on either side of my head, closing my eyes as I rub in a circular motion at my temples. It came from in here, from inside my head. And it sounded like me...sort of. I slowly open my eyes. This is crazy. There's no one here but me.

Am I hearing voices now?

I replay the words again in my mind. Did I think them, or did I hear them? There *is* a difference. If they were words I thought up in my own head, shouldn't they make sense to me? I say it out loud.

"If I had only sat by the dance floor, I would've seen him."

Nope, it makes no sense to me. What the heck is that supposed to mean? What dance floor? It can't be the dance studio, I go there to dance, not sit. And who is *him?* There are no guys in my class.

When is all this nonsense gonna stop?

I run upstairs and find the ointment, and smear it along the welt gently patting it in with my middle finger, relieved it doesn't sting. When I shut the medicine cabinet, I stand there and stare at my reflection in the mirror for a moment. I search my face studying it.

It doesn't show in my face, but there's something different about me. I look the same, but I know something's a bit off. And it's not just what's happened around me. Something's going on inside my head. I can feel an awareness that I've not felt before. Can't pinpoint it, but it's there. I guess it's a sense of *knowing.*

Okay, these words are my own thoughts, and they aren't making any sense to me. A sense of *knowing?* An *awareness?* What the heck does that even mean? Maybe it's just me growing up. After all, I *am* almost eighteen.

Well, there it is, something more to add to my journal besides the fresh welt on the back of my neck which showed up just as mysteriously as the necklace and the voice in my head. Mustn't forget to add the strong hunch or foreknowledge I have regarding this ridiculous family discussion excuse of Michaels. Call it instinct or whatever, but I know his story isn't true.

And what about *the voice?* Could it be some sort of premonition or a clue and I'm supposed to follow its advice? That's crazy. My friends are going to wonder what's going on with me if I go into the studio and take a seat on the edge of the dance floor rather than going directly to the bar for warmup exercises.

That's what *I'd* like to know too…what is going on with me?

13

1966 – Ella Galvez

Today isn't turning out much better than yesterday. I was supposed to be on a fact-finding expedition with my trusty little journal in hand, but so far, I've gotten zero answers and a heap of new questions. The list keeps growing, but I'm determined to tick them off one at a time. I'm on a mission.

On my way downstairs I call out for Cooper, grab his leash, and we head outside for his walk. Even standing under the shade of the big hackberry tree in our front yard, we can feel the heat radiating off the pavement which means it will be a short walk. I slip my sunglasses down to give my squinting eyes some relief.

I love walking in our neighborhood, even in the sticky heat of July. It's filled with so many memories. It doesn't seem that long ago I played baseball out here with Anthony and the gang. With Sadie, I'd play hopscotch, we'd roller skate or jump rope. Once it got dark, we all chased fireflies and played hide-and-go-seek. Mom would lay a bedsheet on the lush St. Augustine grass, and it felt thick and spongy beneath it. We'd lay there naming the different constellations and searching for the Russian satellite, *Sputnik,* as it orbited the earth.

Most evenings after their dinner dishes were done, Mom and Mrs. Bartelli, Anthony's mom, would sit on our front porch, talk and laugh while they kept an eye on us. Anthony's sister, Sofia, who is five years younger than he is, would sit on the steps with her baby doll and watch us play. Mr. Bartelli is Chief of Police, and he and Mrs. Bartelli are part of the elite social scene in Brownsville. Our family isn't. The only reason we were able to live in this neighborhood was that my grandfather, my mother's father, left her the house when he died. It needed a lot of repair, but Dad's a carpenter and was able to do all of the work himself, a little bit at a time.

Lucky for Anthony and me, the difference in social status didn't keep our moms from being best friends which meant we spent plenty of time together from the time we were toddlers. Even after the Bartelli's moved away, they continued their friendship with occasional lunch dates and phone calls. Mrs. Bartelli is one of Mom's regular customers. Mom creates copies of *haute couture* fashions at a fraction of the price for her. And next week, while the Bartelli's are on vacation, she will be working on drapes for their living room and a bedspread and canopy top for Sophia's bedroom. I'll get to help with both, and the money Mom will pay me for helping her goes to my college savings. Well, not all of it, I'll keep some of it to buy fabric for me and some for spending money.

As sweet as life seemed back then, I had the same preoccupations I have now. Mom's sadness has always worried me. She has her quiet moods, stares out the kitchen window a lot, or she'll sit on her arbor swing alone. It's as if she's in a whole other world. A cloud seems to follow her around, but she swats it away when she sees me. Her frown quickly turns into a smile. For her sake, I let her believe I bought the smile. Maybe she worries Dad will leave us. I know, I do. They often argue and sometimes go days without speaking a word to each other, making me their go-between.

I lead Cooper in the direction of our neighborhood park, the center of our subdivision. Michael asked me to go steady here. There are benches and picnic tables nearby. The first table was our let's-go-steady table. There's a heart engraved at one corner with *M loves E* on it. That's us. It was a memorable spot until things changed. All my photos and notes in my scrapbook were quite telling this morning; he really did change. I guess I didn't notice anything in particular because it happened gradually until one day it hit me. I no longer recognized Michael.

At the far end, there are swings, monkey bars, and a slide which is so tall it towered over our heads when we were small. There's also an old mesquite tree with a couple of long branches so low to the ground we could straddle them like horses. Mom and Mrs. Bartelli would bring Sadie, Anthony, and me here, and they would watch us play from a nearby bench. We always knew their eyes were on us. Of course, we would always push the limits to see what we could get away with.

Hmm, that's what I think Michael's doing, pushing the limits, wants to know what he can and can't get away with. I stand there chewing on my lower lip, eyes locked on Cooper who's wrapping himself around a tree trunk. Instead of helping Cooper, I'm stuck here wondering why it hurts me to think that Michael is cheating on me when he's not even the guy I want any more. Me and my insecurities.

I snap myself out of it and once I get Cooper unwrapped, we head to the graveled walkway. The rocks crunch beneath my feet with each step I take. Trees line the curving path and are staggered on either side. They provide intermittent shade which helps on sunny days, but not today. It's scorching out here. That's why there's no one else out here, just Cooper and me.

But then I notice him, the guy walking alone on the other side of the park who seems to be looking in our direction. I ignore him and walk along slowly as Cooper pauses at a fire hydrant, tree trunks, and bench legs along the way. I stop at my favorite spot under a shady tree. Cooper hops on right beside me, places his pointy little head on my lap. I fan my face with my hand, stopping when I notice the guy across the park has also taken a seat on the opposite side of the playground area. I manage to dart hidden glances at him and decide he's way too obvious for my liking. *I'm outta here.*

"Come on, Cooper."

From the corner of my eye, I see the guy wearing the cap has gotten up too, and he just stands there without taking a step. When Cooper and I head toward home, he heads in the same direction. I wonder if he waited to see which way I was headed. I know I have an over-active imagination, but sometimes it's a good thing to have. Like right now. I head home as fast as I can without being too obvious.

As I reach the end of the park, I'm startled when a car jerks into a spot alongside the curb.

"Hey, Cooper, whatcha doing, taking Ella for a walk?"

My breath gushes out. "Rita! You scared me!" I say, holding my hand to my chest. Cooper yanks me in the direction of Rita's car. He loves Rita. She has a Springer Spaniel named Oreo, and Cooper knows she always has doggie treats with her.

My eyes light up when I notice what she's driving. "Whoa. Awesome car!"

She's driving the red Valiant she got for her eighteenth birthday last weekend. The perks you get when your daddy's rich. It's a beauty and Rita looks fantastic in it. She's cute, outgoing, and loud. Very loud. But when she's with our friend, Anna, Rita's even louder. They tend to feed off each other and are a riot to watch.

"Hop in," she says, as she hands Cooper a treat. "Check this baby out!"

"Where are you headed?" I ask, looking around to see if I can spot the blue cap guy.

"Library with Anna. Called you, but your line was busy. I wanted to show off my new wheels. Anna saw it this morning when she came by the house."

"I need to let my mom know and change out of these shorts."

"No problem-o, hop in," she says, fluffing up her blond, shoulder-length wavy hair. She wears it in a no-nonsense style, no clips, bows or hairbands. Just fluffs it up with her hand to give it body, something she does all the time.

I put Cooper in the back seat, and as I go to slide into the front seat, the stick shift which is attached to the floor rather than the steering column catches my eye. The knob you grab to shift is a smooth white ball similar to a billiards cue ball, but it has the diagram of the shift locations on it. I can't pull my eyes away. I've seen this before. The realization startles me, so does the chill that goes rushing through my body and makes me shudder.

Where could I have possibly seen it?

I honestly don't think I've seen it before, but I do recognize it. Does that even make any sense? So is it déjà vu? Impossible. Well, *generally*, it would be impossible, but I'm in my own *Wonderland* now where anything is possible. Wait. This is exactly what I was thinking about earlier – a foreknowledge.

Rita snaps her fingers in front of my eyes. "Hey!"

I quickly speak up without even blinking. "Uh...wow, look at the stick shift." My eyes are locked on this very familiar steering column.

"Cool, huh? I've got four-on-the-floor." Rita smiles, oblivious of what's going on in my head.

"Four on the floor?"

She taps the ball with her finger. "Yep, four gears, see the diagram."

I look up at Rita and smile wide. "Your car is the coolest! I've never seen anything like it, ever." *Except for that cue ball stick shift, I've definitely seen that before!*

"Candy-apple red," she says, reaching over the seat to give Cooper another treat.

I look at the cue ball again. How could I have possibly known what it would look like, but I did. It's definitely not the first time I've laid eyes on it, and the freaky part is that I think I saw it in this car, with Rita's yellow smiley face key chain hanging from the ignition like it is now. The image of the cue ball stick and the key chain seem to be etched in my brain like a distant memory. I make a mental note to add this incident to my journal. Everything's a clue. To what? I have no idea.

I shake my head to rid myself of those crazy thoughts and talk about what's happening now. "Rita, you got here just in time." I lower the volume on the radio. "The guy across the park creeped me out. See? He's right over there." I point to where I'd seen him last. "Weird, he was right there."

"Maybe Cooper, the ferocious man-eating Chihuahua, scared the big, bad *hombre* away! Good boy, Cooper."

"Stop it, Rita! I'm serious! There *was* a guy. He was wearing a blue baseball cap, with the bill pulled low. He sat on a bench on the other side of the playground. What was creepy was he stared in my direction."

"Stared? Are you sure?"

"Okay, maybe I'm not sure. Maybe I'm just a little sensitive. I didn't sleep well last night, so I'm kinda tired."

"Well, he's gone, and so are we," she says, turning up the volume louder than it was when I turned it down.

She puts the car in gear and pulls away from the curb. I clutch the hand rest with one hand, the other grabs the edge of my seat to keep me from lurching forward as she tries to put the car in gear.

Rita looks at me and laughs. "Sorry, don't quite have the hang of it yet."

One more jerk and we are on our way. When we pull up to my house, Rita slaps my thigh with the back of her hand. "*Pronto.* I'll keep this baby running."

I run inside with Cooper right behind me. I let Mom know what I'm up to, then run upstairs to my bedroom. I push off my sneakers, switch into white slacks, a yellow summer top, and sandals. I grab my purse, library book, and lip gloss which I smear over my lips with my finger as I run down stairs. Stop halfway, run back up and grab my journal out of my drawer and stick it in my purse. *I gotta keep this handy.*

"Bye, Coop. Bye, Mom."

"Next stop, Anna's," Rita says. Doesn't wait for me to close the door before pulling away from the curb, but it's a much smoother take-off than the last one. I give her a thumbs up.

Anna's on her front porch when we arrive. She's dressed in a black, sleeveless buttoned-down cotton blouse, white slacks, and sandals.

Her fabulous tan adds to her striking good looks. Her long, dark brown hair is always parted down the middle and sways side to side as she walks. She takes long strides to the curb. There's no bounce in her walk. Rita calls it a slither. Everything about Anna is proper and poised – except her mouth. The things she sometimes blurts out could make a sailor blush.

"Ella, where the hell have you been? I called you to ask you to join us, but I kept getting a busy signal," she says as she climbs in the backseat. "Glad Rita got a hold of you."

Rita revs up the motor. "*Vamonos!*"

Rita loves to throw in a Spanish word every chance she gets. She has an impressive, ever-growing collection. We met Rita when her family moved here from Boston at the beginning of this past school year. We loved her accent, and she loved how we could flip flop between English and Spanish with ease. It was a novelty for her since she'd never had friends who spoke Spanish. We used to kid her all the time about being friends with us "little people" the poor folks. We asked her about it.

"Well, I'm kinda like Anna, I like hanging out with people who aren't as wealthy as I am. And Anna only hangs with people who aren't as pretty as she is. We like being *numero uno.*" This is what she said, and we accepted it.

"You're gonna love my new polish," Anna says as she lurches forward and places her hands between us. "See, how do you like my new shade? It's fuchsia. Looks fantastic with my new sandals." She leans back and sticks a foot between the front seats and wiggles her polished toes.

I laugh. "I love it!"

Rita tickles her toes. "Nice tootsies, Anna Banana."

Anna pulls her foot back with a giggle then leans in between us. "Did you know the guys are planning to go to Padre Island for an all-guy's beach party next weekend? I can't believe they're going without us," she says pounding her fist on the edge of my seat. "We should put a stop to it unless they're willing to take us along, of course."

"Michael can go on this beach thingy for all I care. In fact, he'll do me a favor; I'll enjoy the break!"

"Uh-oh, there's a story there," Rita say's all sing-songy.

Anna leans in between the seats, puts her face right up to mine and nudges my shoulder.

"Come on El, spill it," she says, pushing at my shoulder a couple more times. "What's going on with Mike? We want details. No holding back, either."

"Yeah, spill it, Ella Bella, let's have it," Rita chimes in.

"Well?" Anna asks shoving my shoulder a little harder.

"Okay, okay, I'll spill. Michael said he can't go to the movies with us tomorrow, *supposedly* he has a, get this, family meeting which he said will run late."

They suck in simultaneous gasps.

"Family meeting?" They ask in unison. These two often talk in stereo.

"Lame excuse, right?" I ask.

"The last one about working late was lame," Rita says.

"Yeah, but this one? Beyond lame, it's flat out ridiculous," Anna adds. "A family meeting? Really, Ella? Come on, who makes up shit like that?"

I twist around in my seat to face Anna. "My thoughts exactly! I know he's lying. First, he's a no-show for pizza at my house. Even after I told him it was my reward for helping Mom with an important drapery job last weekend. It didn't impress him that we made his favorite dessert especially for him, either."

My thigh gets three quick slaps from Rita. "The pineapple upside-down cake was the best! I asked your *mamasita* to give my *mamasita* her recipe, *pronto!*"

"Right, it's that delicious. The mention of it always makes Michael drool. I don't get it."

"I'll bet I know," Rita says with a laugh. "He found something else to drool over."

I glare at Rita. "Must you?"

There's a mischievous grin on Rita's face when she nods at me.

"Okay, maybe you're right," I say. "But I still want to know what Michael's been up to. I want to give him a good reason when I break up. *Sayonara* buster."

"El, people talk. We'll get the scoop, trust me. Then you can strangle the jerk," Anna says, gesturing Michael's demise with her hands then gives me comforting pats on my back.

Louie, Louie, comes on the radio, and Rita's head bobs to the beat. Mine would be bobbing too, but I'm thinking about the peculiar things that keep happening, and it's kinda hard to concentrate on the beat. When the song ends, Anna leans in, whispers in my ear. "If you want him to stick around you're gonna have to put out, you gotta give him some. You know what I mean, El?"

"Ha! I heard that. She's right, Ella Bella," Rita yells over the loud music.

I lower the volume. "Put out? I don't have those kind of feelings for him."

Anna yells into my ear. "Let him touch you where he wants. You'll get those feelings really quick," she says through laughter.

"Are you kidding me, I don't even want Michael kissing me. His breath smells like cigarettes. I might as well lick an ashtray."

I'll bet Gabriel doesn't smell like cigarettes. Hmm, I hadn't thought about Gabriel since I saw him in line at the Majestic with his date. Well, except for this morning. *Try every morning since you saw him in line at the Majestic, Ella.*

How I wished he was with me instead of that nose-in-the-air blondie. I guess I gotta count the times he's in my daydreams too. I relive one of them as I sit here in the front seat, get absorbed in it, and a pleasurable ache leaves me squirming. Not for long. I'm sucked back to reality when Rita's voice rings out loudly telling us of what our mission is. "Listen up girls. We go directly to the fiction section and find *Peyton Place.* We'll drop it in my satchel, then scram. If you look suspicious we'll get caught, so don't.

14

1966 – Ella Galvez

I remember the first time I read *Peyton Place*. Read it without Mom's permission, of course. Teens were told by their parents it was too racy for young minds, that it would encourage impure sexual desires and activity. Their reason for not allowing us to read it was exactly why we wanted to. We were curious. I finally got my hands on the book when Rita took her sister's copy to share with Anna and me. We had to skim through it then pass it on to the next person, so Rita could sneak it back into her sister's room before she realized it was gone.

I read the part where Allison McKenzie said she would lay in bed at night and touch her tummy, run her hands to her breasts, finger her nipples, and think of Rodney Harrington. She said it would cause a tightening somewhere down between her legs, and it felt pleasant. Just reading it made me swallow hard. I re-read that part twice, my heart beating fast the whole time.

Before laying on my bed, I locked my bedroom door. I stared up at the ceiling going over in my head what I'd just read, then closed my eyes and touched myself the same way. It felt very nice, and for some weird reason, I felt ashamed that it did. It forever remained my secret.

So here I sit recalling how I felt at that moment when I touched my breasts, my tummy, and the sweet softness of my satin panties as if I were right this instant, in my own private place. I've totally crawled into that secret little attic in my head which only I can enter.

But not for long. I'm jerked away when Rita pulls into a parking spot and stops with a jolt. It's then I realize it's not Michael I'm thinking of, but Gabriel. My heartbeat quickens, and I'm sure my face is flushed. I quickly straighten up in my seat.

Rita turns to us, snaps her fingers. "Let's go, let's do it! *Andale!*"

I take a deep breath then wipe the perspiration off my forehead. I look back at Anna.

"What's that mischievous smile on your face, El?"

"Uh, nothing. Just thinking about how I don't need Michael in my life." *Liar, liar, pants on fire.*

Rita bangs her hand on the seat rapidly. "*Vamonos*, already!" She slams the door shut. "You girls dilly dally and guess what happens. Someone else beats us to the book. What are we left with? *Nada!* We'll be left trying to recall all that good shit from memory. Is that what you want?" She stomps off ahead of us fluffing up her hair.

"Cool it," Anna yells. "We're going, okay?"

Anna looks back at me. "You expect me to believe that, El? Your face was all flushed, plus there's this look of *oh shit I've been caught* all over you."

I giggle. "Oh poop, I've been caught."

"Ha! I knew it," she says. "What were you getting all hot about? Or should I ask who?"

I look at her knowing there's no way I can get out of this, and being that she's probably the expert on all things *sexual,* I ask.

"Do you ever wish you could know how it feels to have a really cute guy touch you, you know, like all over?"

"Which cute guy?"

No way am I going to tell Anna who I'm talking about. I know her, she'd tell Gabriel the first chance she'd get. "You know, a movie star." Hope she'll buy my answer.

"Sure, but you don't have to wish it, just do it," she says, looking at me with a wiggle of her eyebrows.

"Just do it?"

"Yep. You can have pretend sex with him. You know, just the two of you in your head, in your bed, or in the shower, pretty much anywhere, really. With your own hands, of course, not his," she says, waving her freshly manicured fingernails at me.

I swallow hard, just the thought stirs something in me all over again. "And it works?"

"Hell, yeah," she laughs. "So who's the guy? Don't even think of saying Frankie Avalon or Troy Donahue, not even your Paul McCartney. You know I can tell when you're fibbing."

"Okay, Bobby Darin, you got me." I smile.

"Liar," she says with a wink.

Rita's standing at the entrance of the library with her arms crossed at her chest giving us *the look*. We quicken our step.

"You girls totally exasperate me," she mutters as she opens the door. It's funny how her English accent always sounds more pronounced when she's scolding us.

Our good friend, Julia, who's working as a library assistant for the summer, sees us walk in, smiles, and gives us her finger fluttering wave. Her light brown hair is tied back in a long ponytail, with a pastel pink, grosgrain ribbon. She always looks so cute. She's talking to a customer, smiling attentively and twirling the end of her ponytail around her fingers.

I place my book in the drop-off slot then follow Anna and Rita to the fiction aisles. Rita mentioned she'd heard all the naughty pages are now all dog-eared. It'll be kinda nifty being able to turn to what we're looking for, quickly. But no luck, it's not there.

"Damn!" Anna says in a whisper when she doesn't find it.

"Not giving up, we'll split up and check the shelves, book by book, someone might've stuck it in the wrong spot," Rita says, directing us in different directions.

"Let's ask Julia," I whisper.

"Are you crazy?" They both exclaim, no longer whispering.

The head librarian looks in our direction. "Shhhh."

Anna, back to whispering says, "I don't need a lecture from Jules about the evils of sexually explicit literature and its ability to entice teenagers into having sex."

"Julia already knows Greg Bates is all the enticement you need," Rita laughs.

We're shushed again. We move to the next aisle and keep looking. It takes a while, but we check all the likely spots, book by book. Nothing.

I go to the card file and spend time looking for something interesting to check out. Anna catches up to me moments later and grabs my elbow.

"Let's go, El. We're going to Zesto's for fries and cherry Coke," she whispers.

Antsy Rita's already at the door waiting for us, motioning with both hands for us to hurry.

As we head to the car, we see Anthony, who is ambling along in our direction.

"Hey, Antonio, you're going the wrong way," Rita calls out.

"Follow us, Tone," Anna chimes in.

Anna enjoys shortening everyone's name, and Anthony hates being called Tone. He hates being called Tony even worse. Rita calling him by his name in Spanish doesn't bother him, says his mom often calls him Antonio.

He quickens his step to catch up. "Where are you three headed?"

"Zesto's, please come with us, please, please, please," I say with three little jumps, one jump with each, please. I pull Anthony in for a hug.

He laughs, jabs a thumb sideways in my direction. "What's with Ella? Where did all this energy come from?"

"My guess? Nervous energy from dodging the boogeyman at the park," Rita answers. "She's acting weird, said she saw a mysterious guy following her, but I think he's imaginary."

"First of all, I'm right *here*, I can hear you talking about me. Secondly, he's not imaginary, Anthony, he's real. But he was on the other side of the playground, and I really couldn't tell for sure that he was watching me. It *is* possible I over reacted, but I don't think so."

"Let me drop off my book. I'll meet up with you at Zesto's, and you can tell me more. Don't let Anna eat up all the fries!"

"Very funny, *Tony*," Anna yells back.

At Zesto's we all order fries and cherry Coke. Anthony comes in and orders the same and joins us. "Hey, Rita, that's gotta be your new Valiant out there."

She nods. "You like?"

"Hell, yeah! Four on the floor?"

"You know it. Hey, we're gonna meet at Fisher's at six tomorrow before the movie," Rita says.

"I won't be able to go after all," I say. "Dad's taking us out to dinner. Michael isn't going either. Has some sort of a family meeting."

"Meeting, my foot!" Anna exclaims.

Anthony gives her a questioning look.

"Tell ya later," she whispers as she walks off with Rita to chat with friends at another table.

"Wish you were going, Ella," Anthony says as he wipes ketchup off the corner of my mouth. "Hey, that reminds me, do you know Gabriel Marquez?"

I nod my head while trying to swallow down the fries I just stuffed in my mouth. Flashes of the necklace I have in my jewelry box with the name *Gabriel* on the back, and the throbbing my imaginary Gabriel caused in the parking lot all pop into my head, one right after the other. I swallow my fries in a lump then take a long sip of my drink, hoping the thoughts that flashed in my head aren't plastered all over my face.

I blink innocently at Anthony. "Never met him, but he does have an adorable smile, he's handsome, and seems nice. Did I mention he has a great smile?"

"I take it you like his smile," Anthony says through a laugh.

"Yes, I do. But why are you asking?" I nervously rub my shoulder and then my neck. When I feel the scratch, I quickly take my hand away. I don't want anyone noticing the scratch because I can't tell them how I got it. Right now I don't have answers to a lot of things, so it's making me kinda nervous.

"Nothing, really. We were sitting out on the bleachers, resting from a four-mile run. I said something about going to the movies tomorrow and mentioned who I was going with. He said he knows Anna and Rita. Then, he asked what you were like."

"And you said...?" I ask, pleading with my eyes for more.

"I told him I've known you since we were this high." He holds his hand down to about a three-year-old level. "And that you used to be a tomboy in a tutu." He looks at me waiting for my reaction.

"You didn't...did you?"

"I did actually. You would've loved the look on Gabe's face!"

"What look? What did he do?"

"He smiled," Anthony says a big grin spreading across his face.

"Hmm." I nod my head in approval. *He smiled, I like that.*

"Oh, and you should have seen his expression when I told him I had a picture of us in a pool with you topless," he says, smiling and doing a little upper body dance.

"It was a kiddie pool! And we were three years old!" I throw my straw at him, he catches it mid-air and hands it back to me.

"I know, but you should've seen his face - priceless."

"You *did* tell him about the three-year-old part, right?"

"Yeah, but too late, he couldn't stop smiling."

"Ugggh! You are sooo bad!" I throw my napkin at him. He catches it too.

"You used to be so nice, Anthony. You need to stop hanging out with Rita!"

"I'm still nice. I was just having fun teasing Gabe, and now you. Besides, you were just three years old, you said so yourself."

Anthony finishes his fries and starts his interrogation. "Okay, Ella, about the guy in the park, was he young or old, tall or short?"

"Definitely not a teenager. He was across the playground so I couldn't see him very well, so it's really a wild guess. Same thing with his height, too far to tell, but I think he was kinda tall."

"His complexion?"

"Fair."

"What about his build? Scrawny like Michael?" He grins. "Or muscular like Gabe and me?" This time he wiggles his eyebrows and makes me laugh.

"You are so bad, Anthony. In Michael's defense, he's not scrawny, he's slender. But yes, he looked Superman-ish like you and Gabe."

"Superman-ish. I like that." He grins and nods his head approvingly.

"Car? How was he dressed?"

"I didn't notice a car. He wore a navy-blue baseball cap, red short-sleeved shirt. That's about all I remember. Thanks for not thinking I'm going crazy imagining this guy."

"Of course, you're not going crazy. You're the only sane person in the bunch," he laughs.

He'd take that back if I told him about the things I've seen in my backyard. How I wish I could tell him, but even *I'm* having trouble believing it, and I saw it with my own eyes. How can I expect him to? Rita and Anna would laugh so hard they'd pee in their pants.

Julia would take it seriously, tell me not to worry, it'll all go away soon, then blab it all over town. Not in a mean way, but in the usual sympathetic manner in which she shares all gossip. She'll tell them she's worried about poor Ella seeing weird supernatural things in my backyard. Then she'll wonder if maybe it's real and whether or not she should call the Brownsville Herald and have them do a story.

No, I definitely can't tell her. I can't tell anyone. I could risk getting hauled away in a straightjacket. I wonder if they come in pink. I keep myself from laughing at the vision in my head of me in a pink straightjacket in a room full of crazies wearing white ones.

Julia drives up in her baby blue Volkswagen, grabs a front parking spot.

"Hi, y'all," Julia says with a big wave. "I was on my way home, saw Anthony's truck so I thought I'd stop in for a cold drink and say hello."

She walks over to us and stands there with her arms across her chest, taps her foot a few times and waits till she has everyone's attention. "By the way, I know what you girls were doing at the library down in the fiction aisles."

"Oh really, why don't you tell us," Rita says, jutting her chin out and crossing her arms mirroring Julia's stance.

"You were looking for a book that I'd already pulled off the shelf."

"Oh no, Jules, are they banning it?" Anna asks.

"Nope, I took it off the shelf, put it in my bag. It's in my car." She giggles. "And guess what. The pages with the steamy parts are dog-eared."

Anthony's clueless and the only one not laughing. Rita and Anna quickly get him up to speed then follow Julia who said she was going to order something to eat. If I know those two, they're probably trying to talk Julia out of the book she's got in her car.

Anthony sucks on his straw till the ice in his cup rattles. He smiles at me when I laugh. "So what's up with this family meeting you guys were talking about?"

When I explain the whole thing, he asks whether it makes any sense to me. I tell him, nothing about Michael makes sense anymore. I thought Anthony was going to be more reassuring, but no, he wasn't. Instead, he said it may be time to end things with Michael.

"You deserve someone so much better than Michael."

I smile. "I think you're right, but I just don't know what to do."

"At least think about it, Ella. Maybe you should go with your gut feeling."

I look at him, give him a half smile. "It's not that simple, Anthony."

The girls join us again at our table. "You two look somber," Rita says. "Let me guess you're talking about Michael and his stupid family meeting."

"Wait, wait…Ella, oh my gosh…that reminds me!" Julia looks at me with her face lit up the way it does when she's about to drop some juicy gossip. I brace myself.

"You're gonna flip. I forgot to tell you my neighbor was at the library today. You'll never believe what she said about Bridget Dubois. Do you know Bridget?"

"I know who she is, but we've never met. She seems kinda—"

"Trampy? Yes, that's the one."

"Well, I was going to say kinda moody, but now that you've said it, yes, she does wear her clothes a little too tight."

"Oh boy, this is sounding good already," Anna says, rubbing her hands together in anticipation.

"Delia said Bridget's a real swinger and she's mentioned Michael a few times. I think she's interested."

"*My* Michael?"

"Yes. She said Bridget was asking her if I might have mentioned whether or not you two were still going steady."

"We might not be for long." I tell her about Michael's family meeting, and how I'm not buying his excuse. "I wish I could have been talking to him in person. I'd have a better idea if this gut feeling I have is real. I just know he's hiding something."

Julia pats my hand in a comforting way. "Well, just because Bridget is interested in Michael doesn't mean Michael's interested in her. I just thought you should know what I'd heard. I'll see what else I can find out, and I'll tell you about it when we go shopping tomorrow."

"Ella," Anna says. "Girls like Bridget don't wait for guys to break up with their girlfriends. I'll betcha Bridget's the reason stupid Mike stood you up!"

Anthony looks at me. "So *now* what's your gut telling you, Ella?"

"I think it just said *I told ya.*"

15

1966 – Ella Galvez

On the way to the fabric shop, I remind Julia that we can't waste time. I've got dinner with my folks, and she's got movie plans with the gang. So when we get to the fabric shop, we go straight to the pattern books. While Julia flips through a book looking for just the right blouse, I browse through another hoping to find my next outfit.

I pull out my journal and note the pattern number of one I like, then draw a summer A-line dress, so I'll remember what the dress looked like. Do the same with a top with crisscross straps in back. The patterns are only sixty-five cents, so I could buy them now but what if I find something I like better between now and when Mom pays me for the work we're doing on her drapery project. I'm thrifty that way. Julia shows me a couple of designs she likes. We pull the pattern packages from the drawers then walk along the rows of fabrics until we find something that works well with the pattern she picked out.

When we pull up to my front yard, we see Mom stooping to pick up the *Herald*.

Julia sticks her head out the window. "That pastel pink is the perfect color for you, Mrs. Galvez."

"Why thank you, Julia, you are a sweet one," Mom answers.

It's not flattery on Julia's part, Mom looks radiant in pink with her dark shoulder length hair and complexion.

"Thanks for helping me," Julia says as I get out of the car. "I can't wait to get started."

"Sure. Talk later."

Once Julia's gone I decided to ask Mom about her lunch date with Aunt Tilly and their canasta friends. While we were out shopping, I saw Aunt Tilly walking down the sidewalk on the opposite side of the street. I watched as she got into her car alone. The canasta ladies weren't with her, neither was my mom.

"How was lunch with your friends?"

"It was fun," she says as she rolls the cotton cord off the paper.

Looks like Mom is sticking to her lunch with Aunt Tilly story.

The first thing I notice when I walk into my room is the picture of Michael and me face down on my bedside table. Without looking at it, I stuff it in the drawer. I run through my head just how many times I've thought about Michael since he cancelled our movie date. Geez, day before yesterday there were shimmering lights in my backyard. Add to that, a necklace magically appeared in my hand, and a statue of a little boy showed up. Well, it didn't just show up, I just don't remember it ever being there in the first place, which is equally disturbing. I'm living in my very own *Twilight Zone.* Yet, I'm wasting time worrying about Michael and how Julia said Bridget was interested in him. If insanity has taken up residence in my life, how can I possibly be worrying about anything else? What if aliens were lurking in the midst of all that shimmer, Mrs. Alien dropped her necklace, and she and Mr. Alien plan to come back to retrieve it...and me!

Really, Ella? A romantic alien named Gabriel?

Okay, forget the aliens, but the never-to-be-forgotten light show should at least merit more concern than Michael, especially since Gabriel Marquez keeps slipping in and out of my mind.

I open the drawer and pull out the picture and stare at it. A feeling of emptiness hits me as I glance between his face and mine, a hand goes to my churning stomach. I place the picture back in the drawer and wonder what exactly is going on here?

There's more to this than if Michael is or isn't cheating on me. The emptiness that I'm feeling is what I'm afraid of. It's the void I'm beginning to feel now that I know Michael will soon be out of my life. But being with Michael isn't making me happy. Knowing he's fooling around is pretty much making me miserable. *I can't do this anymore.*

I grab my jewelry box, sit on the floor with it in my lap, and take the medallion in my hand. I look at it with so much longing.

"Who do you belong to? Who is Bella Ella?"

There's something so sweet about the words. It paints such a beautiful picture of true love, the kind you read about in fairy tales. Once upon a time, there was this romantic guy who loved this happy girl.

Get over it Ella, there's no such thing as fairy tales.

This guy, Gabriel, poured all his love into this simple little medallion for Bella Ella. It's smaller than a half-dollar yet seems to hold a promise of love that will last through the ages just like in a fairy tale.

That's it, enough! I'm going to forget about Michael and go for what I really want, and that's the same love Bella Ella has found, and I want the promises Gabriel made to her on his gift. I know I have to do what's right for me, and somehow this necklace, which isn't even mine, is giving me the strength I need.

Mom pokes her head in. "Let's not keep your father waiting."

"I won't, I'll be ready soon."

No more thinking about Michael. I know we're over and I'll deal with it...later. I pick out a summery pastel yellow dress that mom and I made together. The bodice is fitted, has a white Peter Pan collar and self-made belt loops. I slip in a thin white patent leather belt which matches my stack heels. Pearl stud earrings and a string of pearls finish the look I want.

I noticed Mom's wearing her three-strand pearl necklace, just like Jackie Kennedy's. Well, not exactly, Mom's necklace is a cheap imitation, but still, they are a fashion statement, and she loves them. Mom is always able to look like a million bucks while being very frugal since she sews almost everything she wears. We go shopping together at stores that sell designer clothing. I take out my journal and draw sketches of what we like then find similar sewing patterns and fabrics and make what we want for a fraction of the cost. Besides saving money, we enjoy our outings and working on our sewing projects.

On our way to The Drive Inn, the voice I heard in my head earlier chimes in again. This time I'm sure it's coming from within. Like a memory. But if it's a memory, why don't I remember it?

If I had only sat by the dance floor, I would've seen him.

What dance floor? I know it's not the dance studio. Maybe the civic center? We danced there at our prom. Oh, wait, The Drive Inn has one, maybe that's it. But we never sit near it, we always sit toward the back. *I could use a clue here.*

When we enter the restaurant, my eyes light up. We've been here many times, but I'm always in awe of the elegance. The lights are dim, and the dance band playing *The Girl from Ipanema* invites us in. This restaurant is about as fancy as it gets. It's the place you take your family or a date on special occasions. This is where we come every time my dad completes a big project. He loves that for a few hours we're taken to an extraordinary place.

The maître d' leads us to one of Dad's favorite tables in the back. As we pass the dance floor, I remember the words that I'd heard. Without hesitation, I tug on my dad's arm and whisper to him. "Daddy, can we *please* sit by the dance floor just this once?" He looks back to where I'm pointing then smiles at me. He lets the maître d' know my request, and we're taken to the table I'd hoped for. "Thanks, Daddy, this is perfect."

So here I am sitting by the dance floor. No more *if I had only...*but now what? What happens next? Will *the voice* go away now that I've obeyed? What the heck. Not only am I hearing a voice in my head I'm also taking its advice.

Well, for one thing, I'm going to enjoy this. I get to watch the dancers, and I also have a view of the entrance, and I can admire the beautiful dresses. A lady walks in wearing a simple light blue shift. The fabric is sateen which makes it look so elegant. I point it out to Mom, and she turns to look.

"I love the bodice," Mom says. "I do hope you have your journal with you. I would love a sketch."

I nod, pull out a pencil and my journal, and draw the top portion of the dress we admired. Mom points to my drawing, tapping at the edge of the shoulder.

"The edge comes across the collarbone just a little more rounded than that," Mom traces the curve on my notebook with her fingernail.

I make the correction then below the drawing I write, *baby blue sateen.* Mom pats my hand then goes back to talking with Dad. The next person I see is much younger and kind of sleezy. That red satin fabric is wrapped so tight around her body she has to take baby steps. Or maybe it's because of the stiletto heels she's wearing. I'm guessing this girl doesn't own a full-length mirror. And look at her boobs popping out of that low-cut dress. She kind of reminds me of Bridget.

Michael? Is that...yes, it is, with Bridget Dubois!

My mouth gapes. A sideways glance at Mom and Dad and I'm relieved they didn't notice Michael nor the shocked look on my face. Michael says something to the maître d' and points to the far corner. They're seated in a dimly lit and really cozy spot.

You stupid, two-timing jerk!

I am such an idiot! He worked all those extra hours for this floozy? I'm disgusted with him, especially when I look over and see Bridget kissing him, and not just kissing him, she's about to swallow him up. You'd think he was the dessert *du jour.* How slutty! Breaking up with Michael is going to be a cinch. *Adieu*, Michael Damon!

I force myself to turn my focus back to our table, hoping no one else has noticed where my attention has been. My folks haven't a clue, they're occupied with their dinner. I pick up my fork, look at it and decide there's no way I can stomach any of this food. Besides, with my hands shaking the way they are, I'd end up wearing my mashed potatoes, they'd never reach my mouth. I place my fork down and rest my shaking hands in my lap. Now to still my racing heart. I make an effort to take longer breaths, and it does help calm me down. I promise myself not to look back at Michael and his floozy again.

I'm lucky my parents have plenty to talk about and are ignoring me. They're in the middle of Dad's favorite subject, politics. Then the subject changes to his current construction jobs and mom's sewing project. I hear Mom tell Dad we worked on drapes and window cornices this morning. When Dad asks what cornices are, she explains they are boxes covered in fabric to match the drapes and go at the top of the window instead of a ruffle.

As Mom shares what we did this morning, I recall how she was unusually quiet. Maybe it's all the details she has to worry about, or maybe it's a personal situation she just can't talk about. I didn't mind the quiet. I had plenty of noise going on in my head - Michael and the wild world of Ella Galvez.

"Sounds like you were busy," Dad says.

"Yes," Mom says, "plus I did some laundry and of course my housework."

"And you had lunch with Aunt Tilly and your canasta friends," I add.

Mom nods. "Yes, yes, that too. And I've been thinking, I'd like to add a border of marigolds around the bird bath, and possibly some more salvia blooms alongside the stepping stones."

Gardening is Mom's signature lets-change-the-subject topic. She looks down at her hands while she's answering Dad, rather than looking right at him as she normally would. I was hoping Mom would say she left early, or she decided not to stay. Anything to explain why she wasn't with Aunt Tilly when I saw her downtown alone. *She's still sticking to that story.*

I go back to playing with my food, Mom and Dad continue with their conversation. I've never been so happy to feel completely invisible.

I'm in a daze here pretending to be interested in the couples on the dance floor. After all, that's why I asked to sit here. As I watch them, I can't help but wonder how many of them are truly in love or are they just going through the motions. Why do people do that – settle?

Good question, Ella, why do they?

Before leaving the restaurant, Mom and I go to the ladies' room. Bridget walks out as I pull the door open. She gives me an unusually big smile but says nothing, I do the same.

She's flaunting it in my face!

When we return to our table, I see her looking at me. Probably wanted to make sure I can see who her date is. I give her a little beauty queen wave and a smile. I don't think Michael even knows I'm here. She probably hasn't told him that she saw me, thinking it might kill the moment. What would he do if he knew? I imagine him rushing over to me. *Ella, baby, it's not what it looks like.*

Or maybe not. Maybe Michael would continue with his date and assume we are over. It doesn't matter, either way, we were already over before he walked in the door. He just didn't know it yet.

On the drive home I wonder how many other times he's gone out with her. She's probably the reason he didn't come to my pizza party. Glad he didn't get to taste his favorite cake. Mom's pineapple upside-down cake will never, ever pass his lips. Oh, how I wish I'd never given Michael the time of day. Just glad that's all I ever gave him, not that he wasn't always trying to help himself. Damn him!

Once we cross the bridge into Brownsville and past customs, I lay my head against the window and ask myself why am I so angry, and why do I even care? I shrug my shoulders and close my eyes.

Mom's nudges awaken me. "Come on, Ella, we're home." Dad waits for me to get out and we walk inside, his arm along my shoulder.

"Thanks for the nice dinner, Daddy."

"Are you alright, Ella?" Mom asks. "You fell asleep soon after we left the restaurant."

"I'm fine, Mom. Just tired."

Please don't make a big deal of it and start checking my—

She puts her hand to my forehead. "You don't feel warm."

"That's because I'm fine. I told you, I'm tired."

"Goodnight ladies. I'm tired too, going to bed." Dad walks off yawning.

"See, Dad's tired too."

She purses her lips, picks up the Reader's Digest she'd been reading earlier today. "Goodnight, Ella."

"Sleep tight, *mamacita*." I smile knowing I'd please her using this affectionate form of mom in Spanish.

Mom's face softens, she smiles back. I hate it when I'm short with her. I didn't mean to be. I bound up the stairs anxious to get into my bedroom and close the door. Need to get the feel of my usual routine. Michael and I are over, time to get on with the rest of my life starting now.

I kick off my shoes at the door, turn my lamp on. I take my earrings and necklace off and put them away.

"I'll bet Gabriel's not a two-timing jerk." I sigh. I slip off my dress and put it on the hanger I'd left on my bed. "I can't believe I saw him with Bridget with my own two eyes."

Holy cow! I saw them because I listened to what the voice said and asked to sit by the dance floor. Just like that, without thinking I asked, and boom, there he was. As I hang my dress in the closet, I wonder if

I'll ever be able to wear it without thinking about tonight. I push away the vision of Michael and Bridget walking in together, and I head to the bathroom. I smear on the Noxzema then take a wet washcloth and wipe it off. I examine my face now freshly cleaned of the little bit of face powder I'd put on.

"Bet she's plain under that slab of makeup." I throw the wet washcloth in the sink taking another look at myself before walking away. As I close my bedroom door, I hear the clickity-click of Mom's dust mop.

At least some things I can still count on.

I grab my brush and begin my ritual of 100 hair-brush strokes which is supposed to keep my hair healthy and shiny. I fall into a nice relaxing rhythm of running the bristles through my hair, and it begins to relax me.

"What's the big deal?" I grumble. "It's not like she has much more to offer."

I catch my reflection in the mirror. "Or does she?"

I go back to brushing my hair, hanging my head forward to brush from my neck down to the ends several times. I stop, straighten up and check myself in the mirror again, run my hands along the slight curve of my breast. "Agggh!" I slam my brush down on the bed. "Beautiful hair just can't compete with *those* things!"

Feeling frustrated, I get into my new baby doll pajamas, place the needle on The Beatles album that's on the turntable, and sit on the floor resting my back against my bed. A smile creeps onto my face when *I Want to Hold Your Hand* comes on, and a feeling of satisfaction sets in knowing Michael wasn't able to ruin this song for me. In fact, I don't think there's anything I love that he can take with him. It's just

Michael that's gone which is fine with me. I take our picture out of the drawer and place it inside my wastebasket.

The phone rings, and I leap for it. It's Julia. "Oh, Ella, I hate to be the one to tell you, but you'll never guess who I saw driving down Elizabeth Street. They were all cozy in the front seat." The words spilled out of Julia's mouth so fast, but I got every single word she said.

"Michael and Bridget?"

"How'd you guess?" she asks, sounding a little disappointed it was no longer late-night breaking news. I give her all the details on the Michael and Bridget saga. She is so easy to talk to, so I spilled my heart out.

"I knew it. I just knew they were up to no good. Bridget's had the hots for Michael all along, so I figured she—"

"Stop it! I don't want to hear anymore Michael crap." I take a deep breath. "Sorry, Julia, I didn't mean to be rude. Michael is the past, so please, can we drop it?"

"Of course, but if you need to talk, you know I'm here for you."

With Julia, good news travels fast, bad news travels faster. So ten minutes later Anna calls. I repeat the same story knowing in the back of my mind Rita will be calling next. Anna's all about payback and how we're going to show Bridget you don't mess with someone else's boyfriend and get away with it. Moments after we hang up, Rita calls.

"Damn it, Ella. Your phones been busy for forever."

"I wasn't on the phone that long. Anyway, you've already heard the story from Julia. So what's the rush?"

"Yeah, I did, but I want to hear it from you. Details, girl, I want details."

So I repeat it once more. Having told the story three times, the fact that Michael cheated on me is sinking in deeper, and it's starting to really mess me up. I finish off the last of my conversation talking through gritted teeth. When we say goodbye, I breathe out a heavy sigh.

Apparently, Anthony hasn't heard, or he would have called too. I'm so glad he didn't. Don't know if I could relive this miserable evening one more time. Anthony will hear about it soon enough since I'm meeting them all for breakfast tomorrow morning. I reach into my nightstand drawer, grab the pink satin ribbon with a key hanging from it and my diary. Flip it open to today's date.

"Dear Diary, Michael Damon is a jerk. We are over!" I snap it shut and place it back in my drawer. "You're gonna miss me a whole lot more than I'm gonna miss you, Michael Damon."

It feels good saying this with such convincing clarity and determination. But I know only a part of me believes it. A small part. It's actually a teensy-weensy part that lays deep within my soul, right next to the tiny part that thought there might have been angels in the sky. Yes, it's tiny, but I know it's there.

16

1971 – Ella Marquez

If Gabriel had told me we'd be spending two whole weeks at this lakeside cabin, I would've definitely said *no*. But now that we're here, I would gladly stay on for a month. Although we haven't even begun to work on all those memories I've kept locked inside, the serenity of this place is healing.

During my visit with Nancy, I was able to face one piece of my story which was shoved somewhere in my head. Yes, it was difficult and painful, but I survived it. And I actually felt my burden had lightened. Now I wish I had been able to deal with my rape back when I was eighteen when it was fresh in my mind rather than hiding it all away. I think life would have been much happier for us. I'm almost sure of it. Now there's no telling what lies beneath all the cobwebs in my head. Hopefully, those memories haven't been melded together, made impenetrable to protect a fragile me.

Plus, there have been a few more bits and pieces that have somehow worked themselves out of a dead sleep in my memory. The day of Gabe's accident I saw a vision while I was sitting on the lawn swing, just after I saw shimmering lights and flickering fireflies in broad daylight. I saw a vision in the backyard of the home I grew up in. It was as clear as day and exactly as I'd seen it the day we arrived. I saw the little girl statue which I always remembered being there, but I also saw the little boy holding the puppy, just like the one sitting outside this log cabin. They were both there beside Mom's rose garden, and I couldn't understand what he was doing there.

Then I was holding the necklace Gabe had just given me for our anniversary, which I've already lost. It must've come undone and fallen to the ground somewhere. I've tried retracing every step I've made hoping to find it. The last time I recall seeing it was when I was sitting on the swing praying for Gabriel soon after I'd learned of his accident. What was really strange is the hand I saw in my vision holding the necklace, which Gabe gave me four days ago, was mine as a teenager. I recognized the ring I was wearing. It was gold and had a small emerald heart. And I heard a voice, my voice, say, *What the heck! Where'd this come from?*

Later on I saw myself walking toward the backyard of that same house I grew up in and deliberately turned my face toward the neighbor's upstairs window. A tingle ran down my spine, and it made me shiver. I wiggled my shoulders, and I ran my hands along my arms. Just as I was turning away, a shadow moved then the curtain closed. I quickly walked away.

I knew it was me...no, *felt* it was me as a teen. I know this because I looked down at my bare feet and saw my pink polished toe nails as I stepped upon each stepping stone. The sundress I was wearing was the light yellow one Mom and I made. I sewed on a chain of little white daisies all around near the hem and embroidered a large one on the center strip of the bodice, white petals with a big yellow center. There was no mistaking that dress.

It felt so strange to see these visions, and I would've tossed them off as daydreams, but I know the difference. I wasn't watching me go through these movements, I was seeing everything through my own eyes as if it were happening to me. And something deep inside me tells me there's something more to that little boy and the creepy neighbor's upstairs window.

While Gabriel naps, I pull out my work journal to entertain myself, then work on costume designs for my students' next recital. He's been sleeping a lot. The medication they gave him when he was dismissed from the hospital makes him sleepy. Plus, his mom and dad came by so it was a long day for him. I hoped he'd be awake for this evening's sunset, but guess I'm on my own for this one.

I make myself a cup of tea and head outside. It is gorgeous out here, and I think it might actually be a sin to remain indoors on a day like today. Although I haven't seen any more of those fizzling fireflies, I make it a point to look around for a hint of sparkle. I'm sure they're still out here. The twins saw them, and so did I...twice.

Even before I take a seat on the swing, my conversation with God is already beginning. While thanking him for this day, I take in the horizon turning a beautiful red-orange, blending with violet and blue. I want to memorize what I'm seeing. We can't take things that are physical with us when we're gone, but what about memories? God's sunsets are some of the ones I'd like to hold on to.

I imagine that at this very moment there are hundreds of photographers clicking away longing to capture this amazing sunset, and artists brandishing their paint covered brushes in hopes of recreating God's breathtaking masterpiece. As for me, I just sit here and thank God for this amazing end to another day. I also thank him for bringing Gabriel back home to me, and I pray for Mom.

I turn toward the sound of the screen door opening.

"Guess I missed the sunset," Gabe says as he steps out to join me, a glass of orange juice in his hand.

"Yes, but there's always tomorrow." I reach my hand up to him. "Come over here, sit with me awhile."

"Thanks for saving me that spot. When I got the juice from the fridge, I noticed a lot of food in Tupperware containers. You've been cooking." He takes a sip of juice and sets the glass down next to my mug of tea.

"Nope, not me. Larry and Tina dropped by with all that food. Sat around for a while chatting with them. They also brought the newspaper sitting on the table. Larry drives out to pick it up each day, says he'll drop one off for us if we'd like. I said yes, and gave him some cash I had in my purse."

"That's got to be quite a drive for a newspaper. I don't recall seeing any stores on our way here," Gabe says, lightly stroking the scratch on his cheek, the only visual clue that he was in a car accident. He was so lucky. *We* were so lucky.

"Larry said it's about four miles in the opposite direction of where we came in."

Gabe drinks up the rest of his orange juice then sets his glass down. "Well, it was nice of him to drop it off. What about the twins. Any word?"

"Yes, the girls and their mom have been interviewed by the sheriff's department and the FBI. The girls have also spent time with a child psychologist."

"Any leads?" Gabe asks.

"Nothing the Horton's told me makes any sense. The authorities and the parents believe the girls were in Paris."

Gabe looks at me with a furrowed forehead. "So what doesn't make sense?"

"Everything the twins have said has convinced everyone they actually were there. They speak French, said they went to the Eiffel Tower and were able to draw a picture of it. Not very well, but can they said there was no denying the A-shaped picture they each drew was the Eiffel Tower. They shared a lot of what happened there including that they lived with other little girls. Sounds like an orphanage."

Here's the weird part, neither Elizabeth nor Amelia has been able to tell anyone how they got there. When asked if they rode in an airplane they both said *no*. They also asked them if they might have crossed the ocean on a ship, again that was a negative. Everyone has gone to great lengths to describe every mode of transportation imaginable, but the girls can't recall any of them. And listen to this. When asked if they could describe the person who took them there, they said, no body took them, just the fireflies."

"Okay, you're right, that is weird. So the twins haven't been able to say how they got there, and how they returned?"

"Do you remember when Tina asked the girls who brought them back to the cabin? Elizabeth said fireflies did and Amelia agreed."

"Yeah, I remember."

"Well, they're sticking to their story. Sparkly fireflies took them there, and sparkly fireflies brought them back to the cabin." And then I laugh. "I think the twins got roundtrip tickets on fireflies."

Gabe sits there staring at me. I laugh because I'm pretty sure it's the same expression I had until I remembered seeing sparkly fireflies myself, or at least something similar to them. Hmm, roundtrip tickets to Paris on fireflies. That's funny—or maybe freaky. Ella, you saw sparkly fireflies...what if they had snatched you up and taken you to Paris?"

I laugh, "Oh wait a minute, don't tell me you're thinking they actually were—"

"Hey, stranger things have happened. Well, not *that* strange," he laughs. "They'll figure it out one of these days. But carried away by fireflies? That didn't happen."

Gabe turns and looks at me with a curious look on his face. "You just reminded me."

"About what?" I ask.

"Fireflies. I was somewhere between being asleep and waking up, and I recalled something from when the officers questioned me when I had the accident."

"Gabe, the police officer told me you were hardly coherent when they talked to you."

"Maybe my speech was off, but baby, I saw the cops and guess what else I saw." A smile spreads across his face. "Fireflies, or something like them. Three of them, and I saw Anthony, and you, we were at Fisher's."

"So you were dreaming this?"

"Nope, eyes opened. Then I thought of you at the cabin, and it went away. The lights fizzed out too."

"Umm. That's weird. We've sat out here watching fireflies at night, and none of them ever flickered away. What are these things? Vampire fireflies that come out during the day and die?" I laugh, so does Gabe. "Well babe, I've got another weird thing to share. Interested?" I ask.

"Visions or more fireflies?"

"Both."

He smirks. "Oh, boy...I'm ready whenever you are."

I share everything I saw in my old backyard and how it looked like I was seeing things through my own eyes. When I tell Gabe about the voice, and the vision of me checking out the necklace in my teenaged hand. It hits me.

"Gabe, the voice...the one I heard. Did I mention that it sounded like me?" I stop and try to recall the sound of it again.

"Ella, your voice would've said, *what the hell*, not *what the heck,*" he says, laughing.

"Not when I was a teenager, I never cussed. Well, maybe a few times."

"Yeah, I guess you're right. Don't recall you swearing much back then."

"It's just so peculiar, my seeing events from my youth like this, especially now that I'm working on trying to recall details about my rape. I did say I wanted to go back in time and change things." I laugh knowing how silly what I just said sounded.

"Maybe part of you already has, you did say you saw shimmers and fireflies."

We sit there staring at each other and then, on cue, we shake our heads and say, "Nah." Then we laugh.

Once inside I head to the shower and make it a quick one, slip on some shorts and a crop top and go into the den to join Gabe who I find talking on the phone.

"I can't believe this Prada guy is living in Houston."

His words reverberate in my head, and I go numb, my body leans itself against the doorframe. Gabe's silent so I can only wonder what's being said on the other end of the line, or who it is.

"No, I'm not saying he's the guy funding Ella's dance school, I'm just saying I'll make sure he comes nowhere near her. This is the wrong time for him to pop into our lives. Yes, you're right, no time is a good time for Prada to show up. I just don't want to upset—"

Gabe turns back and sees me standing there. "Oh no, baby did you—"

I nod, "Yeah."

"Hey, Anthony, I'll have to call you back, just keep looking." Gabe's eyes look back at me. "Yeah, she heard. Later."

I sit on the sofa, and Gabe joins me. "So are you going to tell me what's going on? What were you and Anthony talking about?"

Gabe wraps his arm around me, and I rest my head against his shoulder.

"Telling you would only worry you, so I decided not to say anything."

"Well, I heard you say he's living in Houston. I'm guessing you think he's my benefactor. Is that it?"

Gabe nods and pulls me in tighter. "Yes, I'm scared he might be. At this point, we may want to consider returning the money he's given you and decline the offer."

"But if we do that, we might never know." I look at Gabe. "I'm hoping there'll be a slip up and I'll be able to get his name. We need to know."

"That's true," he says. "We have the attorney's name, Mrs. Hernandez, right? And we know his. It shouldn't be too difficult to hire someone who can track them down. You have a few months before classes begin, so maybe we can rule him out. But should the attorney contact you to meet with the benefactor, make it at a public place, and I will go there with you."

"And then there's Mom's lunch date."

"Ella, you know darn well that's definitely got to be a coincidence."

"Yeah, you're right."

"Wait a minute...the upstairs window I saw. That's where this guy Prada lived. That's why it gave me the shivers. Oh wow! I remember he lived there and I ended up keeping my blinds to my bedroom window closed as well as the shades on the side of my practice room."

I think about what I just saw. "Gabe this is so weird. In my vision, I turned and looked straight at it, but I didn't know the significance of it. Before my rape, I never knew that window even existed, so it makes sense not to make anything of it. But it was me, a grown up me, who was looking at it through teenage eyes. That's why I felt the chills. Are you listening to what I'm saying? I sound crazy. Don't pay any attention to me. This is nuts."

"That's right, he owned the house, so that parts not crazy. But I found out from Anthony that it was his mother who lived there. Of course, he'd go visit her, and that's probably when you'd see him looking out that window."

"So why didn't you tell me it was the reason I reacted the way I did when I saw it in my vision. No...wait. I'm getting things in bits and pieces because it's probably all I can handle. You were right not to say anything. I think everything will come back to me all in good time. Oh, Gabe, I'm so sorry you have to go through all of this, be a part of it."

"I am a part of it. You're my wife, and I love you. It's gonna be okay, baby, we'll get through this."

No, our anniversary week didn't go as planned, and we'll probably not get much further since Gabe is still healing and on meds. But I think the revelations I'm having will help me deal with all these issues once we're back home. Why wouldn't it? My frame of reference has changed. I was trying to heal a wound I couldn't even admit was there.

How can you fix something you don't believe in your mind even exists? You can't, and that may have been the problem. But now that I've allowed myself to see the truth, Gabriel and I can work through it together. I go to my bag and get my other journal where I keep my personal notes.

So let's see, need to make sure I get every detail down. Don't want to miss a thing. *Wow, Gabe said he saw fireflies too.*

I smile thinking about something Gabriel told me early on in our relationship. He said the truth should never be masked, even if it hurts. If the truth is in the way and causing problems, it must be dealt with and worked through. Only problem was that I'd already locked away what I needed to work through. In my mind, it no longer existed. But things are starting to slip through, and I'm doing things Gabe's way now. I'll pull out the trusty truth meter and deal with things whether it be here at this cabin or at home. I have a feeling it's going to hurt a little...or a lot. But I'm ready for it. I've got Gabe, and we've got God.

17

1966 – Ella Galvez

One step into Texas Cafe and I can smell what's on the menu for breakfast. If only I had an appetite, I'd order one of each. I spot Anthony and Julia with their heads together. I'll bet Julia's bringing him up to speed on the new developments. Anna and Rita are deep in their own conversation.

I wave. "Sorry guys, I overslept."

Anthony pats the seat next to him. "No problem, kiddo, you're here now." I take a seat, and he immediately starts in on this morning's hot topic. "Okay, I just heard, and I'm so sorry, I can't believe what that insensitive jerk did!"

"You mean insensitive *jackass*," Rita says loud enough to garner stares from the customers at the table next to us. Rita mimics the same shocked look back at them, and they quickly drop their gaze.

As soon as the waiter leaves with our order, Anna looks at me squarely in the face. "So when are you going to deal with that two-timing boyfriend of yours?"

"Well, he's not my boyfriend anymore," I say in a hushed voice. "I'm done with that slime ball! *Basta!*"

"You broke up with him?" Anthony asks. Anna and Julia lean in with wide eyes.

Rita's distracted. "Wait, hold on. What did you say? *Basta?* How do you spell it?" She has a pen in her hand ready to write it down on a napkin.

"Damn it, Rita! Shut your mouth already," Julia mutters through gritted teeth. "We have a crisis here!"

Julia's a sweet kid, but if you upset her, she can go from cute girl to crazed woman in a matter of seconds. You do *not* want to make Julia mad. Fun to watch when she blows up, but if you're on the receiving end – stand back!

Anna's all over it. "How'd he take it, El, did he cry?" She half-way crawls over the table to make sure she gets every last detail.

"Well, he doesn't know it yet, we haven't talked."

I pick up the salt shaker Anna knocked over then look up at everyone. They all have the same expression – disbelief.

"What on earth are you waiting for?" Anna demands.

"I'm not ready to talk to him, don't want to hear his voice, nor his lies. I'll let him know it's over soon enough."

Anthony cups my chin and turns my face toward him. "But it *is* over, right?"

"Yes. Of course," I say to Anthony who's giving me a squinty look. "Really…it's over."

"So what's the holdup, El? I don't get it." Anna's obviously not buying it.

"It's not that easy. I'm angry, and I'm hurt. The last thing I want is for Michael to hear the tiniest quiver in my voice. I don't want him to think I'm wishy-washy in my decision, or that he still might have a chance – which he doesn't. I want to be in total control."

"Makes sense to me, be strong and then wallop him. Way to go, Ella Bella!" Rita was never a fan of Michael.

"If you need help finding the right words, I've got a few choice ones that will let him know just how pathetic he is," Anna adds.

"Come on, guys, I really am okay. I know my life will be much happier without Michael in it."

Anthony puts his arm around me. "You deserve someone so much better, much, much better."

I turn and give him a half-smile. "So you keep telling me."

"So when's it gonna happen? When are you dumping him, El? We wanna be there," Anna says, pointing a finger back and forth between her and Rita.

"And me," Anthony chimes in. "I'm a big fan of photo journalism. I'll capture the whole shebang for you."

"Y'all are crazy." I laugh. "You're making it sound like it's *the* event of the season."

Anthony does a drum roll on the table with his hands. "It *is*." This cracks everyone up.

The waiter shows up with our order, and I'm happy for the interruption. "Okay," I say. "Our food's here, let's eat, and by the way, Michael, Bridget and I are no longer the topic of conversation, you got it?"

"Okay! So who's registered for classes?" Anthony, asks, picking up a strip of bacon with his fingers and popping it in his mouth."

"I just wish Texas Southmost had a football team and a marching band," Julia grumbles. "My little piccolo is tired of playing *Stars and Stripes Forever* all alone."

Anthony's a big football fan. "Hey, we're still showing up for the games, right guys? The Eagles are still our hometown team."

"What about you, Tone? Won't you miss beating those drums?" Anna asks.

"Yeah, my days with the Golden Eagle Band were the best. At least I can still play my drums with the guys when we're jamming together."

"Hey, do you need a piccolo player?" Julia asks.

"Unless you have an electric piccolo, we won't be able to hear it over the noise we make. We're loud!" Anthony says, laughing. We laugh with him.

"My guess is what you'll *really* miss are those cute Eaglettes hanging all over you," Rita says.

Rita loves teasing Anthony about the drill team. A few of the girls followed him around at the games like little golden baby chicks. They loved being around Anthony, and he loved the attention.

"Yeah I did, but for me it's all about our Eagles, especially when they play against the Edinburg Bobcats," Anthony says. "That's what I think was the best part of my high school years."

"I hope we'll get to see our old friends at the games. I think the saddest part of graduating is losing touch with old friends," I say.

Julia looks at me with a frown on her face. "I don't want to lose touch with my classmates. Maybe someone will form a committee and keep us all connected somehow. You know, gather us together for special events."

"Hey, I like that idea," Anthony says. "They can call it The Gathering of Eagles."

Julia sits there smiling, nodding her head. "I like that idea a lot."

I like it a lot too, but don't bother keeping up with the rest of the conversation, too much on my mind. I quietly eat my toast as I do a rerun in my head of Michael and Bridget's grand entrance at The Drive Inn last night. Then I put my napkin and enough money for my breakfast and a tip on the table and take one last gulp of juice.

"Hey guys, I hate to eat and run, got an errand to run for Mom. Later," I say with a wave. The girls wave back.

"Later, gator," Anthony says, sending me off with a salute.

I suppose I could have stayed longer, but these days I seem to crave a lot of peace and quiet. Although quiet time can quickly turn into crazy let-me-outta-here time when the weird stuff starts replaying in my head. Each day I seem to be grasping for normal. But it's not there. Seeing firefly lights isn't normal. Hearing voices in my head isn't normal either. Nothing is.

Will I even recognize it when it shows up? Will it ever show up?

As I go to open the car door, I notice how invigorating it feels to breathe in the fresh morning air and decide to walk to the fabric shop instead. I grab the envelope with swatches in it that mom asked me to drop off and put it in my purse. I've walked three blocks and I'm still stuck on one question. What am I going to say to Michael when I break up with him? But really, what's to think about? He cheated. It's over. Hah! That's exactly what I'm gonna tell him. *You cheated. It's over.*

When I get to the fabric store, I tap on the door and wave the envelope just like Mom said. Miss Irene opens the door and greets me with a big smile. She takes the swatches from me, but not before giving me a hug and asking me how my summer is going. She is such a sweet lady, always so friendly. That done, I take my time walking back to the car. Window shopping is always fun.

"Uh-oh," I say under my breath when I spot a guy wearing a blue cap. He's walking on the opposite side of the street headed in my direction. I know, lots of men wear caps, even blue ones, but the hairs on my arm stand straight up when I see him. I don't know why, but it's as if something deep inside of me senses that it's him. My upper body tenses up, and I pick up my pace hoping it's not the guy I'd seen in the park.

I think it's him!

I turn the corner so that he can't see where I'm headed. I tell myself I'm being silly, but my quickened heartbeat tells me otherwise. The shops don't open till nine, Irene's fabric store is too far, so there's nowhere for me to duck into. I'm a block away from City Hall. They probably open at eight. I check my wristwatch. It's about five minutes till eight, so maybe, just maybe I can get inside. I quicken my step, then run.

Please be open!

I yank hard on the heavy door not expecting it to open, but it does. I look back and gasp when I see him crossing the street in my direction. He's running.

"No, please, no," I cry as I hurry inside. I decide to take the stairs hoping he'll think I went straight ahead since it would be the fastest getaway.

Leaps, Ella, leaps!

I'm able to fly up those stairs taking two steps at a time. I know exactly where these stairs lead. The switchboard station is in the open area on the second floor. I came by with Mom to drop off flowers for Miss Tere, the switchboard operator. But when I reach the top of the stairs she isn't there. Nobody is. I hurry around her L-shaped desk and scoot in beneath it. I'm crouched there waiting, scared to death. I try to still my shaking body knowing he could be coming up any second now.

Where is everybody?

I look at my watch. It's a couple of minutes till eight.

I hear someone coming up the stairs, but the footsteps sound too light to be a guy's. I wait as I listen to whoever it is come around toward the desk.

It's Miss Tere. I startle her. "What—"

I place a finger over my lips. "Shhhh, I'm being followed."

She looks around. "Honey, there's no one here," she whispers back.

We hear other footsteps come up the stairs, but they sound like high heels. I crawl out from my hiding spot. Even if he shows up, he couldn't possibly do anything in front of Miss Tere.

"Good morning, Maria," Miss Tere says to the lady who walks past us. She gently puts her hands on either side of my shoulders. "I remember you. Your mom is Mary Galvez, right?"

I nod my head. "Yes," I whisper and look back at the stairs.

"Oh honey, you're shaking." She puts her arms around me and holds me tight. "Who are you hiding from?"

"Oh, Miss Tere, you are an angel. There's a guy following me. And it's the second time I've seen him. When I saw him running toward me, I was so afraid he would catch up to me."

"You want me to call the police department or your parents?"

"They aren't home, but I have a friend I can call. He should be home soon. I'm sure you know him, Anthony Bartelli."

She smiles. "Of course, the mayor's son. Here, put on my headset," she says, turning her chair toward me. It will be easier for you to sit here and dial the number."

With shaking hands, I spin Anthony's number. When Mrs. Bartelli answers I try hard to keep my voice steady, and I'm relieved when she says Anthony's supposed to be dropping by here at eight to pick up something from his dad.

As I hand the phone back to Miss Tere, we hear quick footsteps coming up the stairs. I grab hold of her arm, and we both wait to see who it is. My breath gushes out. "Anthony!"

"Hey, what are *you* doing here?" He places his arm along my shoulder. "My God, you're shaking. What's wrong?"

My eyes pool with tears as I try hard not to cry. I bite down on my lip to keep from doing so.

"Stay right here, Ella, I need to get something from my dad, I'll only be a second."

Miss Tere hands me a tissue. He gives her a quick hello wave, and she gets busy with incoming phone calls.

I watch Miss Tere as she answers "Good morning, City Hall." They come in one call after another, and she sticks those long cords all over her switchboard, crisscrossing them into a tangled mess. She looks at me, winks and keeps talking, plugging and unplugging phone lines. "They keep me busy," she says when she's finally free. I smile at her. She has the sweetest smile.

Anthony returns and takes me by the hand. "Come on let's go to my truck, we can talk there."

I pull my hand away and run around the switchboard and give Miss Tere a hug and thank her. She hugs me back and kisses my cheek. "I'm glad I was here for you, honey."

I wave at Miss Tere as we head down the stairs.

"Did Michael—"

"No, it wasn't him."

"So what's going on?"

On the way downstairs I tell him about the blue cap guy, and how he ran after me when I headed into City Hall. When he hears the part about me hiding under the desk, he stops and holds me. "You poor thing. You must've been so scared."

"I was scared to death."

Once outside we look around, but that guy is nowhere in sight.

"You need to go to the police station and let 'em know."

"Yes, I know, I'll have Dad take me."

"My truck's close by, let me drive you to your car," he says.

"How close?"

"Half a block down in front of The Victory Place, the red, white and blue building."

We walk to his truck and sit there talking about who this guy could be.

"It's weird that you've seen him near your home and now downtown," Anthony says, pushing the cigarette lighter button.

Anthony smokes?

Anthony quickly lowers his window when he notices a man finish up a conversation with a couple just outside the red white and blue building. "Mr. Rodriguez," he says loudly. The man comes to the window ducks down, says hello to Anthony, and then looks at me and smiles.

"Did you happen to see a guy with a blue cap come by a while ago?"

"Yeah, I did. I noticed the guy because he came running out of those double doors," he says, pointing to the side entrance to City Hall. "He ran to the end of the street checked around the corner there at The Texas Cafe then walked back and got in a faded red truck, a Ford, and drove away. Is everything okay?"

"Yes, but he was following my friend, Ella, a while ago. If you should see him again, would you please see if you can get his license plate number?"

"Of course. I've got your dad's number. I'll give him a call if I do." Mr. Rodriguez, ducks down to look at me, smiles and waves goodbye.

"Wow, what luck. Nice man, glad he was out here."

"Yeah, he is. He's one of my dad's big supporters, brings in a lot of votes for him. Well, we know what he drives now," Anthony says, nodding his head. "Ella, he could've followed you from home. Maybe he lives in the neighborhood. But wherever he's from, this guy's following you. At least now we can keep an eye out for a faded red truck."

Anthony punches the lighter in again. When it pops out, he lights his cigarette, inhales, and blows the smoke out his window. He sees me wrinkle my nose.

"I only smoke when I get edgy or tense," he says, flicking ashes out on the curb. He takes another puff and exhales the smoke out the window, again. "Where are you parked, I'll drive you there."

He smashes his cigarette out inside the ashtray then drives me to my car and follows me home. Once there, he walks me to my door and tells me not to leave the house by myself.

I run up to my room, turn on the radio, and then open the blinds. My eyes go straight to that window. I shut the blinds and fling the cord against the wall. Before plopping myself on my bed, I grab Blue and hold him close. I lay here looking up at the ceiling, see the outlines of the star stickers which Julia and I stuck on there so long ago. They used to be gold and silver, but they've been painted over. I love that I can still see their outline. I often lay here and count them, and I love how it calms me. Today it doesn't seem to help

I wipe a tear away. I'm feeling sad, but not about Michael. The necklace, it isn't mine. That's what makes me sad. I know it'll never be mine. Gabriel isn't mine either. Not the one written on the medallion nor Gabriel Marquez, the one who has awakened me to pleasures I'd never experienced before, without ever having felt his embrace or kissed his lips. I crush Blue against my heart and hold him tight. Why couldn't I have been with him at the movies instead of his date that other day? I bet he kissed little miss blondie, and she kissed him back. I softly touch my finger to the corner of my mouth, wondering what it would feel like to kiss him right there where his lip turns up when he smiles.

The smiles I've seen and the quiet make-believe moments I've had are all I'll ever have. Can these memories hold me for a lifetime? Yes, I think they can, why wouldn't they? Thoughts of him have taken up space deep within my memory, where time, and time again, I take myself within and experience him.

I know it isn't real, but sometimes it sure does feel that way. I brush a finger against my lips once more and lose myself in my imagination.

18

1966 – Ella Galvez

The smell of bacon comes seeping into my room and jars me out of a dead sleep.

"Good morning," Mom says as I walk into the kitchen yanking up the zipper of my shorts. "There's nothing like the smell of bacon to get you moving. You got here just in time, how about making some toast for us."

"Good morning." I wash my hands in the sink, dry them off on a towel and then turn the knob to heat up the griddle. "I sure do love these griddle toasts!"

"I know," Mom says, "three slices at a time."

"That's right." I take two pats of butter and place them on a thick slice of bread before putting it on the griddle, butter-side down. I listen to it sizzle then scoot it around so the butter spreads evenly over the bread. Let it brown a bit, and then flip it over to toast the other side.

I love griddle toast. It's so delicious in all its melted buttery-ness. When the first one is done, I scoop it up with a spatula and place it on a napkin. As I go to take a bite, mom quickly snatches it.

"No, no, *mijita*. First your dad."

She puts it on a plate and winks at me. My head and my shoulders slump in defeat. Yes, Dad's first, he's always first. In every Mexican and Mexican-American household, the father is always first. It's our culture. Another thing that's us is Mom sometimes calling me *mijita* - my little daughter in Spanish. I'm a second generation American, and she doesn't want me to forget my Mexican roots. Like the *tamales*, *frijoles a la charra*, and *chorizo con huevo*, or any kind of Mexican food would ever let me forget. I love that stuff! I proudly claim my Mexican heritage, and all the glorious food it has to offer! She'll also converse with me in Spanish when the mood hits just to make sure I remain bilingual.

Dad walks in and takes a slice of toast and places some of the scrambled eggs on it. Finishes it off with a strip of bacon. "Love these tacos, American style," he says, placing one on a napkin. "I hate to eat and run ladies, but I've got to get going. Stopping off to talk to Chief Garcia before I go to work. Want to talk to him about getting some sort of protection for Ella."

"Thanks, Daddy."

He plants a kiss on mom's cheek, and then on mine, grabs another napkin, two more slices of toast, and he's out the door.

This is my life with my dad, we are like passing ships in the night. He's a workaholic, so he's hardly ever home. I never get enough of him, but when he *is* around, he's bigger than life to me. I know he loves us, but his life is his work and his politics. He's learned if he plays nice with the politicians they'll send him some business in appreciation for his political support. When Dad's able to give us his time or attention, Mom and I savor those moments. Sure, he's there for Sunday dinners, dinners out, and sometimes church, but it just isn't enough for me.

I take my seat at the table with Mom. "Dad seems a lot calmer than he did last night when we told him about this blue cap guy."

"Much calmer. He came this close," she says, holding up her thumb and forefinger to indicate an inch, "to calling Mr. Bartelli at home last night to see if he would talk to the police chief for him. I convinced him he should wait till morning. Told him you were safe at home, and nothing was going to happen to you here."

"Glad he waited, what's the guy gonna do, knock on our door and ask to talk to me?"

"So tell me, Ella," Mom says as she pours herself another cup of coffee. "How are things with you and Michael?"

Her question catches me off guard. Her back was to Michael when he and Bridget showed up at The Drive Inn. She couldn't have possibly seen them.

Crap, she does have eyes on the back of her head.

I pick up my orange juice and take a gulp. Decide it's one of those coincidences mothers seem to pull out of nowhere and tell her everything is just fine. I know I'm lying, but I don't want her starting up with her my-poor-baby routine. Her eyes stay on me, unblinking. My cue keep on talking.

"Actually things are fine, but is fine *really* good enough? The way I see it, I have the most incredible soundtrack playing in the background of my life."

"Let me guess, The Beatles?"

"Yes, The Beatles' music can inspire extraordinary dreams and a love that promises a happily ever after. The word *fine* just doesn't really do it, Mom. It's just not good enough."

"What would you say is? What do *you* want?"

"I want to fall crazy in love, I want someone who will make my heart to go *boom* just like in that Beatles' song."

She giggles softly. "Ella, you want something really special, all girls do. I think it takes a while longer for boys to figure this out."

"Yes, but settling isn't working out for me. Does this mean I'm selfish?"

"Not at all! And don't you *ever* think that." She stirs a spoon of sugar into her coffee. "You're only seventeen. In time you will find the love you want, and you should take it, and cherish it. But boys are not as tuned in to these things as girls are. Not yet."

"I know. Most guys are idiots and only think about their own personal needs." *Especially Michael.*

She takes a sip of her coffee as she watches me place my eggs on a slice of toast. Then sets her elbows on the table and props her head in her hands, as she looks out in the distance for a moment. Her lips curve into a sweet smile as she turns to look at me.

"Well, it makes me happy to know that you are not going to settle when it comes to love. Life's too short."

I get up and give her a hug. "Thanks for the pep talk. But I need one big favor. I'd like to work things out on my own before I talk to Michael, so if he calls...*please* just tell him I'm out." I give her a pleading look and a show of praying hands.

"Oh, Ella," she says, shaking her head, "I don't want to lie."

"Please, Mom, I just want a little time. I'll talk to him, but the better prepared I am, the less painful it will be for Michael and for me."

"Well, if you put it that way, okay, I'll do it for you, but please work on this and don't drag it on longer than you need to."

"Okay."

I sit down again and continue eating my breakfast. Mom excuses herself as she takes her dishes to the sink. I can't help but wonder if Mom's thinking about her own life and what she might have settled for. I hope what I'm thinking isn't so, but Dad's never around, and she doesn't always look happy.

"I'll be upstairs in my workroom should you want to talk some more."

"Thanks, Mom."

I go to my room and grab a book to read when the phone rings.

Please answer it, Mom.

"Ella," Mom says, tapping on my door. "Anthony's on the phone."

"Thanks, I got it."

Place my book back on my table and make myself comfortable on the floor, my back against the bed.

"Hey, Anthony."

"Hi. How's it going?"

"I'm good. Actually, I'm a lot better than I would've thought I'd be."

"Good, I was hoping you weren't curled up in your room licking your wounds. But just in case you were feeling down, I cooked up a plan."

"Plan? I'm all ears."

"Since we're leaving for vacation, I asked Mom if I could invite friends over to our lake house this afternoon, and she said yes. Interested?"

"You bet! Who else is going?" I ask as I grab the phone cord   and walk to my dresser to see what shorts I'll wear.

"Just you and me, haven't asked anyone else. Thought you could use an ear and a shoulder. Didn't tell Mom, of course."

"But just the two of us? Alone?" I take out my white shorts and navy polka dot halter top.

"Sure, why not?"

"Umm, because our parents will totally flip if they find out. Are you ready to meet their wrath?"

"We won't let them find out. Come on, you need this."

"Let's see, when was the last time we pulled one over on our parents? Wait, I know, you helped me pull Cally, the calico kitten up through my bedroom window," I say.

"Yeah, we put her in a basket and yanked her up to your room with a rope."

"It was hilarious! It took my Mom a while to find out."

"Good job giving it away, kiddo."

"Hey! How was I supposed to know I was allergic to cats? My wheezing gave poor Cally and me away," I laugh.

"Yep, but we almost pulled it off."

"So unless I'm allergic to your lake house, we should be able to get away with your little plan."

"So we're on?"

"Sure, let me check with Mom, she's in her workroom."

I knock on the door and poke my head in. Mom's at her desk writing a letter, a personal one. I notice the box of Eaton's onion skin stationery we bought together at Hargrove's. The paper smells like Estée Lauder's Youth Dew, really nice. It's definitely not for business. *Who would she be writing to*?

"Mom?"

She slips a sheet of paper under a magazine. "Yes?"

"Mrs. Bartelli said Anthony could invite friends to the lake house for a few hours this afternoon. Can I go?"

"How nice, just remember the new rule, you must have someone at your side at all times."

"Okay, Anthony will make sure of it. I think I'll make sandwiches to take with us. He'll be here in a while."

"You kids have fun, and please be careful."

"We will."

"Okay Anthony, she said yes, as long as you don't take your eyes off me."

"My eyes will be on you and only you, promise. Can I pick you up in thirty?"

"Sure. Hey, I'm taking sandwiches and cookies."

"Great, I've got drinks and chips. Bring your swimsuit."

I'm working on our sandwiches when the phone rings. "So what did you forget?"

"Ella, finally! I've been dying to talk to you," Michael says.

Not now! I'm not ready!

"I can't talk right now."

"Ella, please, I just miss you. I wanna see you."

"Sorry, I gotta go."

"Wait, Ella, you're still my girl, right?"

He didn't just ask me that?

"Sorry, gotta go." I hang up.

How can he do that? Act as if he didn't just cheat on me with Bridget? What nerve! I grumble under my breath as I finish fixing sandwiches then take a few calming breaths. I refuse to allow Michael to ruin my day. As I place the last of our snacks in a bag, that darn phone rings again, and it keeps ringing, then it stops. He either gave up or Mom answered.

This needs to end...soon. One thing still bothers me, though. Why was I not enough for Michael? Was it all about sex? But what if it wasn't, what if it's me? Anthony says *Mr. Right* is out there waiting for me, but if I'm not good enough for stupid Michael, how can I possibly be good enough for Mr. Right?

Stop it! Michael's the problem.

He really is the problem. He called and acted like nothing happened, still playing me. Worse yet, called me *his girl*. I'd say that pretty much put the cherry on top. No more quiver in this girl's voice, I'm dead serious now. I'm getting rid of this problem. Next time he calls, I *will* confront him and tell him it's over and he lost.

When we get to the lake house, the sun is shining bright, and there's a light breeze. It feels wonderful out here. We walk up the steps to a porch which wraps around one side of the house.

Anthony lowers his head, squints at the lock then inserts the key. I push my sunglasses up and check out the room.

"This place is beautiful."

"Thanks, make yourself at home."

The main room is a rustic, elk heads and bear skin rugs kind of place with a light scent of cedar in the air. There's a trophy mounted above the fireplace and a fur rug on the floor in front of it. The sofa looks comfy with four decorative pillows spread out across it. A coffee table made of what looks like lacquered pine sits on a braided rug. I love the comfortable, lived-in feel of the room.

It feels so open with its vaulted ceiling and a loft off to one side. There's a step ladder attached to the wall that leads up to it. And what a view. You can see the lake and a natural wooded landscape through a wall of windows.

"Wow, we get to spend the afternoon here. The view is amazing."

"Yes, we do, and so now it's just you and me. What would you like to do?" he asks as we place our stuff down on the counter.

I look up at Anthony. "What are my choices?"

"We can sit and talk, listen to music, eat, take the rowboat around the lake, go for a swim, or just lay around and take in some sun."

How about everything except for the swim. Just washed my hair and meeting up with the girls for pizza and a re-run of Dracula at Anna's house. Although I could wash it and pull it back in a ponytail. Maybe we can just wade in it and dry off in the sun." I smile.

"Okay, you're on!" He grabs a couple of beers out of the cooler. "How about we start with these?"

He gives me a sideways look and bites his lip when he sees my half smile.

I shrug my shoulders. "I've never had one before."

"Oops. I have root beer."

"You know what? I'm feeling daring," I say with a wink. "Let me try a Lone Star."

"You sure?"

I nod. "Positive."

He smiles broadly, hands me one and waits for me to take the first sip. I swallow down a couple of gulps of icy cold beer. My eyes water and I shake my head. "Wow! That was fun!"

Anthony grins, pulls me to him and hugs me with one arm and rubs my back with the other.

"Alright," he says, taking me by the hand toward the double doors that lead out to the porch swing. "Now just relax, let yourself go, and shake all the Michael shit outta your system."

We have a wide-open view of the lake, which is amazing. There are so many trees, and they line the curve along the bend. Talk about privacy. There's only one other structure I can see, a covered area with a picnic table and a short pier just in front of it.

"This is the best spot to drink a beer and talk," Anthony says, pointing to the swing.

We sit and talk for a long while, we recall a lot of the fun we've had growing up together.

"You were always there for me, Anthony. Even when you had to go up against the other boys playing baseball."

"We sure did have fun playing baseball with the gang," he says, attempting to knock my thong off with his foot.

Yeah, I loved it. I was Lucy out in right field, and you were Charlie Brown on the mound."

"And when you'd drop a fly ball, you'd yell back all those same dumb excuses Lucy did when she missed a fly ball." He knocks my foot with his and sends my thong clear across the porch.

Our laughter makes the swing shake, and we're caught up in bursts of giggles just like when we were kids. I finally get a breath, look at Anthony. "Thanks, Charlie, I haven't had this much fun since we landed in a deep mud puddle which was almost impossible to walk out of."

"My pleasure, Lucy, but if I remember correctly, we *crawled* out of it. It was a hole, not a puddle."

"I think you're right." I turn to look at him. "Anthony, do you know what my favorite thing was? When I was grounded, you'd climb up the tree outside my bedroom window, and you'd sit there on that big ol' limb, and we'd talk in whispers."

"Yeah, I loved that too, great memories, huh?"

"They sure are. Are you ready for another drink?"

I check my bottle. There're only a couple inches of beer left in it. I stop and shake my head.

Anthony leans in close. "What's the matter?"

"My face feels fuzzy," I say, shaking my head once more. "It must be the beer, huh?"

"Fuzzy face? Never thought of it that way, but now that you mention it, yeah, that's kinda close." He grins and takes what's left of my beer from my hand. Gets up and brings me my thong. "Maybe you should stick to root beer for now."

"Good idea."

After more reminiscing, we go inside to change into our swimsuits.

"Bathroom's past the kitchen, to your right," Anthony says.

I grab my bag and head to the bathroom lightly slapping my face, trying to get the fuzziness off. I hear Anthony chuckle.

"Stop laughing at me, Bartelli." He laughs again.

By the time I get back, Anthony's already in his swim suit, getting himself another beer.

"Here you go fuzzy face." He hands me a towel and a root beer.

I slip my feet back into my thongs, and we head outside. Anthony pulls the boat close to the pier. I was glad I managed to get on without tipping the darn thing over.

"I love this place. How often do you come out here?"

"Not very. It's usually my parents who spend time here, either alone or to entertain."

"It's been so long since we've spent time alone like we used to," I say, smiling. "This is nice."

"I know, I've missed it," he says. "I really have." He takes a long sip of his beer.

"Me too. This is just what I needed." *Especially since nothing weird has happened in the last couple of hours!*

"And now I think I know what I have to do."

Anthony picks up a rock from a small pile on the floor of the boat and skips it across the lake. "And what's that?" He looks at me, skips another rock.

"Tomorrow I'm calling Michael to tell him we're over. Not going to wait for him to call me." I watch the rock make one last jump before sinking into the water.

I can see the relief in Anthony's face. His shoulders and body slump and there's an audible breath that escapes.

"You have no idea how happy I am to hear you say that. You're making the right decision, Ella," he says, handing me a rock.

I toss it, it sinks. "I never did learn how to skip rocks."

"I know, it used to drive you crazy!"

"Yeah, but I'm over it now," I say with a smug look on my face. "Besides, my friend Carol taught me how to whistle like a guy. That's right up there with skipping rocks."

"Noooo. You whistle like a girl. Guys don't use their pinkies. Pinkies are for sissies," He grins at me.

Anthony just called me a sissy, and he's waiting for me to explode. I just know he is. It used to drive me nuts when the other guys would call me that. I often beat them at their own game, how dare they call me a sissy. I hated it when Jimmy Corona would call me that. When I didn't make a throw from outfield to home plate, he'd yell out, "Lucy throws like a sissy." Well, I'm going to be all grown up about it and not blow up.

I smile at Anthony. "Okay, whatever, but it *is* a loud whistle."

"Yep, it is."

"But wait, what about the Texas Longhorns? You know, the Hook 'em Horns hand signal."

"What about it?" he asks.

"Well, it's a fist with the pointer finger...and...a...pinky. Right?"

"And?"

"And I thought you said guys don't use their pinkies, just us sissies."

He stalls a moment. "Oh yeah, well, it's a little more complicated than that, Ella. Look here, you have the fist and the pointer finger." He demonstrates it with his hand. "Very manly digit, huh?"

"Okay, but you still have a sissy little pinky out there."

"Yes, but the fist and the pointer, man-up the pinky. Yeah, that's how it works," he says, a smug look on his face.

"Seriously? You expect me to buy that?"

"Yes, I do."

I stare him down. "Really?"

His shoulders slump. "Okay, you got me."

Not satisfied, I decide to continue picking on him. He's a big Longhorn fan, so I know this one's really gonna get him.

"Oh, and the Aggie's Gig 'em hand sign is a fist and thumb. No pinky anywhere, no need to man up, huh?

"What are you getting at?"

"All that manliness wrapped up in one hand—"

"Ella! You're not going to drop this are you?" He stares down at me looking past his beautiful long eyelashes.

"Do I hear you say, uncle*?*"

"Agggh, okay. Uncle. You, Eleanor Galvez, whistle like a guy, not a sissy."

I give him a triumphant, smirky grin. He tilts his beer back, finishes it up and sets it down hard on the boat bench beside him. "Sometimes you make me so crazy, Ella!" Then his face softens, and he takes my hand and smiles. "But you're the best friend I've ever had, Galvez."

We talk some more, but this time I ask about his new girlfriend, Doreen. He tells me he's finally found one as sweet as me. "But she's a lot less smart-alecky and not as funny," he adds.

That makes me smile.

"Okay, smarty pants," he says, pinching my cheek. How about we go for that wade in the lake and then lay out in the sun to dry?"

We splash around in the water just enough to cool off, and then lay out on our towels. Anthony rolls over to face me. "We've gotten most of what was on our list done."

I turn toward him, supporting myself up on my elbow. "I've loved every minute of it."

"So tomorrow it is, huh? You'll talk to Michael?"

"Yes. Michael Damon is going to get dealt with."

"Tomorrow. I want to hear you say, *tomorrow,*" he says.

"Tomorrow." I nod.

"Good. I think we should celebrate when I get back from California. I'll take you to Fisher's for a root beer float, we can hang out, and later we'll have dinner."

"Perfect. And I'll fill you in on all the gory details."

"Great, now let's go eat, then we can change and head home."

The mood on the way home is unbelievable. Walking down memory lane with Anthony was a blast. The only thing better would've been if we could figure out a way to zap ourselves back to the past for a quick visit. I would definitely change a few things.

"Today was perfect, Anthony. It was fun talking about how we've gone from playing in the sand box to being in our teens. We've been there for each other through it all."

"Yep, we'll always be there for each other," he says. "Pinky promise?"

"Yes, pinky promise! And just so you'll know, I've never told anyone you, *Mr. Cool,* give me pinky promises."

"Wait, before you get off, did you know the Aggie who started the Gig 'em hand signal was named Pinky Downs? So the hand signal actually began with a pinky."

"What? What kind of name is Pinky? And you let me go on and on?"

"Hey, you worked hard for that one, you deserved the win."

"Are you saying you *let* me win?"

"Okay, I confess. I didn't *let* you win. It didn't occur to me until just now when I said pinky promise."

"So technically, I did win, right?" I ask, nodding my head.

"Yes, Lucy, you won. I'll call you when we get home from our vacation. Don't forget we have a date." He winks. "See ya."

"Later."

Mom's in the kitchen making dinner, and it smells like we're having fried chicken. I remind her I'm eating pizza at Anna's. She asks about our outing. I tell her we had fun, but that I'm exhausted and need a shower. Don't want her asking for details. I'd have to be very creative to share my afternoon with her without mentioning the rest of the gang. I ask if she needs help and if I can take a shower first. I was happy to hear Aunt Tilly will be over for dinner shortly and will help. Aunt

Tilly always has stories to tell, so we'll be talking about her and her funny mishaps and not about what happened at the lake house.

Once I'm up in my room I decide I'm not waiting until tomorrow to break up with Michael. I dial his number. It feels so good knowing it will be the last time I'll ever spin his number around the dial on my pink princess telephone. My outing at the lake house with Anthony was so fantastic it helped give life to my once non-existent determination. *You got this, Ella. Do it!*

'Hello."

"Hello, Michael."

"Oh baby, I'm glad you called, I need to see—"

"First of all, I'm not your baby, and second, I just called to let you know we're over. We. Are. Through!"

"But, Ella, I love you."

"Oh really? Were you loving me while you were having dinner with Bridget Dubois at The Drive Inn?"

"What? Me? Uh-uh, not me. Somebody's lying to you, Ella. When I find out who—"

"Michael, I saw you with my own two eyes. And Bridget saw me. Hmm, I guess she didn't think it was worth mentioning."

"Oh God, Ella, I'm so sorry, it was a mistake, she means nothing to me. I love you and only you."

"Here's the thing, Michael, I don't love *you.*"

"But, Ella, I can make it up—"

"Listen to me, *we* are finished. Don't call me. Don't call my mom. Don't come by my house. I have nothing more to say to you—"

"But, Ella, I—"

"Stop it! I don't want to hear another word."

"I know you're upset."

"Upset? I am millions and billions of miles past upset! It's over!"

The sound of my phone slamming onto the cradle should tell him just how serious I am.

I've got an hour before pizza and a movie at Anna's, so I head to the shower. I can't wait to tell them what I did. I think I just earned me some atta-girls!

Before I leave for Anna's, I give Anthony a call. His line's busy. Probably on the phone with Doreen so it could take a while. Guess he's gonna have to wait to hear about it when he returns from vacation.

Finally! I'm in control of my happiness, not Michael, and I'm so happy right here, right now without him. Not alone – I'm just without Michael.

19

1966 – Ella Galvez

Two days after Anthony left on vacation, his parents let him call me long distance from their hotel in Anaheim, California. He just *had* to know if I really dumped Michael. Of course, I scolded him for not having faith in me. But I can understand why Anthony thought I might not follow through...he knows me all too well. Hate to admit it, but I'm kinda surprised I pulled it off, myself.

Anthony's back, so when the phone rings I rush to answer it knowing it's going to be him. The first thing he wants to know is how my week went without Michael in it. It's hard to believe it's been a week since I broke up with Michael and I'm feeling fantastic. Anthony's thrilled when I tell him this. I am so at peace with *me*. It's just me and nobody else. Sure, I think about Gabriel. Boy, do I think about him. But I'm not feeling a void in my life because Michael's out of it, nor that there's no one in his place...yet. This is pretty cool when you consider Anthony's been gone the whole time. He would have been my crutch. Glad it worked out this way.

"What did you do to keep your mind off of the old boyfriend," Anthony asks.

"Well, Mom and I worked on your mom's sewing project. Sophia's bedroom turned out divine. I can't wait to hear how she likes it."

"I hope you and your buddies didn't get into any trouble," he says.

"I didn't, and neither did Julia, she was visiting her grandparents at their farm and just got back yesterday."

"Okay, let's hear it. What did Rita and Anna get into this time?"

"You'll love it. They went across the border to The Mustang Club with Greg and Jack. Anna's mom found out and told Rita's mom. They were both grounded for a whole week – no phones, no going out. Yesterday was their last day, so I got a call from both first thing this morning. They loved hearing Michael had called several times and that I hung up without saying a word. He finally gave up."

"Stupid jerk. Glad he got the message. So how'd they get caught?"

"On their way from their car to the club, a man walked by selling corsages. Anna and Rita oohed and aahed, so the guys bought them each one. They wore them home, and Anna's mom questioned her about it. Turns out gardenia corsages are very popular in Matamoros and not here in the U.S. Poor Anna, Mrs. Rivera read her the riot act. Anna also mentioned something about Mexican currency in her pocket. You know, it's not the first time she's been caught crossing the border."

"That's hilarious," Anthony says with a laugh. "You really were all alone. You poor thing."

"It wasn't bad at all. I think being alone without Michael and my closest friends was exactly what I needed. I was busy with Mom's sewing project. I worked a lot of the detail work for Mom and was able to get lost in my thoughts. Gave me a new perspective, and I now know

I'm totally capable of standing on my own without anyone else around. It feels pretty darn good, Anthony."

"That's great, kiddo. So let's go for that celebration dinner. We're still on, right? Wanna go to Fisher's? Can I pick you up at five?"

"Are you kidding? I've been looking forward to it. Fisher's is perfect, see you at five. What about Doreen?"

"Nope, she'll join us later when she gets off work."

I decide to wear my white spaghetti-strap sundress. It will look great with my cornflower blue belt and white flats with cornflower clip-ons. I take care making sure everything is perfect, you never know who I might run into. My hair's parted to the left and looks a bit flat on top, so I tease it up a little to give it some lift. Then smooth it down nicely. I dab on just a tiny bit of eye shadow, some mascara, face powder, rouge and lip gloss. As I'm putting on my pearl stud earrings, I hear Anthony coming up the driveway.

I run downstairs, and from the doorway, I watch him as he steps up to the corridor. He looks handsome in his baby blue, boat collar pull-over which shows off his trim, but muscular body.

After he gives me a big hug, Anthony looks up at Mom who's working in the kitchen. "Hello, Mrs. Galvez."

"Hello, Anthony. How was your vacation?"

"It was great, Disneyland was so much fun."

"Anthony, I've been wanting to thank your mom for letting you invite your friends to the lake house before you left. It seemed to help Ella a whole lot, her mood was lifted. I really never got around to ask Ella how it was or who was there."

Anthony grimaces. "It was fun, thank you. The usual happy characters showed up."

I stifle a laugh. Anthony elbows me.

"That's nice," Mom says. "Well, you two enjoy yourself."

"Thanks, Mom, we'll do our best."

"Bye, Mrs. Galvez."

I yank him out by the arm. "The usual happy characters?" I ask, laughing.

"Hey, I wasn't lying, not really…okay, maybe sort of. There was you, me, Charlie and Lucy."

"Very funny, Anthony."

"Hey, check it out, Dad let me borrow the Lincoln. We are celebrating in style."

"I noticed, and yes, it's definitely a celebration."

When we get into the car, Anthony looks at me. "You, kiddo, are about to arrive at your happy place."

"Guess what, I'm already there."

Anthony nods in agreement and switches on the ignition, revving it up a couple of times. "Let's do it," he says, driving off, drumming his fingers on the steering wheel to the beat of *Hang on Sloopy.*

"So tell me how it went. I'm ready for those gory details."

"Not well for Michael. I don't think he expected it. I guess he actually thought he'd gotten away with his little fling, sounded really hurt."

"Good, he needs to suffer."

He leans over and adjusts his rear-view mirror. "I hope he hasn't been bugging you."

"Nah, I think he's gotten the message. The sound of my phone slamming down each time he called must have set him straight. He is such a liar. He denied everything to the very end. When I brought up his date with Bridget, he said someone was lying to me."

"What a rat! And I guess you told him it was you who saw him, huh?"

"Yes, it pretty much went downhill from there."

When we walk into Fisher's, we see Julia and David in one of the booths. We wave at Anna and Rita who are at a table with a couple of girlfriends. Funny how everyone decided to come to Fisher's at the same time. Usually, we have to plan to make it happen.

There's a girl I recognize sitting alone at a table. There are cards spread across the table in front of her. As we head to an empty booth, I watch her move them around from one spot to another, then shuffle them. When we pass her table, she waves at Anthony and smiles and begins laying them out again.

As soon as we're sitting at our booth, I lean toward Anthony, point my thumb in her direction. "Is she doing some sort of fortune-telling stuff with cards?"

He laughs. "No, silly, those are baseball cards. Sandy's memorizing the New York Yankees' players and stats."

"Oh, okay."

"Don't laugh, but she's trying to land this guy who's into baseball. She wants to memorize everything about his favorite team."

"So she's trying to reel him in with names and stats? Wouldn't think she needs to, she's cute."

"I know for a fact, it's gonna take a lot more then spewing stats and a pretty face to reel in the guy she wants. She's too shallow. She's just looking for a little rich boy, any rich boy."

"Hmm, that's a shame."

Anthony looks past me and seems to be following someone through the window right behind me. When he looks toward the entrance, he smiles and gives a little nod. I turn to look. *Oh my gosh! Oh my gosh!* My heart skips a couple of beats. It's Gabriel Marquez!

I haven't seen Gabriel in over a month and darn if he doesn't look even hotter now. So hot, it hurts. He is *so* handsome, and there's that smile. I love that smile so much! Oh those little stirrings. *Really, Ella? Get a grip!*

Gabriel's wearing a white button-down shirt, with slightly turned up collar and blue jeans. I can't believe I actually stretched my neck out to see he was sporting well-shined boots. He stops to say hello at the first table and leans in to talk to a couple of guys seated there. He walks off, runs his hand through his hair pushing back a few loose strands of his side swept hair, but they quickly fall back into place right where they belong, hanging slightly over his forehead in a sexy sort of way.

Little-miss-baseball-cards quickly gathers up her cards, stuffs them in her purse and proceeds to follow Gabriel up to the soda fountain counter. Oh no! Gabriel's her next conquest. I sure hope her little card trick doesn't work. *Hmm, I didn't realize Gabriel was a rich boy.*

I'm caught drooling over Gabriel. Anthony smiles. "So what would you like me to get you?"

"I'll have a root beer float, and I think I'm also kinda craving a Gabriel Marquez."

Anthony laughs. "Got it, coming right up," he says, turning to look at Gabriel.

As he walks off to place our order, Anthony turns back and smiles at me and then walks up to Gabriel. I watch as they lean into each other, engaging in conversation. I turn away to check out the songs on the little wall jukebox but continue taking sideways glances to see what they're up to. When I notice Gabriel walking in my direction carrying a tray with two root beer floats, my heart skips what feels like at least a half-dozen beats. He walks right up to my table, clears his throat and smiles.

"Hi, I'm Gabriel Marquez."

"Hi," I say and quickly look away. *Don't blow this Ella.* I look back at him and smile.

Gabriel sets the tray down. "I understand you're kinda craving a root beer float."

I smile again. This time I hold his gaze. *He's gorgeous.* "Yes, I actually *was* kinda craving one. I'm impressed you just happen to know this little bit of information." *I hope that's all Anthony mentioned I was craving.*

"A little bird told me," he says with a tilt of his head in Anthony's direction.

"Ahh, an Anthony bird."

"Yep, that kind. Is it okay if I sit with you?"

He smiles, the cutest smile I have ever seen. Well, I have seen it, but not this close. I linger on it a tad too long for a girl who's trying to act cool.

"Sure, I'd like that."

"Great," he says and slides himself into the booth then stops half-way.

"Dang, forgot the straws. Hold on a second, sweetie, be right back."

"Sure." I watch him walk away. *Sweetie?* What comes next, *darlin'?* Don't tell me he's one of those guys that flatter the girls by spreading their charm like honey. The last thing I need is another lover boy who thinks he can sweet talk his way into my silky panties. I don't care what passes his adorable lips. If this is fake bait, I'm not biting. *But I sure hope I'm wrong!*

"Here you go." He places a straw in our drinks. Slides in, keeping his eyes on me and smiles. "As I was saying, I'm Gabriel Marquez."

"I'm Ella Galvez." I nod. "I actually already knew who you were."

"Oh really," he says with a big grin on his face.

"Yes, I went to all the home baseball games last spring, watched you play right field. You hit a lot of home runs."

"*You* watched *me* play?"

Oh, that smile again! "Well, I saw the whole team play, but yes, I'll admit I watched you play too," I say with a little shrug.

"We're even then, I saw you dance."

"No you didn't...did you?*" I think I'm blushing.*

"Yes, really, I did. It was your end-of-year recital. Tagged along with Anthony. The ballet was nice, but the jazzy thing at the end, wow it was so sex—"

He stops, bites down on the corner of his lip. "Sorry...special. Yes, it was so special."

Now *he's* blushing and I can't help but smile. I'm actually trying not to laugh.

"Sorry, Ella. I apologize for my mouth, it sometimes gets me in trouble," he says, shaking his head as if to rid the thought.

"It's alright," I say, thinking about his mouth and what it might do to get him in trouble. I think I'm blushing again.

"Are you sure? You're still blushing...I really am sorry."

Okay, he's apologetic, I like that. Maybe I was too quick to judge. Let's see where we go from here.

"Yes, you made me blush," I say with a smile. "But I accept your apology. Now back to my root beer float, it was sweet of you to bring it to me."

I stir it around with the straw as I continue to look right at him, study his face. I love his face. He watches me as I stir my float, then looks up at me, and a smirk appears. *What did I ever do to deserve this?*

"Okay, Ella, here's the thing, the whole truth."

He places his hands flat on the table in front of him, side by side, thumb tips touching. The tips of his fingers meet the center mark of our table. He leans in and looks right at me. Don't know why, but I do the exact same thing with my hands mirroring his. The tips of my pink fingernails touching his fingertips. I lean in, look at him and smile. *Stop being silly, Ella.*

His mouth curves into a big smile. "Anthony was so right about you."

I raise my eyebrows at him. "*That* was the whole truth you were going to tell me? That Anthony was so right about me?"

"No, you threw me off," he laughs. "I don't get thrown off easily."

"Hmm, do I get a check or a demerit for that?"

"A check, definitely a check."

I give my head a quick nod. "Good." *Make a note of it, Ella, silly is good.*

He smiles again and says, "The truth is I've wanted to go out with you since the first time I saw you, but you were going steady with Michael Damon. I bugged our pal, Bartelli, to introduce us. Sure, I could've introduced myself, but he said if I really cared about you, to please wait. So I did because I *did* really care about you. He said it just wasn't the right time." He pauses, swallows. "Plus, I'm shy."

"So am I, and yes, that sounds like Anthony, he's protective."

Gabriel just said he really cared for me. Oh wow!

"He wanted us to meet, but he kept telling me to hold on a bit longer."

"Hmm, that's interesting." I chew on my lower lip as I think about what he just said. "You know, I was kind of taken back that Anthony would take it upon himself to decide when you should or should not approach me. But now thinking about it, he was right; it was *never* the right time."

"Never?" A small frown shows up on his face.

"No, no. I didn't mean never, *ever*. Anthony knew it wasn't the right time until today."

His eyes brighten. "So you're saying today is okay?"

Ah, there's the smile I was looking for. "Yes, today. What perfect timing." I smile. "He knew exactly what he was doing. That's Anthony."

He knew I needed to be in the place where I am now. Happy and confident in myself knowing that I was perfectly fine without Michael in my life, in fact, I'm better off without him. Anthony probably didn't want me to run into another relationship to fill a void. Wow, my very own fairy god brother. Only thing missing were little singing birds showing up to help me dress for dinner. I take my straw and wrap my lips around it, take a long cold sip.

He smiles. "Well, in that case, will you go out on a date with me?"

I look up at Gabriel, swallow hard. Take my middle finger and run it across my lips to wipe off any dribbles, then smooch it off my finger. His smile gets even bigger.

"You're asking *me* on a date?" I ask, pressing my fingertips against my chest.

"Yes, you," he says, pointing to my hand on my chest. "I would really, *really* love to take you out on a date."

I look at him and hold his gaze. He not only has the cutest smile; his eyes are so beautiful - can't seem to pull myself away. He waits.

"The suspense is killing me, Ella."

I take a deep breath. "Yes, I would really, *really* like to go out with you, Gabriel."

"Wow. Oh wow," he says then takes a deep breath. "That's just what I was hoping to hear." He smiles as he raises his hand and gives a thumbs-up signal high in the air, looking back behind him. I peek around past Gabriel, and sure enough, there's Anthony, who looks at me and yells out, "Woo-hoo!"

I laugh out loud. "That's a side of Anthony I've never seen before. The guy's never rowdy."

"Anthony's right, this calls for a celebration," he says with an adorable wiggle of an eye brow.

"Oh yeah? And how do you plan on celebrating, the old Tarzan chest-thumping thing?"

Gabriel throws his head back and laughs. *I love the sound of his laugh.*

"I love it," he says. "You're as funny as Anthony told me you were, and believe me, it's helped. You have no idea how nervous I was."

"Aww, you poor thing, and here I thought it was just me."

He gives me a sly smile, straightens one of his legs out under the table. While keeping his eyes on me, he digs deep into his front jean pocket. Comes up with some change which he places on the table.

I can't believe I'm sitting here with Gabriel Marquez and to think Anthony knew it was going to happen. He had every opportunity to tell me what he was planning while we were at the lake house. But I understand why he didn't.

Gabriel pops several coins into the jukebox, quickly punches the buttons as if he already knew what he wanted, and where they were. The Beatles', *I Wanna Hold Your Hand* begins to play, we both smile.

"I take it you like The Beatles?" I ask.

"Yep, I do." He takes a long sip of his float.

"I love them too, but I also like Beethoven, Bach, and Mendelssohn."

"My Mom's a big fan; I hear their music all the time," he says.

I think he just said he likes them too. I'm too busy watching his mouth, then quickly turn my attention to his eyes. They totally suck me in. I'm defenseless against anything Gabriel's got to offer. And he doesn't even seem to be trying.

"So we have something else in common," he says with the lift of an eyebrow. "But I gotta say, The Beatles have those old guys beat on one thing."

"Oh really," I say, focusing back on our conversation. "The grand masters of music? What?"

He smiles. "The lyrics."

"Ha, ha. Very funny, Gabriel."

We laugh at his response, then his laugh quiets down into a smile which quickly fades away. As he reaches his hands across the table. I instinctively do the same, and he takes my hands in his. Gabriel looks into my eyes deeper than anyone ever has. He tells me how he enjoyed getting little tidbits of information about me from Anthony. Said he'd get them in small doses to hold him over, but that it wasn't ever enough, so he would always be searching for me at the movies, in the shops, at dances, hoping I might be there. He smiles when I tell him I did the same thing.

All My Loving comes on, and as I've done with each song that plays, I smile. "I like the song selections. Did you select the Beatles' songs we've just heard?"

"Yep. These guys play the best music, both lyrics, and guitar chords," Gabriel says.

"Do you play?"

"Yeah, but forget about me, when can we go on our date?"

"How about Saturday?" I suggest then take another sip of my drink.

"The way I'm feeling right now, that's *way* too long," he says, biting his lip again.

"Okay, let's put us out of our misery. Why don't we just meet up somewhere tomorrow? We can still have our date later."

"Tomorrow! Perfect!" Gabriel says. "Hey, you said *our* misery?"

I give him a couple of nods. "Yeah, me too."

That made him smile, but he doesn't say a word. Just looks at me. Me, Ella Galvez. And now I can't stop thinking about the necklace I found. I've got myself a Gabriel, but I'm still short one Bella Ella.

Gabriel looks at me as if he's studying my face. When he licks his lip and smiles, it takes everything I have, not to lean over and kiss him on the mouth, right there where his smile lifts at the corner. Yes...right there. But I don't.

Anthony and Doreen come up to our booth, and Anna rushes over and beats them to our table. "You two were heating it up over here!"

Rita comes up right behind her. "Yeah, Ella Bella, you and lover boy here – steamy!

Gabe looks up at Rita. "Ella Bella, how perfect. It means Ella Beautiful." He turns to me and winks.

Doreen, Rita, and Anna get into a conversation about some flick showing at the Majestic.

Gabriel turns and leans into me and whispers. "Bella Ella would be much better. Beautiful Ella, not Ella beautiful. What do you think?"

It takes a moment for me to respond. My mind is swirling unable to believe what I just heard Gabriel say. Finally, I whisper, "Did you just call me Bella Ella?"

"Yeah, I think it's the perfect name for you, beautiful Ella. And it has such a nice ring to it, don't you think?"

I smile as I breathe out a sigh. "Yes, it does. You just earned yourself another *check*, Gabriel Marquez."

He smiles so big. "My *first check*, is what you mean."

"Nope, I meant another one."

"Oh really, what was my first?"

"You smiled. I like your smile."

"Dang, that Bartelli. He really knows his stuff." I think Gabriel's smile just might be here to stay.

"What do you mean, he knows his stuff?"

"I asked him for any tips he could give me to get you to go out with me, and all he would say was, *just smile.* He left me thinking what kind of advice is that? Smile? Really?"

I laugh recalling the conversation Anthony and I had at Zesto's where I told him that I loved Gabriel's smile. That crazy Anthony. I can't believe he didn't say a word. All he did was tease me about the things he told Gabriel about me being topless in the kiddie pool. Whoa, I forgot about that, so glad Gabriel didn't bring it up just now, when he mentioned things Anthony shared with him about us growing up together. Gabriel just got himself another *check,* and he doesn't even know it. Definitely not mentioning this one.

While everyone's talking, my mind is at home with my jewelry box, where I have a necklace with two names on it – Gabriel and Bella Ella.

20

A guy named Gabriel has just asked me on a date, and he called me Bella Ella. Nothing unusual about that. Except a necklace which magically appeared in my hand is sitting in my jewelry box with *both* our names engraved on it. Now *this* borders on crazy. No, it *is* crazy. *The plot thickens.*

"Come on, Rita," Anna says, pulling on Rita's arm. "Time to cut out."

"Tell me you're not going to Matamoros," Anthony says with a laugh.

"Oh, but we are," Rita says. "The Mustang Club for some *Mar-ga-rrritas.*"

Anthony's eyebrows arch. "What? Didn't your folks just come down on you for sneaking off across the border?"

"Yeah," Anna says with a shrug, "but I took notes. Not wearing a Mexican corsage home. I stuck to my story and denied it all, but then my mother found Mexican pesos in my skirt pocket when she did the laundry. Trust me, that's not gonna happen again either."

"Anna's gonna tell the waiter to keep the change," Rita laughs.

Once our friends have left, Doreen and Anthony join Gabriel and me for dinner. I order fries smothered in gravy, everyone else orders burgers and fries. Anthony and I share some of our adventures from our day at the lake house. I can tell Gabriel and Doreen are really enjoying our trip down memory lane. I think the four of us are going to get along great.

Then Anthony starts in on how Gabriel kept bugging him to introduce us. "Well, I think the timing was perfect, I don't think I could have held Gabe back much longer," Anthony says.

Sorry, buddy, I know I was being a real pain. I came so close a couple of times. Thought it would be so easy, well, not that easy, after all, I *am* shy, to go up to Ella and ask her for a date," he says, looking at me and smiling. But no one knows her as well as you, so I just talked myself out of it."

Doreen clears her throat and smiles shyly. "When I first started hanging out with Anthony and his friends, all he talked about was you, Ella. I figured I didn't have a chance with him, and I was starting to get jealous," she says with a half shrug. Finally, someone told me you two were like brother and sister.*"

"Gosh yes, that's what Anthony and I are. We're like family, and I love him to death."

"Same here, kiddo," Anthony says.

"Well, let's just say I was relieved," Doreen adds. I smile back at her.

"We were quite a twosome growing up. I'm sure Anthony will share some more of the crazy things we got ourselves into. You'll have to ask him about what he wanted to do with me when I got the chicken pox a month after he did."

"Hey, I wanna know," Gabriel says.

Anthony laughs. "I completely forgot about that. I was such a funny kid, huh?"

"Well, tell us the story," Doreen says, nudging Anthony.

"I'd already gotten over my pox, and now Ella was covered with them," he says.

"Yeah," I continue. "And the day Anthony came over I was wearing a halter top sundress that tied around the neck, and my shoulders and back were bare. And of course, I was covered with those ugly spots."

"I kept staring at them - there were so many! Finally, I asked Mrs. Galvez if I could play connect the dots on Ella's back to see what kind of picture they would make."

We burst out laughing. Gabriel and Doreen insist on hearing more stories, so we share a few more. We finish eating dinner listening to Gabe's stories about growing up in Odessa and then moving to Corpus Christi in his early teens. Said that's when he decided that for the rest of his life he wanted to live near the ocean.

"When it's time to leave, Anthony says, "Hey Gabe, why don't the three of us drop Ella off at home then Doreen and I can bring you back to your truck?"

"I would love it, how about you, Bella Ella?"

"Sounds perfect," I say. Hearing Gabriel call me Bella Ella in his own voice caresses my whole being, and I'm hoping my face doesn't give away the effect it has on me. I know darn well that this could all be a dream. But we're both in it, and that's all that matters right now.

When we arrive at my house, Anthony pulls up to the curb. "Gabe, you can go ahead and walk Ella to the door, I'll go around the bend then turn back to pick you up." Okay with you, Ella?"

"Yes, perfect."

"Great." Gabriel says, "Hold on, I'll get your door."

I give Anthony a little wave. He smiles and says, "Call me."

Before they pull away, Gabriel leans into Anthony's window.

"Drive really slow, okay, Bartelli?"

"You got it, Marquez."

Gabriel takes my hand, and we walk down the long driveway toward the front porch.

"What a night," he says, giving my hand a little squeeze. "I've been wanting to do this since the first time I saw you."

"I didn't think you even knew I existed, much less want to be with me."

"Well, I did, and it's been a while now," he says."

"You were one of the reasons I went to the baseball games, the other was Anthony. Plus, I love baseball."

"I love the Yankees," Gabriel says. "How much do you know about them?"

I tilt my head and think about it. "Umm, maybe three things," I say with a shrug. I watch his gaze linger on my shoulder and then he smiles. "They're from New York. They play at Yankee Stadium. I know who Roger Maris is."

"Right fielder, just like you and Lucy from the Peanuts comic strip."

I laugh. "Is there anything, Anthony *didn't* share with you?"

"Well, he did tell me how you'd make up excuses every time you missed a fly ball," he laughs, "and how your excuses would change just like Lucy's do."

I turn to him and place a hand on my hip. "Are you done having fun now?"

"I'm not laughing *at* you, I'm laughing because I think you're so cute. So that's it? That's all you know about the Yankees?"

I look up and frown at him. "What? You want *batting* averages?"

"No, please, not that! It would've been a demerit if you did."

"Don't tell me! You're talking about Sandy. Did she really do that? Go around throwing stats at you?"

"Yes! She's been driving me nuts!"

Well, Marquez, you're safe with me, that's all I have on the Yankees."

"Good," he says, nodding. Then I watch as the corner of his lips slowly curves into a smirk. "Hey, I need to tell you something."

"You *need* to tell me? Uh-oh, should I be worried?"

He laughs. "Nope. I just wanna say that you have the most beautiful shoulders."

I smirk back at him. "Shoulders?" I ask, raising my eyebrows trying not to laugh.

He chuckles. "Yes, shoulders." He runs a finger from the beginning of my collarbone across my shoulder and to where it curves down sending tingles everywhere.

"You gave me goosebumps."

"I noticed. Sorry, guess that was a bit too personal. It's just that your shoulders are so—"

"Beautiful?"

He laughs again. "Yes, beautiful," he says then slowly pulls me in close for a hug.

It was a hug I didn't want to end, but it was short and polite. We say goodnight, and I watch Gabriel as he walks away. He turns back, kisses his finger tips and sends it to me with a wave and a smile. I kiss my finger tips and wave back. My heart is so happy.

I tap on Mom and Dad's bedroom door. "I'm home, goodnight."

I get ready for bed then take a quick look at the necklace that has an even more special meaning tonight. Maybe I'm getting ahead of myself. It may have been a cute little one-time deal. Gabe might never call me Bella Ella again. *But then he might.*

"Ella," Mom says, tapping on the door. She peeks in, and Cooper scurries in past her and jumps on my bed.

"I just wanted to let you know Michael called. He told me he's very sorry about what happened and wishes you'd give him another chance."

I plop down onto my bed, arms folded across my chest. "He had no right to involve you. I've made my mind up, so please, Mom, don't try to convince me otherwise. I'm done with Michael, I've been done with him since I caught him cheating."

"No mijita, I wasn't going to suggest it at all. Do you want to know what I believe? She steps in and closes the door behind her. "I truly believe when someone cheats, something is lacking in that relationship." She walks over, sits on the bed next to me and strokes my hair. "The one being cheated on is left wondering what they've done to deserve it, or what is lacking on their part."

"No kidding." I turn and grab *Blue.*

"The truth is there's probably nothing you have done to cause the cheating or that you can do to change the relationship. The heart wants what it wants."

"Wow, I've said those exact words."

"Well, I believe them to be true."

I look down at my waste basket where I dumped our picture over a week ago.

She reaches for my hand. "Sometimes people stay together when they shouldn't. You did what was right for you. Michael may not realize it now, but it's probably the best thing for him too."

I give Mom a big hug.

"Oh Mommy, thank you so much. I believe the exact same thing. In fact, I met someone tonight, someone so special. Anthony got us together. I know you're going to love him. His name is Gabriel Marquez. He's exactly what I described to you the other day, he's the one, Mom. He's the one I've been waiting for."

"I'm so happy to hear this. Marquez? Gabriel Marquez. Yes, I know him from the lunch line at school. I know his brother, Marco, as well and his mom. I've designed a few gowns for her. I've always liked Gabriel, very polite. And so handsome, mijita," she says, giving me a sweet knowing smile.

"I think he's handsome too. He and Anthony have so much in common. I'm so happy that you know Gabriel. So you know why he's so special to me."

"Yes, and you're right, sometimes feelings are so deep they defy explanation; only the two involved can understand it."

"I guess that's you and Dad, huh?"

She stands, kisses the top of my head. "Honey, it's getting late for me, I'm exhausted, and I didn't sleep very well last night. I'm looking forward to seeing that handsome young man again. Oh, and he loves enchiladas. I could always count on him being in the lunch line on Wednesday, which is enchilada day," she laughs.

"That's funny. You just might know more about Gabriel than I do," I say with a smile. "Good night, Mom."

"Sleep tight," she says. "Come on Cooper, downstairs."

Cooper jumps off the bed and joins her. Just as she closes the door, the phone rings, and I immediately hope it's not Michael.

"Hello."

"Hi Ella, I got your number from Anthony, I hope it's not too late to call. I just couldn't help myself."

"No, no, no, Gabriel, not at all, I'm so glad you did."

I carry my phone to my bed and snuggle in.

"Just wanted to tell you how much fun I had. I already miss you."

"And I already miss your smile," I say.

"Oh wow, I love hearing you say that. So we're on for something tomorrow?"

"Yes, what do you want to do?"

"I get the feeling I'm not gonna fall asleep right away, so getting up early tomorrow may be a problem."

"So call me in the morning once you get your sleepy little head up off your pillow," I say.

"Okay, I'll do that, we'll decide the time and whatever we'd like to do then."

"Goodnight, Gabriel."

"Good night, Bella Ella."

Tonight, I met the boy I've been dreaming of for so long, and you'd think the only thing I would be thinking about is him. But this isn't just any ordinary boy-meets-girl story. No, not even close. Lots of strange and unusual things have happened since the day I found the necklace with Bella Ella and Gabriel engraved on it. And there doesn't really seem to be any connection between them...except for two.

The necklace with our names on it and the voice in my head which seemed to prompt me to ask Dad to switch tables at dinner, I think, are in a way connected. How? I don't know. But I know one thing for sure, without that voice prompt, I would never have asked Dad to switch tables. And I wouldn't have seen Michael cheating on me. That means I probably wouldn't have broken up with him, and I wouldn't have been free to meet and accept a date with Gabriel.

So something else to add to my journal, and it's a whopper. I take the journal out of my drawer, and after reading over all the oddities since the day of the backyard shimmers, I write down everything about this evening. This entry fills up a whole page. When I'm done, I think about it all and smile. Then decide this entry needs a title, so I add one at the top of the page.

Bella Ella Meets Gabriel.

I put my journal away, crawl into bed with Blue, and I whisper in his ear. "Gabriel called me Bella Ella."

21

1966 – Ella Galvez

I find myself sitting straight up in bed. Slivers of light along the edges of my blinds pierce the darkness in my room. My alarm clock's lighted hands appear outstretched. It's three-forty-five. *Why am I up at this ungodly hour?*

I close my eyes and let myself fall back on my pillow. As I lay here, I begin to see flashes of shimmering lights and flickering fireflies that seem to fizzle out and then light up again. Wait, I remember now. I was in the middle of a dream. I saw these lights while sitting on an arbor swing, just like the one we have in our backyard, but covered in dried up vines. No roses, no flowers of any kind. I was sipping a cup of tea. *Weird, I don't drink tea.*

I shut my eyes tighter and try to recall more of my dream. I remember sitting there, looking at a beautiful lake surrounded by lots and lots of trees. Didn't know trees came in so many different shades of green. Then I got up, looked around, and oh yeah, there was an honest to goodness log cabin.

I sit up when it hits me. "No, no. Please, no." I cover my face with my hands and suck in a deep breath. "It can't all be a dream!"

This is not good. It's exactly what I saw in my own backyard—the shimmer, firefly lights. Oh no, all that was a dream...Fisher's and Gabriel, the necklace, all of it. I look over at my jewelry box, scoot out of bed, and stand there staring at it, not wanting to open it. I'm scared to look inside, afraid of what I...I might not find there.

"Please, please, please don't let it be a dream," I whisper.

My hands tremble as I wipe the tears from my eyes, and my heart is beating so fast. I slowly lift the lid. It's there! My necklace is there!

Then everything else must be real too. I *did* meet Gabriel, and he *did* hold my hand and hug me. And the kiss he waved at me, that was real too. I take a deep breath then smile when I realize I called it *my necklace*. It feels like it's mine, it's got Gabriel's name on it, and now it has mine too. He called *me* Bella Ella.

A yawn tells me I won't have trouble falling back to sleep. I crawl back in bed and snuggle myself into my pillow, but I don't drift off. The log cabin...I've been there. *Right, Ella. You've never stepped a foot out of the Valley. There are no cabins in our neck of the woods.*

I sit up in bed again. I've seen that cabin before, just as I'm sure I saw the cue ball stick shift in Rita's car. As far as I can remember, I've only seen pictures of cabins in school books when we were reading about Abe Lincoln. I thought they were the coolest things, houses made from cut down trees, stacked up one on top of the other. I even wondered what it would be like to live in one. Then, of course, there were the Lincoln logs I used to play with at Anthony's house. But no, it's not that. I've seen this one, the one in my dream surrounded by trees and next to a lake.

Another déjà vu moment? These things I'm seeing feel like memories and voices in my head nudge me to do things. That's exactly what that voice did. It made me do something without even knowing why I was doing it. Good move too. It made me switch tables so I could catch my lousy, two-timing boyfriend cheating on me. Geez, I'm talking like I have a fortune teller living in here. I slap my head a couple of times immediately hoping I didn't wake her up in there. I'm not ready to hear anything else from her right now...or ever. *Oh, boy, I just might be going crazy.*

"Oh, no you don't. Don't you dare go crazy on us now that we finally landed Gabriel Marquez!"

I lay back down, curl myself into my pillow and picture Gabriel sleeping in his own bed. Maybe even dreaming of me. I wonder what he would think if he knew everything I'm going through. He would probably laugh and then scram. I need to get to the bottom of this. Need to add this log cabin stuff to my journal and work out some sort of chart, start connecting the puzzle pieces. With that plan in my head, my eyes close and I feel myself drift off.

When the phone rings, I jump to answer it and knock it off the base. It flies off the table and lands as far as the coiled cord will allow.

"Oh shit!" I say, scrambling to pick it up.

"He-hello?"

"I heard that Ella. Your momma needs to wash that little mouth of yours out with soap," Gabriel says in a husky, I-just-woke-up voice.

"Ugh, I'm so embarrassed. I was so anxious to hear from you that I totally knocked my phone to the floor!"

"I know. I heard it crashing, and then I heard you cursing," Gabriel says through laughter.

"That's exactly what happened. I'm sorry you had to hear my 'bad girl' rear her naughty little head."

"Hey, no problem, I can dig a little bit of naughty." Sorry, I couldn't resist."

"That's okay, I'll let this one slide."

"Thanks. But hey, I like the thought of my calling you had you throwing yourself at the phone. I feel wanted."

"Well, you are wanted. What time is it anyway?"

"It's late, almost twelve. I stayed up way too late, thinking about you, doing a complete playback of last night. I pulled out my guitar and lowered the volume way down low on my amp so I wouldn't wake the dead. Lucky for me, my parents are out of town. My brother didn't even stir."

"I didn't know you had a brother. Younger?" I cover my mouth trying to suppress a yawn. "Sorry, excuse me."

"Yes, he's a freshman, and plays catcher on the B-team."

"Nice. So how long did you play your guitar?"

"Long enough to figure out one song."

I'm enjoying the sound of his voice. I can tell he just woke up, and it's so relaxed and lazy sounding. Kinda sexy, especially since I'm imagining him still in bed.

"Oh yeah? Which one?"

"A sweet, romantic one, *Till There Was You.*

"Ohmygosh, I love that song. Cute Paul sings it."

"Cute Paul? You're trying to make me jealous, right?"

I giggle.

"Just teasing," he says. "But hey, I need to see you soon - real soon. I'm hurting here."

"Good," I laugh. "Me too. The girls and I are going to meet up at Zesto's. The guys will join us also. You want to meet up there?"

"Sounds good, but I've got a better idea. Why don't I pick you up and take you there myself?"

"I like that. You want to come by for me at two-ish? Do you think you can drive me by the dance studio after Zesto's? I have to be there between three and four to pick up my order."

"Sure," he says, suddenly all chipper. "I guess I'll see you at two."

"Okay, see ya."

I dash downstairs. "Mom, Gabriel's coming by to take me to Zesto's. We're meeting up with friends there. Is that alright? He also said he'd drive me by the studio to pick up my stuff."

"Yes, mijita, looking forward to seeing him again."

"Thanks, Mom."

I decide to wear the plaid summer skirt I just bought and a white sleeveless top. I pull my hair up in a ponytail, tying it with a navy-blue ribbon to match my skirt. When I see his truck come up the driveway, I quickly slip on my white Keds and bounce down the porch steps to greet him.

"Hi, Gabriel." I greet him with a little wave.

I can't believe I get to see his gorgeous face again. He looks darling in a black ringer T-shirt, with off-white rings and off-white jeans and brown loafers. No socks. Really cool. He takes my hand in his and looks at me with the sweetest smile. He steps in just a little bit closer causing me to take a deep breath and exhale with a sigh.

"I know," he says, "I feel the same way."

He brings his hand up to my cheek and strokes it softly from the corner of my eye down to my chin. As he tells that all he's been thinking of is seeing me again, he reaches behind me to play with my ponytail. He strokes it with his hand, following it to the end where it curls into a little turn. I can feel him twirling the end of my ponytail in his fingers when he reaches it, the way I do when I'm reading a book.

"So here we are again, you and me," he says with such a satisfied smile and a little dance of his head.

"Yes," I say, taking his hand and leading him inside. "How'd we ever get to this point? It seems like forever since I first noticed you in school. I was coming in from the main entrance. You were wearing a black turtle neck sweater, fumbling with your books."

"I know exactly when that was, you were wearing, pink on pink. I remember thinking you must like pink a lot. And I *was* juggling my books. I wasn't looking where I was going and ran into someone. I was watching you."

"Wish I would've known that," I say.

"By the time I looked up, you'd already headed down toward the cafeteria, and you were talking with your friends. Plus, you were with Michael."

"Yeah, and he was being a jerk. But you're right, I was wearing a pink pull-over sweater with a pink cardigan over it. But wow, I can't believe you actually remember what I was wearing."

When Mom comes out of her sewing room, I wave her down. "Gabriel's here."

She smiles broadly as she takes quick steps down the stairs.

"Hello, Gabriel. It is so nice to see you." She offers him her hand.

"Thank you, Mrs. Galvez. It's good to see you too."

"I'll bet you're missing those cafeteria enchiladas."

Gabe laughs. "You remember! I loved those things. And yes, I miss them."

"I think everyone remembers your love of enchiladas. I happen to have the recipe," she says with a lift of an eyebrow. "We'll have to have you over soon."

"Oh boy, I would love that so much," Gabe says, nodding his head. "Thank you."

"Okay Mom, we're heading out."

"Nice to see you again, Mrs. Galvez. By the way, you have a lovely daughter."

"Thank you," Mom says with a smile. "Enjoy your ice cream."

We're the first to arrive at Zesto's. We get our ice cream cones and head to an outdoor table.

"I love ice cream," he says, swirling his tongue completely around the tip of the ice cream cone just like a five-year-old.

"That was cute," I say with a smile.

"What was? Me? Which part?"

"Uh, the tongue part." I giggle.

He winks. "There you go, watching my mouth again."

"How can I not, you swirled your tongue completely around the cone just like a little boy."

"Oh really? Let's see you show me how I did that."

"You're serious?" I ask.

He nods.

I swirl my tongue completely around my cone. "Like that," I say, trying to lick off the smear of ice cream left on my lips.

I watch as a smile lifts the corner of his mouth. He clears his throat. "You know you're killing me, don't you?"

I smile.

"Can I have a taste?" he asks.

I offer him my cone. He shakes his head and instead lifts a smudge of ice cream off my lips with his finger, then I watch him touch his finger to his mouth. Not sure if he kissed it off or licked it off, either way, I thoroughly enjoyed it. "Now look who's killing who," I say.

He smiles, giving his head a little shake. "*Aye*, I am *so* in trouble."

Rita, Anna, and Julia climb out of Rita's car, noisy as ever, except for Julia, she's smiling, adjusting her headband and smoothing out her skirt. They come over to where we're sitting.

Julia thrusts her hand out with so much enthusiasm, grinning ear to ear, and Gabriel makes a sound that's somewhere between a muffled laugh and a snort.

"Hi Gabriel, we weren't introduced properly when I saw you at Fisher's, I'm Julia McInnis, pleased to meet you." Her ponytail bobs back and forth as she speaks.

Rita scoots Julia aside. "Hola, I'm Rrrrita!" Gabriel and I laugh. "But you already knew that."

"Hi Gabe, Ella's been drool—" I elbow Anna, shrug and give Gabriel an I-don't-know-what-she's-talking-about look. He's loving it.

Rita leans into me and says in a whisper loud enough for everyone to hear. "So Ella, how hot was he?"

Anna rolls her eyes. "Rita, you can't just go asking stupid things like that in front of everybody. That's private!"

"Come on Ella," Anna says, loudly. "Let's go indoors where we can have some privacy, and you can tell us if he's hot or not." She smiles at Gabriel as she tugs on me to follow her.

"I think you're being followed," Gabriel says, jerking his thumb in the direction of David and Jack who are waving at us. They join Gabe at the table as we head inside.

We spend our time laughing at Anna's antics and talking about boys.

"Anna, where's Greg?" I ask.

"I'm putting him on hold for a bit, need to check out some other options, if you know what I mean, El."

"But Anna, he's so sweet," I say.

She rolls her eyes.

"I'm serious," I say. "He's attentive and caring."

"My *dog* is attentive, that's how dogs are supposed to be, not guys. I need him to be cool and nonchalant so that I have to charm him to get his attention or have my way. Otherwise, it's no fun!"

"Huh?" I ask.

Rita and I look at each other with scrunched up confused looks on our faces. Anna darts a look at us and tosses her hair back. "Oh brother, when are you two ever going to wise up?"

Gabriel comes inside. "Hey, Ella, are you ready to go? You mentioned you wanted to be at the studio around three o'clock."

On the way to the dance studio, Gabriel tells me about how he's been spending the summer. Says he works part time at his dad's architecture firm. I tell him about how I help mom at home with her sewing business. It's obvious to me that Gabriel's very fond of Mom just from the questions he asks and, in his expressions as he talks about her. That touches my heart.

Gabriel pulls up to a parking spot at the dance studio and turns off the ignition.

"I won't be but a moment," I say, scooting over to my side.

When Gabriel sees me walking back to the truck, he reaches over to open the door for me. As I jump in, I notice the blue-cap guy looking at us from the far corner of the building. "It's him!"

"What?" he asks as he turns to see who I'm looking at. What's wrong?"

I point toward the corner of the building. "That guy." I point to a guy who's no longer there.

"The one Anthony told me about?" Gabe asks.

My eyes are on Gabe's hand on his door handle, scared of what I think he's about to do.

I nod my head. "Yes...I think so," I say about to cry.

Gabriel bolts out and runs toward the rear of the building. I'm stunned. I get out and run after him. I watch as he dashes around the corner and I'm terrified. I can't see what's happening, but hear the banging of metal garbage cans. I finally reach the back of the building, and I'm relieved to see Gabriel running back toward me.

"Oh baby, I'm sorry, I'm so sorry, I couldn't catch up to him. I have no idea where he went after he turned the other corner." Gabriel asks if I'm okay and holds me. "No, you're not, your heart is pounding! That son of a...I'm sorry, Ella, I'm just so mad!"

A police officer pulls into the parking lot and stops near us. He walks around his car. "Ms. Galvez, are you okay? I followed you here, and I circled the block while you were inside, and then I saw you running."

"Followed? Wh-why were you following me?" I ask, my voice still shaky.

"Mayor Bartelli's request. We're to drive by your home during our patrols, and if you're spotted anywhere in town, we're to make sure everything is okay. Just doing my job. So what just happened here?"

"But I'm not even in my own car," I say.

"Yes, ma'am. We were given vehicle information for any that you may be a passenger in, including three that belong to the Marquez family."

Gabriel speaks up. "I'm Gabriel Marquez, Ella's boyfriend. While I was waiting for Ella, I saw a guy standing at that far corner of the building. He was there the whole time Ella was inside, but never looked my way, so I didn't get a really good look at him. He was wearing sunglasses, and his visor was pulled down low. When Ella got into my truck, she saw him and said she thought he was the same guy that followed her downtown. I ran after him, but he made a quick turn going north. I lost him when he ducked between the other buildings."

"What was he wearing?"

"White T-shirt and dark navy-blue pants," Gabriel tells him. "And a navy-blue cap."

"Got it." He gets into his patrol car, talks into his walkie-talkie thingy, and heads north.

"Ella, come here."

He holds me, and I can feel my heart beating against his chest.

"This guy needs to be caught. I wish I could have gotten my hands on him."

"No, no, I didn't want that. The thought of you catching up to that guy scared me even worse. I was afraid you might get hurt."

"I'm sorry. Hey, I'm glad Anthony's dad is getting you some police protection. Guess you're kinda like a daughter to him since your families are so close."

"Yes, we're very close. The Bartelli's watched me grow up since I spent a lot of time in their home playing with Anthony and our friends. Sometimes I'd play with Sophia."

"Hey, I'm getting a little hungry. How about we go to The Vermillion for a bite."

"Sure," I say, then smile thinking about what Gabriel told the officer. "You just told him you were my boyfriend."

"Yeah, it kinda slipped out," he says with a shrug of a shoulder. "I guess because I want to be. Umm, you wanna go steady?"

"Yes. Yes, I do." A smile quickly spreads across his face. His head drops back, eyes closed. "Finally!"

When we arrive at The Vermillion, my stomach is still tied up in knots. I decide to stick with just soda, but Gabriel orders two burgers and fries. Gabe must be starved. Or maybe he's hoping he can talk me into having some. By the time the carhop arrives with our order, my tummy's a little more settled. Gabriel convinces me to take a couple bites of his sandwich, says it might help to calm me. I can see he's relieved when I tell him it made me feel better.

"Isn't that Miss Bates?" Gabe asks.

I'm confused. Miss Bates has dirty blond hair which she always wears pulled back in a bun. "Miss Bates, the government teacher?"

"Yeah," he says, handing me his burger for another bite. "It *is* her. A different her."

As she passes by I realize Gabe's right, it *is* Miss Bates. She's dyed her hair brown. It's parted at the side, and it's long down to her shoulders just like mine. Or it's a wig? She's also changed her style of dress, but then I've never seen her outside the classroom. Could be this is her casual look, but it's more youthful. "Wow, it sure is. I recognized her face, but I couldn't place it."

"It's the way she twists her lips like she's thinking about something, that gave her away," Gabe says. "She did it all the time in class."

"Quite an improvement. She's not a bad looking lady; she just always looked so dull...and much older than this," I say.

"Yeah," he nods, "you're right. She always looked kinda old maid-ish."

It's so much fun sitting here with Gabriel, getting to know him. He tells me about his parents.

"Mom has blond hair, blue eyes and *I* think she's beautiful," he says. My dad's tall, with light brown hair, hazel eyes, like mine and has a tanned complexion. They're really neat together and don't fight much, well, not anymore. They used to, often. My dad has a short, very hot temper, which he's worked hard to control. I'm afraid I've got a short one myself. And we're both controlling."

"That explains you jumping out of the truck and chasing the blue-cap guy. Uh, remind me not to make you angry. And as for controlling, that won't sit right with me." I frown and then give him a half smile.

"You don't ever have to worry," he says with a concerned look on his face. "I could never lose my temper with you, Ella."

"And what else," I ask.

Gabriel's eyes dart from one side to the other as if trying to figure out what I'm referring to. "Oh, and I promise never to be controlling," he says, looking concerned again. His face softens when I smile at him. "Ella, I'm glad you know what you want and what you expect from a guy." Then he smiles that cute little smirk. "I'm gonna be *that* guy."

I smile. "I was hoping you'd be the one."

"I didn't mean to paint a bad picture of my dad, though, he's really a pretty neat guy. I can't wait for you to meet my parents. Mom's gonna love you. She thought Carolyn was way too clingy. I had to keep reminding her there was nothing between us. Mom was driving me nuts."

Then Gabriel tells me he also spent time at his grandparent's home in Odessa. Said his grandfather's eyesight is failing and every summer when he and Marc visit them, his grandfather has them read the Bible to him. Gabe says he began to wonder if his grandfather asked them to read it to him for his own benefit or was it for his grandsons' benefits.

"My grandpa treats my grandma like a queen. He told me a couple of summers ago that I should never forget that women should be treated with love, respect and tenderness. He really didn't need to tell me that. As far back as I can remember I've seen it. Yeah, even as a little kid I noticed it."

I smile at him. I'm so lucky to have someone like Gabriel in my life.

On our way back to my house I think about how I felt when I saw the blue cap-guy again. It was the very same feeling I get from the little boy statue and the neighbor's window. That is so weird, there's absolutely no connection between the three. Well, there is. They all suck the air out of me.

Gabriel turns to me and reaches out to take my hand. "I'm not going to let that weirdo come anywhere near you."

I guess he was thinking about him too. "Please promise me you won't go chasing after every guy you see wearing a blue cap."

"Sorry," he says, shaking his head, lower lip drawn between his teeth. "I can't promise that."

22

1966 – Gabriel Marquez

Anthony's phone rings six times. *Come on buddy, pickitup!*

"Hey, Bartelli. I thought you'd never answer!"

"What's going on, Gabe?"

"Nothing and everything, man."

"Oh boy, let me guess. Ella's gotten under your skin."

"Has she ever. So sweet, yet so hot."

"Whoa, hold it there. Don't tell me you've—"

"Heck no, nothing like that. Haven't even kissed those sweet lips. It's just that she can say the sweetest things, but in a way that leaves me weak in the knees."

"Ha! The knees?"

"Okay, you got me. She totally turns me on. And the thing is, I don't think she's even trying. Even her shoulders get me going. I mean it's such a beautiful thing, her shrugging a shoulder. It's so seductive, when all she meant by it was *I don't know.*"

Anthony laughs, "She's got you good, Marquez."

"Boy, does she ever." I grab the phone, walk to the window and see that Marc is out there wiping down Dad's Mustang for me. Gonna pick up Ella in it...with the top down.

"Hey, I'm gonna make a tennis date with Ella, and then have her over for pizza with Marc and me. Parents are out of town. You and Doreen should join us. How about it? I'll pick up the pizza on our way home."

"Doreen's working, but I can make it. Why don't I get the pizza for you? Her favorite is shrimp pizza from Gio's."

"Shrimp pizza? Are you kidding?"

"Nope, it's the best. You gotta try it. It will make a believer out of you."

"Okay, so how about we meet up at six, my house."

"Later, gator. Hey, just a warning, Ella's really good."

"Great, it'll be fun!"

As I head for a shower, I start having the same hot images of Ella I've had since that unexpected romp I had with Carolyn in her car. I keep damning Carolyn because she started it, but I could've stopped her. I'm left with these images of Ella and me that played out in my head while I was getting it on with Carolyn. Now I'm kicking myself in the head. *God can't be too happy with me either.*

The thing is, the night it happened I was going to tell Carolyn I wasn't interested in her as a girlfriend, and we shouldn't go out anymore. It was the night I saw Ella at The Majestic; I thought about her through most of the movie. Later, when Carolyn was driving me home, she pulled over and pretty much threw herself on me while I still had Ella on my mind. Talk about bad timing. Can't help but wonder what Ella would think of me if she knew. I should've stopped it! Dammit!

Once I'm showered and dressed, I grab a bowl of cereal and take the phone with me to the kitchen table and dial Ella's number. I can't wait to hear her voice.

"Hey, Ella," I say when I hear her sweet hello. "Been thinking about you. How about a game of tennis?"

"Tennis? Oh gosh, I hope you won't be too disappointed. I'm not that good."

"That's not what Anthony says."

She laughs a deep warm laugh. Must be her morning laugh. "The fact that I'm better than Anthony doesn't necessarily make me a great player."

"Oh, I get it," I laugh with her. "I still want to play with you. Tennis...play tennis with you."

Ella giggles.

"Since my parents are out of town again, I thought we could have dinner at my house after our game. Anthony said he'd join us for the pizza. Marc will be here too."

"Sounds great. Hold on for a second, Mom's out in the hall, need to get her okay."

Just talking to Ella seems to have calmed me down. I was feeling a little bit desperate there. It's just that I haven't seen her in three whole days. No one's ever had this effect on me. I'm liking it, though.

"Okay, Mom said yes."

"Great. Can I pick you up at four?"

"Four's good. See ya then."

"Later." I place the receiver back and stand there smiling. *I've fallen in love with Bella Ella.*

When I drive up, Ella's outside waiting on her front porch. She smiles and quickly gets up to greet me. Look at that little tennis skirt. *I like it.*

I pull off my sunglasses and wrap my arms around her.

"I've missed you something awful." I take in a deep breath. "And wow do you smell good." Okay, here's my chance. I grab her hand and quickly lead her to the backyard.

"What are you doing?" She giggles as I continue pulling her along.

"You'll see." When we get to the backyard, I stop and turn her toward me. "Ella, I can't wait any longer." I touch her chin, lifting it up just a bit. "I'd like to kiss you," I whisper and move my lips as close as I possibly can to hers without actually touching them.

She takes a quick breath causing her soft lips to lightly brush mine and whispers a sweet breathy *yes.*

I press my lips gently to hers for the sweetest kiss I've ever tasted. When I look at her, her eyes tell me all I need to know. I kiss her again, this time my lips press a little more firmly, causing her lips to slightly part and I ache when I hear her tiny, sweet moan.

"I've been dying to do this."

She smiles. "Me too."

"Oh yeah?" I ask, smiling back. "When we were at Fisher's I actually thought you might lean over and kiss me. If Anthony and Doreen hadn't come up when they did, I was ready to do it for you." I laugh, pretty sure I read her right.

"You noticed!" she says, placing a hand over her eyes.

I think I embarrassed her, but at least she's still smiling.

"I sure did." I nod my head a couple of times and smile. "You were looking at me, well, at my mouth, when I was biting down on my lip." I feel my smirk turn into a big grin.

"Oh, really?"

"Yep, I was watching your lips too. They parted slightly, and I just knew a kiss crossed your mind. So was I right?"

She gives me a sly little smile. "Uh-huh, you were. Kissing you crossed my mind at that exact moment. Very perceptive."

She smiles again when I wiggle my eyebrows at her. I bring her head to my chest and hold her close. When she pulls away, she moves her hands up to my shoulders. "How about you kiss me again?"

"Oh yeah," I say.

I kiss her deeply and tenderly. And this time she presses her lips against mine. The pleasure works its way through every single cell in my body, and I'm hoping she's feeling the very same thing.

"That felt so good," she whispers. She licks her lower lips as if to taste the kiss we just shared. "You know, I can't believe that we're standing here in my backyard kissing."

"Well, I prayed for you, and here you are."

Her eyes open wide, her face brightens. "You actually prayed for *me*? I mean really prayed, like bend your knees, close your eyes kind of praying?"

"Yep, I did."

"Wow, Gabriel, I don't think anyone has ever prayed for me. Well, they have, like *God bless Ella*, but not *for* me. You know what I'm trying to say?"

I smile at her. "Yes, I do, but that's exactly what I did."

She smiles up at me so sweetly, her eyes sparkling.

"I know we haven't been together long." I search her face, not sure I should continue, but I do. "I think I've fallen in love with you."

Ella closes her eyes, takes a deep breath, and I hear her sigh.

"I'm sorry. I guess I shouldn't have...shouldn't have said it...yet," I stammer.

She looks up at me, her eyes a little misty. "Did you mean it?"

"Of course, I meant it."

"Then you shouldn't be sorry."

"But...but you didn't say anything. Thought I said the wrong thing."

"No, you didn't, it's just that I'm afraid," she says, her eyes locked on something distant, avoiding mine.

I run my hand along the side of her face, cup her chin and lift it toward me. I want to look directly into her eyes, want to see what's there. "What are you afraid of, Ella?"

"Of what I feel."

"I don't understand," I say, keeping my gaze on her.

She taps her hand against her chest. "I guess I'm afraid for me. It was easier to know I might never have something that I wanted than to know I could lose something I already have."

"You're afraid of losing me? That I'll stop loving you?"

She nods. "Somehow falling in love with you was easier when I knew you didn't even know I existed."

"Are you saying you've been falling in love with me?"

"Yes, I have...a little bit at a time, for a while now."

"Really?"

"Yes, really," she says with a sigh, and then she smiles. "This morning when I woke up, even before I'd opened my eyes you were on my mind, and the first thing I did was tell my teddy bear, *I think I've fallen in love.*"

"Oh, Ella," I say and exhale a breath I had no idea I was holding. "You *do* feel the same way. You've got no idea how happy—"

A smile creeps onto my face. "Wait. Hold on a minute. You have a teddy bear?"

"Uh-huh, his name's Teddy Bear Blue, but I call him Blue. And yes, I do talk to him."

"Teddy Bear Blue. And I'll bet Blue sleeps with you every night."

She smiles, nods her head.

"What a lucky bear."

She laughs. "Tsk, tsk, Gabriel."

"Uh-oh. Demerit?"

"You're in luck, I'm fresh out of demerits."

"I'm in luck, alright, you're falling in love with me."

I take her in my arms breathing in the sweet smell of her hair. "Let me love you, Ella. I promise I'll never leave you."

Her chest rises against me as she takes a deep breath. Then she totally relaxes in my arms as she releases the breath she'd held. I rub my hands up the length of her back and up over her shoulders. My fingertips rub the soft sides of her neck.

"Mmm, that feels way too good. I think we need to stop," she says in a husky whisper.

I can see the desire in her eyes, and it warms my whole body, and I *don't* want to stop.

"I think you're right. Come on, let's go hit some tennis balls."

She stops at the porch and picks up her racket and a straw bag with a yellow scarf tied around the handle.

"Fancy car, Gabe, your dad's?"

"Yep, he lets me borrow it when he's out of town."

I open the door for her. "There's an extra pair of shades in there," I say, pointing to the glove compartment.

"Got mine, thanks." She pulls out a pair of white-rimmed sunglasses from her bag and slips them on, then takes the scarf off the handle and ties it around her head. Her ponytail pokes out underneath it. I reach out and stroke the ends, and it makes her smile. She looks so happy and so sweet sitting here beside me. *Damn, I'm such a lucky guy!*

I start up the car. "Who's your nosy neighbor?"

"The upstairs window?" she asks, turning to look at it.

"Yes, that one. I saw someone standing there, couldn't see a face, but there was someone there. I saw the curtain move when we came to drop you off the night we met."

"I've never met them since their front door faces the other street, but I've recently started noticing stuff too."

"Tomorrow, I think I'll drive around and see who comes in and out of that house. I may be over reacting, couldn't really tell if it was a guy," Gabe says as he looks up at the window once more.

"That's sweet of you, Gabriel. Just don't go after anyone."

It's a noisy drive to the courts with the top down, radio blaring. But all I need is to feel Ella close. When we pull up to a stop light, another car zooms up and screeches to a stop next to us. It's Carolyn, and she's in her daddy's car and has the top down too. I give her a hesitant wave. Ella leans forward to see who I've waved to. Carolyn smiles and blows a kiss in my direction then gives me the universal *call me* sign while mouthing the words. She takes off the instant the light turns green, arm up in the air waving goodbye.

"Sorry about that," I say.

"Is that the girl you were dating, the one I saw you with at the movies?"

"Yes, but she wasn't really a date, we're old friends. We just did things together." *All kinds of things, dammit!*

"Well, what I just saw looked more like something an old girlfriend would do just to make the girl sitting next to you jealous."

"So are you?"

"Nope, I'm sitting here, and she isn't."

I turn and smile at her. "Love the attitude, Ella."

The courts are all taken when we get there. We sit and talk and watch a doubles match being played in front of us.

"I like that," Ella whispers as a girl walks by. Ella grabs her bag and pulls out a small journal and a pencil. "Sorry, I need to do this. I love the cut of her sundress, the angle of the open sleeves," she says, flipping through the pages.

I watch as she draws a picture of the sundress in her journal. "I didn't know you liked to draw."

"It's not drawing I like, it's sewing," she says as she continues her sketch. "Would like to make myself one just like it. It's obvious hers is expensive. I could never afford it."

"You sew all your clothes?"

"Not all of them, but quite a few. I enjoy sewing. I also like wearing something no one else will have."

"But if you make a dress like hers—"

"It won't be the same dress. I'll choose a different fabric, different color. It's the cut of the dress that I like."

When our court is free, we warm up volleying back and forth, but once we start our set, I find out Ella's pretty good on the court, quick on her feet and actually makes me hustle a few times. I'm playing hard, but not as hard as I would play against the guys, although I do make it hard enough for her that she breaks a good sweat. We both do.

"You beat me again," Ella says after our second set. "So who taught you how to play?"

"Actually, both my parents did. They'd take us out for tennis drills. I loved it. Got to spend time with my folks *and* do something fun."

"You're lucky, my dad rarely spends time with Mom and me. But one thing my dad does when we're together is use our time as a teaching moment. Just wish they'd happen more often."

"Sorry." I notice a sadness in her face, and at that moment I decide I want to be the one to make the sadness go away…forever.

I grab our towels and hand her one. I dry my face off then give her a quick kiss on the lips. "Hope you're hungry, we've got pizza waiting for us."

When we get there, Ella looks around, checks the landscaping and the *resaca*. When we moved here, Mom insisted Dad buy a house with a water view. We found out that in Brownsville that water view will be a *resaca*. It looks like a small lake, but it's actually some kind of a river channel.

"I love the view you have from here," she says.

The sound of Herb Albert greets us as we walk inside. She smiles back over her shoulder at me. "It's beautiful. I love all the modern, clean lines, and the mix of the beige leather sofas with brown and lime green accent pillows."

"Thanks."

"This fireplace is enormous!"

"Yep, it's a big one."

Anthony's sitting in the kitchen with Marc. Those two are already digging into the pizza.

"Ella, this is my brother, Marco, who prefers to be called Marc."

"Hi, Marc. Hi, Anthony."

"Ella, this one's shrimp," Anthony says, pointing to the one in front of him.

"Fantastic, I'll have two slices of that, but I think I need to wash up and change first."

I reach for her hand. "I'll show you the way to the powder room."

"That's okay, I know where it is."

"What?" I ask.

Ella stops, she turns to me, eyes wide. "Uh, what am I saying? I have no idea where it is." She shrugs then takes my hand and follows along.

I point to the cabinet. "Fresh towels are in there."

Ella returns wearing a sundress and sandals and has taken down her ponytail. She looks beautiful head to toe, and here I sit with my bare feet propped on the barstool rung.

Marc cups his hand over his mouth. "She's a babe, Gabe."

Anthony and I nod, "Yep."

Ella laughs. "Okay. I'm ready for some of that shrimp pizza. I see you've changed too. I like you in black." Her approval makes me smile. She runs a finger down my back, making me wiggle as she does. "Ticklish?" She asks.

I smile. "A little bit."

"Ella we've got RC, 7-Up and Grapette to choose from," Anthony says.

"I'll take a 7-Up, please," Ella answers.

A new album drops on the turntable and side two of *Rubber Soul* starts up. Ella looks at me and smiles.

"So was she good or what?" Anthony asks, scooting the shrimp pizza in front of Ella. She reaches over and slides it out and takes a slice then pushes the rest of it back into the brown paper bag it came in.

"Actually, she *was* pretty good."

"Gabe is excellent at placing those balls, and what a serve," she says and then takes a bite of her pizza. She holds her hand over her mouth as she smiles and chews it up quickly. She looks at me. "Gabe, you have got to try it. It is by far the best pizza ever," she says, dabbing her lips with a napkin.

Anthony nods in agreement while stuffing a slice in his mouth.

I reach for another slice of pepperoni pizza, "I just might try a slice. You know, I would've done much better playing against Ella had she not been wearing that little tennis skirt."

Anthony laughs. "You let a tennis skirt interfere with your game, Marquez? Unreal!"

"Well, Ella's did," I say then bite into my pizza.

Anthony grins. "Hey, Ella, I think we've discovered his Kryptonite – short little tennis skirts."

She rolls her eyes at him. "Okay, now I'm stuffed. You guys can have all the rest."

"I've decided to give your beloved shrimp pizza a try, but first I'll add some jalapeno slices." I take a huge bite, Ella watching me as I chew it down, waiting to see what I think. "Hey, not bad," I nod. "Much better than I expected."

"We told ya," Anthony says. Ella smiles and nods.

I finish up the rest of my drink and look at Ella. I know what song is going to play next, so I walk over and take her by the hand and pull her to me. When *In My Life* begins to play, Anthony and Marc go upstairs leaving Ella and me on our own.

"Come on, dance with me."

Ella slips off her sandals and pushes them off to the side. "You're barefoot, wouldn't want to step on you with shoes on."

I know it's crazy, but it feels as if we've danced this song before. Her body melts into mine, and we move as one. It's like she already knows my very next step or turn, and she's getting it so right.

"How do you like the bridge in this song, a little Baroque-sounding, huh?" I ask.

"I love it. Sounds like a harpsichord."

"Yes, that's what I thought it sounded like too."

When the song ends, I pull back to look at her. "I hope I'm not rushing you because I've fallen for you like really hard."

"Gabriel, you can't rush my heart into anything it isn't already feeling on its own. My heart's been making room for you since I saw you that one night at the movies. At first, I thought you might've noticed me too. It was a short moment between us, just a look. I finally convinced myself you hadn't noticed, and it was just me."

"Noticed? Are you kidding? I noticed it from my head all the way down to my toes." I laugh. "Come on, let's go outside."

I hold the door open as she steps through, watch as the breeze plays with a few wisps of her hair. With a sensual tilt of her head, she takes her hand and slowly lifts them off the side of her face and smiles at me.

Anthony comes out right behind us. "Guys, I've got to get going. I promised Doreen I'd meet up with her."

"Thanks for everything, Bartelli. You're the best," I say.

Anthony and I do the big buddy, back slap, then he gives Ella a kiss on her forehead and takes off.

I lead Ella toward the patio, to a private spot with a view of the water.

"I just want to do a little bit more of this before I take you home," I say. I kiss her cheek, then her neck, and move along, across her shoulder. "Did I ever tell you that you have beautiful shoulders?"

I feel her laugh vibrate in her throat as I kiss her neck again. "You did, and I still think it's funny. Who notices shoulders?"

"I do." I kiss her passionately, my arms taking her into me so close. I move my body against her, and oh man, I love how she's completely melting in my arms. We press into each other, and it feels so good, way too good. *Oh shit!*

Ella gasps and I take a quick step back, rub my hands over my face and rake my fingers through my hair. *That wasn't supposed to happen.*

"Wow, that was feeling so good," she says as her chest rises and falls.

I tilt my head back with a laugh. "I'm glad you're enjoying yourself, but baby, you're killing me. *That* was not supposed to happen. Maybe we need to stop."

She pouts and pulls me toward her. "Come on, just a tiny bit more...well, maybe not so tiny." Then she kisses me long and hard.

"Uh, you have no idea what you're doing to me," I moan.

"I just wanted one last kiss. No more, I promise. I can feel your misery and your reaction, I mean *really* feel it," she says.

I laugh. "I love your choice of words. You said, *my reaction*. Was that a sneaky little play on words?"

"No, I meant *reaction*. But now that you mention it, yes, I did feel your...ohmygosh, what am I saying!" She covers her face and muffles a giggle. "I can't believe I just said that! I'm so embarrassed!"

I pull her close to me and give her a hug as I try not to laugh, but I do. I've definitely won the prize. "You are something else. And by the way, misery doesn't come close," I say, laughing again. "You, are a bad, bad girl, Ella Galvez."

She looks up at me and winces. "Demerit?"

"Not a chance. And darn, I hate having to take you home, and oh how I wish I were Teddy Bear Blue tonight."

She smiles and puts her hands around my neck, holding me without allowing our bodies to touch.

I take in a long, deep breath. "And to think this is just the beginning – we are so in trouble, baby. And now I have to take you home to that lucky little bear."

When we pull up at Ella's, I grab her tennis racket from the back seat and walk her to her front porch. We kiss, and as I hug her good night, I notice the light at the neighbor's window go out. Don't say a word, don't want to concern her. But I do make myself a promise that I'm not gonna let anyone harm my Bella Ella.

23

1966 – Ella Galvez

The stairs just outside my room squeak. That's my five-second warning that Mom will be opening my door. I look at the clock and see it's been ten minutes since I told Mom I'd be out in a minute. She pokes her head in my doorway. "Ella? Weren't you supposed to be helping me with the sheets?"

"Okay, okay, gimmie another minute, Mom, pleeease."

"Only one, Ella, not five. And *it's, give me*, not *gimmie*."

I laugh. "Okay, how's this? Give me one more minute, please."

She smiles and gives me a nod. I put my journal and pen away. Just had to make sure I added last night's minor mishap at Gabriel's house. How could I be so stupid to say I knew where the powder room was? And how did I think I was going to explain that one?

The problem was I didn't have time to think; the words just popped out. And that's because even before Gabriel opened the door, I *knew* exactly where it was and that it had ornate gold-toned mirrors and fixtures that clashed with the sleek modern lines in the living room. I deserve an Academy Award for my performance. I pulled it off, and the guys never had a clue that while they were stuffing down pizza, I was still freaking out over having a déjà vu moment yet again.

But then something happened once Gabriel held me as we danced. From that point on nothing else existed but us. Not my life without Gabriel, nor a world filled with mysterious and unexplainable happenings. Well, except for the unexplainable thing that happened out on the patio. I was joking about reactions and erections like if I'd been possessed by my good friend who's queen of all things sexual, Anna Rivera! Where the heck did that come from? I'm the shy and coy one. Stuff like that just doesn't pass *my* lips. I was so embarrassed. Thing is, I had as much control over that as I did with the powder room incident. I am so in trouble!

When I got home, I came straight upstairs, took the necklace out of my jewelry box and wondered if Gabriel might love me as much as this Gabriel loves his Bella Ella. For the first time, I decided to try it on and imagine how she might've felt when her Gabriel gave it to her. But I couldn't, the clasp was broken.

At first, I was upset that I couldn't try it on, but then I remembered Mom's comment when she checked the welt on the back of my neck. She told me it looked like a necklace had been yanked off. Seeing the broken clasp really shook me up. My mind kept tossing all kinds of scenarios around, but each one was illogical or just plain 'ol wacky. I convinced myself I was being silly letting my imagination go wild; it was just a coincidence. That settled, I was finally able to fall asleep. I'm thinking differently this morning. I know there's got to be more to all of this. The coincidences are starting to pile up.

As I head outside, I see Mom gathering the corner of a sheet. She pauses as she looks up in the direction of the neighbor's upstairs window. She bends down and grabs another corner and looks up there again. She's never mentioned those neighbors before. Since the front door to their house faces the cross street, we don't get to see who comes in and out of it. So I doubt she would know them. But yet, there was a pleasant look about her as she looked up at the window, I'd say she smiled quite fondly.

Mom hands me the two corners of the sheet she had just gathered. "Here you go." She grabs the other two corners and hangs her end on the line with a clothespin. I do the same with my corners. If I didn't have issues with that darn window to start with, I wouldn't question Mom's attention to it. Even Gabriel mentioned how it appeared someone was peering out from behind the curtain.

"Ella, you seem a hundred miles away. Take the corners, please."

"Sorry, I'm just sleepy," I say.

Once we're done with the sheets, I take the empty laundry basket and head inside, holding the door open for Cooper to come in. Later, I'll have to ask her about those neighbors.

While changing into my leotard, I think about how sexy Gabriel looked last night in his snug black V-neck knit shirt and blue jeans. Sat there with his bare feet propped on the chrome barstool rung, looking so cool and relaxed, yet so hot. He was so romantic and sensitive. Kinda reminded me of this Gabriel, the one who gave his own Bella Ella a beautiful necklace with his promise to her engraved into it.

The phone rings and I rush to answer, hoping it will be Gabriel.

"Hello," I say, grabbing the phone and taking it to my dresser with me.

"Hey, Ella Bella, checking to see if you're riding with Anna and me tomorrow, or is lover boy taking you."

"Riding with Gabriel."

"So did you guys do *it* last night?"

"Noooo!"

I hear giggling in the background, then Anna's voice. "What'd she say? Did she say yes?"

"But you wanted to, right?"

"Ohmygosh, yes!"

"Well, well, well. The sexual awakening of Ella Bella."

"What? They had sex!" Anna exclaims in the background.

"Hold on, Anna," Rita says. "I'm trying to—"

"Gimmie that phone," I hear Anna say. "You had sex with Gabriel Marquez?"

"No, Anna, I—"

"I'll bet he was so hot! Tell me everything!"

"Anna! You're not listening!" I yell into the phone. "We...did not...have...sex."

"Oh man, I thought you—"

"I know what you thought." Then I sigh. "But what I wanna know is how am I gonna remain a virgin when my body's begging me not to."

"Being a virgin is overrated," Anna says. "Go ahead, let lover boy give you a thrill. Hey, we gotta go. See ya tomorrow."

Now I know something's wrong with me. Anna and I are talking the same language!

Before starting my warm-up, I pull up all the shades. I enjoy dancing with the sunshine streaming in and love how the rays of light are displayed against the wall and how the dust particles linger in the air like magical pixie dust.

I place my new album on the turntable and take my position at the barre before the music begins. My barre exercises are strenuous yet relaxing and help remove all the rubbish that accumulates in my head.

So much going on in there these days. But once the music begins, my focus is on the music and the movement.

When I'm done with my barre exercises, I put *Feeling Good* on the turntable to dance the jazz number Gabriel said he watched me perform at the auditorium. I love the movements of this piece, but today each step, turn, leap and reach is for Gabriel, and I try to imagine what he might have thought as he watched me perform this very dance on stage.

24

1966 –The Blue Cap Guy

Don't know why I didn't think of this before. The things I could have seen. I carefully pull my new telescope out of the box. My hands are shaking as I pull out each piece and line them up side by side on the table where they wait patiently for me to connect them all together. I take a long sip of my beer to settle my nerves. It's the anticipation of being able to see her up close that's driving me crazy. I'm moments away from a front row seat into the life of this girl named Ella.

I've watched her for a while. Unfortunately, binoculars have only taken me so far inside her world. But she's given me plenty to look at. She's a teenager, and they just don't think. She leaves her blinds open on occasion. My favorite is when she does it at night with her lamp on. So far, I've seen her in her sweet little night clothes and in her bra. Damn window's not low enough, so I can't see much more, but I do have a vivid imagination that takes me right down to the details. I've thought of climbing up the trellis to the roof and looking down through the window, but with my luck, someone will see me, or I'll slip and fall in the middle of a very inopportune moment. I've thought about doing it, right down to the point of wondering what it would feel like to free-fall during a moment of bliss. What a way to die. Splat! Right there on the concrete. That would definitely turn her off. I'm sticking to the window.

Okay, my tripod is up and at the perfect height. I place the telescope on its rest. I'm ready to put it in the service of my perverted needs. Well, that's what the experts call us voyeurs and peeping Toms – perverted. But in my case, it's entirely different. She's not just any girl, she's *my* girl, my sweet little dancer, my delicate flower.

The magnification of this little scope here will put me right inside both rooms and at the right angle into part of her backyard. Whoever built this house couldn't have planned the placement of this window any better than this. Smack center between her bedroom and the room where she dances and does stretches on those wall bars. I love watching my sweet Ella.

I'll never forget the moment I learned her name. I'd seen her coming and going from the dance studio she went to once a week. Then one day I saw an announcement. There was going to be a dance recital at Jacob Brown Auditorium it said. So I attended the performance in hopes of watching her dance. I even got there early so I could sit up front. And with the program in my hands, I waited until I finally saw her there on stage.

She stood there with three other girls. The program listed four names, but I didn't know which name was hers. I had to know. I had four names to choose from but guessing just wasn't good enough. My choices were Sandra, Maria, Ella and Janet. I checked the other dance groups that were going to be performing, only Sandra and Ella would be in two different routines. Sandra would be dancing in a group of seven and Ella would be performing a solo. It would be the last performance. So I waited patiently.

Finally, the dance with Sandra and six other girls was about to begin. The curtains opened to an empty stage. The first girl stepped forward from behind the curtain, performed a few dance steps moving forward toward the center, then kicked and spun around. The next girl did the same thing. I watched with so much anticipation waiting to see if it would be my girl stepping out. Finally, the seventh girl appeared. It wasn't her. Well, that told me her name wasn't Sandra. So I had to wait and see if my girl would be the one dancing the last dance alone on that stage. It had to be.

When the final dance began, the curtains were drawn open, and the stage was dark. As the lights slowly brightened I saw her. She was standing there in the center of the stage wearing black satin and fish-net stockings with a gold sash around her waist. It was my girl, and I finally knew her name – Ella Galvez. She was the star of this number. My star. I felt such pride for my girl, my Ella. The music that began to play was *Feeling Good.* And boy was I. It was a jazz number, and she was hot. And right then I realized inside my sweet little girl was a passionate woman who one day soon I was going to make mine.

Well, she has been mine for a while. She had a boyfriend, but she was not into him at all. I could tell. I studied every little nuance between them while he was around. I'd see them saying goodnight on the front porch. Little pecks were all she allowed. He'd try for more, oh boy did he ever, but she'd stop him and shake her head. I watched them in the park, at the movies and even at a football game. It was always the same thing. My sweet Ella was saving herself for me.

Then something changed. I watched Ella for over a week and that pestering, idiot boyfriend of hers was no longer coming around. That's when I realized she probably dumped him. I knew I would have my chance.

But then one night some other guy showed up. He returned the next day and the next, and the next. He ruined everything. She changed, she was no longer my innocent Ella. She let him kiss her, and I could tell she wanted him, she still does. Their kisses are getting longer and hotter. I've even had to endure watching him kiss her delicate shoulders. That's the night I almost blew it. I was ready to go out there and tear him away from her.

Yes, I've gotten off watching them. Well, until my blood begins to boil. I won't allow him to have my Ella. I'm going to make her mine before he gets a chance to ruin everything. It's going to happen soon. But I'm afraid I won't be that nice about it. She'll need to be dealt with for misbehaving with him, letting him kiss her the way he has, allowing him to rub his body up against hers. Soon, real soon, I'm going to take her and make her mine before he does.

Well, the moment I've been waiting for has arrived. With my heart pounding and my fingers still shaking, I slowly pull aside the curtain and place the scope there. I look into it, making adjustments to sharpen the image. Damn! Talk about perfect timing! I watch as the shades of her dance room go up one at a time. And there's my Ella in a snug-fitting pink leotard. The beauty of this room is that the windows are much lower than her bedroom windows. Depending on where she is I can see her whole torso and most of her thighs. I'm able to enjoy every curve of her beautiful body and her face. And better yet, there are mirrors along a wall where the exercise bars are attached, so I get to see both sides of her. This is going to be sooo good. *Come on baby, do something special just for me.*

I watch, and I wait. Ella walks up and stands sideways at the bar facing me and places her satin ballet slipper on the bar. I can actually see the arch of her foot as she points her toes. She reaches her arm over her head and leans into her leg, her ponytail draping over it. When she pulls her torso up, her foot remains on the bar, and I move my scope slowly to the right. See the pink ribbon which wraps around her delicate ankle. I then zoom in on her muscular calf and slowly move it further down where it curves in underneath her knee. As I move along her shapely thigh, I swallow hard as I'm about to reach her—

Damn, she brought her leg down. Why right now? Damn it! My heart beat picks up again when I readjust my lens and watch as she turns around, her backside to me. She lifts her other leg onto the bar, and I watch as she leans over her leg and I follow her from her head, down to the small of her back, then follow the curve—

The downstairs door slams shut. Damn it! She's back! I end up knocking the lens off to one side. My heart is about to jump out of my chest. I quickly fumble with my telescope and stuff it in the closet along with the box it came in. I place blankets on top of everything. I make sure nothing shows and close the closet door.

When I hear her footsteps coming up, I grab a magazine and quickly take a seat in the chair, an open magazine in my lap.

"Hey," I say with a smile, "I didn't expect you back so soon."

25

1966 – Ella Galvez

As we approach the beach, we begin taking long, deep breaths of that fabulous salty air. There's nothing like the first sight of the enormous ocean and the sound of the crashing waves. Amazing!

When Gabe steps out of his shorts and pulls off his T-shirt, I like what I see. He's trim and muscular. Rita's right, he *is caliente*. Something tells me the Ella I was with Michael, is not the same one I am now. Rita said there's been an awakening, but after night before last on Gabriel's patio, I'm thinking someone else has taken over the reins. I no longer seem to be in charge. Call me crazy, but I think that voice in my head has something to do with it. *Yikes, I'm starting to sound like I have a split personality!*

"Come on," Gabe says. "Let's introduce you to some of my friends." With my hand in his, he leads me toward a canvas canopy. Some of his friends are sitting on a long beach-weathered log, others on lawn chairs.

I notice Carolyn's in the bunch. *How nice, his ex-sort-of girlfriend.*

"Everyone," he says, swinging his arm around my waist and pulling me close. "I'd like you to meet my girlfriend, Ella Galvez."

"Look at you two, all couple-y," Carolyn says with a noticeable slur.

I smile, look at Gabriel, who ignores her as if she's invisible to him which I think is kinda strange. That's what you do to an ex-girlfriend maybe, but friends don't break up. I guess that kiss she blew at Gabriel on our way to the tennis courts doesn't make sense either. I recognize a couple of other faces as he calls off their names. I smile and say hello, but the only thing I'm focused on is this nagging thought that maybe there's more to Gabriel and Carolyn.

"Hi everyone," I say with a smile and a little wave.

Gabe excuses us, and we head toward the cabanas where we were told the refreshments are located.

"Sorry about that, she must be someone's date."

"It's okay, it's not like you were lovers or anything, right?"

He looks at me for a moment, his lips twisted to one side while his eyes dart to where Carolyn's sitting and then back to me. "You are the only girl I've ever loved. Everyone else was just, well...everyone else." He smiles and then nods which I think was meant to reassure me.

We get our drinks and see Anna and Rita wave and head in our direction. Rita checks Gabe out from head to toe. "Hey, if it isn't Gabe, the babe." Sounds like Rita's already got a nickname for him.

"So what kind of drinks do we got here?" Rita asks.

"There's all kinds of soda pop." Gabriel points to the cabana and takes a sip of his. "Wow, these things are icy cold!"

Anna wrinkles her nose. "And what else?"

Gabriel laughs. "That's it, but if you look around you'll see some of the guys brought their own coolers."

Anna pulls on Rita's arm. "Come on girl, let's go find us some beer."

They take off to mingle with everyone, including Gabe's so-called friend. Gabe notices. "Do they know Carolyn?" he asks, scrunching up his eyebrows.

"Maybe, if not, they will soon." I see a half-smile, but he's still frowning.

Gabe takes my hand. "Come on, let's go for a walk."

The smell of lighter fluid is strong as we walk past a couple of pits with hot glowing embers. I stop and slip out of my beach cover-up and drop it on the table. Gabe looks at me and gives me that smile I love so much. "I like it a lot," he says, then takes my hand and walks us toward the shore, looking me over again as he smiles.

We walk hand in hand for a while along the beach sharing stories, taking in the scene, and making time for kisses along the way. I stop to watch the seagulls playing in the surf, leaving their cute little birdie prints on the wet sand only to be washed away by the waves.

Gabe pulls on my arm. "Come on let's get wet, it'll be fun." He takes me into the water which is cool and feels so good.

We walk against the waves, our eyes fixed on the horizon. We stop when the waves rush up against our bodies, as they make their way to shore. Once the water starts hitting me at hip level, Gabriel holds me steady as the waves flow past us. Then a big one comes crashing in pulling us under.

He catches me by the arm and pulls me toward him holding me while I rub my salty eyes and push strands of hair away from my face. Another wave, much stronger than the last, slams over us, and I wrap my arms tighter around his neck and hook my legs around his waist. Gabriel stands firm, and we're able to remain upright. Once the wave passes and rushes to shore, I pull away, look at Gabriel, and what I see in his beautiful hazel eyes is exactly what I'm longing for. He presses his lips to mine passionately, the warmth of his kiss flowing to every part of me. Gabriel moans low and slow, and another wave of these delicious sensations overcome me.

"Baby, I don't wanna stop."

"Then don't," I say, resting my head on his shoulder enjoying the movement of our bodies as the swirling water moves us to and fro.

I just told Gabriel not to stop. Where did that come from? I'm the prude, the one who's on the receiving end of Rita and Anna's virgin jokes. But yet, I just said *don't stop*. I could blame it on the voice that's taken refuge in my head although I haven't heard from her in a while. But I know she's there, I can feel her there. Saying stuff like this is starting to sound normal to me. Not good.

Just when I thought I'd steadied my desires and longings, another strong wave comes through, causing me to slip further down Gabriel's hips. To hold on, I pull myself tightly against him with my legs. The wave going out to shore is followed by a strong current making its way back to sea. Together, they rhythmically and strategically move our bodies slowly back and forth against each other.

"Oh, Ella, this feels so good," Gabe says in a low raspy voice.

I whisper, "I know, I know." Then I sigh. "But I think we're supposed to stop."

"Yeah, we should...we will," he says, pressing his lips to mine.

I'm totally melting into him with that kiss. "Oh, Gabe," I moan when he presess himself against me.

Anna's words rush through my senses along with those incredible feelings he has just stirred in me. She said I should go ahead and let Gabriel give me a thrill...he did.

"Oh, Ella," he says in a deep whisper.

I'm amazed at how the sound of his voice saying my name like that can caress me all over leaving me so weak and with no will left to say let's stop. I need to say it, but I don't. Neither does Gabe. A colossal wave catches us off guard and throws us forward, arms flailing. Just what we needed! I wonder if Gabe will say God sent that crashing wave. Knowing Gabe, he probably said *please God, help me,* and that's what God did.

Gabriel picks me up out of the water, and I hold on to his arm. "Oh man," he moans. "This is so hard, I mean unbelievably hard!"

His words make me laugh. I shove the hair away from my face and look at him. "Are we talking about *reactions* again?"

"Ha! You caught the *hard part*," he says with a smirk on his face.

"Yeah, and I kinda actually felt it," I smirk back.

He squints at me. "What am I gonna do with you? Well, I know what I'd *like* to do."

"Gabriel, that's not helping."

"Yeah, I know, I know. God's gonna get an earful tonight."

"I knew it! You do talk to God about stuff like this."

"*Especially* about stuff like this. Right in the middle of it, I said *God, please help me.*"

"And so God sent that big ol' wave that knocked us to our senses," I say.

Gabe laughs and pulls me to him. "Yep, it's quite possible. I'll have to remember to thank him for that," he says as we head back.

We make it to shallow waters, and are able to walk without fighting the waves. I look at him and smile and get such a warm feeling. He's the only person I know who talks about having conversations with God. My folks pray when they go to church, and of course, they say their prayers before they go to sleep each night, and Mom sometimes prays the Rosary. I say my bedtime prayers too, but mostly it's just ones I learned to recite growing up.

No long conversations with God and definitely not grown up stuff like this. But then none of my sins are serious. A white lie here, eating a hotdog on Friday there, skipping out on Holy Communion so I can sneak out of church early to meet up with Rita and Anna. That kinda stuff. I'm sure my sins bored Father Robles to tears. Well, except for the Holy Communion one. Don't remember how many *Our Father's* I had to say, but that one got his attention. I knew I wasn't about to commit that sin again, or at least not tell Father Robles about it.

Once Julia scolded us for sneaking out of church. She said it would never cross her mind and often stays long after the service is over to help with refreshments at fellowship. Julia huffed when Rita told her she probably only shows up for that because it's where she gets all the latest gossip. As Julia walked off, she gave Rita the most obscene gesture sweet little Julia could conjure up – she stuck her tongue out at her.

"Ella, I'm doing awful and should've had more control. I guess I was kinda hoping you'd have control for the both of us."

"Me," I ask. "You kinda got me all hot and bothered too."

I frown at him when he wiggles an eyebrow at me. "Stop with the dancing eyebrow, already, I'm serious."

He nods. "Alright, okay, I'll be serious too."

"We need to set boundaries," I say, trying to run my fingers through my wet, sandy hair. "But not when we're in the heat of the moment. Got to decide those limits *before* we get all caught up in the...you know."

"Boy, you are so right, once it started feeling good, stopping was not what I was thinking of."

"And I wasn't much help," I say, feeling a little low. "Like you said, I should've been in control for both of us."

He gives me an apologetic look. "No, Ella, I didn't mean to stick you with the hard part."

I scrunch up my face and narrow my eyes at him. "Don't say *hard part.*"

"Ha! I knew it as soon as I said it!

I shake my head. "Oh boy, we're in trouble."

"No, we'll be fine, we'll figure this out." He gives me one sweet kiss then we walk hand in hand back to the party.

As we approach the group, we hear someone playing a guitar and singing. "That's Steve," Gabriel says. "He usually brings his guitar." As we get up close, Steve hollers to Gabe. "So did you bring it?"

"Yeah," Gabe answers, "It's in the trunk." Gabe excuses himself to the little boy's room, says he'll be right back.

Anna comes up to me holding a plate of cheese cubes and chips. "Why aren't you with Frank?" I ask. "I thought I saw him from a distance. Was that him?"

"He's gone off to the restroom too," she grumbles.

She puts a cheese cube in her mouth and yanks the toothpick out angrily.

Someone's not happy.

She waves the toothpick around like a little sword. "I'm telling ya, El." She stabs the toothpick in Carolyn direction. "That floozy can't keep her paws off of Frank, making eyes at him, coming over and grubbing on him," she says, waving the toothpick in the air then stabbing another unsuspecting cheese cube.

"Grubbing?" I ask.

"Grabbing and rubbing," she says, kindly demonstrating by grabbing her breast with her hand then rubbing on her hip. Grubbing. El, you've got a lot to learn."

"Yeah, maybe so, but I'm catching on fast."

"Frank's not being very effective in pushing her away."

"You gotta give him a break, Anna. A guy can't be forceful with a girl without coming across as a brute, don't you think? It's not like he can slap her, or fling her away, huh? Gotta be a little more understanding, especially since it's not his fault."

"I *am* being understanding. Otherwise Frank would be sporting this toothpick in his eye," she says as she stabs another piece of cheese.

I see Carolyn walk up to some guy, and she wraps her arms around him and smooches him. He's not complaining.

"Think Carolyn's forgotten all about Frank," I say. "She's busy grubbing with someone else."

Anna follows the direction of my gaze, lets out a sigh of relief. "Maybe I should go find Frank." She places her plate on a table and hurries off adjusting her bathing suit top to show more cleavage.

Funny, I never knew Anna to be insecure. But then, there's never been anyone she's had to work hard for, until Frank. If I recall correctly, this is precisely what she said she wanted, someone cool and nonchalant that she has to charm to keep his attention. *Well, that should keep her busy.*

When Gabe returns he pulls me by the hand. "Come on let's go listen to Steve."

We listen to him sing a rocking *Kansas City.* When he's done he lifts his guitar toward us and asks Gabriel he wants to play one. Gabe looks at me and smiles. "Sure, just one for my girl, Ella." And that's exactly what he sings, *My Girl.* I'm swept off my feet by that. So much for bashful guy. Gabe sings that song beautifully and makes a show of walking over to me and making me blush.

"I loved it, Cute Gabe," I say when he's done.

"Cute Gabe, I like that," he says and then gives me his smirky smile.

We get ourselves some burgers and chips and find a spot to sit. We watch everyone having fun and talk about everything except what happened out there in the waves. Gabe looks so gorgeous. His wet hair's slicked back except for a few strands that fall over his forehead. I love watching him, his beautiful eyes narrowing when he's serious and wide eyed when he talks about things he did growing up. I also love watching his lips as he speaks. As far as I'm concerned, his mouth is the main attraction.

Everyone else ate while we were gone and are either dancing to the music, playing volleyball, splashing in the surf, or sunning on towels. Carolyn, however, is still all over this one guy, but now it looks like he's had his fill and is trying to discourage her. I give Gabriel a questioning look.

He leans in and whispers. "She doesn't know how to take *no* for an answer. I feel sorry for that poor chap."

"Gabe, that's not a nice thing to say."

"Hey, I've been on the receiving end," he says, sounding a little angry.

"Wait. You and Carolyn?"

Gabe nods, he shifts his eyes away from me and looks at the surf.

"What are you saying?" I ask, hoping my annoyance isn't obvious. "I thought you and Carolyn didn't have that kind of relationship."

"We didn't...not really...well, kinda," he says, looking at me with a frown. "But I don't want to talk about it here. Later...I'll tell you everything...later."

Kinda? I don't like the sound of that, and I'd rather not wait for later, but I keep my mouth shut. I already had it in my head that something was off about their relationship. Guess I'll find out soon.

It looks like everywhere we look, there's Carolyn and when she's not grubbing on someone she watching us. It's starting to make me uncomfortable. I think it's bothering Gabe too.

"Come on baby, let's get outta here," he says.

Gabe turns on the ignition and turns to look at me for a moment. We sit there idling while he closes the convertible top. Then I see it. A somber look comes over Gabriel. I've never seen him look this serious before. Gabe's gaze follows my hands as I nervously dust sand off my shoulder and then my thighs. "You know we have to talk about Carolyn and me. Right?"

"Why do I get the feeling a fuzzy face, like the one I got at Anthony's lake house, would be very helpful right about now? You know, a la Carolyn?"

He backs up out of our parking spot, then glances over at me as we drive off. "I've heard alcohol can help mask pain and uncomfortable feelings," he says, reaching over to turn the radio off. "But I don't think truth should be hidden. Sure, it can sometimes hurt, but you just have to work through it."

"Wow," I say with amazement. "That's deep."

His eyebrows raise. "Does it make sense?"

"Yes, I think so. A truth should be heard and dealt with."

He nods. "Exactly."

"Ella, I've fallen crazy in love with you." He bites down on his lower lip, and his face grows serious as he breathes out a long slow breath. "I want us to last and don't want any secrets ruining things." He looks at me for just a moment then looks back at the road. "How do I start?"

he asks, shaking his head. He pauses. "What you saw out there was Carolyn and me several weeks ago."

I swallow hard. "But I thought you two didn't have that kind of relationship, just friends is what you said."

"We *were* just friends. You believe me, don't you?"

I make no effort to respond, just sit there twirling my ring around my finger.

"Like I said, we were only friends. But then she started acting like we were more than that, referring to the two of us as *we* and *us*, being a bit possessive, and giving me *the look* when I noticed other girls. The last time we went out I had already decided I was going to talk to her about it, let her know I wasn't interested in anything more than being friends."

He waves at the guy behind us to pass, then glances back at me before focusing again on the road. "That same night, out of the blue she came on to me. Surprised the heck out of me. I tried to tell her what I had already planned to say. She blew me off." He turns to look at me. "Not saying it's all her fault, I should have stopped it, after all, I'm the guy who likes to be in control." He turns his focus back on the road. "Screwed this one up big time."

I take a deep breath to brace myself.

"She was all over me, fast. Just like with those guys on the beach." Gabriel's fingers curl into tight fists around the steering wheel, his knuckles turn white, and his voice gets deeper. My eyes dart between his fists and his face, wanting to know for sure that what he said was happening between them wasn't something he wanted.

"I told her I wasn't interested in her as a girlfriend. She just didn't care." He shrugs his shoulder. "She went right on rubbing me *there*,"

he says, looking down at his lap right when he says *there,* and I look
there too.

Suddenly it feels like all the air's been sucked out of the car, and I'm
unable to take a deep breath. He runs a hand through his hair, and I
can tell he's upset too.

"Ella, a girl can't do that to a guy and not get a reaction."

"You mean an erection?"

His eyes meet mine. "Must you?" Then looks back at the road ahead.

"Let's be truthful here, Gabe. Which one was it?"

"Okay, you're right," he says, avoiding my eyes.

"I knew it," I mutter.

He takes a quick look at me then looks away.

"So you had sex with Carolyn?" I hold my breath, bite my lower lip,
hard.

"Not exactly, not all the way. But it was still—"

"Sex?" I ask, eyebrows arched.

I sense his regret when he responds. "Yes...it was."

He squeezes my hand, and I almost pull away, but then I think
about what I just told Anna, about how difficult it must be for a guy to
take control without feeling like a brute or having others see him as
one.

"Sooo," I chew on my bottom lip, "you didn't, uh, actually—"

"No...no, we didn't go all the way. I promise you that."

"Okay, so Carolyn got you going. Did all this, and stuff."

He turns to look at me. I flutter my fingers and say, "you know, with
her hand."

"Trust me, Ella, it was my first time, she didn't have to do much."
He turns and gives me an embarrassed look. "It happened this quick,"
he says, snapping his fingers in the air. "And boy, she was not happy.

It was still my fault, I should've never allowed things to get to the point where I was aroused—"

I slap my hands over my ears, close my eyes. "Okay, la, la, la, la, la, I can't hear you anymore."

He laughs, turns on his right-hand signal, pulls over into a parking lot, and puts the car in neutral. He reaches for my hand and says, "I didn't mean to laugh, but how can you be so cute and silly in the middle of being upset? How do you do that?"

"I don't know what else to do. It hurts Gabe, it hurts a lot, and I want it to go away. Kind of like eating Milk Duds with popcorn, the salty makes the sweet taste better, and maybe silly makes the hurt not feel as bad." I shrug my shoulders. "I don't know."

"So you feel better?"

"No! Not even a little bit better. Maybe I just don't want to hear anymore. One can only take so much truth at one time, well, this kind of truth."

He lifts my chin so that I'm looking right at him, his beautiful eyes narrowed and pleading. "I'm so sorry, Ella. I am really sorry. It was a stupid thing to ask."

I look down at my hands, spin my ring around my finger, and watch the little emerald heart reappear every few turns. We sit there silent.

"What if I told you it was you I was thinking about, and it was you who was turning me on?"

I continue spinning my ring, trying to digest what he just said. I turn in my seat and face him.

"Can you repeat that again for me, please...slowly?"

"Of course, it didn't make sense," he mutters.

He swallows and slowly raises his gaze back to meet mine. "I think I'm about to totally screw this up. You just might tell me we're finished, or slap me, but here goes because I'm hell bent on telling you everything, Ella...everything." He takes a deep breath and lets it swoosh passed his lips. "I had just seen you at The Majestic standing in line with Michael. When you passed by me, I saw your face up close, and I wanted it to be me who was there with you and not Michael. When I got my tickets, I hurried into the lobby hoping I would see you again there. I thought about you throughout the whole movie. So when Carolyn did what she did, I took advantage of the situation, and her too. I just thought of you and only you. And well, you already know the ending."

He watches me as I process what he just said. "You can do that? You can have the girl you're with touching you," I flutter my fingers again, "but think of someone else?"

"Yes...and I thought of you."

"But you weren't with me. So how could it possibly work?"

"Oh, believe me, it worked." He shakes his head. "There I go again," he says his shoulders slumping with a sigh. "I'm sorry I said that. Look, I know it doesn't make sense to you, it was wrong, and it was a shitty thing to do. I disrespected you thinking of you like that, and I took advantage of Carolyn - I used her." He turns to me with a hopeful look. "Ella, I love you so much, can you please forgive me?"

I sit there, watch as his hands reach to hold mine, his thumbs rubbing my palms. I'm hurt, upset and so jealous of what they did together. He didn't mention whether he touched her *there*. Now that would make me crazy jealous knowing he'd given pleasure to someone...to Carolyn. I'm not going to ask. *Don't ask Ella!*

"Uh...did you touch her?" *Oh, shoot! Too late. Better brace myself.*

His body slumps forward as does his head, and he rests it against the steering wheel. I immediately jerk my hand away from him.

"Yes, I did. But—"

"Taking a wild guess here, Gabriel. *But you thought you were touching me*," I say, making sure my tone conveys my displeasure.

"Yes."

"Let me see if I got this straight." I feel the sting of tears I'm trying to hold back. "You can be with *whomever* and do *whatever* you want to them, and all you have to do is think of me, and you're good to go? Sounds like you don't need me, well, not physically. You can just keep me hanging around in your head and summon me up whenever it's convenient. Isn't that peachy!"

"Please don't say it like that. It's you that I want to be with, and not just in that way. It's been only you since that very first day I saw you. You can ask Anthony. I love *you*, Ella."

He turns away, his hand goes up to his face, and he rubs across his eyelids with his thumb and fingers. My tears spill and I quickly wipe them away with my hands.

"I know you're upset with me, Ella. I just hope you can give me some credit for being honest with you."

"I'm sorry, Gabriel, but I don't want to talk about this anymore. Can we just go home, please?"

He puts the car in gear, and his eyes meet mine. I can see he's in pain too. And I wonder if it's because he's hurt me or is it that he might lose me. He turns his blinker on and waits for a car to pass before pulling out onto the highway. That's when I notice the beautiful sunset we're driving toward. Sunsets always make me happy, fill me with hope and awe. Well, not this time.

26

1966 – Ella Galvez

The words we just spoke to each other hurt. But what frightens me is the silence that fills the space between us. We've driven for miles and haven't said a word. Gabriel reaches over and turns the radio on. Guess the silence was weighing heavily on him too.

As if on purpose, KRIO plays all the wrong songs, the ones which used to feel so right. Every other song is one we've shared together. At Fisher's, on our drive to and from Zesto's, to and from the tennis courts, and at his home, including one he just sang to me, *My Girl*. That one really gets me. Gabriel and everything he's meant to me since the first time I saw him is deeply woven into every single one of them.

These songs are so much ours that if we should break up, I imagine the songs themselves would cease to exist. The world would no longer recall their melody, their beat, or their lyrics as if the essence of them was swallowed up into nothingness. Well, maybe that would be my wish. It would be too painful for me to listen to them without Gabriel.

What made him pour out his soul...and crush mine? It's not like I had to know what happened before I came into the picture. Do I even have the right to be upset? We weren't together then, he didn't even know I cared. There's nothing either one of us can do to change the past. What's done is done. But there is something I can do to keep it from tearing us apart. I can accept it. I'm Gabriel's girlfriend now. He loves me and only me.

Gabriel was being so open and honest with me. This is how I respond? I finally get a guy who tells the truth and I blow it. I shouldn't have been so selfish. Why didn't I take my own advice? *It's not like he can slap her, or fling her away, huh? Gotta be a little more understanding for his sake.* That's the advice I gave to Anna at the beach. Surely it applies to me too.

Till There Was You, by the Beatles comes on. It's the song Gabe learned to play just for me. Said he would sing it to me some day. I wonder if that day will ever come. Tears begin to spill down my cheeks, and I wipe my eyes, hoping he doesn't notice. Then, from the corner of my eye, I see him do the same. He's sitting there with his forearm resting along his open window. He takes his hand and wipes his cheek. I feel so horrible. I need to get over this...I must. Deep down inside I believe we belong together. After all, I'm Bella Ella, and he's Gabriel.

He drives into a Gulf station, pulls up next to a pump. He apologizes for having to stop, says he's running low. When the attendant comes up to his window, Gabe asks for a fill-up.

"Excuse me," Gabe says, leaning over to reach the glove box. He pulls his wallet out and pushes on the door to shut it, but it doesn't catch and falls open. I close it for him.

"Thanks," he says.

"You're welcome," I whisper.

We sit there quietly as the gas is pumped and watch the attendant go from window to window, squirting them down and wiping them dry. Then the attendant checks under the hood.

Gabe's slipping his graduation ring past his knuckle, then back again. He does this continuously. I'm twirling my ring round and round. At the exact moment, we turn and look at each other.

"I'm sorry," we both say, our apologies blending together in harmony. I couldn't help but smile, it was funny. Gabe smiled back.

"Baby, I didn't mean to hurt you," Gabriel says.

"I'm the one who needs to be sorry, Gabe, and I am. I shouldn't have reacted the way I did. I truly am sorry. Please forgive me. What happened, happened, and you have no idea how jealous I'm feeling right now, but I saw what the poor guy was going through out there on the beach with Carolyn. I never stopped to think how difficult it must've been for you. Besides, it was before we got together."

He breathes out a long sigh and reaches out to take my hand. "Ella, I love you so much."

"And I love you. Let's start again from this point, Gabriel," I say, holding his hand tighter. "Clean slate." Then I smile at him shyly. "And just so you'll know and never have to wonder, I'm still a virgin, and no I haven't—" I flutter my fingers at him, "anybody, and yes, I get teased about it by you know who."

I can hear the relief in his laugh. "I'll bet Rita and Anna are vicious!" He takes my hand and kisses the fingers I'd just wiggled and winks at me. "You really need to stop fluttering your fingers at me like that."

I squint my eyes at him. "You do have a one-track mind, Gabe."

"You've noticed," he says with a smirk.

"Can I ask you what made you want to spill your guts like that? We weren't even together then."

"*Not* telling you never entered my mind. I knew I had to, and when I saw Rita and Anna talking with Carolyn, I decided it had to be now. I wanted you to hear it from me and not from your buddies."

"Hearing it from them would've been awful!"

"That's what I thought," he says.

"Thanks for being so honest." I pause, study his face a bit. "Can we promise we'll always be as honest and open as you were today, even if the truth hurts? Like you said, we just need to work through it, and I know I can do it because I love you."

Gabriel takes a deep breath.

"I learned a lot about you today," I say. "And you're right, we should never hide the truth."

"That's right, keep no secrets," he says then kisses me.

He puts his car in gear and as we drive off the thought hits me. *Gabriel said no secrets.* I've been holding on to secrets myself. They're on an entirely different level, but all the same, I'm keeping stuff to myself Gabriel really ought to know. Especially if it turns out I'm losing it. He may not want to stick around. Besides, his name is on the back of my *Bella Ella* necklace. *That's the best part of my secret.*

As we pull into my driveway, he turns to me. "Hey, can we talk out back for a bit?"

"Sure, not about, you and uh...I really am okay about it."

"Nope, not that. I wanted to give you part of your gift right now. I just can't wait for you to see it. I'll give you one more tomorrow."

"How sweet, you're anxious."

"Yep." He grabs his shirt and pulls it on, then takes a small gift-wrapped package from the back seat, while I'm putting on my cover-up. Before we reach the swing, he stops.

"This is good right here, under the light." He kisses me sweetly then hands me the gift. "I hope you like it."

I remove the wrapping, then open the long, black box. I can't take my eyes off what's inside. I feel as if I'm looking at something very special to me, something that I'd lost, except I've never owned one. It's a silver charm bracelet with three silver charms: a heart, ballet shoes, and a guitar. My eyes well up with tears.

He smiles. "You get one more charm tomorrow."

I look up at him, give him a kiss. "I love it, Gabriel, I love it so much." I hug him and hold him tight.

"You're crying. What's wrong?"

"I'm okay. Although I'm not too sure you'll be when you hear what I'm about to say."

"Ella, you're scaring me. You said everything was okay with us."

"Everything is, I promise. But I've got a secret to share too. I've had some weird things happen to me the past couple of weeks which I haven't told anyone about. I can't even start to explain them."

His eyes go wide, and his eyebrows arch. "Weird? What kind of weird?" The wrinkles across his forehead tell me he's more than a little bit concerned.

"I'm kinda nervous telling you this." *Nervous? I'm scared to death.* "I guess I should start with the beautiful bracelet you just gave me. I think I've seen it before."

"At Lackner's? I bought it there," he says, nodding.

I laugh. "I wish it were that simple." I pause, look at him and grimace. "Don't say I didn't warn you." I take in a huge breath. "Here goes...I saw a vision of it." I watch, waiting to see how that sinks in.

"What do you mean? As in not *really* there, but you see it anyway?"

"Sort of, it was a bracelet like this, but it had other pieces. Four of them stood out. These three and a little teddy bear with a blue—"

"Stop, don't say it...a blue sapphire heart?"

I smile. "How'd you guess?"

He laughs a short nervous laugh. "It's not a guess. That's the other charm I got you. You're saying you actually saw it?"

"That's what I'm saying. Premonition or what, who knows. That's why I said maybe *you* might not be okay with me. Who wants a wacko for a girlfriend?"

"Ella, you could say you were a vampire, you were going to bite my neck and that whole blood-sucking scenario. I'd still stick around, so tell it to me - all of it."

"It's nowhere as bad as vampires and dodging sunlight. I can promise you that."

He laughs. "It doesn't matter. Like I said, I'll never leave you."

"You say that now, but what I have to tell you is a little freaky. Ready for some crazy?"

He nods. "If the crazy has anything to do with you, I'll take it. Here, give me your hand so I can put your bracelet on you."

The excitement suddenly kicks in, and I'm ready to share it all. "When I was sitting there on the swing, before we met, out of the blue I found a necklace with a pendant in my hand. I've got to show it to you, Gabe. Wait here. You're not going to believe it."

He nods grinning from ear to ear. *He's actually enjoying this.*

I rush toward the house, my heart racing because I'm finally going to share my secret with Gabriel. I open the door slowly. *Thank you, Daddy, you fixed the noisy door.*

I creep up the stairs, skipping the squeaky step, second from the top. I take the necklace out of my jewelry box and peek outside my door - all clear. I quietly head back down skipping the squeaky step again. Once outside, I see Gabe standing there waiting and still smiling. I love how the moonlight casts light on his face.

"Look." I place the necklace in his hand. He moves so he's directly under the light and looks at the front of the medallion, rubs his thumb over the *Bella Ella* inscription. His eyes dart from the medallion to me, then back again. He runs his finger over the words once more.

Gabriel looks puzzled. "Who else calls you Bella Ella?"

"No one. Just you."

He smiles as he reads the inscription. "Here, There and Everywhere. That's really nice."

"Quick, look on the back."

He flips it over, and a grin spreads across his face as he reads it. I watch him mouth the words. He looks at me, then back at the medallion. *"I'll never leave you, Love Gabriel.* Baby, this just gave me chills."

"I know. Isn't it crazy?"

He flips it back to the front. Looks at it again.

I laugh. "I know, it's hard to believe."

"This is beautiful. It has our names on it. And where did you say it came from?"

"Nowhere, Gabriel, it came from nowhere! Just like that, I found myself holding it in my hand. But the weirdest part was what I saw all around me. First, I was jerked off my swing, then there were lights like sparkly fireflies that fizzled away. And then everything around me shimmered."

"It's the first time I noticed him," I say, pointing to the little boy statue. "I'd never seen him before in my life although Mom says it's been here for four years."

Gabe walks over to it and touches it. "Weird, in your own backyard, and you don't remember him."

"It's as if I've been blocking it. Every now and then the little boy gives me shivers, like the upstairs window you asked about."

"So all this shimmering thing is recent, huh?" he asks, still smiling. "Man, oh man, baby, this is so cool – I think."

"Gabe, either I'm having premonitions, or part of me popped in from somewhere in the future. We go on to have a life together, and you buy me this necklace, which is the most romantic thing I've ever seen, and maybe it means we already have a beautiful life ahead of us or had one. Geez, Gabe, I don't know what it means." I laugh.

"This is so crazy, but it's making me feel so good," he says, smiling.

"Imagine how I felt when you called me Bella Ella."

"Yeah, I remember. You even asked me to repeat it. But you were so calm about it," he says, brushing my hair back away from my face.

"Ha! On the inside I was flipping summersaults." I laugh.

"I guess you would be. Baby, this...you and me...it's amazing."

He moves closer, looks at me and smiles, running his hands from my shoulders down my arms lightly brushing my breast with his thumb. It's barely a touch, but I feel it. He pulls his hands away. I guess he did too.

"Sorry, I accidently got fresh with you there."

I giggle. "It's okay."

"Hey, I was just thinking. Maybe, since there's a good possibility we're married out there somewhere in time." He gives me that smile and a couple of eyebrow raises.

I hug him. "You're cracking me up, and here I thought I was going to turn you off. You know, this girl's a freak, I'm outta here."

"Not a chance. I want you to share everything with me. We're in this together, even the necklace says so." He smiles.

I reach my arms around his neck. "You believed me! I was worried."

"You never have to worry, Bella Ella, I'll never leave you."

"You say that all the time."

He kisses the tip of my nose. "I mean it all the time."

"Oh my gosh, the engraving, it says *I'll never leave you.* I just said you say it all the time. Maybe you continue to say it, and it becomes a sentiment between us, so you had it engraved on the medallion."

"Whoa, you just sent chills down my spine!"

"I know, mine too!"

He hugs me tightly. "Wow, this is so cool." He takes my hands in his. "So I guess I'll see you for your birthday lunch and then again later with your other buddies." He kisses me. "Don't forget to put our necklace away."

"*Our* necklace?"

"Yes, our necklace – you Bella Ella, me Gabriel," he grunts.

I laugh. "Thanks for the bracelet. See you tomorrow."

27

1966 – Ella Galvez

Since my early teens, there's been an unspoken rule between Mom and me – no chores on my birthday. Before Mom began offering her dressmaking skills to friends, there wasn't much splurge money around for birthdays and Christmas gifts. I suspected the birthday rule was Mom's way of trying to make my day a little more special. Her dress designing business has grown which means she now has some extra spending money, but the rule remains in place.

Birthday breakfasts are no different than any other day. Dad grabs a few quick bites then rushes off to work. While Mom and I finish our pancakes, I tell her about Gabriel singing *Las Mañanitas,* the Spanish version of *Happy Birthday*, on the phone first thing this morning and how excited I got when he said he and Anthony will be taking me to lunch at The Fort Brown Resaca Club.

I've only been there once when Rita's mom invited Anna and me to dinner with her and Rita to celebrate our graduation. Before going into the restaurant, we walked along the winding paths. It was like a tropical paradise with palm trees towering over us, waterfalls, and sparkling streams. Mrs. Perkins had us pose for pictures on a small bridge which was surrounded by beautiful tropical plants and flowers.

The restaurant was elegant, and we sat at a table with a view of Horseshoe Lake. During dinner, Anna and I elbowed each other every time we saw someone walk in wearing something voguish. But the best memory I have was observing the stark difference between the rude, unrefined Rita that Anna and I know and the polite and dignified one sitting right in front of us next to the prim and proper Mrs. Perkins. Their British accents added to the elegance. Mrs. Perkins would surely faint if she heard her lovely daughter's colorful language. Later, when we mentioned our observation to Rita, she made us laugh when she gave us a tight little smile, tilted an invisible tea cup to her lips while holding her little pinky up in the air. "I know, I know, uppity can be soooo boring," she said.

Mom gets up to serve herself another cup of coffee and returns with a gift covered in the same giftwrap as the wristwatch she and Dad gave me first thing this morning.

"Here's something from Nana," she says, handing it to me. "It was so sweet of Nana to ask Mr. Garcia to get you something special while on his most recent visit to Greece. He goes there often. She had him send it directly to me so it would be here in time for your birthday."

Nana's gift is a beautiful silk scarf. I've never owned a silk scarf. Heck, I've never owned a silk anything. Nana has always been in my life. She helped care for me since the day I was born. Even when I was a teen, she'd often be here helping Mom around the house, keeping her company and spending time with me like any grandmother would, except we aren't related.

Her name is Estella Garcia, but I call her Nana, and she filled the role of grandma in my life. Nana couldn't have loved me more if I'd been her own flesh and blood. I loved her just as much. I remember how happy she'd get when strangers would say I favored her. She never told them we weren't related. She would just smile and say thank you. She's not well now and is in the care of her relatives. I miss her.

Nana's son, Mr. Garcia, was also special to me. He was very kind and loving to Nana, Mom and me. I would see him often when I was younger. Around the time of my ninth birthday, he stopped showing up at Nana's house during my visits there. He'd be there every now and then. One day he said he'd be leaving the country and I never saw him again. When I asked Mom why we didn't visit him anymore, she said his business had flourished and required him to travel for months at a time.

I really missed his visits, the stories he'd read to me and the time spent at Ringgold Park. He seemed to love me as much as Nana did. Mom would always tell me we shouldn't share with Dad how much time Mr. Garcia spent with me because it would make Dad sad since he wasn't able to do the same, and it wouldn't be nice to hurt his feelings. So I didn't say a word - not about the time we spent together, nor the gifts, and especially not how much fun he was to be with.

When we're done with breakfast, Mom goes to the sink to get started on the dishes. I set mine down on the counter and watch her slip her slender petite hands into rubber gloves.

"Mom, let me help you with the dishes."

She tilt's her head in my direction and looks at me past her long dark eyelashes. "I've got this all under control, birthday girl," she says as she swirls a soapy dishcloth across the plate's surface.

I peck her cheek with a kiss. "I figured, but thought I'd offer anyway."

I pour myself another glass of juice and head outside to sit under the shade of the arbor swing. As I walk toward the swing, I notice the little boy statue's toppled over. I gasp when I realize his head's been broken off. I feel the blood drain from my face, and I turn away as if I'd witnessed a gory crime scene. They're just lying there, the boy and his head. No blood, no gore, but the concrete carnage is still kinda creepy. I make myself look back, and when I do, I find the little boy is standing upright, and his head is propped on his shoulders where it belongs.

"Ella, what's wrong?" Mom asks, poking her head out the door.

"What? Uh...nothing, why?"

"You yelled out!"

"Oh, I did. I'm sorry, uh...I saw a lizard, two of them. Freaked me out! But I'm okay now. Lizards and me just don't get along," I say with a shrug.

"You look like you've seen a ghost, Ella. And all because of two little lizards?" Mom laughs. "I'm sorry, I know it's not funny, I react the same way with spiders," she says then closes the screen door.

She heard me scream? I didn't even hear *me* scream, how's that possible? Oh wait, I forget, things around me don't happen because they're possible, they happen in spite of being impossible. At least now I can be glad that I'll be able to share it with Gabe and not feel so alone in my own distorted world.

Speaking of...I need to let him know what I just saw, gotta keep him up to date. Up to date? Heck, I still haven't shared all the other stuff that's happened. The weightlessness, the shimmering curtain, nor the cue ball in Rita's car. Wait till he hears about the fortune teller living in my head! *Oh boy.*

I dial his number and cross my fingers. Just hope Gabe can handle all this weirdness. Having him to talk to about it is the only thing that's going to keep me sane.

"Hi, Gabriel. Can you talk?"

"Uh-oh, why are you whispering, Ella?" He sounds a little concerned.

"I wanted to share what I just saw," I say as I close the door. "Are you really sure you want to hear some more? It was so weird."

"Yes, really. Come on, tell me."

So I tell him what just happened with the boy statue and I wait for his response.

"Wow, that's weird."

"Told ya. But I don't even know if it's already happened or if it's gonna happen. Wait, it's not broken now. So does it mean it's going to break later on?

"Okay, we really need to talk about this. How about when we're done with lunch after Anthony leaves. You've got some really crazy stuff going on, and I want to help."

"Thing is, Gabe, you haven't heard the half of it. You may not want—"

"Ella, you're not scaring me off. You're stuck with me, I'm not gonna go away."

I laugh. "Okay, okay. I hear ya. Guess, I'll see you guys in a bit."

"Yes, we'll pick you up around noonish. See ya."

Mom took off to do some last-minute shopping with Aunt Tilly so she's not around to help me decide what I should wear. I'm torn between two dresses. One is a summery yellow fitted dress which is sleeveless and has a boat collar. The other is a spaghetti strap dress in cornflower blue that has a matching short-sleeved bolero. I go with the blue one, but without the bolero. I lay out my *Que Sera, Sera* necklace and pearl stud earrings to wear with it. I'm also wearing my new charm bracelet, but I'll have to ask Gabriel to help me with it when he gets here. Putting on a bracelet by myself is next to impossible. I place it next to my purse, so I won't forget it.

I decide to polish my toenails. I love it when my hands and feet match. Just wish I hadn't waited so long. Now I'll have to wait to put on my stockings. I don't want to smear them. I finish getting dressed and sit there fanning my feet with my hands to hurry up the process.

Cooper walks in and stands there wagging his tail looking up at me. Figure he needs a bathroom break. The guys will be here soon, but I've got time to go out there with him. I grab my hairbrush and head downstairs with him and wait on the swing brushing my hair. Once I notice Cooper's curled up in the shade and obviously done, I head inside with Cooper at my heels. Cooper jumps on my bed and curls himself up for a nap. When I realize I left my brush on the swing, I head back outside. As I walk across the lawn, I admire my freshly manicured fingernails, courtesy of mom. No smudges when she does it for me.

Movement from behind the tree distracts me, and my gaze moves to the flowers that encircle the large tree trunk. I see men's rugged black shoes come out from behind it, scuffed and dirty. My eyes move up to old faded jeans. Then I see hands, one gloved, the other not. My breath catches in my throat when the realization of what I've just seen kicks in. Shock gives way to fear, and that's when I hear the loud sound of my heart beating in my ears.

This can't be happening!

I scream and then turn to run. He puts a hand around my waist and pulls me in. His gloved hand goes to the side of my head and shoves me down. I twist my body and hold my hands out as I watch the ground coming toward me. My knee, wrist and then the side of my head feel the brunt of my fall. When he flips me around and pins me down on my back, panic shoots right through me. I yell out as loud as I can then feel his bare hand hit across my face jerking my head to the right.

Before the pain from that blow has a chance to subside, I feel the sting of his fingernails scratching deep into my breast as he yanks the front of my dress down ripping it and snapping the straps off. When he leans into me, I'm hit with the smell of sweat and stale cigarette smoke. It almost masks the scent of Aramis cologne, but it's there, and the blend of all of it sickens me.

I scream out again, but this time his gloved hand smashes into my cheek and mouth. It muffles my cry for help and forces my teeth down on my lower lip; I can taste the blood. His other hand holds my hands above my head. For a moment, nothing but fear exists.

But then I think of Gabriel. The smile I see snaps me back to the moment...the moment when I know I must fight back with all I've got. I manage to slip a hand away, and I bang my fist as hard as I can against his chest. His hand over my mouth slips, and I cry out Gabriel's name. He grunts a curse at me and flips me over again.

My face hits dirt and grass, and his body crushes into me as he straddles me. His fingernails scratch into my backside as he yanks down on my panties. He continues pulling on them working them further and further down my legs, while I repeatedly thrust my legs back behind him. As hard as I try, the heels of my feet don't reach him, and I wish I could just die, right here, right now. My muffled cry for help goes unheard.

He grabs me and rolls me over face up again. That's when I see his grotesquely stretched out eyes looking at me through a beige silk stocking, I shut mine tightly, wanting desperately to push the image out of my mind. With his gloved hand once more firmly placed over my face, my desperate cries are trapped. Barely able to breathe, I bite into his hand but can't get past the thick leather. I continue grabbing at his wrist, but nothing I do can push his gloved hand away.

Now the weight of his body holds me down, and I realize I'm helpless. My screams are muffled. And as loud as they are no one can hear them. They have nowhere to go.

He's fumbling with something - his pants!

Oh God, this is really happening!

My mind turns to everyone I love wanting to hold some warmth and goodness close to me, wanting an assurance it will all be okay. The bells of a nearby church begin to ring signaling the faithful to pray. *The bells sound at noon! Gabriel, where are you?*

That expectation quickly vanishes when he yanks down on the front of my panties. He pulls on them repeatedly. When I feel him, his rough hand touching me, invading me, my screams turn into sobs, but their sound is trapped against the glove pressed hard over my mouth again.

With his head against mine, I hear a whispered growl. "You're mine." Then I feel agonizing pain, he's tearing me apart! I scream out a muffled plea, begging him to stop. He grunts loudly as he thrusts himself inside me, and then again. With each thrust his hand shifts and each time it does, I'm able to breathe in quick inhalations of air. I cry out with everything I've got in me, but all my screams do, is scrape the back of my throat. I desperately keep pulling on his wrist below his glove. I can't breathe!

My eyes open when I hear a car coming up our driveway. *Gabriel's here!*

The man crushing the life out of me looks over his shoulder and thrusts himself into me again, hard! My fingernails finally catch his watch, and I yank on it with all my might. When it flies off his wrist, he turns in the direction that it went, and his gloved hand slips off my face.

A car door slams and with the first breath of unobstructed air, I scream out. "Gabriel!"

Once again, his nails scratch against my chest, and as my head is jerked up, I feel a sting along the back of my neck. He presses a hand down against my chest, and with nimble agility, he pushes himself off, and he's gone.

Ignoring the pain, I swing a bent leg over my body to roll my hips forward, then extend my arm to reach for a handful of grass to help pull me onto my side so I can hide my bared breasts, my body, but I can't, don't have the strength. The beat of my heart quickens knowing Gabriel is about to find me like this. That very thought saddens me; I feel my soul die a little.

"Gabriel," I whisper into the grass beneath my face.

28

1966 – Ella Galvez

I lay here looking toward the side of our house knowing I'll see either Gabriel or Anthony coming around that corner any moment. But a moment feels like forever. "Gabriel," I whisper when he turns the corner. My heart breaks when I see the pain in his face when he finds me laying here. "Oh, Jesus! Ella! No, noooo."

I watch through tears as he hurries toward me unbuttoning his shirt. He gently drapes it over me as he kneels close by my side. He bends down low, so he can look directly at me. "I'm here, baby. I'm right here," he says, crying. My lip quivers as I try to hold back the tears and suppress a sob.

He lifts a few strands of hair away from my face, carefully tucking them behind my ear. "My poor baby," he says, brushing blades of grass off my cheek. He pulls a handkerchief out of his pocket, and I see a faint smile as he gently dabs my lips. "I'm going to take care of you, it's going to be okay."

A car door slams. "Anthony," Gabriel says then yells out to him, letting him know we're here. He takes his eyes off me for a moment to look around. Then yells out to Anthony again then turns back to me. "Is your mom inside?"

I shake my head. And then I begin to cry when I think about what it will do to Mom when she finds out what happened to me.

"I'm sorry I wasn't here to protect you, Ella," he says through a sob. "But I'm here now. He wipes away my tears and then his. "Anthony can call for an ambulance," Gabriel says, looking at me, searching my eyes.

I shake my head desperately, as I grab on to Gabriel's hand. I don't want to go to the hospital. I'm too ashamed. I can't let anyone else see me like this. They'll ask me to tell them things that I just can't repeat...things I want to forget. "No." I shake my head again.

"My God!" Anthony says when he sees me. "What did he do? I'll call for an ambulance!"

"No," Gabe says, "we'll take her. Check to see if Mrs. Galvez is inside. If she's not, call your dad and have him get ahold of Ella's dad. Let him know we're taking her to the hospital."

I begin to cry again at the thought of having to go to the hospital. I can hear Gabriel trying to hold in his sobs. It causes his chest to jump. All I hear is the short, staggered breaths that come with each one. It hurts so much to know he's holding the hurt inside, trying so hard to be strong for me.

He takes one long breath through his nostrils. "Ella," he says as he exhales the breath he'd just taken, "are you hurting anywhere?" I shake my head although I am. "Let me try to sit you up so I can carry you to my car." Then he looks at me, closely. "Do you think we can do this without hurting you?"

Although I'm not sure, I nod.

"If you feel any pain at all, we'll stop. Okay? I just want to make sure we can do this, if not we'll call for an ambulance."

"No." I jerk my hand up to his chest and shake my head then look at him and plead. "Please, no ambulance," I say in a small raspy voice I'm unable to recognize, but I know it's mine because it hurt to speak those few words. "I can't," I say, shaking my head again.

"Okay, no ambulance. Then let's try to sit you up." He squats beside me. "I'm going to lift you just until you're sitting up. Are you ready?"

I nod, but I'm afraid my scrunched-up face tells him otherwise.

"Don't worry, we'll do it slow and easy. Shake your head if you need me to stop."

When he sees me nod again, he asks, "Can you put your arms around my neck?"

I nod and do as he says. Scooting an arm beneath my back, he lifts me so I'm sitting up. As if it wasn't enough that my world has already tilted on its axis, something rocks the earth beneath me. I gasp and the hair on my neck prickles causing my shoulders to shudder.

"Sorry, where did it hurt?"

I point. "Look!" I whisper.

Gabriel's gaze follows my arm to where I'm pointing, and when he sees the little boy statue laying on the ground with his head lobbed off, his hazel eyes grow wide. He stares at it for a moment. "It's just like you described."

I nod as new tears pour out as if the flood gates had just been opened. With his hand on my chin, he gently turns my face away from the same creepy scene I witnessed in a vision a couple of hours ago. My head turns, but I keep my gaze on the broken little boy until he's no longer in view.

"Ella, push it out of your mind. I'm going to take care of you." He moves himself closer and holds me as I sit there crying. I try to will my mind to make it all go away, the image of the little boy, the pain and the shame I'm feeling. "It's going to be okay, baby." He reassures me with a squeeze of his hand.

Anthony comes rushing up to us.

"Mrs. Galvez isn't home, but talked to my dad," he says, sounding breathless. "He's doing everything necessary. They'll send officers to the hospital to get a statement from Ella, and here to secure the scene."

Gabe looks up at him, nods his head. "Thanks."

Anthony stoops down beside me. "Oh, kiddo, I just can't—"Anthony heaves two deep breaths of air and sobs into his hands. It breaks my heart to seem him so broken.

"I'm okay," I whisper. "Don't cry."

Gabe reaches out to him, placing a hand on Anthony's shoulder. "Ella's gonna be fine buddy. We're gonna take care of her."

"I'm sorry," he says through ragged breaths.

Gabe rubs his hand across his eyes and cheeks. "We need to get Ella to the hospital."

Anthony runs his sleeve across his face, and then I see his puzzled look as he focuses at something behind me. He squints at it. "I think I've found some evidence." He takes a dishcloth hanging on the clothesline and then walks toward the rose garden. "It's a man's gold watch," he says.

He uses the cloth to lift the watch off a thorny branch, shows it to Gabriel then wraps it up in the towel and sticks it in his pocket.

Gabe gives him a nod, then places his hands beneath my arms. "I'm gonna pull you up with me."

Once we're standing, Gabe holds me there giving me a chance to adjust my body. Then he looks at me. "Any dizziness?" I shake my head.

"Okay, I'm going to lift you up and carry you to the car." He lifts me up into his arms and smiles at me. "Good girl. I'm glad I brought my dad's Lincoln. With the top down, it'll be easy to get you into the car. You and I can sit in the backseat. Anthony, you'll have to drive."

Once I'm settled in the back seat, Gabe climbs in and sits beside me. He drapes his arm along my shoulder, and I snuggle into him. We wait there while Anthony moves his truck, so we can back out. Then it starts. My head begins to explode with questions. How could I let this happen? Where was he? Why didn't I see him? As I start recalling what I've just been through, the chills begin to weave their way through my entire body. How can I ever forget what he did? Then the most painful question of all enters my mind. How can Gabe possibly love me now?

We drive off, and the thoughts swimming in my head cause the chills to turn into shivers, and my body trembles. I press my face against Gabe's chest breathing in the clean scent of Ivory soap and a hint of patchouli. Deep inhalations of his fragrance calm my heart, but they don't stop the tears from flowing.

Gabriel notices the new tears and wipes them from my cheeks. He leans in closer and in a low voice begins singing *Till There Was You*, the song he said he learned just for me. He sings it so sweetly in my ear. My thoughts turn to us, how we met, how we so easily fell in love. The memory of all we've shared soothes me, and I smile through the tears up at Gabe. He winks at me as if nothing has changed.

As I turn my head my neck rubs against Gabe's arm. I feel a sting along the back of my neck and along one side. That's when I realize my necklace is missing.

"It's gone," I say, touching my fingers to my collarbone. "My necklace."

"Your *Que Sera, Sera* necklace?"

I nod.

"Don't worry, tomorrow I'll come and look for it in the grass. I'll bet it's there." Gabe lightly strokes my arm. It's calming, my eyelids flutter before finally closing, and I sink further into his warmth.

As I'm being wheeled into one of the ER examination rooms, I begin to shiver, I rub my hands briskly along my arms. It's freezing in here.

"Can you please bring her a blanket?" Gabe asks the attendant. "And can we stay with her at least until a family member arrives?"

"You can, but once someone comes to examine her, you'll have to leave," he explains as he takes a flannel blanket and drapes it around my shoulders.

From the examination room, I hear Dad's voice. "Anthony, where's Ella?"

I run my hands across my face to wipe away any sign of tears, any sign of anything. I breathe in deeply and paste a smile on my face.

"Right in there, sir, we just got here. Gabe's with her now."

"Daddy," I whisper.

He leans into me and kisses my head. "Oh, my little girl, what has he done to you?"

He's stoops over and cries on my shoulder. I cry with him.

"I'm alright," I say, looking up at him. "Just a small bump on my head." I smile through my tears, point to the side of my head so he can see, it really is nothing at all.

He kisses my forehead. "Your mother is on her way."

"Excuse me, Mr. Galvez, we need you to go to the front desk and provide information to administration. Go straight down this hall, you'll see the sign," a nurse tells him. He looks at Anthony and Gabriel. "Please, I need both of you to stay here with her." They nod.

Gabe comes back to my side and touches my shoulder, lightly. I look up at him and smile. I can do this. I must do this. I can't bear to watch my dad look so sad.

Anthony leans over and kisses my forehead, stoops down at my side and takes my hand. "Ella, I know you. You *are* strong. Heck, you were often stronger than some of the guys growing up. You were one tough little tomboy." A big smile spreads across his face. "But I've also seen you as dainty, delicate, and as fragile as the ballerina spinning around in your jewelry box."

I nod and smile.

I hear the tippy tap of high heels coming down the hall. "Can someone please tell me where Ella Galvez is? Where is she?" I turn toward the direction of Mom's voice. She begins to sob when she sees me.

Be strong Ella, be strong.

I want to be strong for Mom especially. She always seems so fragile to me. But I'm also afraid if I let myself fall apart, I won't be able to put *me* back together again. So I *must* be strong.

Mom walks in with outstretched arms, sobbing. "My baby," she cries.

"I'm okay, Mom, really," I whisper.

Mom hugs me lightly. "Are you in pain?"

I shake my head.

"Mijita, I'm so sorry I wasn't there," she says through tears, "but thank God Anthony and Gabriel showed up." She turns around and hugs them both. "Thank you so much for being there. You two are a God send."

Dad returns, extends his hand to Gabe then pulls him in to wrap an arm around his back. "Gabriel, I can't thank you enough for getting to Ella when you did." He reaches an arm around Anthony. "You too, son."

Dad takes Mom in his arms. She breaks down in his embrace.

After a while, a doctor and a nurse come in. Dad and Anthony walk toward the door. Gabriel brushes his hand across my shoulder as he joins them. I smile at the nurse. There's something comforting about nurses. I think it's the hat. Nuns and nurses have always made me feel cared for as a child growing up. Here at Mercy Hospital you get to see both.

The nurse smiles at me, the doctor nods and turns to speak to mom who is dabbing her face with dad's handkerchief. I sit here spinning the ring on my finger, watching the little emerald colored heart hide beneath my finger and then reappear again.

When the nurse pulls the curtains around us, Mom turns to me and says she'll be here with me through the exam. I'm thankful for that. First, the nurse tends to the scrape on the side of my face which probably looked like it needed cleaning. It hurts to the touch, and it stings when she dabs on it to clean it. After taking care of everything that needed to be attended to, they have me stand while they visually scan my body. *Can this ordeal get any more embarrassing?*

As the doctor begins to describe the first injury, the nurse writes it down. My eyes move to the furthest corner of the room, and my gaze is fixed there. As the doctor mentions each one, in my mind I see what was happening while the wound was inflicted. They make note of bumps, bruises and scratches I didn't even know I had.

My ordeal *does* get more embarrassing. I lay back on the table for my examination, and the nurse places my feet in the stirrups. I take a deep breath knowing what's about to happen—I'm going to be violated again. But this time my mother is standing there holding my hand and allowing the doctor to do it.

The doctor sits there between my legs already too close for my comfort, yet he asks me to please scoot myself closer to him. I lay there staring up at the ceiling and tears begin to run down the side of my face. I don't want to move closer. I want to sit up and get off. I turn and look at Mom. "Do I have to?"

She nods, dabbing at my tears with Dad's handkerchief. "It will be over soon," she says.

I look back up at the ceiling, grab hold of the edge of the pad I'm lying on, lift my bottom up and scoot further down.

"Very good," he says, placing his hands on the insides of my knees. He presses against them to spread my thighs apart, while I attempt to press them together. It's like an obscene version of arm wrestling, and I'm winning.

"I'm sorry Miss Galvez. I need you to relax and spread your legs a little further. Can you do that for me?"

Well, it looks like I'm gonna have to concede. I take a deep breath and slowly breathe out as I allow my knees to lay flat just as I do on my mat at home during my floor exercises. With my eyes closed, I listen to Beethoven's Moonlight Sonata playing in my head and count imaginary pliés, visualizing myself performing each one slowly and in perfect form. No one is here but me, I'm alone in my head, if only for just a little while.

I'm extremely tender, and his intrusion into my body hurts, but the pain isn't the worst part. The worst is the shame of the most private part of me being on display. It feels like I'm being violated all over again. Except this time, I don't scream. I don't even whimper. Mom's holding my hand and I make a conscious effort not to squeeze back so she won't know I'm hurting. Instead, I clench my teeth and grab onto the examination table with my other hand hidden under the sheet they've covered me with.

When it's done, the doctor extends his hand to help me sit up. I say thank you, and he leaves the room without me ever making eye contact with him. He's already gotten way too personal with me, but to allow him to gaze into my soul would be too much. The nurse lets me know I'll be taken for x-rays shortly.

When Gabriel returns, he comes up to me and kisses me on the cheek. "We prayed for you. I hope it helped."

I nod at Gabriel, recalling how I was able to remove myself from the situation for the most part. I smile at him, and it's a genuine smile. I know I can get through this, because of Gabriel and his God.

29

1966 – The Blue Cap Guy

I went to great lengths to find out when my sweet Ella's birthday was. Paid a friend who knows someone who works in vital statistics for the city. I got my money's worth. I saw her date of birth, and I couldn't believe my eyes. It was only two days away, and I knew exactly what my gift to Eleanor Galvez was going to be. That's what the copy of her birth certificate shows is her legal name, Ella's her nickname. I like it much better – sounds so innocent. My innocent Ella.

It's been over a week since we were together on her birthday. Making love to her was going to be my special birthday gift to her. It didn't go too well. She jerked away, and I had to shove her to the ground. I know it hurt, but she really needed to learn her lesson. I've seen the change in her attitude, swooning all over *Pretty Boy* just because he's got money. I know that's why she wants him. This guy is really rolling in the dough. I've followed him, seen his house. She better not be expecting roses and diamonds from me when I finally make her my girl.

Once I had her down, I was all over her. I held her close, and I was overcome by the scent of her hair. She smelled delicious. Oh, how I wanted to kiss her, stake my claim on those sweet lips and make her forget those kisses left behind by Pretty Boy. But I couldn't. Damn stocking over my head kinda got in the way.

Something I didn't expect was the look on Ella's face when her eyes finally met mine for the first time as we laid there on the ground about to make love. It was a look of disgust. It was because she couldn't see the real me. She couldn't gaze into my eyes the way lovers do. That's when I got really pissed. When Pretty Boy kissed her, they gazed into each other's eyes, *that's* why she let him kiss her the way he did. It's also when I decided Ella had to be taught a good lesson. Things didn't turn out so nice for my little girl.

I let my body press heavily on her, and my aggression heightened my pleasure. She begged me to let her go, but in my mind, she really didn't try very hard. And the way she trembled under my touch, I knew she was enjoying it. Soon after, I heard the church bells ringing and I told myself, as soon as my body presses into hers, it will be heaven. And it *was*, but not for long. I heard a car come up the driveway, but I wasn't done yet. I wanted more, I needed more, and I kept on.

She managed to grab my watch, and it flew into some rose bushes. When the car door slammed I lost the pressure of my glove on her face and Ella was able to call out. "Gabriel," she said. *His name is Gabriel. Damn you, Gabriel!*

Moments later I was back upstairs. I just sat here, didn't dare look out. Didn't want to get caught. I'm glad I took something from Ella. Something she touched every day, something she wore around her precious neck. Ella and I will forever be linked because of it. Every time I see it I'll think of her. That should be enough for me, but it isn't. I need to finish what I started, I *need to go back for more.*

I haven't seen my girl since making love to her on her birthday. I'm guessing Gabriel won't be coming back. She's used goods now but not to me.

As I enter my observatory and head toward the window, I hear a truck come up Ella's driveway. I pull the curtain away slightly, and I see him get out of his truck, and he's smiling. "Dammit, it's Gabriel. He's back!"

30

1966 – Ella Galvez

My eyes open at the sound of little taps on my door. The left corner of my mouth lifts into a half-smile when I see Gabriel poking his face into my room. He walks in holding a bouquet of flowers, twine wrapped around it in a tight little bow, and the smile on his face is the one I fell in love with.

"Hi," I say pausing to let the sweetness of this moment sink in. "I was just sitting here talking to Mom. I must've dozed off." I sit up and prop myself against my pillows.

"Yeah, she mentioned you fell asleep mid-sentence, just after you said *I wish he were here*." He holds out the bouquet of flowers. "Well, here I am."

"Thanks." I take them and slowly turn them around in my hands, examine them carefully. I smile. "Hmm...they look kinda familiar."

He smirks. "Yeah, they used to be part of our landscaping."

"They're beautiful, and who'd you steal the twine from?"

"You've pegged me for a little thief now, haven't you?" he says with a chuckle.

I smile. "Yep." I lay the flowers on my bedside table.

"I remember asking for you," I say, sounding a little bit groggy. "I guess that's when I dozed off. I'm so glad you're here, it's been way too long. I've missed your face."

He smiles. "Missed you too," he says and places a kiss on my forehead. "How do you feel?"

"Fragile...emotionally and mentally. If I were to step outside, a gentle breeze could easily scatter all of that's left of me." My hands go to my face when I recall the dark circles under my eyes. I noticed them in the mirror this morning when I washed my face. They're from laying wide awake for a good part of the night. The alternative is to close my eyes and fall into a dark dream that I can't seem to escape, but when I do, I find myself sitting on my bed sobbing. Or I can take a Valium and end up moving as slow as a slug the following morning. I chose door number one.

"Oh my gosh, Gabe, I look horrible."

He lifts my fingers away from my eyes with his. "Not to me. But are you sure you're up for a visit? I can come back later."

"No, no, I want you to stay." I run my fingers under my eyes knowing darn well I can't wipe the unsightly rings away. "Thoughts of you are the only things that have been holding me together, also your calls to tuck me in at night. Having you here with me is exactly what I need. I'm sure of it."

He sighs. "Well, then I'm glad I came. Can you imagine how happy I was when your mom called to say I could come see you? Especially since Anthony and I had already been told we would have to wait at least a month. Anthony called me as soon as he heard from your mom. He should be coming around soon."

"I'm glad she did, I needed to see you. Things have been rough off and on, but I've been telling myself our love is bigger than any of the *demons* lurking around in my head." A tear spills over onto my cheek.

"Ella, those demons don't have a chance," he says, taking a seat beside me on the bed. He gently wipes the tear away with his thumb then presses it to his lips and kisses my tear away. And just as heartwarming is the smile he gives me when he sees mine.

"Well," Gabe says, "you've definitely made *me* feel better already. But I'm sorry it's been tough for you," he says, stroking my cheek.

"Physically, I feel okay. Mentally, it comes and goes. The doctor gave me Valium to help me sleep. I never take naps, but I did just now. I dreamed of us."

"Oh, yeah? Let's hear it," he says then gets up to place a chair by my bed, so he can sit facing me.

"We were at the beach laying on the sand, side by side, looking at the sky above us. We could hear the gentle rhythmic sound of the surf, its calming inhale and exhale. And when we spoke, our voices, our words, seemed to mimic its rhythm. The water would come, play at our feet, we'd say a few words as the water rushed back out to sea. And as the water returned, we'd share a few more. This continued throughout our conversation."

"You painted such an awesome picture. What did we talk about?"

"Well, I asked, *am I going to be okay*? It took three waves coming in and going out for me to say it. My words were broken up into *Am I – going to be – okay?* Matching the rhythm of the three waves. You said *God knows your needs, let it go*. And again, it took the pace of three waves for you to say *God knows – your needs – let it go.* It was lulling."

"Wow!" he says eyes wide.

"It was just a dream."

"A beautiful one. I think we need to pay attention to everything happening around you a little closer. You know, all the visions, signs, and dreams. And yes, God *does* know your needs."

A smirky smile appears as he looks around my room. "Hey, I'm in your bedroom. It's pink."

He can be such a kid, and that makes me smile. He gets up and walks up to my bookcase and studies each shelf. "It's exactly as Anthony described." He picks up a baseball, tosses it up, catches it, and puts it back. "Can't wait to play ball with you, Lucy," he says over his shoulder. I laugh softly.

He runs his finger along the side of one of my satin ballet shoes and smiles. "I remember the day I saw you dance."

Gabe notices a picture of Paul McCartney on my wall which he couldn't have seen when he walked in. He points a sideways thumb at it. "Cute Paul?" Gabe asks in a whisper.

"Yes," I whisper back then giggle. A brightness seems to wash over Gabriel's face, and his eyes glisten as he watches me respond to his teasing.

"I love seeing you happy, Ella."

The look in his eyes tells me he's equally affected by this moment. He made me laugh for the first time in almost a month. I've felt so much sadness, I wondered if I could feel like this again. I take a long breath and savor the warmth that his being here is causing in me. The look in his eyes tells me he's happy being here too.

He notices my jewelry box and lingers there, rubbing his fingers along the length of it.

"You can open it," I say.

He does. "Hey, the little ballerina Anthony was talking about at the hospital, right?"

I'm totally enjoying his expressions as he learns a little bit about me. There's so much we haven't shared about each other.

"She *is* as delicate as you, Ella. That's how Anthony described her."

I giggle. "Tell me you jocks didn't sit on the stadium bleachers talking about a little ballerina that twirls to *Dance of the Sugarplum Fairy*."

He turns grinning ear to ear. "Yep, we did in fact, do *exactly* that. And you're gonna love this, we made a pinky promise not to tell anyone. Dang, I guess I just broke that promise," he laughs. "You know I'm kidding about the pinky promise, right? We jocks wouldn't be caught dead doing girlie stuff like that." He laughs again.

I laugh too, and it feels good, and I end it with a sigh. I think it's the first time laughter made me sigh so deeply, it's just that it felt so good, so warm inside. I want to remember the feeling it left me with. It may sound like a silly thing to say about a laugh, but it's not. Not really. We seem to go about our life taking so much for granted. Laughing hasn't come easy lately, and smiles don't appear as often as they used to either. I value both now more than I ever have in my life.

Gabe turns his interest back to my jewelry box and bends over to look inside. Picks up *our* necklace and checks it out up close. He's only seen it at night under the porch light.

"Wow, this is really nice." He looks over at me. "Why don't I take it with me? I'll get the clasp fixed for you."

"I would love that." I lean over and take an envelope from the drawer. "Here, put it in here, so it will be safe."

He takes the envelope and holds it up to his nose. "Smells nice," he says, dropping the necklace carefully inside.

"*Youth Dew,*" I say.

"Huh?"

"The fragrance you just sniffed, it's called, *Youth Dew.*"

He moistens it with his tongue, seals it and folds it up. Then he smiles as he lifts it to his nose again before putting it in his pocket.

When Gabe comes back to sit by me, he sees *Blue* lying there next to me. "Hey, I didn't notice this little guy." He picks Blue up and studies his little face. This makes me smile. But when I see him give my little Blue a kiss, it completely melts my heart.

"I already love this guy," he says.

We hear Anthony's truck drive up, and then his footsteps bounding up the stairs. He walks in smiling and hands me some grape taffy.

"Taffy! Thank you, Anthony" I turn to Gabe. "My favorite, well, this and caramels. Anthony's favorite is Junior Mints, what's yours?"

Gabe smirks. "Would you believe grape taffy and caramels?" He then looks at Anthony, who nods in agreement.

"Neato, just like me. Learned something new about you,"

"Hey, are you doing okay, kiddo?" Anthony asks, his eyes begining to glisten. "Oh dang, I'd planned not to get all emotional."

"Hey, join the club, buddy," Gabe says, patting his back.

"Sorry about the scare I gave you guys," I say.

Emotions kick in without warning, and I can't hold back my tears. "I'm sorry, just seeing you two together reminded me of what might've happened if you two hadn't gotten there when you did. I remember hearing the church bells ringing at noon and hoping you'd be there soon. But then I was so embarrassed, you found me in such a horrible state." I look down at my hands.

Gabe sits beside me on the bed. "There's nothing to be embarrassed about. When we found you, it was like a switch was flipped and we did what had to be done." Then he goes silent. He looks at me, tears begin to pool in his eyes, and he breathes in a couple of sniffles. "I don't think I've ever felt so much pain. It felt like a dagger struck me deep inside." Gabriel's face scrunches up. It makes me sad that he's still having to deal with the pain of that day. "I'm sorry," he says, choking on his words trying hard not to cry. But he does. His hands go to his face, and I hear a deep sob. When I reach my arm out to him, he leans in close and lets me comfort him.

"I'm so sorry." He pauses, shakes his head. "I wanted to be strong, but just now so much flashed through my mind."

I look at Anthony and he's wiping away new tears from his eyes. *Being strong just isn't gonna happen here today, but that's okay.*

I reach for a tissue, wipe my eyes and blow my nose. "Guys," I say, looking at Gabriel and then at Anthony, "I love you so much, and I get it, you want to be strong for me, but I say we're allowed to cry, let whatever is hurting out. One thing I learned from Gabriel is we need to accept the truth and deal with it whether we like it or not. Healing starts with accepting the truth."

The day following my rape, what I wanted to do was to push the painful thoughts aside, place them where I'd never be able to find them and hope that one day they would disappear and no longer exist. I told myself this surely had to be easier than dealing with the painful memories every waking moment.

But then like an unexpected gift, I recalled Gabe's words: If it's a truth, deal with it a little at time. If it's a lie, toss it out. I made a conscious decision to meet every thought head on. It hasn't been easy, but I think it's better than having them pile up into an unsurmountable mass hidden in my brain. It would be horrible to have these unresolved memories unexpectedly sneak out on their own at any given time. The worst would be to have that mass explode all at once, shattering my world and everyone in it. No telling what kind of life I'd have.

The three of us agree that's where we are. We've accepted what happened and now we need to move forward one day at a time.

Anthony rubs my arm taking in a deep breath which he exhales as he stands. "I have to run guys. I've gotta get Sophia to practice. Ella, I'll come by and see you soon, pinky promise."

A huge grin spreads across Gabriel's face as he looks at Anthony. "Pinky promise? Bartelli, did I just hear you say *pinky promise?*"

Anthony turns to me, his eyes are wide, eyebrows arched. "Shit, I've been found out." We laugh so hard and boy does it feel good.

"Not to worry, buddy, your secret's safe with me," Gabe says.

A smile slowly spreads across Anthony's face. He looks straight at Gabe. "Pinky promise?"

I think Gabe knows what he needs to do. He looks at me, and I nod, grinning from ear to ear.

"Okay, Bartelli," Gabe says. "Pinky promise."

"What a sight, my favorite superman-ish guys hooking their pinkies right before my very eyes."

They turn and look at me laughing. I smile and hold an imaginary key to my lips and twist it shut. They look at each other again and burst out laughing, and I lean back on my pillow wearing the biggest smile I've had in a very long time, and I watch...and enjoy.

When Anthony's leaves, Gabriel sits on my bed beside me. He holds my hand, stroking it, playing with it as he tells me what he's been doing at his dad's office and about his fishing trip with his dad and Marco. And then he asks what television shows I like to watch and I tell him I like Perry Mason, That Girl, Bewitched, and Dark Shadows. He smiles and says he likes Dark Shadows too.

"So you like scary movies, huh?"

"Yeah," I say with a nod. "The scarier the better."

"Brave little girl," he says.

"Not at all. You wouldn't believe the number of boxes of popcorn that have gone flying out of my hands when I jump out of my seat. I swear, I'll half-way crawl over you," I laugh.

Gabriel's head drops back with a laugh. "That's funny, I just pictured the whole thing. You, sitting in a dark theater and corn kernels flying up in the air. And I bet you scream too," he laughs again.

I look at him and love the sound of his laughter. This right here is living, and we're both enjoying life right now. We should never take things such as these for granted. Gabe would call them blessings. I may not be religious like Gabe, but Mom always taught me to count mine before I go to sleep each night and I do. Tonight, I'll count all the smiles that we shared today and the laughter as blessings. I'll also count the tears and the healing that came from allowing them to surface and to flow.

31

1966 – Ella Galvez

Daylight flickers brightly along the edges of my blinds. The rays of sun sneak through and touch my skin like warm fingers rousing me from a deep sleep. I yank the covers over my head and roll over. *I'm nowhere close to being awake.*

The sound of a lawnmower passes near my window then fades away into the distance, only to return to the edges of my window again. The back and forth rhythm holds my attention for a while. I roll onto my back and stare up at the painted stars on my ceiling for a while. My eyes jump from one star to the next as I continue to listen to the droning buzz. Why is the noise from some old lawnmower so comforting?

Come to think of it, so is the humming of the oscillating fan in my room at night. It's like its standing guard over me when all it does is turn back and forth blowing air from one corner of my room to the other. Same goes for Mom's clicking dust mop moving from side to side around the house and outside my bedroom door each night before bedtime. All those things are what *normal* sounds like. It tells me everything's okay with my world. That's what I long for—normal. I kick my covers aside and lay there letting the moving air from the fan send a gentle breeze over my warm body.

A glance at my alarm clock tells me not only have I missed breakfast but also lunch! Can't believe I slept so long. I get out of bed with a yawn and head downstairs to the kitchen and notice Mom in the living room reading. She looks up and scoots her reading glasses past her forehead, pushing her hair back like a headband. "Mijita, you're awake, how do you feel?"

"Groggy," I say, opening the fridge. "I didn't even take a Valium so don't know why I slept so late."

"You *did* take one. I gave it to you to help you get back to sleep after the nightmare you had."

"Nightmare?" I close the refrigerator door and turn to look at Mom. "Did I say what it was about? Don't remember having one."

"Honey, you were sitting up in your bed when I ran into your room. You looked straight ahead screaming. You looked horrified. You said, *They're coming,* and then you said, *They're here!*"

"Yes, I remember! I *was* horrified!" I cover my face with my hands wanting to blot out the vision that popped into my head. "Five guys on motorcycles were at the foot of my bed revving up their motors. And the louder they got, the more afraid I was. One of them got off and walked toward me, a stubbly faced guy with a wicked grin." Picturing it again makes me shudder. "I know it wasn't real, but it sure felt like it," I say, opening the refrigerator door again. I pull out the orange juice and place it on the counter.

"It's past lunchtime, you must be hungry. I can make you breakfast or lunch, whichever you want." She places her reading glasses on the table beside her *Reader's Digest* and joins me in the kitchen.

I pour myself some juice then turn to look at Mom. "Do you think we'll hear something about the watch today? It's been long enough."

Mom looks doubtful. "I don't know," she sighs, "we can only hope." She hugs me, gives me gentle pats on my back. "So is it breakfast or lunch?"

"Maybe some toast." I yawn again. "And some coffee, I'd like some coffee."

"Coffee? When did you start drinking coffee?"

"Today, right now. I want to be wide awake and aware. I'm tired of trudging through life at a snail's pace. I want to feel normal again, Mommy."

"My poor baby, of course, you do. Let me make us a fresh pot. I think I could use another cup too."

The phone rings, and I can tell by Mom's responses the conversation is about me. I take the percolator from her hand and pour in some water.

"No, Madge, that's quite alright." She pushes the coffee canister toward me along the counter. "No, no bother at all." She turns and looks at me, rolls her eyes and shakes her head. "Thank you for calling and for your concern. Goodbye, Madge."

I love it when she turns toward me and makes a face as she points a finger to her head and pulls the thumb trigger as if she's just shot herself. "No, we haven't heard anything yet. No, don't have any information I can share at this time. Of course, Madge. Goodbye."

Mom brushes her hair back with one hand and puts the phone back in the cradle with the other. She stands there for a moment shaking her head.

"I can't believe friends are still calling." I add the coffee grounds and then plug the cord into the outlet.

She sighs. "Lots of well-meaning callers, wanting to let me know they heard, and they will be praying for us in this *oh, so difficult time,*" Mom says, mimicking an insincere caller. "I don't understand these so-called friends who seem to be digging for details rather than expressing sincere concern. I should leave the darn thing off the hook. But then there are those who say they are sorry to hear about what happened, say they will keep the three of us in their prayers and nothing more. No questions, no digging for details. Those are real friends, Ella."

She stands there looking at me, shaking her head. "I think I'll start a list of these friends. They'll get a beautifully embossed Christmas card from Hargrove's selected especially for them. The others will get the cheaper ones out of a box of identical cards which I get from Woolworth's or Kress."

When the phone rings again, Mom's look is one of exasperation. She takes a deep breath before answering it.

"Yes, hello Sandra."

I start to lift myself up on the counter but decide I'll just be scolded, and not quite sure I have the strength to pull myself all the way up. Instead, I grab a chair and wait there as mom listens to whatever is being said on the other end of the line. She nods and offers an occasional *uh-huh,* keeping her gaze on the coffee bubbling up inside the glass knob of the percolator top, it's color slowly deepening.

"That is so sweet of you. I sure do appreciate your call and prayers. Yes, we'll talk soon, please give our regards to Harry. Goodbye, dear." Mom hangs up and turns to look at me with a smile on her face. "Sandra and Harry will definitely be getting a beautifully embossed Christmas card selected just for them."

It's July, and my mother's already making Christmas card lists. But I get it. This is probably an easier way of pushing those snoopy friends out of her mind rather than dwelling on how nosey they were. Sticks them on the cheap Christmas card list and she feels better. In her mind, they got dealt with.

"Oh, I almost forgot," she says, taking two of her brand new colorful Melmac coffee cups from the cabinet and setting them in front of the percolator. "Julia, Anna, and Rita called again. They've been worried. I told each one you would give them a call as soon as you were up to it. They seem to understand. Poor Julia, I could tell she was struggling. She finally broke down and cried."

"Oh, poor Julia," I say, through a yawn. "I feel badly for her. I hope they know the only reason I asked to see Anthony and Gabriel is because they were there when it happened, so I didn't have to explain anything and relive any part of it. I take in a sharp breath. "I guess I should do it soon. I think I'll ask them to come by together. I won't have to repeat myself that way. It'll be one emotional blowout instead of three. See, that's what I dread, the emotions."

"I know, honey. Take your time, do it when you're up to it, but I honestly feel that the more visitors you have, the quicker you'll get back to that normal life you're longing for. I could see the difference after Gabriel and Anthony left."

"You're right. I think it's time," I say as I head up to my room. "I'll be down in a bit." I breathe in the aroma streaming out of the percolator. I'm really enjoying the smell of the freshly perked coffee. Funny, I don't think I've ever paid much attention to it before. Kinda looking forward to my first cup.

I sit on my still-unmade bed and call Gabe. He mentions that I sound half asleep. I tell him about my nightmares and the Valium. Assure him the grogginess will be gone as soon as I shower. In a deliberately perky voice, I ask him what he's been up to today.

"Laid around and thought about us and how my girlfriend's a time traveler. My very own time traveler in a tutu," he says, and we both laugh. "Listened to the Beatles for the soundtrack. Think you, Bella Ella, and I would make one hell of a movie, *Gabe and Ella.* A love story, of course."

I laugh. "A time traveler in a tutu sounds more like a character in a children's book, than someone in a love story. How about, *Tina, the Tiny Time Traveler in a Tutu.* When she's not time traveling, she lives in a little girl's jewelry box."

"Cute, the ballerina in your jewelry box. But how does she get out of there to travel?"

"Hmm, well...how about she gets her power when the little girl who owns it winds the music for the ballerina to dance. Yep, that's where she gets her power. If the kid closes the box before the key unwinds completely, Tina has power left to time travel. If the little girl leaves the jewelry box open long enough to completely unwind, then there's no power left for the ballerina to go tippy toeing anywhere and she's stuck there inside the box. And she's pissed," I laugh. "How's that for a fascinating illustrated children's book?"

"Wow, you've got one heck of an imagination. I like it. So when do you think you'll be up for a visit?"

"Can you come over now? It won't take me long to shower and dress."

"Heck yeah. Okay with your mom?"

"Yes, she encouraged me to spend time with friends. I'm about to have coffee and toast, you can join me. A fresh pot's perking."

"When did you start drinking coffee?"

"Oh brother, you too? I haven't started yet, this will be my very first cup. I think I need one."

"I've already had juice and cereal, but I'll have toast and coffee with you."

"So you're a coffee drinker?"

"Nope. This will be my first cup too," he says with a laugh. "So okay, I'll see you soon."

I let mom know Gabe is coming and to please make enough toast for him. She says okay, and then as I go into the bathroom, I hear her say something about Gabe being a big eater and she should make him several slices.

I take a quick shower, put on a pair of shorts and a waist-high sleeveless summer top and I rub on some lilac scented lotion. I look at myself in the mirror, and I'm glad to see the horrible experience is no longer written all over my face in black and blue. I put some concealer on the bruises which are now barely there. Better than the yellowish-green from several days ago. I smear on some lip gloss and take another look. Decide I should wear my glasses rather than contacts to hide my still-sleepy eyes.

When I hear a truck come up the driveway, I go out to the front porch and wait there. I breathe in the humid summer air. I rarely come outdoors; it leaves me feeling so exposed, too vulnerable. I realize how much I miss the sunshine.

"Hey, look at my girl. You look cute in glasses," he says, smiling. He hugs me gently and kisses me on the cheek.

"Mmm, you smell nice," he says, breathing deeply and gives me another kiss on my neck.

His kiss tickles and I wiggle my shoulders.

"I love how your shoulders do that quick little dance."

"You and my shoulders," I say as I open the door and invite him in.

Mom says hello and tells Gabriel how happy she is to see him. She hands me a tray with a stack of toast and coffee.

"That's a tall stack of toast," I say.

Gabe laughs. "Ella, I think your mom remembers what a big eater I am."

Mom smiles. "Yes, I do. And if it's not enough, I'll be happy to add more to that stack."

"Thank you," Gabe says.

I carefully negotiate the two steps that lead down into the screened porch. I ask Gabe to close the door behind us, so we can have privacy. Cooper manages to sneak in before the door is closed. As I set the tray on the coffee table, Gabe takes a seat on the couch, and Cooper lays on the rug in front of the back door. As soon as I sit beside Gabriel, he wraps his arm around my shoulders, and I lean against his arm. But then I sit up abruptly when I notice Mom's lowered every single Roman shade including the one on the door leading outside.

Mom had told me I shouldn't go outside for a while, she took care of taking Cooper outside for bathroom breaks and even took him for a walk a couple of times. I obeyed but now sitting here, I realize that on the other side of these windows is where it all happened. She has totally blocked it from my view. I mention the shades to Gabe, and he agrees it's probably best for now. I guess it's possible that I might have walked out here and gotten upset seeing where my rape took place. But suddenly all those blue and white nautical themed Roman Shades seem to cry out *Crime scene. Do not cross this line.*

I push the thought of what's out there away and lean over to serve our coffee. "Cream? Sugar?"

"Good question," he laughs. "Let's try it all."

While I prepare our coffee, Gabriel digs into his pocket. "I got something for you. After everything that happened, I'd forgotten I didn't give him to you on your birthday. Mom found it in my pants pocket when she took them to the cleaners." He holds his fist out. "He's in here, dying to meet you."

"I actually thought about him last night. I forgot to ask about him when you called to say goodnight."

What's weird is I know exactly what he'll look like, but I still can't wait to see him. I hold out my hand, and he drops the little bear with the sapphire heart into it. A fleeting vision that rushes by is so clear and just long enough for me to grasp what I saw. I look up at Gabe, tears pooling in my eyes. "My Baby Blue."

"Cute, you've already named him."

"No, Baby Blue *is* his name, Gabe. He was already mine."

"What do you mean, did you like feel a connection to him or something, and not just a vision?"

"Yes, I think everything I've seen has been part of my future, *our* future. Crazy, right? Like my necklace, think about it, it's got both our names on it. Not just Ella and Gabriel but *Bella* Ella and Gabriel. Who's gonna call their kid Bella Ella? Well, maybe if they're in Italy. I could see an Italian father saying, *my Bella Ella, come to papà,"* I laugh. And from Gabe's smirky grin, he seems to be enjoying this.

"What I'm saying makes sense to me, kinda sorta." I laugh. "Listen to me, I must be totally nuts. I said my coming back from the future makes sense." This time Gabe laughs with me.

But my laughter quickly fades knowing how crazy I really do sound and my smile almost slips away, but then I hear his words.

"Wow, Ella, I'm loving this. I wish I knew where I got the *Here, There, and Everywhere* line from." He sits there looking at me intensely. "I think maybe we're getting closer to home."

"Home...as in *our* home somewhere out there?"

As he nods, his expression turns serious. "Yeah, I do...I really do." After a deep breath and an exhale, he takes a drink of his coffee. "Not bad, I like it." He then takes a bite of his toast. "Whoa, this is great!"

"Glad you like it."

"I think I turned out to be a pretty romantic guy. I mean, look at the gifts I've given you," he says, breathing on his knuckles then buffing his fingernails against his chest.

I laugh. "Well, Mr. Romantic, I have to agree. There's something about the words on the necklace, the desire to have someone always present. They actually touch the soul."

I lift my cup to my lips and not knowing just how hot it's going to be, I slowly take my first sip of coffee, ever. "You're right, not bad."

"Back to the visions," Gabe says. He puts his cup down. "You really do feel it's something from the future instead of a premonition?" He takes another bite of toast, licks his lips.

"Yes. In my mind, seeing a future event, such as in a premonition, isn't as personal as having experienced it yourself before. Say, looking into the future, as in things which haven't happened yet. If it hadn't already occurred, you know, like a memory of it, I shouldn't feel a connection to the charm bracelet. It would be like window shopping and seeing something beautiful and wishing I could have it."

I smile at Gabriel as he picks up his second toast and totally devours it. He smiles back.

"Okay, what I was gonna say is if I saw something from *my* future, one I've already experienced, there should be a bond and a closeness since it's personal." I put my cup down and take a bite of toast.

"Yeah," he says, squinting and nodding as if he's thinking about what I just said. "I think I know what you mean. So how do you feel about the two right now?"

I take a napkin and dab at my lips. "It's definitely a strong emotional bond between the bracelet, the necklace, you and me. And another thing, I think the day we met, not the first time but this time..." I hear those words pass my lips and I see my mind flashing me a neon warning: *Crazy! Crazy! Crazy!* But I keep on going anyway. "...the love, our connection was already there."

He grabs his cup takes a couple more sips.

Something comes over me, and I start crying. Gabe quickly puts his cup down.

"Uh-oh, what did I say? What's wrong, Ella?"

"No, it wasn't you. These days my emotions kick in for no reason and without any warning." I sniffle, take my glasses off and use the napkin to wipe my eyes and nose. "I was thinking about us, everything was so perfect, and then *he* shows up. He invades my thoughts with *his* disgusting memory."

"I'm sorry, baby. Go ahead and cry, it's okay to be sad. Come here, I'll hug you as long as you want."

We sit here on the couch, my head tucked in the crook of his arm. He rubs his fingertips along my arm softly and it soothes me. I can feel myself calm down.

"Gabriel, I've gone through so much. I can say my attack is in the past, but all my crazy visions, those are still happening, and I don't know what the heck is going on. I'm not sure that I could make it if I didn't have you to share everything with."

He takes my hand. "Maybe if you start from the very beginning it will make more sense to me."

"Ha! Good luck," I say, putting my glasses back on. "I've *lived* it from the beginning, and it doesn't make sense to me! That's how crazy it is!"

"Try me. Tell me how it all started?"

"Actually, you've already heard the very beginning, you know, the swing and shimmering lights, but I haven't given you the details." I smile at him and wink. "Hold on to your seats boys and girls."

Gabe chuckles and rubs his hands together in anticipation, the most adorable little smirk on his face.

"Wait, I have a better idea. I'll be right back."

"What? Hey…wait…don't leave me like this."

I run up to my room to fetch my journal and when I step onto the porch, Gabe motions with his hands for me to hurry. "You left me in suspense, girl!"

. "You are such a child," I say. I hold up my journal for him to see. "I've got it all written down and illustrated right here between these pages."

"Wow," he says as I sit down beside him. When I flip it open to a bookmarked page, Gabe scoots up close. "Can I look over your shoulder?"

"Sure," I say and begin telling him in detail what happened in my backyard as I point to each entry. I read it slowly and with so much detail that it takes me back and I pretty much relive each incident.

"I like how you colored in your illustrations," he says.

"Yeah, I went back and added that later. I did it mostly for my entertainment, but it did make it a little more vivid for me."

I then tell him how it was the first time I noticed the neighbor's second story window. Not that I just happened to look in that direction and saw it there, but more like something made me turn my head to look. I described how it made me feel, especially when I saw someone move away behind the curtains. Next, I tell him about the cue ball stick shift incident in Rita's car.

The look on Gabe's face is one of amazement. He listens with so much interest. "Wow, this stuff is unbelievable."

I look at him, my forehead scrunched up wondering what he's going to think when he hears what I have to say next. "Well, you haven't heard the half of it," I say as I turn to the next page. "This one's the kicker."

He looks at me and wiggles his eyebrows. "Let's hear it."

I smile, bite down on my lip. "I heard a voice in my head, a lady's voice."

His eyes grow wide. "You're kidding!"

"Nope, not kidding. This happened about a week before you and I met."

Gabe listens intently while I give the whole rundown from the point where I heard the voice and how it conveniently repeated itself when we were at The Drive Inn prompting me to ask Dad if we could sit by the dance floor. And how the logistics of our new sitting arrangement made it possible for me to see Michael and Bridget walk in.

There's a look of revelation on Gabe's face. His eyebrows arch making his forehead wrinkle. "Ella, if you hadn't caught them, you and Michael might still be together."

"Yeah," I sigh. "That scary thought has played around in my mind too."

"I like that, a gypsy in your head."

I look up at him, holding back a smile. "Uh...I didn't say she was a gypsy, I said it was a lady's voice."

"I know, but that's what I pictured. A pretty one, though. You know with a scarf tied around her head and a fluffy white blouse hanging off her shoulders."

"Oh, I see," I say nodding my head and giving him a knowing look. "It's not just *my* shoulders you like."

"Only yours, Ella." He winks, then leans over and places a kiss on the tiny part of my shoulder that my sleeveless blouse allows him to see.

"I got your number, lover boy." I turn the page and keep on reading.

When I tell him that last night as I was getting into bed I imagined someone else in Sophia's place as Alice in her theater's production of *Alice in Wonderland*, it dawns on me.

"Oh no, Gabe. It just hit me! Why wouldn't Sophia be able to be there to play the part of Alice? And why do I get a horrible sinking feeling it has to do with the blue cap guy? Wait a minute, we saw him at the parking lot by my dance studio. Sophia's Performing Arts Center shares the same parking lot!"

"Ella, you're not thinking she could be next, are you?"

"I was, maybe. What if that guy waits for her there when she goes for rehearsals? Anthony has always said Sophia, and I look like we could be sisters, in fact, he says she reminds him of me when I was her age. So if he's after a particular *look* then yes, she could be a target."

"Scary. Well, for one," Gabe says, "Anthony drops her off and picks her up. And he mentioned that since your attack, his mom has been vigilant about making sure Sofia is safe. Until this guy is caught Sophia's not allowed to go anywhere alone."

"That's good to know."

"Okay, I need to get going. So would you like me to take Baby Blue and your bracelet with me so I can have him added?"

"Gee, I just got to see him again, but yes, the sooner he's on the sooner I'll get to wear it." I run upstairs and get my bracelet, place it in the box it came in and add Baby Blue. "Here you go."

"Great, I'll get it taken care of. Call you later tonight. Or you can call me. Either way works for me."

I walk Gabe to the front porch to say goodbye. Gabe kisses his fingers and touches my lips. It's sweet, but I know he's still being careful with me. I think he might be afraid of how I'll feel or react.

I smile at him and lightly trace his lips with my finger. "I know you're being cautious, and I appreciate it, but I think I'll be alright if you kiss me on my lips."

He smiles. "I'd like that. Umm...are you sure?"

I nod.

He gently cups my face in his hands and presses his lips lightly onto mine. When he pulls away, he moistens his lower lip as if he's savoring something he had missed. And then he smiles. "I've missed your kisses."

"Me too." I want you to be normal around me. You and I are the only things I feel that are real. Please don't stop being who you are. I want you to be you, and if you ever stop smirking or wiggling your eyebrows at me I swear, Gabriel Marquez, I'll give you one big fat demerit." I laugh, so does Gabe.

"Okay, I get it, Bella Ella."

I love that Gabe is being so careful. And I also love that every day since my rape, he has shown me he loves me, that I'm still his Bella Ella. Gabe and I hadn't been together that long so my attack could have easily happened when I was with Michael had I not met Gabe when I did. How would Michael have acted had he been with me instead? The thought sends shivers through me.

I watch as Gabe walks to his truck and sends me a goodbye kiss, which I return with a little wave. He smiles back. As I stand there watching him, I think about how lucky I was that a voice in my head nudged me to ask my father to please let us sit by the dance floor.

32

1966 – Ella Galvez

My life has always been somewhat boring. But when I met Gabriel, it was perfect, and then it wasn't. I was raped—that changed everything. Now I'll do anything to get that life back.

Things are far from normal, but at least I'm no longer sitting around staring at the same spot on my wall. The first few days following my attack I felt like a child. I needed to be checked on, to be told what to do. If Mom said a bubble bath would do me good, I'd take one. If she said a cup of chamomile tea would calm my nerves, I'd drink some. The one I heard most often was that I should try to eat something, so I'd force down what I could. It left me queasy, but at least it made Mom smile.

Then one day, I decided to acknowledge and confront all of it. What was done to me was something no young girl should ever be put through. I had to accept that it really happened. Each day something new comes to mind, not every little detail and not in the right order...random is what it is.

My mind seems to be the keeper of my sanity. I think it's being selective. Holds on to memories too painful for me to handle. Dishes them out in manageable bits and pieces - each one as startling as the last. I allow the emotions to flow and analyze every single thing I see and feel, but I remove myself from the situation, kind of like I did in the hospital. I decide which things are true, deal with them, and if I can't, I set it aside to work on later.

The first truth I dealt with was there is no fear in the past. It's over and can't hurt me anymore. All I need to do now is deal with what's true and accept it, and that's what I'm doing. And the lies? Told myself it was not my fault. I did nothing to entice this sicko to rape me. Simple as that. The officer's insinuations during my questioning were false. All of them lies. End of story.

One thing I haven't dealt with is the anger and the hate. It makes me cry. I'll have to deal with it too. Later.

Something that keeps showing up in dreams is the concrete boy which I loathed since the day of the shimmering lights. He seemed to taunt me, didn't know why he did, nor why I didn't remember him. The vision of him on my birthday with his head lobbed off, both pieces laying on the ground, has continued to haunt me. Now I know it was a vision of what was about to occur. It was almost like a warning.

I laugh at myself, at what I'm saying. Vision? Warning? This is a whole other ballgame I need to be able to grasp. Thank goodness, I have Gabriel to share that part of my mixed-up life with. Otherwise, I'd be a total nutcase.

But not all my dreams are bad. This morning I woke up to my voice saying *I think the twins got roundtrip tickets to Paris on fireflies.* Can't remember what the dream was about, but it sounds cute. Teeny tiny twins riding on the backs of fireflies. Hmm, that's as cute as Tina, the time traveler in a tutu. Both would be cute books to have on my shelf.

My only outing has been to the police station where I was verbally raped. That set me back another couple of days until I ran it through my truth meter. Aside from the times Gabe and Anthony came by to visit, my best day was when I went with Mom to Den-Russ to fill my prescription. Got a copy of the latest *Seventeen* magazine and a box of colored pencils. Decided I'd brighten up all the drawings and illustrations in my journal. I wished the set had come with a pencil color called iridescent. I sure could've used that. I ended up blending several colors together for the iridescent lights. Of course, the colors don't change, but it was much closer to what I saw that day than my original black and white drawings.

Gabe calls to see if he can come by, and of course, I say *yes*. There's something I need him to do for me, so I wait anxiously, and I'm at the door before he even knocks. As soon as he walks in, we hear the thunder and the rain comes pouring down.

"You got here just in time!"

I turn and look at Gabriel as I chew on my lip.

"What's up," he asks.

I squint at him. "How'd you know something was?"

He laughs. "If you're biting on your lip or spinning your ring around your finger, something's up. So what is it?"

"There's something I'm about to do, and I'm kinda scared. I'd like you to help me."

"Uh...what are you about to do?"

I get up, take a deep breath. "I know Mom has all the shades completely pulled around the porch for my own good, but I *need* to look outside. I can't go on like this. I must face what's out there, and the longer I wait, I think the worse it will be. Can you please come outside with me?"

"Ella, this might not be a good idea. Maybe you should check with your mom."

"It will just worry her. No sense putting her through any more than I already have," I say as I walk toward the door. "If it makes you feel better, I'll stay inside and just take a peek from here. Besides, Gabriel, isn't this part of me facing my truths?"

He sits there, looking at me. Now *he's* chewing on his lip.

"Well?"

"Okay," he says as he stands, "but let's do it slowly."

He walks over and places his arm around my waist. I wrap my fingers around the knob then pause for a moment. I take a breath, close my eyes and then start to pull the door toward me. I hesitate again.

"Second thoughts?"

I nod. "Maybe."

"Just take your time."

"I am, that's why I'm standing here with my eyes closed."

"Good, that's good," he says, moving his hand from my waist to my shoulder, rubbing it lightly.

I take another deep breath before opening the door really slow, like centimeters at a time slow. I'm afraid to open my eyes, but then I do. And I see him. The little boy is on the ground, just as I'd seen him the day of my attack and in that crazy vision with his head broken off. Everything is soaking wet out there because of all the rain. It makes the scene even more frightening. And then I see something I never expected. It all begins to play out before my eyes. I watch it as a spectator, but I also feel the pain of what's happening, as if I were there. *That's because I was there*! This is no premonition! This really happened! And it happened to me. I clutch my stomach. Gabriel closes the door and looks at me.

"Oh, Ella. What happened? What did you see, baby?"

"I remember, I finally remember! I *did* name the puppy Daisy because the little girl has daisies in her basket." My eyes pool with tears. "It was just as Mom said." I turn to look at Gabriel, my tears spilling over. "I must've blocked the memory of the boy and his demise because he was part of the memory of being raped here in my own backyard. I blocked him out, I didn't want to remember. Oh, Gabriel. It really happened."

"I don't understand. I know you didn't remember him, but what does it have to do with suppressing the memory of your rape? It hadn't happened yet."

"Ella, your trembling, come here."

He holds me then takes me by the hand back to the couch. I allow the pain of what I've just seen sink in. I honestly believe this is what I needed to experience to help me heal. No more suppressed memories. We sit side by side. Gabe takes his handkerchief and dabs away at my cheeks and holds me.

Finally, I look at him. "That's just it, Gabe, it *had* already happened to me. I think there's been a wall of denial shielding me from the truth. I'd blocked everything. It's all been buried in the dark recesses of my mind, so I wouldn't remember, I didn't want to. Oh, no, no! That's it, I didn't want to remember."

"Remember what? What were you trying to block out?"

"Being raped, Gabe. I just saw it! Not what took place recently, but the first time it happened. Oh, Gabriel, it really did happen!" I hear those words come tumbling out of me over and over and the realization of what I've just said sends a cold shiver through me. "Please hold me, Gabriel." I catch my breath and hold it there. Then an audible breath swooshes out of me, leaving me weak and faint and I cry as Gabe holds me close.

"I don't understand what you're trying to tell me, but that's okay, I'm here. Let me just hold you."

We sit there for a while, my body relaxing as Gabe holds me until the tears subside and I'm calmed.

"Gabe, please don't freak out." I finally say as I turn to look up at him, wondering what he's going to think when I tell him what just flashed past me and the emotions that came with it. I can see he's still waiting for me to say something.

"Okay, *now* I'm freaking out. What did you see?"

"I only saw a glimpse of the first time I was raped. It wasn't you who was there, it was Michael. I was laying on a gurney being placed inside an ambulance. I was so scared. I didn't want to be alone. I lifted my head and looked around trying to find Michael. The right side of my head throbbed when I tried to pull myself up. My right eye was swollen shut. I was looking for him, I needed him to hold my hand. And then I saw him. I saw Michael walk away. Didn't even turn back to look at me...he just...walked away."

"No, that can't be," Gabe says with a shudder in his voice, shaking his head. "Oh, Ella," he says, running his hands through his hair.

I choke back a sob, and Gabe pulls me to him and holds me tight. After a while, I pull myself away and continue. "I so desperately needed him to come back to me or at least turn around." I shrug my shoulders. "Turn around and what? Wave? *See ya*? *Later*? How could he do that to me...walk away...leave me like that?"

"I'm so sorry, baby," Gabe says.

I wipe away new tears that spill from my eyes and sit there thinking, gnawing on my lower lip. *Why am I going through all this horror?*

I breathe out a sigh and look at Gabriel. "Maybe that's the reason I'm here, why I came back," I say, glancing from one side of the room to the other thinking about what harm I might've done. "Gabe, I've messed with the past. With Ella Marquez's help, I was able to catch Michael cheating. Maybe I'm here to help things turn out better. This time you were with me and not Michael. You've stayed by my side. He walked away. Who knows, maybe I shriveled up into some pathetic basket case the first time around." I turn and look at Gabe. "I'm sounding like a crazy basket case right this minute, aren't I?"

"Guess I'm turning into one too, because you're starting to make a lot of sense."

"Really? You're not just saying that? I was starting to sound really insane to me, but I honestly do think the visions I've seen are part of some sort of a collage of a life we've had somewhere in time, in a parallel world we're not even aware of."

"How I wish I could peek into that world with you."

We sit there not saying a word. But I'm sure Gabriel's head is trying to sort everything out just like mine is. We sit here for a long time. I'm finally able to talk through what I saw. What's calming is knowing that I honestly believe this is part of my healing. Not just for this time around, but for what I went through before.

Gabe glances at his watch and says he's going to have to leave as soon as the pouring rain stops. We sit and talk as we wait. When it finally stops we get up, but before walking out Gabriel hugs me and says, "I have faith that everything is going to be just fine." We go out the back door, and I walk him to his truck. We see a rainbow that arches from one side of town to the other. We look at each other and smile and kiss goodbye. I walk back inside as quickly as I can without looking in the direction of the neighbor's window.

Mom's in the kitchen on a stepstool dusting her cookbooks, her prized possessions which she keeps lined up on a shelf above the bar that divides the kitchen and the dining room. Mom's an excellent housekeeper, but lately, there's been an extra shine to our home. Her way of keeping her mind occupied is to dust, clean and polish.

Aunt Tilly is at the kitchen table sipping a cup of coffee. She stands when she sees me. "Oh, honey, you've been crying, I'm sorry." She gives me a peck on the cheek and a hug.

"I'm okay, it comes and goes. It doesn't happen as often now.

"Thanks for waiting, Tilly. I'm just about done here," Mom says.

I'm heading upstairs when the phone rings. I come back down to answer it, but Mom's already off her stool and gets to it first, so I head back to my room.

"Yes sir, this is Mrs. Galvez, Ella's mother, how can I help you?" She pauses. "The owner of the watch?" she asks.

Her words stop me in my track, and I run back down. "Yes, of course, we're anxious to know. Can you give me the name?"

"Did you say it belongs to a neighbor? Sebastian Prada?" Her voice quavers when she says his name and her head snaps in my direction. The color drains from her face. Aunt Tilly notices too and moves toward Mom.

"Oh, my baby," Mom says, her eyes spilling over with tears as she slumps to the floor, clutching the phone to her chest.

"Mom!"

I rush to her side. Aunt Tilly takes the phone, clears her throat and speaks to whomever it was Mom was talking to on the phone.

"Mom's fainted!" I shake her shoulders but get no response.

Aunt Tilly stoops down. "Mary, Mary, can you hear me?"

I grab a wet dishcloth and place it over Mom's forehead. Her eye lids flutter and then she slowly opens them looking back and forth between Aunt Tilly and me.

"They gave you the name of the bastard who hurt our Ella, didn't they, Mary?"

Mom looks up at Tilly for a fraction of a second, nods then looks at me following me as I position myself so that I'm sitting next to her. I wrap my arm around her back to help support her. Her tears turn to sobs. She holds on to me as she continues to cry uncontrollably.

"I'm so sorry he did this to you, mijita."

Loud thunder reminds me that it's been raining heavily which means work's been shut down at Dad's construction site. He should be walking in soon. Aunt Tilly and I manage to lift Mom from the floor to a chair. She's calming down but just sits there shaking her head slowly back and forth, wringing her hands.

When Dad arrives, Aunt Tilly goes to the door to meet him.

"Tom, Mary just got word about who the watch belongs to."

"Good, I hope they hang him," he says as he pulls off his raincoat. He hears Mom crying and looks at her astonished. Her eyes are red and puffy, and her skin is blotchy. Her hair is in disarray from running her hands through it.

"Mary? What's wrong?" Dad asks.

"Daddy, when she was given the name she just fell apart. I guess it felt so real now knowing his name."

"Ridiculous, it was real the moment I saw what he did to you. It can't possibly get any more real than that!"

Mom sit's there quietly, tears streaming down her face, she doesn't look up at Dad, nor does she acknowledge that he's there. Dad goes to the kitchen and pours Mom a glass of brandy. She takes it without looking up at us and drinks it down in one quick gulp and begins coughing.

"Water please, Tilly," Dad says.

When Mom finishes her water, Dad suggests she lay down. He guides her to the bedroom and moments later he returns. He comes to me and hugs me, asks Aunt Tilly if she heard the name Mom was given.

She nods. "Sebastian Prada."

Dad seems to be thinking about the name but says nothing.

"It's so sad to watch Mom fall apart like this," I say, crying again.

"I know," he says, hugging me tighter.

Once in my room, I try to relax. Instead, I think about what I witnessed with Mom downstairs and then the visions and memories that surfaced. I can't believe I experienced my rape twice. To endure one rape is bad enough but two?

Later, when I go downstairs, Mom's in the kitchen drinking a glass of water. She attempts to give me her I'm-okay smile but fails miserably. She asks how I'm doing and I say I'm alright and then we hug. We hold each other longer than usual. I somehow think Mom needed it more than I did. I just don't understand why.

33

1966 – Ella Galvez

Since my attack, each new day begins with doubt and a little bit of fear. That's because each day I sense the lies I've already dealt with trying to wiggle themselves back inside my head. And despite the new revelations that showed up in a vision a few days ago of having been raped once before, I'm still winning. Gabriel and I discussed the new vision at length over the phone. We kept coming up with the same truth. The first rape was in the past, and the past can't hurt me.

When the phone rings, the quick breath I take is one of hopeful anticipation. I doubt Gabe has any idea what his calls mean to me. He asks how I'm doing and says he'll be praying for me while I'm at the station. I tell him that I'm beginning to feel hope when he says those words…that he'll be praying.

"I love hearing you say that, Ella," he says.

"Well, I'll really need them today. I dread going back there. My last visit was not very pleasant. But at least we're getting closer to this whole thing being over."

"Yep, it's almost over. Now what we need to do is find us some more clues. Keep rolling that phrase on your necklace around in your head, you never know if a vision will pop in."

"I will, and I'm actually quite hopeful. When I was looking at my journal I noticed the trend. Each discovery seems to bring with it more questions and new answers. I think it's just a matter of time, Gabe. I'm not giving up."

I go downstairs and find Mom in the kitchen. It surprises me she's still in her house dress. She usually puts on a pair of comfortable capris and a cotton shirt when she'll be working around the house. Mom's wiping down the counters with such fervor, buffing up the tile as if the queen herself will be dropping by for tea. She jumps when she senses someone's there. "Sorry, Mom," I say, slipping my arm around her waist. "I didn't mean to startle you. How do you feel?"

She turns around to complete the hug I've started. "A little bit tired."

I see the puffy circles which ring her eyes from lack of sleep or worse yet, crying. It breaks my heart. This whole thing has caused Mom so much grief. Learning the name of my attacker day before yesterday sent her reeling to a very dark place. All I know is that on that night for the first time since I can remember, I didn't hear mom's dust mop clicking outside my door before bedtime. It's the one thing I could always count on.

Mom reminds me that we have an appointment at the police station and that Dad will be here soon.

The stale smell of the police station triggers my memory of the last time I was here to give my report two days after I was raped, and my stomach turns inside. When Dad asks for Detective Aguirre, we're led to his office by another officer. He tells us the detective will be with us shortly.

I know I was here a little less than three weeks ago, but I can't say I remember what it looked like. I kinda wasn't *present* that day. The office is quite small, but Dad manages to be able to pace back and forth. Four steps to the file cabinet and then spins around and takes four steps back to where his chair sits. He does this slowly and in deep thought, back and forth, back and forth.

Mom sits with her hands together on her lap spinning her thumbs around each other. I stare at the wall in front of me trying to decide if it was deliberately painted this color or did it simply fade to this depressing shade of grey.

I also wonder why the officer who escorted us here left the door wide open. Didn't it occur to him that we might want some privacy? I notice people, mostly guys, walking by and looking in at us. They look directly at me. I guess they've heard the story, and now they want to see the *rape-girl*. I don't play the victim and look away. Nope, I stare right back and let them be the ones to drop their gaze. The shame is on them...not me.

I check out this guy Aguirre's desk. Not very tidy. Folded up *Brownsville Herald*, a bunch of pink *While You Were Out* notes stuck through a pointy spindle and scattered about his desk. Manila folders laying around, not in neat stacks, just placed here, there and wherever.

Detective Aguirre walks in holding a cup of something hot and steamy in one hand, one of those plastic-wrapped, vending-machine cherry pies in the other. Based on the state of his office, I half-way expected him to be a bit sloppy in his dress, but his cotton shirt looks crisp and well creased. *I guess there must be a Mrs. Aguirre.*

He says hello and sets down his cup while his eyes scan his desk. He touches the different files with the palms of his fat hairy hands as he tries to bring the one he's looking for to the surface. But then he snaps his fingers as if a light bulb flipped on in his head.

"Carmen," he says, careening his neck toward the door, "could you bring me the file I left on the table in the breakroom."

Well, isn't that peachy? This man leaves *my* extremely personal file in the breakroom for anyone to see. Guess that explains all those passersby.

"Be right in with it," she yells back.

The secretary walks in wearing a cute but very tight skirt. She hands the detective the file, he winks, smiles and she walks out with a wiggle which holds the detective's attention until she's out the door. When he opens the file, his eyes scan it from side to side as he gather's the information to share. He looks up at us, his attention going from my dad to my mom and then to me.

He clears his throat and looks up meeting my eyes briefly. I take a deep breath, and this time the stuffy office smell startles me and the feeling I'm left with is one of dread. I wrap my hands around the arms of my chair tightly and brace myself. *Something's about to go very wrong. I can feel it.*

"We've confirmed the watch left behind at the time of the rape was bought at Weldon's by Mrs. Maria E. Prada for her son, Mr. Sebastian Prada, three years ago." He stops, taps his pen several times against the desk. He slowly picks up his cup and takes several long sips, peering over his cup at something on the wall behind us. His gaze lingers there.

He's stalling, I know he is. "There's something else, isn't there? There's something you're not saying!" I blurt out.

He puts his coffee down abruptly, spilling a couple of drops on his desk which he rubs away with the tip of his finger.

I straighten up in my chair and fold my arms across my chest. "Well?"

My parents look at me. I was *not* brought up to be rude. But then I was never taught how to behave when I sense my rapist is about to be set free either. And right now, I'm feeling...no not feeling...I *know,* yes, in my head I already *know* he's about to send my life into another tailspin.

He takes his glasses off and pinches the bridge of his nose. "Mr. Prada," he says, putting his glasses back on, "informed us he lost his watch several months ago." He looks up at us for a short moment then returns his attention back to the paper in his hand. "According to Mr. Prada, it was taken from his car. He said he removed it before playing a game of tennis and placed it on top of the center panel between the front seats.

Mom gasps loudly, then the next thing I hear is Dad's chair scraping hard against the floor as he stands. He places both palms on Detective Aguirre's desk and leans in toward him.

"Are you telling us you have no problem taking the word of this man? You know damn well he happens to own the house next to ours, has a second story window which looks into my yard and worse yet, has a direct view of my daughter's bedroom and the room where she performs her daily dance exercises. Yet, you're okay with it?" Dad pushes himself away and sits back down.

"The detective continues as if Dad's outburst had no effect on him whatsoever. The paper shaking in his hand tells me otherwise. The detective proceeds to share everything he knows about this upstanding citizen, Mr. Prada. He's a member of the Jaycees, Chamber of Commerce, Knights of Columbus, and on and on. He finishes off with the fact that I couldn't identify him so there's nothing they can do since I didn't see his face.

"That's because this coward was wearing a stocking over his head," Dad says, pounding a fist on the desk and causing the detective, Mom and me to jump back in our seats.

"He...he—" Daddy chokes on his words and holds back a sob. He keeps his eyes closed until he regains his composure. Mom sits there trembling and hugging herself. I get up, go to Dad and wrap my arm around him.

"There must be something we can do, isn't there?" I question as I return to my seat.

Detective Aguirre rakes a hand through his thinning hair and scratches the top of his head. He leans forward and places his forearms on his desk, clasps his hands, and looks directly at me.

"Unless we obtain any new evidence, I'm afraid there is nothing more we can do Miss Galvez. We have to drop the charges on Mr. Prada. I'm sorry."

We sit there for a while, stunned at what we just heard. Finally, Dad gets up waving us to follow him out the door without a word.

On our way home, I sit in the back seat quietly thinking about how I was so certain something was going to go wrong. I don't know how I knew it. I just did. Maybe it was a vague memory. I did come across a bit bold and well, rude. That's not me. I would never talk to an adult the way that I did, especially not in front of my parents. But I did. Boy, the look they gave me. Maybe a tiny chunk of my *older Ella* slipped in and did the talking for me. *The complicated life of a time traveler.* Dad drops us off at home and heads back to work.

Once home, Mom says, "Ella, I didn't sleep well last night, I'm laying down for a nap." She helps herself to one of my apple slices. "Will you be okay?" she asks, scooting a strand of hair away from my face.

I tell her I'm fine and remind her that my friends will be dropping by this afternoon. She puts her glass in the sink and retreats to her bedroom. This whole ordeal has been so hard on her, and it's hard on me to see her this way.

Gabe arrives and asks me to share what happened at the police station. He's particularly interested when I tell him I felt, for just a moment, I'd gained a *big girl* attitude from the other Ella, the one that's all grown up. By the look on Mom and Dad's faces, I know it shocked them too. I guess under the circumstances neither one of them felt it was necessary to scold me.

"Hey, you know the voice in my head from the other day?" I ask, tapping a finger against my head. "I recall thinking she sounded like me but maybe an older me. It could very well have been a memory of something I said in the future. Maybe she's five or ten years older than I am now. That must be it. I conjured up a snappy attitude."

He laughs at that.

"Think that's funny? Listen to this. We had to sit and wait in the detective's office with the door open. A few people walked back and forth, mostly guys, and they looked right at me like if I was on display. How rude, huh? Normally I would look away embarrassed. But no, I didn't look away. I stared back at them and made them look away. Now *that* is something Rita would do, not me. Oh no, or maybe older Ella would. Geez, I hope I don't turn into a *Rita.*"

Gabe laughs again. "I seriously doubt that could happen, Ella."

"Well, I'm thinking older Ella is poking herself in my life to help me out. Just like she did talking in my head. I know this is a wild guess, but

I'm thinking in my future I could have told myself, or maybe I told you that if I'd sat by the dance floor, I would've seen Michael. So older Ella stuck that memory in there for me to hear to help me out. What do you think?"

"I think you've been given a second chance. You said *if only*. I'm guessing that means things didn't work out so well the first time around. And after the vision you had of Michael walking away, I'm convinced of it."

I've thought the same thing, but I want to know exactly what Gabe's thinking and I don't want to put any words in his mouth, so I let him continue.

"Well, about the voice, could it be you were telling someone that if you'd broken up with Michael before the rape, it would've been me who was there with you. Things could've turned out differently? And with older Ella's help, things did turn out differently."

"As wild as your little theory sounds, Gabe, that's exactly what I've already thought. I got a second chance. This time around it was with you by my side. You never left me."

"And I never will," he smiles. "I know, I know, I say that all the time. Come here, baby, I need to hug you." He takes me in his arms and holds me for a while rocking me gently. He always knows what I need. "Let's forget about the past and the what-if's it comes with," he whispers.

"You know, I've been thinking if the engraving on my necklace is from a song, it may take forever for us to hear it."

"By the Beatles?"

"I kinda have a feeling it might be. I felt it way deep inside," I say, pressing the tips of my fingers deep into my rib cage. "The Beatles' songs are really good at doing that to me. Well, the Righteous Brothers' *Unchained Melody* does it too, but I honestly don't think it's them. For some reason, I'm sensing a really sweet melody, and if it was composed and sung by the Beatles, it's gotta be Paul."

"Of course, cute Paul again! Aggh! You know there *are* three other very talented guys in the group. You do know that, right?"

I give him a half-smile.

He smiles back. "How is it that I love you so much?"

I shrug my shoulders. "I could ask the very same thing."

When the girls and Anthony show up, we gather in my living room. After hugs and a few tears we sit, and I realize I have no idea where to start or what to share. I should've written stuff down maybe on index cards like I've done for book reports. I look at them sitting there silently waiting for me to say something. Gabriel reaches for my hand and I speak up. I run through a watered-down version and tell them about what I learned today at the police station. After a gasp from Julia and curses from Rita and Anna, I assured them I was going to be fine, but that we girls need to be especially careful until he's caught.

I open my birthday gifts from the girls. And I again apologize for not inviting them over before now. Of course, they say they understand. I thank them for their gifts and most of all for their friendship.

Once everyone's gone, I decide a bubble bath will help me relax and take my mind off the police station fiasco. I plug the drain and sprinkle a packet of bubble bath granules in the tub. Let the tub fill with warm water while I undress, then I slowly slip myself in. The scent of lavender consumes me as I allow myself to sink until my head is below the surface and listen to the quiet. Then I hear six distinct notes. I push myself up out of the water and repeat them to myself. *Where have I heard that before?*

As I'm getting ready to get into bed with a book, Gabe calls to ask if I'd like to go to the movies tomorrow. His invitation catches me off guard. I pause and think about what he just said. I've been cocooned in my home for over a month. I've let life go on out there without me.

"Gosh, hadn't thought about this…the moment I'd have to go out there and see people. Or rather have people see me."

"We can wait, Ella. It doesn't have to be now."

"No, I think I should do it. It's a good idea, after all, I've been wanting my life to get back to normal. Glad you thought of it."

"It was Julia who suggested it. She said she and Chris could double with us."

"Can we go to Fisher's afterward? We haven't been back since the day we met."

"Sure. I want you to be sure, so think about it. If you change your mind, let me know."

I yawn as I reach for the book I started reading the week Anthony went on vacation. Haven't been able to get very far. Too much going on in my head, I'm constantly distracted, and tonight's no different. Forget the book, Harper Lee's gonna have to wait to tell me her story.

I roll over on my side and reach for *Blue*, "How'd we ever get so lucky to meet Gabriel Marquez?"

34

1966 – Ella Galvez

When we walk out of The Majestic, I realize Julia's idea was a perfect one. I peek around Gabe to find her and Chris in the crowd of people. I see her and smile. She smiles back. I think she knows exactly what I'm feeling. The movie was great, and I'm once again having fun. Tonight, I got a taste of how good normal can feel. Well, that's easy to say *now*.

When Gabriel and I arrived, all I wanted was to sit in the safety of his truck. We sat there for ten minutes. I was nervous. I just knew everyone would stare at me. Of course, Gabe reminded me that the truth is I've done nothing wrong.

"Sure, they might look at you, Ella, but what are they gonna see? The same Ella they saw before except a happier one because she's with Gabe, the babe."

I laughed when he said it knowing Rita's going to love it when I tell her he called himself Gabe the babe.

As my friends and I have always done after a movie, we head to Fisher's, which is just across the street from the theater. While we're waiting for a car to pass I notice Michael walking along the sidewalk in our direction. I give Gabe's hand a squeeze. He leans in and whispers. "We'll pretend we don't see him."

There's a swagger to Michael's stride – I think he's been drinking. A cigarette hangs from the corner of his mouth, the end lights up a bright orange as he lifts his hand to take it from his lips. We cross the street, and as Michael passes by us, he looks our way. "Hey Marquez, hope you like leftovers, cuz that's all she's got for you." He laughs mockingly.

Gabe loosens his grip on my hand and turns to face him directly. Chris pulls Julia and me back. Michael's cheeks suck in as he takes a long drag of his cigarette. A smile spreads across his face as he flicks the cigarette stub to the curb. I'm scared knowing Gabriel isn't going to let this go. Where's Officer Gomez, he's always around.

"You son of a bitch," Gabe says, squaring his shoulders and taking a firm stance. "Get the hell out of my sight! I'm not doing this here."

Michael moves closer to Gabe, juts his chin out, fists clenched at his side. He's almost daring Gabe to make a move. "About the only way anyone can get inside those sweet, silky drawers is—"

Gabe grabs ahold of Michael's shirt. "You bastard!" he says, yanking him in close.

"Gabriel, please!" I lurch forward, but Chris yanks me back.

Gabe releases his grip, and as he turns to look at me, Michael reaches him with a punch grazing the side of his face near his temple. Gabe turns back to Michael and lands a hard punch right on Michael's nose and sends him flying. Michael, bloody nose and all, scurries to stand and get his fists up, anxious for a fight. He comes toward Gabe who's ready for him. From the corner of my eye, I see faces are lined against the window at Fisher's, and a crowd has gathered outside.

"Try that again, and you'll be sorry," Gabe threatens.

"You don't scare me, Marquez!" Michael swings to punch, and Gabe manages to dodge him. Michael loses his balance and lands on the ground, sprawled face down.

Anthony runs up to us, "Stay with Ella, Gabe. I'll take it from here."

Gabe wraps his arm around me, and we watch as Anthony lifts Michael up by his shirt, shoves him roughly against the wall and keeps him there. Gabe tries to take me inside, but I tell him we can't leave Anthony.

Michael manages to lift his gaze up to meet Anthony's glare.

"Listen up, you worthless piece of shit," Anthony says. "Stay away from Ella and Gabe. If Ella hadn't been here, Gabe wouldn't have held back. It would've been lights out for you. So just stay away, or either Gabe or I will finish you off. Got that, Damon?"

Anthony releases his hold, and Michael slides down the wall to a stoop. Anthony sneers down at him then walks away. A few onlookers give Anthony pats on the back and thumbs up.

I check Gabe's face to see if he's okay. Gabe looks at his fist and rubs the redness on his knuckles with his finger.

Anthony comes up to us. "Ella, are you okay?"

"Yeah, thanks."

"Way to be there, Bartelli," Gabe says, turning to him, and they do their big guy pat on the back.

"I don't think he'll mess with any of us, what do you say, Marquez?"

"You never know with Michael," Gabe responds.

I nudge Gabe. "Let's go inside so I can kiss your boo-boo."

Julia and Chris have a booth for us, and we join them. Anthony looks out the window. "Hey, guys, I see Officer Gomez, I'm gonna talk to him, tell him what happened."

"Maybe I should go with you," Gabe says.

"Nah, Michael hit you first, unless you want to press charges."

"The only thing I want to do is press another fist against his face," Gabe says, rubbing his knuckles again.

Anthony laughs. "He's not worth it. Besides, I doubt he'll be coming around any of us."

I check the side of Gabriel's face. No blood, just a raised red spot where his eyebrow ends. I trace the hurt lightly then barely touch it with my lips.

Gabe smirks. "All better."

He straightens out his leg to reach into his pocket. *Hmm, this looks familiar, I think we're going to hear some music.* He pulls out some coins, hands them to Julia since he can't reach the wall-mounted juke box.

"Do me the honors, please, Julia, I'd like to hear D-7."

Julia finds it. "*I Feel Fine?*"

"And I do," he says smiling at me.

I laugh at his musical humor. "Wait a minute, do you actually know the number for all The Beatles songs?"

"Yep, I do."

"Nuh-uh," Julia says, her mouth dropping.

"I do. Try me."

"Gabe." Julia squints her eyes at him.

"What?" He squints back.

"You're just like Sandy, memorizing those baseball cards to try and catch a boyfriend, in fact, I heard you were her next victim."

"Hey, not even close. I just happen to like those guys. Besides, it's not just The Beatles' songs. B-3 is *Do Wah Diddy Diddy*, B-9 is *Jailhouse Rock*," he says then sneers at Julia which makes Julia and me laugh.

He hands Julia more change. "One more, please – C-6."

"What's that one?" I ask.

"Yesterday."

When *Yesterday* comes on, I notice a sadness in Gabriel's eyes. He looks at me as if he's studying my face, and then he smiles. Not his usual smirk. It was a small and barely-there smile, and it didn't last long. I'll have to remember to ask him what was on his mind.

We manage to get through dinner without mentioning Michael or my rape. Two of my school friends wave at me, smiling.

As we're finishing up, Anna and Rita come charging in.

"Finally, we find you!" Rita exclaims, waving at Anthony to come join us.

"You're not going to believe this!" Anna says. "I was—"

"Wait, I'll tell it, I was the one who saw her!" Rita interrupts.

"But I'm the one who asked her!" Anna says, folding her arms across her chest.

Rita leans into Anna. "Why do you have to be so bossy?"

The rest of us just watch, our head's going back and forth between the two, our smiles growing with each response.

Julia interrupts. "Stop your arguing."

"No, don't stop," I say, cocking my head at Rita, "it's kinda fun to watch."

Anna rolls her eyes at me then turns to Rita. "Okay, I'll set you up in the credits."

Rita nods. "Okay, tell it."

"Rita," Anna says, nodding toward Rita, who is smiling, "saw Miss Bates, you know, the government teacher. We were at Penney's. Turns out Miss Bates is working there for the summer. She was at the register when we went to pay for our stuff. We noticed her new hairdo. It's exactly like yours, El."

Rita takes over. "Anna Banana raved about how pretty she looked and after a gushy *thank you,* Miss Bates said her boyfriend, Jimmy, picked out the new hairdo. Even paid for her trip to the hair salon."

"Here's the important part," Anna says. "Rita noticed Miss Bates' necklace. It's a little rectangle engraved with Que Sera, Sera!"

"What?" I ask in shock. "It's a one of a kind!"

"That's what we thought," she says, looking at Anna, who nods in agreement. "But we weren't positive, so we didn't say anything. Anna admired it, and, listen to this, she said Jimmy gave it to her about a month ago for no special reason. He told her it went perfectly with her new look."

That comment made me shudder, my thoughts are flying all over the place, but then Gabe snaps me back to the present. "That son of a...sorry. I just hope they lock him up!"

"You bet, they will," Anthony says. He heads toward the door.

"Hey, where are *you* going?"

"Payphone, calling my dad to let him know," Anthony says over his shoulder.

Gabe gives him a thumbs up. "This Jimmy guy is in for a rude awakening!"

"I'm scared to get excited about this. He could've had one made for Miss Bates. I mean those *are* the words of a popular song."

"What are the chances?" Gabe asks. "Yours was ripped off about a month ago. He looks at me and smiles. "I think there's a very good chance that Miss Bates is wearing your necklace."

I think about what Gabe said and realize he's probably right. But questions start coming at me in quick succession. Is Jimmy the blue cap guy? Will he have an alibi, too? Will he say he bought it from someone off the street and didn't realize it was stolen? I'm scared I'll be let down again, but I'm just going be hopeful that it's going to work out this time and don't say anything.

I look at Rita and Anna. "Thank you so much," I say, wiping my tears. "You found my necklace. That's something I can be glad about."

"It's kinda creepy, her wearing your necklace and looking like you with her new hairdo," Anna says.

I frown. "Yes, that is creepy. Gabe and I saw her at The Vermillion. I thought her hair looked just like mine. Didn't think anything of it."

Anthony returns. "Dad's on it!" he says, smiling from ear to ear. "Can you believe this? We came down on two bad guys tonight. I feel fantastic!"

"Wait, who's the other bad guy?" asks Rita.

"Oh boy, you missed it. Michael Damon got a bruising," Anthony says with a big grin on his face.

"Whoa, by whom?" Anna asks.

"He got punched by Gabe, talked to and warned by me. He didn't look too hot when we last saw him."

"He showed up blitzed and opened his stupid mouth," Julia adds.

Rita makes a face. "Damn, I missed watching Michael get decked!"

"Yep," Anthony says.

I breathe out a heavy sigh. "I think it's time for me to go home. I've had all the excitement I can handle in one evening."

On the way home, Gabe apologizes for the whole fight scene, insisting it should never have happened while I was there. But of course, we both knew it couldn't have gone any other way. Michael was looking for a fight and wasn't going to let it go. Then I mention that I thought he looked a little sad when the song, *Yesterday*, played on the jukebox.

"Yeah, I was for a moment. The words got to me. I got to thinking if you came back to 1966 to figure out a few things here, what happened to Ella from the future? Did she get zapped away? If so, there's a Gabe out there missing his Bella Ella."

"Yikes! But if I'd been zapped here physically, I'd look different, you know, older and grown up." I cup my hands in front of my breasts to indicate possible growth making Gabe laugh. "Just today I was thinking that maybe it was a time travel glitch and I only came over in bits and pieces. Older Ella is still wherever she is now with little bits and pieces of me. Who knows, it's not like there's a book at the library I can check out on time travel rules and oddities."

Gabriel laughs. "No, don't suppose there is."

When Gabe walks me to my door, we look in the direction of the neighbor's window. There's no one there, but we both have the same question. If this Jimmy guy is the one who raped me then why is Mr. Prada or someone else who lives there looking at my house? At me?

"Do you think Jimmy's his son and lives there, too?"

"Nope, Anthony's dad told him that the only other person who lives there is Prada's mom. There's a nurse who comes to care for her, and Mr. Prada's sister drops by during the evening. They also have a housekeeper. That room facing your house is an extra bedroom, his mom's bedroom is downstairs, so it could be just about anybody."

Before Gabe leaves, he kisses me goodnight. It's sweet, a quick brush of his lips. He pulls back and asks, "Ella, are you okay with this, my kissing you? *Really* kissing you. I know you said it was alright before, but—"

"Just kiss me already, Marquez."

He gives me his usual mischievous smirk and shakes his head. "You, little girl, are asking for it." He pulls me to him and kisses me again. I feel his lips turn into a smile against mine when he hears my tiny moan. It was very tiny, but he liked it. I smile too.

"What a sweet kiss," he says as he exhales. "I just don't want to rush you."

"You're doing just fine. But thanks for taking such good care of me." We kiss again and say goodnight.

Mom's in front of the television when I walk in. She looks up at me, and I can see she's very happy. She gets up to give me a hug and a kiss. "You're smiling, I take it you had a good time."

"Yes, it was very nice, and for most of the evening I felt like everything was back to normal." I don't mention the Michael incident. Don't want anything to take away from the happy look on her face.

"Well, we got a call from Tony Marquez. He talked to your father and told him the news Anthony got from Anna and Rita."

"I'm not putting too much hope on having the guy arrested. The detective was so quick to dismiss Mr. Prada. What if they do the same with this guy? I don't want to be let down again."

"I understand, but this means it really wasn't Mr. Prada. They were right," Mom says.

"Yes, I guess that's true," I agree.

"I go to the kitchen and get a glass of water. As I head toward the stairs, I look down the hall that leads to the back door and decide to peek outside. I don't see the little boy. Dad must've taken away the broken pieces. It's just the little girl and her basket of daisies standing there all alone. It's crazy, but I miss him now.

I breathe out a sigh, turn off the outdoor light and step outside just as far as the steps go knowing I can't be seen from the neighbor's upstairs window standing here. Dad's already started on a patio cover to block the view of our back yard from that window. I hope he doesn't change his mind; a cover would be so nice.

It begins to sprinkle. It's light, sporadic. My mind is focused on the feeling of each drop. One on my cheek, nose, then on my chin, then one eye, making my eyelashes flutter, then my cheek again.

A thought intrigues me. I'm doing it again. I'm living life in slow motion. I remember the sensation while eating my ice cream and how I thought I'd made it an art form, but no, it's more like being in tune with everything around me. And now here I am enjoying a raindrop symphony. This is the second time I do this slow-motion thing. No, I did it once before the ice cream, when I was fixing a cup of tea watching the steam rise.

Wait a minute. Whose tea. I don't drink tea, and I don't know anyone who drinks mint tea. Mint? Why am I thinking about mint tea? What's going on?

As goosebumps surface, I smile. *I get it.* The other Bella Ella drinks mint tea. She was fixing herself a cup of mint tea and watched the steam rise in slow motion. That's what this is about. *Isn't this amusing?*

35

1966 – Ella Galvez

I open the door before Gabriel even makes it to the porch. "I thought you'd never get here; the waiting is killing me!"

"Are you always this excited about going to the record shop?"

"If The Beatles are releasing a new album, yeah! Especially an album that might show us the necklace may have come from the future." I laugh. "Boy does that sound crazy!"

I take Gabe's hand and place it over my heart. "Here, feel that!" I get wiggly eyebrows along with a sly little smile. "Stop it, Gabe, just feel my heart!" I put a little more pressure on his hand.

He cracks up laughing. "Ella, you put my hand on your breast, and you want me to feel *your* heartbeat. Baby, all I can do is feel mine, and you're making my heart bulge...among other things!"

"Darn you, Gabriel Marquez, you are incorrigible! It wasn't supposed to be sexual, I just wanted to show you my excitement."

"But instead I showed you mine." That little smirk-y smile is back, and he knows it's my weakness. "Okay, sorry...really," he says, bowing his head like if I'm supposed to give him some sort of absolution for his sins. "God's still working on me. But I *am* trying. It's not my fault that I'm a sexy kind of guy," he says with a wink.

I can't help but laugh. "Hold on, I'll be right back." I head up the stairs to Mom's workroom to let her know I'm leaving. Three steps up, then I look back at him over my shoulder. He's standing there grinning from ear to ear. I turn around, lean forward cupping my hands around my mouth and whisper loud enough for him to hear. "Sex fiend."

He tilts his head back and just stands there looking up at the ceiling. "Mercy!" *There he is talking to God, again.*

When I return, he's standing in the same spot, hands in his pockets, wearing a mischievous grin. I narrow my eyes at him. "What are you up to?"

"Nothing, just reliving the moment when you asked me to feel your heart," he says, taking my hand and leading me out. I roll my eyes, he smirks.

"Wow, the Mustang," I say as we walk toward the car.

"Yeah, big day, fancy car," he laughs. I had to beg my dad this time. He found sand in it the last time I borrowed it.

I half-way skip to the car holding Gabriel's hand. Once we're in the car, he reaches for my hand again. "I love seeing you happy."

"I have every reason to be. I'm loved, cared for and prayed for."

"Loving you and caring for you is easy for me. The prayers, that's all God."

"You really do talk to God, don't you, in a let's have a chat kind of way?"

"That's exactly what the Big Guy and I do, we chat."

"Chatting with God...I like the sound of that. You'll have to show me someday."

356 LALI SERNA CASTILLO

I don't think I'll ever forget the look I see on his face this very moment. I see love swelling up in him with the long breath he takes.

"We can chat with God together, you and me. One person praying is great, two or more, now that's powerful stuff." He takes another long breath and smiles.

When we arrive at the record shop, Gabe grabs me by the hand and pulls me into a trot, all the way to the store.

"Now look who's excited!" I tease.

There are others holding *Revolver* albums waiting to be checked out, but I think we're the only ones with so much riding on it. "Are you ready for me to flip it over?" he asks in a whisper.

"Yes," I whisper back.

He slowly turns it over to check the list of songs. It jumps out at me. "It's there!" I say, pointing to it, no longer whispering. I go to reach for an album for me, and he beats me to it

He shakes his head. "Please let me buy it for you," he says.

"Aww, thanks, that's so sweet of you."

As soon as he's paid for our albums, Gabe pulls me by the hand, and we laugh all the way out of the store. "Holy cow," he says when we're finally outside, "I was about to burst in there!"

"It's for real!" I yell. "I'm not going crazy after all."

"I never thought you were." He wraps an arm around me and kisses me right there in front of Capitol Record Shop, and his kiss ends with a smile. "Let's go find out what was so special about our song."

When we're in the car headed home, we're both talking non-stop. We talk about all the clues we have pointing to the possibility that I really did somehow get zapped from the future. Gabe suggests we pull out my journal and go over each clue carefully to see if there's anything we might've missed.

As soon as we get to the house, we scramble out of the car, run through the front door and bound up the stairs.

"Hi, Mrs. Galvez."

"Hi, Mom, sorry, but we've got a new Beatles' album we just gotta listen to."

Mom laughs. "You silly kids. I'm making sandwiches, would you like some?"

I look at Gabe, he shakes his head. "No thanks, I'll make some later if we get hungry," I say from the top of the stairs as we enter my bedroom.

Once in my room, I kick off my sandals. Gabe pushes off his loafers and starts opening my album, while I get my stereo ready. He lays the album on the turntable and carefully put's the needle on the right track. I get to my spot on the floor leaning back against my bed, legs stretched out in front of me. He sits next to me, and we listen, holding hands, and we are so excited. We hear the first note, then the first verse.

"You're right, Ella. Paul's voice *is* sweet."

"Told ya."

"Gabriel, this is beautiful." And then I hear it...the melody where the notes go upward at the end, the one that played in my head. I point toward my stereo looking at him with misty eyes. "Gabe, that's it...the part I heard in my head. Those last six notes."

We listen to it two more times, then settle back to listen to the full album.

I gotta hand it to your cute Paul. This is one hell of a song, the lyrics, the melody and his voice. Everything!"

"You own a necklace engraved with the title of the best song on this album, heck, on this planet!"

Gabriel turns to me, a serious look on his face. "Ella, all these visions, voices and melodies weren't premonitions. You've already lived them. Well, *we* have, I'm just not able to see it." He cups my face in his hands. "I want you to take me there."

"I think I can. There are probably clues everywhere, we just have to find a way to tune into them together."

Gabe looks at his watch, "I've got to get going, got stuff to do for Dad. But first chance I get, I'm listening to the whole album again. Gotta figure out how to play *our* song too."

"Gabe, this is funny. You're gonna go home and learn a song on the guitar which you've probably already played and sung to me somewhere in time. I'll bet you play it for me often."

"I'll bet I do." He gives me several sweet kisses and sighs when he stops. "Just wondering, do you think you'll get over cute Paul, you know, like in the future, ten, maybe fifteen years from now?"

I squint my eyes and think about what he asked, then look over to the wall where Paul's picture is hanging. "Hmm...maybe...nah, probably not." I laugh.

"Why do I put up with you?" he asks, smiling and giving my earlobe a little tug.

I laugh. "Because you love me, Gabe the babe, that's why, so just get used to it."

He laughs. "Okay, gotta go. See you in my dreams, Bella Ella."

"Yeah, I'll see you in mine too. Hey, thanks for my album."

36

1966 – Ella Galvez

When I get home from having lunch with the girls, Mom meets me at the door. Her expression tells it all – she's beaming. She tells me Detective Aguirre called to say there's been an arrest, and the man who raped me will soon be behind bars. Detective Aguirre told Mom that he was glad they were able to solve this one.

"*They* were able to solve it? Nope, Rita and Anna nabbed this guy," I laugh, Mom laughs too.

And then I cry. And I can't stop. This was supposed to be a happy day, and maybe it will be but not right now. Everything I've endured plays out in my head as I sob. Then I somehow manage to thank God. It's more with sobs than actual words but somehow feel my spirit lift, just like that. I recall what Gabe once said: *My grandfather told me that sometimes you'll find you can't pray, for whatever reason, the words just don't come or you're not able to speak them. But if there's faith, God takes that unspoken prayer, whether it be a groan or a sigh. to him.* I think that's exactly what happened. God took my prayer.

When I call Gabriel to tell him what we learned from Detective Aguirre, Gabe tells me he'd just gotten off the phone with Anthony. He asked Gabe to meet him at my house. They'll be on their way shortly, he says.

"Wait, Gabriel, there's something else. I thanked God for everything today, especially for your prayers. I think I know what faith feels like now. I felt it."

Gabe's quiet for a moment then clears his throat. "Ella, what you just said was an answer to one of mine."

Mom and Dad leave for an appointment with Detective Aguirre as Gabe and Anthony show up.

"Dad gave me a rundown on what happened," Anthony says.

Gabe notices I've been crying, wipes a tear that fell at the sight of them coming up the steps. "Are you okay, baby?"

"Yes, I'm fine, it's been an emotional afternoon."

Gabe and I sit side-by-side while Anthony shares the information he got from his dad, late last night. Two officers went to Miss Bates' home yesterday. She was wearing my *Que Sera, Sera* necklace. She said it was a gift from her boyfriend, Jimmy Martin. He gave it to her a day after I was attacked. She said the chain was broken. Jimmy told her he hadn't noticed it when he bought it, but he'd get it fixed for her.

"That's unspeakable! How could he give his girlfriend a necklace he took from his victim? What if he says he found it?"

"No, they've got him. He can't wiggle out of this. Miss Bates said she saw Jimmy the day you were raped but not until later in the afternoon. She said Jimmy told her he was helping the lady his sister, Glenda, cares for. Glenda is a nurse and takes care of Mr. Prada's mother, who's bedridden. Jimmy's family owns a company that provides oxygen tanks. Listen to this, the business is in the grey building which shares a parking lot with your ballet studio and Sophia's theater group."

I gasp. "It was him all along." I turn to Gabe. "We saw him there." I shudder at the thought of him.

Anthony continues. "He delivers refilled oxygen tanks to Mr. Prada's mom's bedside when needed. Jimmy also helps his sister move Prada's mom around, making beds, that sort of thing. He also watches the old lady whenever his sister needs to run an errand. Miss Bates said she remembered he was late that day, said something about offering to prune the old lady's rose bushes."

"Doesn't make sense. I don't think you're supposed to prune rose bushes in the heat of summer," I say. "I know Dad doesn't."

Anthony shrugs. "She said he came by really upset. Said he'd lost his watch," Anthony says with a nod and then smiles. "That's when she noticed his arm was all scratched up. He told her it got scratched working in the rose bushes."

"Oh, wow!" I say. "He lost his watch, scratches from rose bushes on the very day I was attacked? It's him, it really is him."

"Here's where it gets really interesting," Anthony says. "Mr. Prada's mom lives next door to you, which is where he delivers the oxygen and where he helps his sister out."

I point in the direction of the house with the second story window.

Anthony nods. "Yep, right over there. And his last log entry before lunch was a delivery to Mr. Prada's house, so it put him next door to the crime scene."

I'm so relieved to hear everything points to this Jimmy person, who turns out to be the blue cap guy who was stalking me.

"So there you go, kiddo. You don't have to worry about him anymore. It's a done deal."

I wait until Anthony's gone to mention something that came to mind. The first time I noticed the window and the blue cap guy was the day of the shimmering lights.

"The window practically slapped me across my face to get me to look at it. It must've been my older self...that sounds so weird, but what else can I call her or the other me?" I ask with a laugh.

A big grin spreads across Gabe's face. "Call her Ella Marquez."

I giggle. "Well, we don't know that we're married, but I do like the sound of it. So okay, part of Ella Marquez or her memories showed up the day of the lights, and her necklace too. Hmm, that really is weird, Gabe." I chew on my thumbnail and look at him. "I wonder why her necklace made it, but only bits and pieces of her memory showed up."

He nods. "Good question...maybe she just couldn't let go of her life there." Then he flashes his cute little smirk. "Or maybe she couldn't bear to leave the grown-up and very romantic Gabe the babe behind."

"Yeah, I'm sure that's it," I laugh. "Well, something apparently made her hang on tight. But what I was going to say is she knew about the window and the pervert who would stare at her from there. Being forced to look in its direction must've been a warning from Ella Marquez to me, Ella Galvez."

"I think you're right. So no telling how long this guy's been looking out that window since you never noticed it was there before."

"Right, it didn't exist. And now I shudder at the thought of him there. To think I've allowed him in my bedroom and my dance room without even knowing it. The first thing I've always done when I enter my dance room is pull up all the shades to let the light in. Stupid, stupid, stupid," I say through gritted teeth.

"Don't blame yourself. There's no way you could have known."

I roll my head around trying to undo the tension. Gabe places his hand on my neck, rubs up toward the hairline. His fingernails softly touch my skin, and graze my scalp, giving me delightful little chills. I drop my head slightly.

"It feels so good," I say, bringing my head up and letting it fall back against his hand.

He leans in and kisses my neck. Several little kisses from the little hollow of it, all the way up to the tip of my chin. I'm melting into the wonderful feeling his trail of kisses is leaving on my skin. My lips part slightly when his touch mine. His kisses are so delicious.

Little moans from me bring deeper ones from Gabriel. His hand reaches down and caresses my calf then slowly moves up and over my knee. I hold my breath when I feel it at the edge of my skirt. But then, he strokes back toward my knee, and I release the breath I've been holding. I'm left with a great feeling of desire for him, yet relieved it didn't go any further. It didn't scare me, I guess I'm not sure what I thought. Gabe would never hurt me. He looks at me. "Ella, I'm—"

"Don't say sorry."

He strokes my cheek softly. "I hadn't planned for this to happen. I just got carried away, and...maybe we should talk about something else. Peanut butter sandwiches. I love peanut butter, how about you?"

I laugh at him. He can be so funny. "Okay, that worked. Now I'm craving a peanut butter sandwich. Good job, Gabriel."

"I know, that little trick does come in handy," he smiles. "But we really need to think about what happened."

"You're right about that, but how do we stop from getting to the point where, *you know*?" Where did we go wrong?"

"We kissed," he says and looks at me with his mischievous, little smile.

"What? We can't kiss now?"

Running a finger along my lower lip, he says, "I didn't say that." He places his hand behind my neck, slowly pulls me to him and kisses me firmly, I kiss him back. We finish off with several lingering kisses.

I nod. "Okay, we can still kiss. But *you* just have to stop us before we go too far."

"Me? *I* have to? There you go again, making me do the hard part."

"Gabe, you *are* the hard part."

He laughs. "Okay, you're right," he says as he nods his head. "Don't you worry; I got this." He stops and thinks for a moment and then turns to look at me. "But maybe you shouldn't wear a skirt...and we need supervision," he says with a smirk and then he laughs.

I laugh too. "Yeah, we shouldn't have let Anthony leave. We're like little children wanting to take something that's not ours to take."

"Yet," Gabe says. "It's not ours to take...yet."

"One things for sure," I say. "The last thing I want to do is have to discuss this kind of stuff with God. It would be so embarrassing."

"Welcome to my world," he says with a laugh. "Hey, I was wondering if we could do something later. Maybe grab a bite at Rutledge Hamburgers and then go to The Capitol for a movie. They're playing an old Dracula movie."

"Yes, I'd love it, but I'm telling you now, I'm scared to death of Dracula. Yes, I watch Dark Shadows, and I'm scared of Barnabas Collins too. I hate how Dracula just suddenly appears in girls' bedrooms. Freaky! I'd rather he'd knock first, then suck the life out of me. It would be a lot less frightening."

"Ella, either way, you turn into his bride."

"Right, but the worst part is when he's suddenly there because—" As I turn away I feel the sting of tears which I'm glad I'm able to hold back.

"Oh no. I'm sorry. We can do something else."

"No, it's okay, this is just how things are. Somehow when I mentioned the part of him suddenly being there, a vision flashed. But I'm okay, and I *want* to see the movie. Not gonna let that guy take one more thing away from me."

"Only if you're sure."

"I'm positive. Just be prepared to have your hand crushed." I laugh.

He looks at his manly hand then lifts my small hand and looks at it and smiles. "I think my hand will be just fine. I'll pick you up at 5:30."

When the movie is over Gabe's takes me by the hand and pulls me quickly out of the theater and to the car. I giggle all the way. When we're in the car he shoves his hand in his pocket and pulls out my bracelet with Baby Blue now hanging there with the others.

"Oh Gabriel, thank you," I say as he places it in my open palm. I look at it swirling in my hand. When I'm finally able to focus on it, I look up at Gabe. He's smiling, and from the eagerness on his face, I think he knows something's going on between the bracelet and me. I look back at my bracelet then shut my eyes for a moment.

"You saw something?" he asks.

"Lots of little charms, Gabe."

"What kind?"

"Besides the ones I already have, I also saw a record, you know, as in music, a daisy, a sand dollar, engagement ring and a wedding cake."

"Ha! I knew it! We're married!"

I also saw a bridge, the Golden Gate Bridge, I think. I couldn't see them all. It went so fast."

Holy moly!" He looks over at me. "You think we're married too, don't you?" he asks as he pulls out of our parking spot.

"This bracelet tells a story and I think it's ours. So yeah, I do."

"Isn't this the wildest thing? Hey, maybe it happens all the time, and people just don't notice," he says.

He makes me go back and tell him again what each charm looked like. I run them by one at a time with as much detail as I can remember. Then he makes a sudden right turn off Elizabeth Street into a driveway and parks the car facing Sam's Stadium right next to The Eagle's Nest, where I'd seen him a couple of times during the school year buying a soda. I remember wondering what kind of drink he'd bought. Wanted to know if his kisses would taste like cola, or maybe root beer and if he'd enjoy the taste of my strawberry soda kisses.

Gabe shuts off the engine and turns in his seat toward me. I tilt my head and think about what he'd said before. "You think people time travel and don't even know it?"

"Maybe, but what if we *do* notice and don't give it much thought, and just say déjà vu?"

My eyes dart around as I think about it. "Ohmygosh! You're right! When I got into Rita's new car, I knew I'd seen that stick shift before. If I hadn't had all the weird stuff happening around me, I might've said exactly that and not given it a second thought."

"Except you didn't toss it off, you kept digging deeper," Gabe says. "I think you're here to find answers and solve crimes. All those Nancy Drew mysteries you've read are starting to pay off."

"Maybe I should start carrying a flashlight." I laugh. "But seriously, I think you're right, I'm here to find some answers. And I also came here to work things out. I'm definitely feeling pretty good, and a lot of it has to do with you and your prayers."

He smiles. "So...do you think we can go back?" I can see he's dead serious. He looks at me and arches his eyebrows. "Do you?"

"I hope so. My bracelet told a story of a life we have together." I look at my hand and give my ring a twirl. "What's scary is my being back could mess things up. Look at how I managed to change you being there for me rather than Michael. We almost broke up on the way back from the beach! Messing things up wouldn't be good." I look back at Gabe, he looks concerned. "Maybe it *is* time to go back, after all, I've accomplished what I was supposed to do." I give him a mischievous smile. "I think I know a way, and the shimmering firefly lights I've seen might be the key."

"Firefly lights! I just remembered something I wanted to tell you."

"Oh no, not you too."

"It happened the night after we uh...kissed a lot on your sofa."

"Oh, oh. Scared to ask, but...what did you dream?"

He laughs. "No, nothing like that. I was dreaming, well, I think I was. I swear I thought I had opened my eyes. It woke me up in the middle of the night, but not sure if my eyes were open while it happened or after." He looks at me, squinting. "Ella, I really do think I was awake. Didn't think much of it then, but now it's a different matter." He stares straight ahead toward the stadium bleachers a moment then back at me.

"Good grief, Gabe, don't keep me guessing, what happened!"

"I saw fireflies or something like them, they'd melt away and then return. Three of them. And then I saw Anthony and you. We were at Fisher's."

"So you were dreaming this?"

"That's what I thought. But like I said, my eyes were open. And then I saw more lights, but I remember thinking about you alone at the cabin, and that scene at Fisher's went away. The firefly lights fizzled out too."

"Did you say *cabin?*"

"Yeah."

"Like in log cabin?"

"Well, now that you mention it, I didn't say *log* cabin, but I somehow know that's what I thought of in my mind. Don't know what you'd be doing in one, but you were, and I blew off dreaming of Fisher's to go be with you there. But it ended so don't know if I made it back to you at the cabin."

"Gabriel, things just got a little more interesting."

"Oh yeah?

"Yes, I had one of those I-think-I'm-awake dreams about fireflies and a cabin by the lake. The thing is I knew I'd seen it before. It was an honest-to-goodness log cabin. It happened just after we'd met. Way before I shared any of this madness with you. But the weirdest part was the fireflies. Well, they couldn't be real fireflies because it was in the middle of the day. They looked like them but fizzled away and then came back."

Suddenly, I feel a moment of clarity as if a light actually went off in my head, just like they say.

"Firefly lights! They *are* the key." I think about what I just said, nod my head twice, slow and deliberately then look at Gabe. "It's those crazy lights I saw in my backyard. And guess what? I've seen them a few times since. I didn't think much about them because there were just a couple of them on one occasion. Then three or four of them at another time. I think I've seen them on you, like on your shoulder once and then in your hair. I just tossed it off as a sun glare or something. And we've probably seen them at night but don't pay attention to them since they look like regular old lightening bugs...until they fizzle out."

"That's crazy, Ella. Do you really think—"

"They multiplied...the lights multiplied. I saw one, noticed it right here on my upper arm. I didn't think anything of it, but I was sad, and I remember wishing I could go to the future to where there is no upstairs window looking down at me, where there is no talk of rapists. I said it out loud, and I saw four more lights. That's when I said there's no way I want to go anywhere without you. The lights just disappeared."

"And in my dream," Gabe says, "the same thing happened, they multiplied when I wished something and fizzled away when I changed my mind." A smile slowly makes its way across Gabe' face. "This is the answer, isn't it?"

"Yes. My backyard was covered with them that day. I don't know why I didn't put two and two together. And you saw them too. Maybe we both longed to be here, and you held back more than I did and less of you showed up. But now I'm wondering why did we long for this place."

"Well, we know you'd been raped, we also know Michael walked away so it could've caused problems, so you had the desire to return to the past to fix things. And remember, I didn't want to leave you behind, so I think we were happy together."

"Gabe, I just remembered a dream I had. Well, it was part of a dream. Actually, I only remember one thing that I said in it. It woke me up."

"So what'd you say?"

"Something about twins getting a roundtrip ticket to Paris on fireflies. It was the morning after I made up that Tina the time traveler story. Maybe I fell asleep thinking about it. My brain just kicked in with this new one. Guess that must be it...unless maybe—"

We look at each other and say, "Nah." And then we laugh

And the laughter disappears, not even a smile is left. "It's too crazy to be true, the firefly lights." He sighs deeply, sounding disappointed.

"But maybe not," I say with a smile.

37

1966 – Ella Galvez

Gabe drops by the house wearing a sleeveless T-shirt and shorts. His skin glistens - he must've just finished his run.

I check him out and smile. "That's a look I've never seen before. You're hot and sweaty."

"More like drenched. You like?"

I smile and open the door further for him to come in. "Yeah, I do, but not enough to let you hug me." I laugh, and so does Gabe.

"Definitely not gonna do that. I hadn't planned to stop by, but an idea hit me on the way home from doing a long distance run with the guys."

"Let's hear this idea of yours."

He smiles. "Our first date."

I'm not sure I understand what he means by *first*. Before we were brutally interrupted, he'd taken me to Zesto's for ice cream and then to play tennis, and we had pizza at his home. He also took me to a beach party, and twice to the movies. I remind him of all the stuff we've done.

"Those were not the same kind of *real* date I'm thinking of."

"Hmm, you got my attention, Marquez, keep talkin'."

"Good. How does a romantic Italian dinner sound?"

"I think it sounds very romantic. But you're a guy, what makes *you* think so? I would've thought an Italian dinner was just pasta, meat sauce and garlic bread on the side for you guys."

He gives me his cute little smirk. "Don't laugh. It's because of the movie *Lady and the Tramp*. You know the scene when Lady and Tramp are sucking on the same piece of spaghetti, and they end up kissing."

I laugh.

"Hey, you weren't supposed to. But no biggie, I knew you would. So how does Gio's sound?"

"Fabulous. I love that place. The dripping candles and the checkerboard tablecloths make it so cozy and romantic. But I've never been there on a date, only with my friends stuffing our faces with pizza. Definitely not romantic."

"So we're on. I'll come by at six."

As I step into my dress, I think about the vision I had last night of Gabe and me. There's no doubt in my mind we are a happy couple in the future. He's gonna love hearing about this one. I'm straightening my stockings, which are in a twist when I hear Gabe drive up. *He's early!* I quickly get my earrings on, put on some lip gloss and slip on my heels. I check myself one last time in the full-length mirror. I'm happy with what I decided to wear. It's a light blue chemise dress which accents my shoulders. I know Gabriel's going to love it.

When I'm halfway down the stairs, I see him sitting on the sofa staring at the same old pictures he's looked at several times before. He turns in my direction and walks toward me as I come down the stairs. He looks so handsome in a white long-sleeved cotton shirt and a navy and grey striped tie. I've only seen him in T-shirts and short sleeved cotton shirts. But it's his smile that captures me and the look in his eyes.

"Wow…wow…oh, wow."

"What? Gabriel Marquez is at a loss for words?"

He grins. "Yeah, totally." He moistens his lips, and his smile settles into that smirk I adore. He pulls his hand out of his pocket and extends it to me. "You look beautiful, Ella." He leans forward and kisses me on the cheek.

We turn to a flash of light and realize it came from mom's camera focused on us. She captured such a sweet moment. Can't wait to get the film developed. I'll frame it and place it on my bedside table. I'll give one to Gabe for his.

Mom comes over, wraps an arm around Gabe's waist and leans into him for a hug. "I think you two are going to love the picture I took. Let me take a few more," she says, and she does.

As we head to his car, Gabe leans in and whispers in my ear. "You weren't supposed to wear a dress. Ever!"

I laugh. "I thought about it while I was dressing."

He winks. "God help us."

As usual, Gio's is busy, and we end up parking in the furthest spot from the door. Once Gabriel has parked, I tell him I have a new vision to share and the smile he's had on his face gets bigger.

"Let's hear it." He says as he scoots around to face me.

I tell him how I saw us standing in a house with a rustic feel to it and that I think it might be the cabin we'd talked about because through the windows, I could see a lake with trees bordering it. Then I share how we kissed passionately, and how his kisses moved to my neck and then to my shoulders and how I, rather Ella Marquez, moaned so sweetly.

"Oh, Ella, don't get us going here."

"I know, I know. But don't worry. We know the rules. Your hands are not allowed past my knees."

"Ah, yes, we know the rules. Now tell me the rest," he says.

"Then I heard you whisper. No mistaking it, it was your voice."

"What'd I say?"

"*You are so easy.*"

"That's what I said?"

"Yes, you whispered it. And then I said something about how your kisses on my neck turn me on, and you asked me if I wanted more."

"Tell me you said *yes.*"

"How could I not!! But the vision stopped before I answered. It had to be a *yes,* why wouldn't it be?"

He looks at me with a mischievous smirk. "I knew it, we are one hot Mr. and Mrs. Marquez.

We agree to *not* discuss this hot little scene, well, not while we're alone and definitely not while I'm wearing a dress. And to make sure we hold ourselves to it I ask for a pinky promise. Gabe scrunches his brow at me, shakes his head then holds up a pinky.

I toss my head to move strands of hair out of my face. "You are so easy." I laugh. He flicks my arm with his finger and immediately rubs the spot he hit.

"Come on, our romantic evening is waiting," he says as he takes my hand and leads me toward the door.

Gio's Villa is a small family restaurant housed in what used to be someone's residence. I think it's charming or maybe quaint, and that's definitely part of its charm. There might not be much to the exterior, but once you step inside you know you're somewhere special. It's the ambience and of course, the incredible smell of Italian food.

An Italian theme is carried throughout. Each table has a red and white checkerboard tablecloth with a wine bottle at the center used as a candle holder. These are fiasco wine bottles, the kind with a straw basket woven around the round-bottomed bottles. They burn alternating colored candles, so they melt one on top of another in a beautiful colorful display. Those same bottles hang from the ceiling and on the walls.

The coolest part is watching Bart toss the pizza high up in the air. I'm betting it's the secret for the to-die-for pizza crust. Gio's introduced pizza to Brownsville and I've been loving those pizzas ever since. It was Nana's son, Mr. Garcia, who brought me and Nana here for dinner. I guess that's another reason why this place is so special to me. Well, that and their shrimp pizza.

"What would you like for dinner?" Gabe asks once we're seated, and we order iced teas.

"I think I'll have cheese ravioli."

"No shrimp pizza? Is this a first?"

"Yes, it is. It's hard not to, but I'm going for something grown up and romantic," I laugh.

"My parents and I come here all the time, and I can vouch for the ravioli. Would you like a salad?"

I look at Gabe and I'm about to answer, but I'm reminded of something I wanted to share with him, so I make a mental note to do it later.

"Ella," he says, smiling at me "if this is an Italian versus French dressing decision you're tossing around in your head, forget it, they only have house dressing. It's all they serve and trust me, it's all you need."

I laugh, "No, that wasn't it. I love their dressing."

When the waitress returns with our tea and asks what we'd like to order, Gabe says, "We'll both have the cheese ravioli with a salad, and I'd also like to order a shrimp pizza to go."

"To go?" I ask, after the waitress has left.

"Yes, for you. I don't want you to lay awake tonight thinking you should've ordered shrimp pizza."

"Thank you, maybe you can drop by for lunch." I smile at him, tilt my head and with my fingers move strands of hair that hang over my eye and brush them away from my face. And then I sigh.

"I love how you do that, tilt your head to the side and brush your hair away with your fingers. Sometimes it's a little toss of your head. I love that too."

I smile at him. He notices the tiniest and most insignificant things about me, and he loves them. How did I ever get so lucky? While we talk and wait for our dinner, I realize this is the first time we've sat like this, just the two of us talking about *us* and laughing about how for a married couple we know so very little about each other.

So we play a game and make our own rules. The game is to take turns sharing tidbits, and our sentence must begin with *I like* or *I love*. The other person has to say, I like or love it too, or I dislike or hate it, whichever the case may be. I take in Gabe's expressions, his mouth when he talks, the way his eyes sometimes squint, one eye more than the other, when he's thinking about something while he tells me a story, and I love the way he sometimes arches his eyebrows. It turns out we have a whole lot in common. Except for liver, he loves it, and I hate it. And he doesn't like musicals, but I love them.

We don't feel rushed to leave, so we take our time with our dinner, talking about the days before Gabe and Ella, and the day we met at Fisher's. For the short time we've known each other, we find so much to reminisce about, and it makes for a magical evening.

I'll bet couples come here all the time and do the same thing we're doing, reminiscing about falling in love. I think it's because there's something extra special about this place. Nothing else like it. It's quaint, cozy and so romantic. And maybe a little bit magical too.

When we pull into my driveway, Gabe asks if we can sit out on the swing for a while. When I see him trying to loosen his tie with one hand, I ask him to hand me the flattened brown paper bag which holds my shrimp pizza.

As we head toward the swing Gabriel loosens his tie then undoes the top two buttons of his shirt. He takes off the cufflinks and rolls his sleeves up to his forearms. I watch him, loving the way the moonlight on his face brings out Gabriel's handsome features. I place the pizza on a table and take a seat on the swing. As he sits beside me, I take his hand and tell him I have something I want to share. And he says he's got a surprise for me.

"You go first," he says.

"Okay. First, thanks for tonight. It was wonderful. And I want you to know I'm delightfully happy, even after everything I've been through. And you are the reason for it, Gabriel."

"Uh-uh. You're giving me way too much credit. You're a lot stronger than you think. *You* did this."

"Well, maybe a little bit," I say. "I've always been timid, shy and a little insecure. But now I realize there was a strength in me beneath the surface. God must've slipped it in there when I wasn't looking."

Gabe smiles. "Yep, that sounds like something God would do."

I smile back and nod. "When I was raped, I didn't want to ever tell anyone what my rapist did to me. I thought saying it out loud would make it true, and I didn't want it to be. But it *was* true, and I had to accept it and work my way through the pain and the horror of it all. I'm still doing that."

He reaches over and holds my hand in his. As he always does, he strokes the soft little spot in the space between my thumb and my finger. It's so soothing.

I smile. "Gabriel, you taught me we need to accept what's true, that it might hurt, but we have to work through it, but slowly and at my own pace. That advice helped me the most."

"And that's what you've done, Ella. I'm proud of you."

"Thanks. But honestly, I was afraid I wouldn't ever be able to be with anyone the way we were a couple of days ago, you and me, kissing and snuggling."

"You mean our make-out session?" he asks with a smirk.

I fan myself with my hand. "Yes," I giggle, "*that.*"

He smiles, biting down on his lower lip. I love his face, and I would really like to kiss him right now. But I need to continue.

"A nurse, who's a friend of our family, shared information with me on what rape victims can sometimes go through. She told me some girls end up resenting men in general, not trusting them, being afraid of them, especially fearful of their touch."

She said how each person deals with it can differ. Some may even become promiscuous. The saddest part is some may carry the stigma of rape for years and years to come, causing failed relationships and marriages. It might have something to do with the severity of the attack and the support the victim gets during recovery."

I touch his cheek with my hand stroking it down and around his chin. "I told her I could never resent you. You were there to hold me just after it happened when I needed you the most. You made me feel safe, loved and cared for. Anthony too. When I told her this, she said it was probably a matter of trust. Anthony is like a brother to me and you, well now we know, you, and I are married. We know that I've been raped before and we probably worked through some problems that may have come up because of the fact I was raped. I guess having my older self in here with me has helped."

"Yes, I think she has."

"What also helped me, Gabriel, is that I knew you would never pressure me to have sex with you. Like you've told me over the phone during our goodnight chats, you want to save sex for marriage, and so do I. That has helped me feel completely comfortable even though I know we can get ourselves worked up. It's because I know we both want the same thing."

He takes a deep breath, pulls me close and holds me there for a long moment.

"I don't know what to say, Ella. I felt I had screwed up letting us get carried away when—"

"No, no, don't even think it. What that man did to me, to my body, and how he touched me was horrible, brutal and disgusting. He was like an animal, and he sickened me. He has nothing to do with who you are or how I feel about you. And that's probably why what happened with him never entered my mind when I was with you. Your kisses were sweet and tender. I liked it. A lot. I didn't want you to ever stop, but of course, I knew we needed to."

"Oh, Ella," he whispers.

He pulls me to him again holding me close, stroking my hair. I'm enjoying the feel of his hands and the kisses he's giving me along my cheek, and then the corner of my mouth, then my lips. I melt into him with a sigh.

I look at Gabe and continue. "I feel sad for anyone who couldn't deal with the truth and instead harbored the pain of what they endured. How sad for them. And for women who didn't have the support I had. Remember how I saw Michael walk away? Like I said before I don't think it went well the first time around for me."

"Yeah, that makes me sad."

"One thing I still have to work through is the anger. I'm angry because he took something from us so precious. And the hate, I know I'm supposed to forgive, but I'm having a whole lot of trouble with it."

"You have every right to be angry. And I know with God's help you'll work through that. But just so you'll know, you are precious to me just the way you are. The hate's got to be the hardest. We both have to work on that."

"But what if, when we're married, and I end up having problems and I'm not able to...you know."

"We'll work through it. I promise you. And remember this: One, I love you. Two, I'm a very, very patient guy."

He moves strands of hair off my face and places his lips on mine. But he doesn't kiss me. Instead, I feel a smile form against my lips. I pull away and look at him.

"Why are you smiling? You were supposed to be kissing me, you know, your lips were on my lips?"

"I know, and I was. But as I was about to, I thought about this." He reaches into his pocket and pulls out tissue paper folded into a square. He carefully unfolds it and pulls out my Bella Ella necklace.

"Let's put this on you."

"My necklace," I sigh. "Bella Ella was me all along."

"I wanted to wait to give it to you right here in your backyard where you found it."

I shift my body around and lift the hair up off my neck. I turn so the outdoor light from the house is shining on it, so he can see the clasp. He places it around my neck.

"You've probably put this on me once before Gabriel. I would love to be able to see what that moment was like, wouldn't you?"

"Hey, that's what I was thinking. Wait a bit, I can't seem to slip it in."

My breath catches in my throat. "Gabe, look," I whisper. "Firefly lights."

Gabriel gasps. "I see it!" He looks around, then turns back to me, his eyes pleading. "Ella, please don't leave me." He takes the chain and holds it in one hand, the medallion dangles from it, swinging and spinning in the light. His other hand clutches my arm and pulls me close.

"I won't." I look at Gabriel. "We just made a wish together. I think it's the reason this is happening. Maybe we need to be more specific and wish to be back to the exact moment I described to you, the one in a house by the lake when you asked me if I wanted more kisses on my neck. We can go back there together."

Gabe's eyes search mine. "But are you sure it will work?"

"I think so. If not, the worst that could happen is I would take the memory of Ella Marquez being here from a future time with me. I'd return to that other Gabriel who's going to think I'm crazy when I tell him where I've been. You'd be left with young Ella Galvez, a teenage girl who is head-over-heels in love with you. And you'll eat shrimp pizza for lunch." I smile. "Besides, if it doesn't work, I'll know how to get back to you. Sparkly firefly lights. Oh Gabriel, can you feel that?"

"Yes, I can, and I'm wishing too, Ella," he says, holding onto my hand. He looks heavenly surrounded by the shimmer. The medallion sparkles in his hand as he reaches up to stroke my cheek with his thumb.

"I feel weightless," Gabe says. "I can't even feel the swing beneath me and look at all the fireflies."

"I know, isn't it awesome?"

"Look at me, Ella, I don't want to lose sight of you," he says as we're enveloped by the iridescent and shimmering lights. And then...

38

1971 – Ella Marquez

"Come here, baby," Gabe says, taking me in his arms. He holds me for a moment, then kisses me when I look up and smile at him and then again, a little more passionately. His kisses move to my neck, along my shoulder causing delicious shivers to run through me. My moan is barely audible, but still, he hears it. "You are so easy, Ella," he whispers in my ear.

"Hey, come on, you know how those little kisses on my neck turn me on."

"Uh-huh, want some more?" He continues to kiss me, making it impossible for me to resist. I lean my head back, and he places more of those sweet kisses from the tip of my chin down my neck.

"I do want more...those toys are gonna have to wait," I whisper.

"The twins can play...with the dog," Gabe says between kisses. "What's her name, again?"

"Uh...hmm...Mrs. Beasley. Yeah...they can play with her."

A strange but very familiar sensation makes me open my eyes. "Gabriel, look! Open your eyes."

"Why," he asks still kissing me. Then he stops and opens them. "I felt that!"

I watch as a smile spreads across his face. "Wow, the shimmer! And look at all those lights!"

He steps back to take it all in, slowly turning around, his eyes scanning the iridescent lights and yes, firefly lights, which fizzle away and reappear just as quickly. He looks back at me quite amused then we watch the shimmering veil lift until it disappears into the rafters. "Did we just—"

"I think we did."

"Wow, I remember it all. This is this wild! We were in your backyard." He looks at his hand. "I have it, I have your necklace!"

Gabe's expression makes me laugh. I remember how I felt the first time it happened to me. While it's still mesmerizing, I'm more of a spectator here watching Gabe experience it for the first time.

"I gave you the necklace at our apartment this morning for our anniversary. And then, moments ago, back in 1966 in your backyard, I started to place it around your neck again. Now here we are back in 1971 and guess what I'm about to do? Oh wow, Ella, this is unreal!"

"And we were eighteen years old, and we were dressed to the nines for our first romantic date, and now we're twenty-three. I'm in a sundress and barefoot, you're wearing shorts and a T-shirt. And there's a shrimp pizza sitting on the table that young Ella and Gabe will be sharing for lunch tomorrow."

We laugh, we hug, and we laugh again.

"What an experience we've had, Gabe. It's fantastically, unbelievably, over the moon, crazy! And it was incredible! It was our very own *Tale of Two Cities*."

Gabe scrunches his brow. *"Tale of Two Cities?"*

"Yes! Surely, you remember. Charles Dickens? I can quote it from memory."

"Let's hear it," he says.

"It was the best of times, it was the worst of times, it was the age of wisdom, it was the age of foolishness, it was the epoch of belief, it was the epoch of incredulity, it was the season of light."

"Whoa, Ella, that's uncanny."

"Yes, our season of light was shimmering firefly lights, and we definitely lived through the best and the worst. And we were older and wiser, then we were younger and took foolish chances by hitching a ride with the firefly lights. We definitely believed and yes, yes, yes, it was incredible!"

"Ella, the resemblance to his quote is surreal."

"Well, this is where I think our comparison to Charles Dickens's quote ends."

I look at Gabriel. The realization of what just happened kicks in. He's standing here in front of me looking so handsome. The same smile which melted my heart at Fisher's the summer of 1966 is melting my heart right now. *Thank you, God!*

Gabe looks at the medallion in his hand and reads it. "*Bella Ella - Here, There and Everywhere.* I think this belongs to you, Mrs. Marquez." He gives me his adorable smirk. "Come here, wife, let's put this back where it belongs."

"Wait I want to hold it first." I take the medallion, read the front then turn it around, and I stroke Gabriel's name several times as I did when I'd have trouble falling asleep after my rape. It soothed me.

"The night before our date at Gio's when I called to say goodnight, you told me on the phone that sometimes you fell asleep stroking the length of my name on your medallion. I didn't tell you, but just hearing you say that turned me on."

"Yes, I say," with a smile. I do remember. You didn't tell me, but I heard you moan," I laugh. "So it turned you on, huh?"

"It still does," he whispers.

He places the chain around my neck, and I lift my hair so he can clasp the ends together. With his hands on my shoulders, he turns me toward him as I let my hair fall. He kisses me deeply and holds me, and I feel myself melting in his arms.

I relish the look on his face as he slips the straps of my sundress off my shoulders. "My favorite part," he says as he watches them go bare. I wiggle my shoulders as the thrill runs through them when he kisses me there.

He smiles again when my dress drops to the floor, leaving me standing here wearing only my white satin undies. "So glad you wore a dress," he says with a wink. His voice sounds deep and warm, and I can see the desire in his hazel eyes, as I watch his pupils grow wide. "I've never wanted you more than I do right now."

I laugh softly. "I don't know Gabe," I say as I step out of my dress, which lays like a puddle on the floor, and watch him fling his T-shirt and shorts across the room. "You were really aching for me on that sofa in my living room."

His smile is a mischievous one. "Yeah, I've been waiting for this moment ever since."

We exchange kisses as he runs his hands along my shoulders and then my breasts, pausing for a moment there. We continue to kiss as his hand moves further down.

I feel him smile deliciously against my lips. "Mmm, I love the feel of satin," he whispers. Then he gently lays me down.

We've done all this before, so many times. The same touches which always start out so gentle and so, so slow, as if he had all the time in the world. Sweet agony is what it is. We share the same kisses, the same strokes, the same sweet words of love, the same passion and the same sighs and moans. Yet, there's something so different. My desire is heightened to an unbelievable level. We kiss, and our mouths can't seem to get enough, continually wanting and searching for one more kiss. And then another and another. His lips leave a trail of sweet sensations, and I close my eyes as all of my senses are awakened there and let myself enjoy the feeling his touch brings. The pleasure comes in continuous rhythmic waves.

And then, my attention turns to him, I touch, I hold, I stroke, I taste. When he looks at me, we smile. And I help myself to the smile I love so much. He makes love to me with his body, his words. The passion builds until we feel the incredible waves of true love flowing over us.

"This is the closest to heaven I've ever been," I say softly.

He kisses me and smiles.

We hold each other for a long time. Smiling, touching and whispering about how beautiful life can be. Gabriel's love came just before I entered the worst possible time in my life. God put him there to allow me to see love and passion for what it really is. Something extraordinary and capable of healing the soul. The love between a husband and his wife has got to be one of God's greatest gifts.

He pulls me to him so that I'm on my side and up against his beautiful bared body. I wrap my leg over him, lay my head on his chest and close my eyes. I feel myself drift. I'm very sleepy now.

I wake up from my nap to find Gabe laying there beside me on his side, his head propped on his hand watching me. He smiles, I smile back. "Come on he says, pulling me out of bed with him.

"Where to?"

"To take a shower. You my darlin' are a moveable feast."

I giggle. "Gabriel, I don't think that's what Hemingway had in mind."

He turns back and gives me a cute little smirk, and so I willingly follow him into the bathroom.

Once showered, Gabe pulls on his jeans and says he needs to get a fire going in the grill. While he does that, I unpack our bags and put everything away in the chest of drawers. I throw on my white shorts and a yellow floral halter top then pull my damp hair up into a twist on the top of my head. I finish off with some moisturizer, blush, and lip gloss. As I put on my charm bracelet, my eyes tear up. I finger the charms recalling the story that goes with each one. Now the bracelet, along with all the charms attached to it, carries its own phenomenal tale. Our story, and how a vision of it helped us get back to our life right here where we belong.

"Fire's lit, and I'm starving," Gabe tells me when I walk back into the living room. "You know, we just had dinner at Gio's so why am I so hungry? I should've held on to that shrimp pizza in my other hand," he laughs. Gabe pulls out the cheese tray I'd put in the fridge. "I think we fed our young bodies not these."

I grab crackers from the cabinet. Gabe rubs his hands together in anticipation. "Alright, where's our anniversary bottle of wine?"

I point to where I'd placed it when he brought it in and hand him the wine opener. I grab a couple of wine glasses from the cabinet and set them on the counter.

"Happy anniversary, baby. And happy first date, happy time travelling, happy everything."

I smile. "Happy. It's such a wonderful word, and I can tell just how happy you are. You've been talking non-stop, and I'm loving that smile on your face, Gabe the babe."

He tosses his head back in a beautiful warm laugh then looks at me. "*Salud, mi amor*," he says as we clink glasses.

Gabe notices the tinkling of my charm bracelet. "Wow, here it is in real life. I still can't believe it." He runs his finger along each charm.

"I know," I say. "I keep thinking I'll wake up and find out it was one big crazy dream. I don't want it to be."

I finish getting our sides heated and start to set our cutlery on the bar. But then decide sitting side-by-side here in the kitchen just wasn't going to do for a romantic anniversary dinner. I find two tablecloths in a drawer. One is white, the other is red and white checkerboard. I take one and place it over the coffee table and stand there smiling. I move the girl's chairs and throw cushions down on the floor for us to sit on facing each other. I like it. *Just wish I had a fiasco wine bottle and a candle.*

Gabe walks in with our steaks, smiles when he sees my table setting. "Hey, check out the table," he says and places the steaks on it. He pulls me in for a hug and kiss. "Déjà vu?"

I laugh, "That's exactly what it is."

We enjoy our dinner. The steaks are fantastic, and the conversation is a revisit of 1966 starting with the day we met at Fisher's to this moment here at the cabin. Not the shortcut we took via shimmering firefly lights, but the original one that led to his proposal and our marriage. By all accounts, it's been a blissful, perfectly married life.

While Gabe makes us some coffee, I clean up and pull out the top layer of our wedding cake. We take our cake and coffee outdoors. I lay out a blanket on the grass, and we sit there facing the lake, which has a shimmer to it cast by the moonlight. It's a beautiful night, and the stars are out in abundance. We sit there sipping our coffee and take turns feeding each other bites of our delicious year-old dessert. Our kisses between nibbles are especially sweet.

"Look Gabe, fireflies."

"Real ones, they don't fizzle out," he says.

Gabe looks at me, it's a pensive look I see as if he's searching for the answer to what he's about to ask. "When you spoke the words that young Ella heard...you said *if only*, right?"

"Right, *if only I'd sat by the dance floor.* Why do you ask?"

"Well, I mentioned this before. *If only.* That's a term of regret Ella. You must've been wishing you had sat by the dance floor."

"Yes, there was regret in it. As young Ella, I acted on it. I *did* sit by the dance floor." I lean back on my lounge chair and look up at the stars. I breathe out a heavy sigh thinking about the implications of what I did and what happened after that. "I made it happen – sat by the dance floor, which changed things. There's no doubt in my mind."

"Lucky for us, Ella."

"Gabe, as far as our old past is concerned, I only remember the vision young Ella had. But we both know you weren't part of my life then. We hadn't met. We know it's been altered - our memory includes everything we experienced, said and heard during our temporary stay in 1966, so we know we've changed our lives for the better, and it didn't all turn out perfect."

"It probably wasn't perfect, but it sure does feel perfect now and that's what counts."

"Hey, where are you going? Why'd you get up?"

"I'll be right back," he says.

While Gabe's inside I think I remember some of the things that happened while I was here and part of me was with young Ella. Yes, part of me did leave, maybe even a little at a time, because not long after I started having visions of the house next door to me and I was drawn to the window as I walked toward my house. Later I remember being in the kitchen. I could see it all. Sometimes it was me seeing it, at times it was young Ella. So hard to explain.

I saw myself holding my necklace. Part of me knew that it was me as a teenager holding it. I was totally blown away by it. I saw the cue ball stick shift in Rita's car. Poor young Ella was so confused. And the little boy statue. I had no idea I had blocked it out until young Ella mentions it after one of her visions. I felt like I had a split personality, part of me at times was the age I am now, and other times I was a teenager. No wonder I thought I was going berserk.

I hear the door open. I turn back to look at Gabe. I smile. He's got his guitar in one hand and a bottle of wine in the other. He smiles back and takes a seat on the blanket with me.

"Happy anniversary, Bella Ella."

I bite down on the corner of my lip, emotions stirring, tears welling. "Happy anniversary, Gabriel. Another song for me?"

"Yep, I hope you'll like it. It's really sweet."

I shrug a shoulder. "Try me."

He nods, his gaze remains on me as he strums the first chord and begins singing our song, *Here, There and Everywhere*. And he smiles. I smile and wipe a happy tear away from my face.

"It's such a beautiful song and holds so many memories for us. Even more now that we've taken it on tour all the way to 1966 and back."

Gabe laughs. "Yeah, we did." He places his guitar aside and moves over next to me. "It was so much fun reliving those early days. You were so sweet. You still are. I told you there's no way you could ever turn into a Rita," he laughs.

"Thank God! Because I really was sweet. And you, lover boy, were sexually frustrated."

"I definitely was. But you had your little hotness going on too, you know."

"That's true. It's amazing I was able to remain your virgin bride all the way to the altar, well, as virgin as one can possibly be after being raped." I give him a half smile.

Gabriel looks at me - my eyes, my mouth. "You were a virgin to me," he says as he takes a finger and taps my head and then my heart.

He kisses me tenderly then pulls me close. "I love you so much, Bella Ella."

I kiss him back. "I think I just might love you more."

"Ella, maybe we need a plan just in case one of us accidently wishes for something and gets whisked away."

"Good idea. How about if either one of us finds the other one missing we wish for this spot, right here right now. We can just wait for the other to show up."

"How about we wish for the same one we wished for to get us here in the first place. You know, the one where I tell you, you are so easy. We can give it a code name. How about we call it *Hot Spot.* Maybe we can train those firefly lights to zap us there anytime we say *Hot Spot.*" He laughs hard.

"You really liked that, didn't you?" I say through laughter.

He smirks. "Yeah, I did."

"I love that idea, Gabriel."

Gabe pours us some more wine, and we sit out here and gaze at the stars. And we see shooting stars too. And we count fireflies. The real ones. The ones that don't fizzle away. Had they fizzled, we probably would have simultaneously yelled out, *Hot Spot!*

39

1971 – Gabriel Marquez

While Ella gathers what she needs for our breakfast, I sit on a barstool at the counter and keep her company. I sip my coffee and watch as she places the ingredients in whatever spot that's available in this tiny space they call the kitchen. The bread, butter, and jelly are by the toaster. Onion, tomato, and fresh jalapeños are next to the cutting board, and eggs cracked and dumped into the mixing bowl are next to the stove.

"Ella," I say, refilling my cup, "you realize the twins were telling the truth, right? Well, kind of – fireflies took them away."

She pops the bread into the toaster and looks up at me and nods. "Uh-huh. I think they were zapped to Paris and back a year later."

I watch her over the rim of my cup as I take a sip. "So what would make four-year old twins wish to be in Paris? What would they know about Paris that would draw them there?"

"I think they happened to be near those magical firefly lights when they made a wish." She adds the eggs to the sautéed veggies and looks back at me. "Just like we did, but why, I don't know."

"You got me."

"Hey, I think I know *exactly* why." Her eyes go wide. "I know what they wished for, Gabe!" Hold on a minute, I need to cook this up and get it off the flame, or I'm gonna overcook them."

Dang, she's always keeping me hanging! I watch as she moves the eggs around till they're ready and places them on plates. She sets the spatula down and looks back up at me.

I raise my eyebrows at her. "Well?"

"This has got to be it, I'm almost sure of it."

"What? Tell me, already!"

"They wanted to go to Paris and claim one of Genevieve's pups. You know, from the story their mom said she read to them over and over again?"

"What's it about? Any clues in the story?"

"Well, according to Tina they'd been asking for a puppy, but their mom kept telling them there weren't any available. In the story, Madeline falls in the River Seine and is rescued by a dog. They can't find the dog's owner, so she gets to keep it, but Cucuface, the landlord, hates dogs and has someone take it away. Well, Genevieve, that's what they named the dog, returns and ends up having a litter of puppies."

"So you think they wished to go to Paris for a puppy?"

"That's gotta be it! Remember, the twin's mom was allergic to dogs, but rather than explain the illness she kept telling them the pet store hadn't gotten any new puppies."

Ella places the toast on our plates and comes around to sit on a barstool beside me.

"Hey, we're planning a trip to Paris, maybe we can take a free ride." I smile.

"Gabriel, you're not seriously thinking we could zap ourselves to Paris, are you?" She narrows her eyes at me. Then she gasps. "Oh my gosh, you *are* serious!" She picks up her fork and takes a bite of her eggs shaking her head.

"Hey, it's a thought. Maybe we can play around with the idea," I say, scooping some of my egg and veggies onto a slice of toast. "Or maybe zap ourselves back to your mom's sofa. You know, new times – new rules."

She puts down her fork and gives me an exasperated sigh. "How about to see my dad again?"

"Sorry, I hate it when I'm selfish."

"I swear, Gabe, I think you've regressed. You've pumped yourself up with raging teenage hormones."

I wiggle my eyebrow at her then take a bite of my toast taco.

"Alright, maybe we could go back to mom's sofa...once," she says with a sly smile.

"Pinky promise?"

She holds out her pinky. "Yes, pinky promise."

"You know, you'd think there would've been something on the news about four-year-old little girls who spoke English roaming the streets of Paris," I say.

"Except they spoke with a British accent, and they certainly could pass for little British kids. They probably assumed they were from England so why broadcast it in America. Besides, the book was written in the 1950's so maybe they were transported way back in time to that period. The twins weren't born then so there'd be no parents to claim them."

I pour more coffee into Ella's cup. "Here's a weird thought. You know the news clips they always showed at The Majestic back in the old days? If the twins were zapped last year back to 1950 would they have appeared in one of those black and white clips way back then? We could've been sitting in the audience as young kids watching them talk about lost four-year-old twins in Paris that we end up finding here at the cabin yesterday."

"That's one of those time travel conundrums. You could short-circuit your brain thinking about it," she laughs.

"No kidding, it's already starting to hurt."

"Question for you, Gabe. Are we going to mention our fake firefly theory to anyone?"

"Absolutely not. They'd laugh us out of town. If the twins were still missing, then *maybe* we'd risk being hauled off to the funny farm. But that's not the case. The kids are home safe, so not a word. You know, one thing I'm curious about is when you were zapped to 1966 why weren't you missing like the twins were. When we were zapped back to our kissing spot, I didn't say, *Ella, where the hell have you been?* That tells me life was still going on with you here. Is that too weird to wrap your head around?"

Ella laughs. "That's so funny. Speculating here, but I think *time* exists continuously. It never ceases to exist. When I zapped back to 1966, it may be more of a mind thing, not a body thing since I'm already there. At a different age but still there. And when I was wishing I was thinking of me as a young Ella, not Ella Marquez lurking around. I think a part of me took up space in young Ella. Part of who I'd become, who I was in 1971 melded into her. She sensed a few of my thoughts and my visions, and I sensed some of hers."

She shakes her fork at me. "Another thing, since the twins didn't exist at that time in Paris, they were zapped completely, and so they were missing. And even if they'd zapped themselves in present time to Paris, they don't exist there, so they had to physically go there. That's what I think."

"And why would they appear now at the cabin when we're here and not show up at a time when their parents were here. Or wherever their parents are now?"

Ella looks pensive, as she takes a sip of her coffee. "Uh, first of all, the firefly lights aren't always around. They might've wished to go home to their parents many times when those lights weren't nearby. Maybe they were talking about their toys, and they both wished they could have their favorite dolls at the same time firefly lights were nearby."

"That's a possibility. The good thing is they don't live at the lake house anymore so no chance of being zapped away again," I say.

Ella drinks up the rest of her coffee and begins cleaning up. "Babe, here's something else. And yes, it's crazy. The flickering fireflies stuck around after they brought me to my backyard in 1966. Remember how I said I'd seen them flicker around a couple of times, but I didn't pay attention to them. Totally disregarded them. But now I'm thinking if I'd had a great desire to be somewhere when those little suckers were near, they would've multiplied and brought the shimmering lights, and I'd be who knows where."

"Wow. There's suddenly a whole new meaning to the saying *be careful what you wish for*," I laugh.

Ella's eyes suddenly widen. "Hey, I wonder if we can catch some of those lights in a mason jar. You know, use them for later. Maybe even take some home with us?" She laughs. "I'm kidding, Gabe, don't look at me like that."

She said *I'm kidding,* but there's a pensive look on her face, she's clearly lost in that thought. And I've gotta say, she's got me thinking too.

Ella takes a blanket out of one of the chests and says she's going outside to do some yoga stretches. I decide to join her. Not to stretch – I'm gonna sit there and relax, watch the fish jump and watch Ella.

She goes through those yoga stretches so easily. I can't believe how flexible she is. While she holds a stretch, she looks at me and smiles. I smile back and think about how much I loved her back in 1966 and how much more I love her now.

I take in a deep breath and as I do, I close my eyes, and I swear I can still hear the echo of her sweet moans which I heard while we made love. It was the most amazing thing.

The phone's ringing when we walk inside. Tom's booming voice is on the other end of the line. He says the Carlton's are visiting them and would like to drive by and pick up the girls' toys and stuff left behind. I tell him they're welcome to come by and he said they'd be here in a bit.

When we hear a car coming up the road, Ella and I walk up to meet the Carlton's. Tom and Tina's truck comes right behind them.

The girls ask if they can go play in the shed while we talk. We all look at each other. Ella speaks up. "Why don't we all sit out on the picnic table and talk while the girls play, then we can all go inside and bring the girls in with us to gather up their books and stuff."

Everyone agrees that would be best. The girls take off into the shed to play, and we sit and talk about what it's like having the girls back after being gone a whole year. I make it a point to keep my ears open. If I hear the twins counting, I'm getting them out of there. I'm sure Ella's thinking the same thing.

"We still aren't any closer to knowing what actually happened," Martha says. "No clues were found when it first happened. And the girls haven't been much help in telling us how they got to Paris."

Ella and I look at each other tight lipped.

"We've taken them to three different child psychologists," Frank says, shaking his head. They all agreed on one thing. The girls believe they were in Paris, and they were taken there and brought back by fireflies."

"We even humored them and asked them how it felt to fly away with fireflies. And they said they didn't fly, they were swooshed away when the fireflies got all sparkly," Martha says, sounding a bit exasperated.

Elizabeth comes out of the shed smiling, Amelia right behind her. "We caught two fireflies," Elizabeth says.

"Where?" Ella asks a little too abruptly.

Amelia points to the shed, "In there, inside a jar, but you can't see them right now."

"We caught them, but their lights didn't stay on too long. They get invisible when their lights go out," Elizabeth says.

I look at Ella who's already standing up. "Why don't we all go inside? We can start gathering up the books and toys." Then Ella turns to me. "Gabe, why don't you get a box and gather *everything* from the shed."

I quickly get up and tell everyone to go on inside, that I can handle the stuff in the shed by myself. "It's not that much stuff," I say. I hurry to the shed glad no one is following me. I grab the box of toys I'd set aside and go to the kids play area. I see it. It's a mason jar. I look around and find another mason jar sitting on a shelf, put that one in the box and place the girls' jar on the top shelf. They'll think the fireflies are still invisible and will light up later. *Sorry, girls, it's for your own good.*

I gather the rest of the toys and carry the box into the house and place them on the counter. "All done," I say, looking at Ella.

The men have taken care of getting the stuff out of the chests , and the girls' chairs to the car and . We place the books in boxes that Larry brought from his truck and load them into the Carlton's trunk.

We say good-bye to everyone as they leave. We wish the Carlton's the best and say we hope the girls can get past all that they've experienced. I'm thrilled to hear Mrs. Carlton say that maybe it's best to just put it all in the past and not pressure the girls anymore to recall what happened, let them go on with the rest of their lives.

We watch both families drive away then head back to the house.

"So, Marquez, how'd you handle the firefly problem?"

"Switched jars. Gave them an empty jar. Their jar is on a shelf in the shed. Couldn't tell if there's anything there, the lights weren't lit. You want to check it out?"

Ella nods and pulls me toward the shed. We step inside and I point to it. "Holy moly, they're lit!" she says obviously excited. There's two of them. Let's name them!

"Ella, baby, just think of the possibilities."

40

1971 – Gabriel Marquez

I come in from picking up the newspaper Larry left there for us this morning. I drop it on the coffee table and get started making our morning coffee. Ella walks in towel-drying her hair wearing matching yellow top and shorts.

"How about some refrigerator biscuits for breakfast. I know you said you wanted to leave early, but they'll bake up really quick."

"Sure," I say and plug in the coffee. Ella gets started with the biscuits while I go take my shower. When I step out of the shower, I find a cup of coffee Ella's placed on the vanity for me. She's so sweet. I smile thinking about how after all she's been through Ella is in such a happy place. She's always done a pretty good job of keeping herself and everyone around her uplifted, but back in time, we both went through some tough spots. That's all behind us, so it's smooth sailing from here on.

A few minutes later she pokes her head in and says the biscuits are done. I throw on a T-shirt and some shorts.

"Those biscuits sure do smell good. Thanks for the coffee, babe."

"You're welcome. We can have breakfast on the sofa."

I set the newspaper aside, and she places the tray with biscuits, butter and jelly, and a couple of plates with sliced peaches on the coffee table and joins me for breakfast. While we eat we talk about maybe taking a different route home, so we can see what else is out here in this area.

"You'll have to stay awake this time, so you don't miss anything," I say.

"I'm well rested, so no problem. But I'll miss out on your sweet wakeup call. Gee, decisions, decisions." She smiles mischievously at me and laughs. "Hey, we need the checklist your mom and dad worked up for us to use to close down the place before leaving."

"Yep, I placed it on the counter."

When I finish off my fourth biscuit, I grab the newspaper. There's an article with a photograph and I can't believe my eyes. It's about Mr. Sebastian Prada and his sizeable donation of works of art and artifacts to Texas museums. The article is long – I don't read it. Instead, I stare at the picture alongside it. It's Mr. Prada on his sail boat, *The Que Sera, Sera*, docked somewhere along the coast of Greece.

"Ella, you gotta see this."

She leans in to look. "Is that my old neighbor?"

"Think so. Look here, it says he's lived in Brownsville from 1945 to 1970. Ella, this is very interesting. The man who lived next door to you is shown sailing on a boat named after a song so dear to you and your mom, *Que Sera, Sera.*"

"It's gotta be a coincidence. That song was very popular and a well-known favorite. Neither, Mom or Dad mentioned knowing the guy. All we knew about him was we wanted to hang him for raping me, well until we found out it wasn't him. Poor Mr. Prada. Well if it is him, I'm happy things turned out well for him after what he was put through."

She looks back at the photo for a moment. Hmm, there *is* that note Mom received from someone named S. Prada. She could've met him after I left town. Mom didn't volunteer anything though, that was strange. Maybe she's worried how I'd feel. You know, about her replacing Dad."

"How would you feel?"

"I'd be thrilled. Mom needs someone in her life to love her, I mean *really* love her. They didn't have a marriage that I would've ever wanted. I would love to see Mom with someone who can sweep her off her feet. A soulmate." She smiles at me. "Like you are to me, Gabriel."

I fold the newspaper in half and point at the article. "Look here, it says Prada's the son of Maria Estella Garcia Prada and Guillermo Prada. Do you know either of these people? It says the picture was taken five years ago."

"Nope, I don't think I do. But wait, Nana's name was Estella Garcia and, her son bought me a silk scarf for my birthday. But not five years ago, it's the one I just got. Mom said he sent it from Greece. I remember he was always travelling and I recall Nana saying Greece was his favorite place to visit. But his name was Mr. Garcia, not Mr. Prada."

"Ella, the one you *just* got was in 1966."

"Yeah, that one. Oh, right. That *was* five years ago," she laughs. "He *was* in Greece five years ago just like this guy."

"Here's another picture of him and his sister, Claudia Hernandez. It's a closeup. See if you recognize—"

"Claudia Hernandez? Gabe, that's my benefactor's assistant's name. Let me see that picture," she takes the newspaper from me and looks at it up close. "That's her! That's the lady who brought the paperwork for me to sign." And then she looks at Mr. Prada's picture again, then at me. "Gabe, this man they're calling Sebastian Prada is the man I knew as Mr. Garcia. Nana and Mom would call him Sebi, but he was always Mr. Garcia to me. Oh, gosh, I can't believe I'm seeing him after all these years!"

"Are you sure?"

"Absolutely! He's older, but his fine, handsome features are still there. That's him alright," she says looking at me, nodding her head. Her eyes get misty. "And Claudia Hernandez is his sister. I guess we know who my benefactor is. But why is he being so secretive? It's not like he did anything wrong. Jimmy Martin was the one who raped me. There was no doubt about that. So much evidence pointed to him. I don't get that at all."

Ella gets up and takes the tray from the coffee table and heads toward the kitchen. She stops, spins around and looks at me. I can tell her head is spinning. She walks back, set's the tray back on the coffee table and the tears begin to flow. "Why couldn't Mom tell me Mr. Garcia lived next door to us? She knew I'd missed him so much. And Nana, why couldn't I go see her."

"Maybe he hadn't moved there yet," I say.

"Oh, you're right. That's gotta be it. Maybe he moved there just before I was—"

She turns to look at me. "Oh my God. Gabriel, Mom fell apart when she was told the watch belonged to Mr. Prada. How awful that must've been for her knowing he was Nana's son. No wonder she couldn't tell me what was wrong. She didn't tell Aunt Tilly either." Ella turns and looks at me. "I wonder if she told Dad." I shrug my shoulder at her, and she releases a long breath. "How quickly things change. "I need to call Mom."

Somehow Ella's missing the fact that her mom thought the man that Ella saw as a father figure had raped her. It would've been devastating for Ella to have thought that too. It could've broken my poor baby. Thank God that's all been cleared up.

When we get up. I hold Ella for a while then she walks over to the phone where she stands and stares at it for a moment. She dials the number then takes the phone with her to the sofa, sits there and waits. "Please answer, please answer, Mom." She gets up and puts the phone back.

"You can try again before we leave," I tell her.

She nods. "Let me get the breakfast dishes and get us packed. You can run through the checklist. Let me know if there's something I need to do."

It doesn't take us long to get packed and load the car. I take Ella's hand. "I know you're disappointed with the new questions that came up this morning."

"Yeah, I am. We've had an unbelievable first anniversary. I don't want to take away from that. I've got plenty of Prada questions, one that's almost as crazy as us zipping through time. But that's okay. We'll deal with it just like we have everything else," she says with a smile. "Thanks for all of it, it was one fantastic anniversary week."

As I lock the door to the cabin, Ella looks around smiling. "I love this place. I can't wait to come back."

"Yeah, me too. See ya later *lucioles*."

She laughs. "Come on, babe, let's go home."

Ella's not as talkative as usual on the way home, but I kind of expected it. Finding out Mr. Prada is Mr. Garcia really was a shock for her. And it's killing me because I think the rollercoaster ride Ella's been on is about to make one last wild loop. She's seen and read everything I have and has probably made the same observations, but I'm going to have to let her do this on her own, but I'll be here for her.

She undoes her seatbelt, turns around in her seat and leans over the backseat and pulls out the newspaper clipping about Mr. Prada. She looks at me, gives me a half smile. "I just need to think about this some more," she says.

She opens the article, looks closely at the close-up picture of Prada and his sister. Then she reads the whole thing again, some of it out loud. She folds the paper, so she's got the close-up photo of the two in front of her. She looks at it for the longest time, then I see her wipe a tear from her eye. I reach over and touch the top of her thigh, rubbing it softly with my fingers.

"Are you okay?"

"No," she says with a sniffle. "I've missed Mr. Garcia so much. I used to imagine him surprising me one day. I'd imagine him coming to our house, other times it would be us running into him at the park, or at a restaurant. You know, him just showing up. I'd picture the whole thing in my mind. But it never happened. And nothing could fill the void, not even my own dad. And then I guess I got used to him not being around."

Ella drops her head into her hands and cries, her body shaking with each sob. I see an old abandoned fruit stand a couple yards up. I stop there. I undo my seatbelt and move over close to her and hold her until she seems calmed.

"I look like him...Mr. Prada. I can see it in this picture. People used to say I looked like Nana too."

I take a deep breath. "Yes, baby, I noticed a resemblance. I see your eyes, your chin, even your long dark eyelashes." Her eyes pool with tears when she looks at the picture again. She sets it aside and turns to wrap her arms around me.

Do you want to know what the saddest part's been for me? I loved him so much. He treated me like a daughter. He seemed to really care about me. And then as easily as he came into my life, he was gone. Of course, I loved my dad more. It felt so good seeing him for the past few weeks, but I didn't know it was temporary at the time. Dad kissed and hugged me before he left for work. If I would've know it was the last time I was going to see him, I wouldn't have let go." She begins to cry again. "Oh, Gabriel, I want to go back and see my daddy."

She takes tissues out of her bag wipes her eyes and blows her nose. "Suddenly so much makes sense. I noticed so many things while I was just there, maybe because I was looking at it through my eyes and not just through young Ella's. I saw Mom's sadness – I finally understand it.

Mom has suffered so long with her secret. I knew deep down there was no love between my parents. I compared how they were together with that of my friends' parents. I knew something was missing, but I always hoped I was wrong. And I knew Dad saw other women. I heard their arguments when they thought I was asleep. My poor Mom."

The rest of the drive home is quiet. We listen to music, and I let Ella sit there and think, something she needs to do.

41

1971 – Ella Marquez

"Home sweet home," Gabe says as he opens the door for me. The first thing he notices when we walk in is the picture of us with the Golden Gate Bridge in the background. He drops our bags and takes the picture off the shelf. "I love this picture of us on the bay. I hadn't noticed it before."

I laugh. "I know. I put it there about a week before our anniversary. Wanted a memory from our honeymoon. It's one of my favorites. Too bad we didn't take one of us during our anniversary trip to set alongside of it. Wait, we *did* take a picture on our anniversary, sort of."

I go to our bedroom and return with a photo album and place it on the counter. I flip a few pages till I find what I'm looking for. "Look, Mom took this picture of us before we left on our date to Gio's." It was while we were celebrating our first anniversary – sort of." I run a finger across the surface of it. "This is too weird."

"Yeah, I guess you could kinda say that – weird. You should get a frame for it and place it next to our honeymoon one."

Once we put our stuff away and grab some cold drinks and chips, we sit on the sofa side by side. I look at Gabe. "I'm nervous about talking to Mom. I've had a chance to work things out in my head, and I understand her reasons. But for her to have to explain things to me, especially since she doesn't know how I'll feel, it's gonna be hard."

We sit there enjoy our cold drinks and potato chips. To liven the mood, I'm sure, Gabe brings up the new time travel shortcut code we made up. *Hot Spot.* And, of course, it made me laugh.

"That is the funniest idea. I love it! But can you imagine us when we've been married ten, maybe twenty years? We decide it's a lot easier to zap ourselves to *Hot Spot* than to go through all that stuff like me putting on a little strappy top for you to slip off my shoulders and setting the mood for a little romance. You know, that kind of stuff. Instead we forego the regular day-to-day sex and just get the fires burning *pronto* via firefly lights."

Gabe laughs hard. "That's hilarious, baby. You know we could probably make a whole lot of money with these lights! I guess we could always give our honeymoon a code name and zap ourselves there," he laughs again.

"We are so bad, Gabriel."

"So good, Ella, we're so good." He leans over and kisses me. "It's good to be home. I'm happy right here with you."

"Yeah, me too. But you know what? I want to get my phone call out of the way. I need to have it behind me and get on with the rest of our lives. Gonna call her now."

When I hear Mom's voice on the phone, it's suddenly harder than I thought it would be for me.

"Hi, mijita, I was just thinking about you, in fact, I knew you'd be arriving home today, so I was going to call you."

"Yes, we're back. We had a wonderful time. The cabin and lake house were more than we ever dreamed of." I'm amazed at how calm *my* voice sounds, but Mom's is a little shaky.

"I'm so happy to hear that and glad you made it home safely."

She clears her throat, and I hear her take a deep breath.

"Honey, I'd like you and Gabriel to come for dinner tomorrow."

"Um...that would be very nice, thanks. It'll be great to spend time with you. You can tell me how your lunch with your out-of-town friend went." *I guess our talk can wait till dinner.*

She clears her throat again. "Yes, it was wonderful, Ella. I wanted to tell you the friend I went to lunch with was Nana's son. I know how much he means to you. I was hoping he could come to dinner tomorrow night also.

"Oh, Mommy, I would love to see Mr. Garcia. I've missed him so much."

"Mijita," she says, and I can tell she's crying now. "He loves you and misses you too. It's just that, well, we'll talk when you get here."

"Mommy, I already know, I already know what you probably want to tell me."

"You know? Honey, what are you saying?"

"Well, first of all, I want to say that I love you both so much, and I'm happy that he's going to be in my life again. You have no idea how much he means to me."

I tell Mom the whole story. That, I saw the article about Mr. Sebastian Prada, saw the picture of him and his boat, *The Que Sera, Sera.* And how I know that Claudia is my benefactor's assistant and that I'm certain that Mr. Prada is my benefactor.

When I tell her that I loved Mr. Garcia like a father, and I've missed him so much, I break down. I can't hold my tears back any longer. Gabe holds me and rubs my back which helps me continue. I'm finally able to tell her that I think that Mr. Prada is my real father.

"Oh, my baby," she says, her voice choking. I can hear her struggling, taking short little breaths.

"Mommy, I didn't mean to make you cry."

"It's not your fault, all of it is mine," she says. "He missed you so much too. We didn't mean to hurt you," she says through sobs.

"I know, Mom, I understand." Gabe hands me a tissue, and I wipe my tears and blow my nose. "But, he is my father, right?"

Mom takes a deep breath. "Yes. Yes, he is." She pauses, and I wait. "I pray you'll understand why we couldn't tell you. Out of respect for your father, we never said anything. He never knew about Sebi. Sebi and I didn't continue our relationship, but we kept in touch because of you. He bought the house next to ours, so he could watch you grow from a distance. He wanted so much to be near you. Ella, we never meant to hurt your father. Things just weren't—"

"Mom, I understand. I know Daddy was unfaithful. I figured it out when I got older. I understand why you turned to Mr. Prada. I'm not saying that it was right, but as an adult, with a loving husband of my own, I understand completely, and now so much of the advice you gave me about relationships and finding true love makes so much sense."

"What happened caused both your father, I mean, Sebi and me shame. The reason we discontinued our personal relationship was we knew I would never leave your father. We were married in the Catholic Church, and I couldn't break those vows. I asked him to please not wait for me. So he married someone else, and we didn't get back together until recently. Both of our spouses have passed away, and our feelings for each other never changed, and we both love you so much."

"Is he there with you now?"

"Yes, honey, he is."

I break down crying. Crying because I'm missing the absence of my dad once again after spending time with him these past several weeks and now there's tears of joy because I'm going to see Mr. Garcia, the man whom I've always loved like a father and have missed for too long.

"Oh, my little girl, we didn't mean to cause you so much pain."

"No, Mom, right now it's joy. I'm happy for you, and I'm happy I'll be seeing Mr. Garcia soon.

"He'll be here when you come for dinner, if you wish to see him."

I breathe a heavy sigh. "Tell Mr. Garcia, I mean Mr. Prada that I'm looking forward to seeing him again."

"My sweet Ella. You have no idea how long we've been waiting for this day. It's one I've dreamed about often as you were growing up."

"Mom, I love you so much, and I'm really happy for you. I'll see you soon."

When I hang up, Gabe turns me toward him and holds me. "My sweet Bella Ella. You've gone through so much. Are you okay?"

"Yes, more than okay. I love how God can take something so painful and turn it into something beautiful. Yesterday I was hurting knowing I don't have my dad around anymore. I'm thankful I was able to see him again, but I knew it was over and he was gone once more." But Gabe, even having just been back at home with my parents, I don't feel like I spent much time with Dad. He was hardly ever around. I needed him in my life, so did Mom."

"Yes, I remember she was usually with your Aunt Tilly."

"I realize there really was a void in Mom's life. I was all she really had. Well, Aunt Tilly and me. And all I did was hang out in my room, go out with my friends. So now I'm so thankful she has Mr. Prada."

"Yes, and now you have your Mr. Garcia back in your life," Gabe says, stroking the length of my back with his hand.

"Yeah, I do. Talk about God and his perfect timing. It's like God's given me something to ease the pain after feeling the loss of Dad once more. Mr. Garcia, whose memory I've held close to my heart, appears in my life again. And turns out to be my real father."

"Baby, it's got to be hard for you."

"Yes, I'm feeling some conflict. I love my dad so much, Gabe, he'll always be Daddy to me. But it's not like someone out of the blue is going to fill the void. It's someone I've loved for so long. He treated me like his own little girl, his *princesa*, as he used to say. And it turns out, I am." I rub my hands across my face, wipe away the tears.

42

1971 – Gabriel Marquez

Ella is quiet on the way to her mom's. We listen to music and talk, but I can tell she's taking the time to prepare herself for what will be a very emotional reunion. When we pull up to a parking spot in front of her mom's apartment, Ella looks at me.

"You're going to be just fine, baby," I say. "You're about to have dinner with three people who love you very much."

She smiles, nods, and then takes a deep breath. "I know."

Ella never knocks before entering her mom's home, but she does tonight.

"I'm nervous, Gabriel."

I go to put my arm around her when the door opens.

"Ella! Gabriel! So glad you're here."

"Hello, Mama Mary, nice to see you, you're looking as beautiful as ever," I say.

She waves us in with her hand. We hug and kiss just inside the door. Ella holds on tight to her mom, longer than usual. Neither is wanting to let go. Ella pulls away, looks at her mom and smiles.

"Mom, I am in awe of you. You are the strongest woman I know."

"I'm sorry for keeping so much from you," she says, brushing Ella's hair from her face with her fingers and kissing her cheek.

A gentleman steps forward, and Ella turns in his direction. He smiles at her. I can see just how much Ella favors Mr. Prada.

"Mr. Gar...Mr. Prada. I'm...I'm so glad—" She goes to him and hugs him tightly and begins to cry. "I've missed you so much."

"I've missed you too, *mi princesa*," he says, his voice trembling when he says *princesa.*

Wow, the emotions in this room. I'm getting the sniffles myself.

Ella looks up at him. "That's what you used to call me, *princesa*. No one's ever called me that, only you. And it was what made it so special."

"You *were* special. How I wanted to tell you just how special you were. That you were my little girl. There were times when I thought I would just blurt it out, but I knew it would be a selfish thing to do. So I kept it to myself. But look at you now, Ella. All grown up and so beautiful."

Ella wipes tears away. "Thank you."

"Come on let's sit down," Mama Mary says taking Ella by the hand to the sofa while Mr. Prada and I introduce ourselves.

Ella sits next to her mom; they sit there holding hands. Mr. Prada and I sit in two upholstered arm chairs facing them. Ella reaches for tissues from the coffee table and hands some to her mom.

"Mom, you always seemed so sad, I know you tried to hide it, but I'd see it. I always wondered why. And now I know."

"You're right, I often was. Mostly because I longed to tell you about Sebastian, but I just couldn't. I knew you wouldn't understand, you were too young, and it would hurt you and your father. He loved you, and it would have broken his heart."

"So why did Mr. Prada stop coming to see me?" Ella asks, turning to look at Mr. Prada.

"Ella," Mr. Prada says after taking a deep breath. "When you reached the age of ten, your mother and I agreed it would be risky for us to continue trying to keep a semblance of our own little family. We were afraid you might notice something, a nuance, overhear a conversation, and begin to ask questions. You were a very curious little girl. I loved that about you." He removes his glasses and his hand goes up to his face, and he wipes his eyes.

"Walking away was the hardest thing for me to do," he continues. "I went along with the plan, but I told your mother I could not give you up entirely. That's when I bought the house next door to yours. It wasn't even for sale. I had to offer the family a hefty sum to acquire it. I told them it had sentimental value," he laughs. "And that was true. So I was able to watch you grow into a beautiful young lady. When I'd return to Brownsville after being away, it's *that* house I'd go straight to from the airport. I couldn't wait to see you again. And how I loved it when I'd see you wearing any of the gifts I'd sent you. We'd say they were from Nana, but they really were from me. A lot of thought went into each one."

Ella's face lights up. "From you? You'd actually picked them out yourself?"

He smiles. "Yes, *princesa*, I would. My favorite gift I sent you was a pink cashmere sweater set. You wore it often, so I knew you liked it."

"One of my favorites, it was so soft, the softest sweater I'd ever touched. I was wearing it the first time I saw Gabriel at school."

I'm smiling when Ella turns to look at me.

"And you saw me wearing it from the window that faced my room?"

Ella pauses. Her eyes go wide as the realization sinks in. "Oh, Mom, I see it now! When you were told the watch, the rapist left behind belonged to Mr. Prada, you—oh no! Mom, you thought my father—"

Ella throws her arms around her mom, realizing the pain she must've endured thinking that Ella was raped by her own father. It was incomprehensible. They hold each other there until their sobs quiet.

Mama Mary wipes her eyes with a tissue. "Once I got over the initial shock, I knew it wasn't possible, Ella, I knew there had to be an explanation. Sebi and I met to talk, and he told me he would never do anything to hurt you. I knew the man he was, so I believed him without a doubt," she says, looking at Mr. Prada as he wipes a tear away from under his glasses with a handkerchief.

Ella reaches for a tissue and wipes her nose, says nothing for a moment. Turns to Mr. Prada.

"I love you like a father, I always have. You always treated me like I was your very own. And you always made me feel so special, so loved."

He smiles, looks at Ella's mom who gives him a nod. He stands, reaching into his pocket and pulls out a small box.

"*Princesa*, I had this made especially for you while on one of my trips. I thought someday I might be able to give it to you. It's a day I have been anticipating for so long. Today is that day."

He walks over and hands the box to Ella. She says thank you and opens it. She lifts out a gold necklace with a locket. "Oh my. The filigree design on this is so exquisite."

She opens the locket, takes a quick breath and looks up at Mr. Prada and then her mom. She turns and shows it to me, tears streaming down her cheeks. The locket has two framed photographs. On the left is her dad, Tomas Galvez, and on the right, is her father, Sebastian Prada. The top of the locket has a beautiful swirly design which I guess is what Ella called filigree. I hand it back to her.

"It's beautiful, I...I love it," she says through tears. "Thank you so much."

"I never expected you would want to wear it, but I did have hopes you would accept it and keep it somewhere special."

Ella stands, kisses him on the cheek. "Would you put it around my neck for me, please?"

He smiles. "I would..." He chokes on his words. "...be honored," he says, his eyes filling up with tears. They hug, it takes Ella a while to let go.

She turns and shows it to me as it hangs around her neck, just below the *Here, There and Everywhere* medallion. She smiles looking down at them.

We sit and talk for a long while. Ella thanks Mr. Prada for his donation to her dance studio and tells him how excited she is to be able to offer the children the gift of dance. She also tells him how much she loved the letter that Mrs. Hernandez shared with her.

"I guess now I know that you were probably thinking of how shy I was and that it was the reason I was enrolled in dance classes."

"Ella," her mom says, "Sebi and I agreed that you should take dance classes. He made it financially possible for you to attend. His family owned the fabric store where I purchased the fabric for my business. They gave me a sizable discount so that my profits would allow me to pay for your classes. In return, I sewed for Claudia and his other sister, Irene.

"So Mrs. Hernandez is my aunt. She was so sweet."

"Yes, and she fell in love with you, Ella. She said she didn't realize how difficult it was going to be for her to see you and not say anything. She said she wanted so much to hug you, but she knew she couldn't."

"I remember how she was especially warm to me when we said goodbye. I noticed it in her handshake. And then I thought she was a little misty-eyed. I figured she'd just been touched by your generosity."

"I spoke to your aunt this morning to tell her of our upcoming reunion. She said she's looking forward to seeing you again soon."

"I'm looking forward to seeing her again too," Ella says and dabs her eyes with a tissue.

"You know Sebi's other sister, Irene. She ran the fabric shop in Brownsville where I bought my fabrics."

"Yes, I know Irene. I always thought she was so beautiful."

"You favor her, Ella. When she was your age, she looked a lot like you."

Ella learned that she also had cousins her age who live in Brownsville. It was so much for Ella to take in, but she was happy to hear that her family had grown and was looking forward to meeting everyone. Mr. Prada made it a point to mention that he approved of me as a prospective husband right from the beginning. He said Ella's mom kept him up to date on everything Ella was going through, all her growing up experiences.

It's quite an evening for Ella. She's glowing, and so is Mama Mary. Every now and then there are tears, but they all end in smiles.

To my surprise, dinner was my favorite dish – cheese enchiladas. Mama Mary said she made them especially for me. Said she's never stopped thanking God for sending me to Ella at the most perfect time, making Ella a very happy girl. She knew Ella needed someone like me in her life. I let her know that it was I who needed someone like Ella in mine. And I'm glad both Ella and her mom have Mr. Prada in theirs.

I like Mr. Prada. He's a gentleman, proper, and appears to be very well educated. He's very articulate and speaks with a Spanish accent; his voice is deep and crisp. I think I'll enjoy getting to know him. I must admit, I've never seen Mama Mary looking so happy and so beautiful. It's obvious to me, and I'm sure to Ella that her mom and Mr. Prada are very much in love. I can see the admiration Mr. Prada has for Ella's mom. There's a genuine smile on Mama Mary's face. And I thought I'd seen Ella at her happiest at the cabin earlier this week. I was wrong. *This* is Bella Ella's happiest face yet.

EPILOGUE

1971 – Gabriel Marquez

Ella and I have experienced something most people wouldn't believe was even possible. We still have trouble believing it. But we know it happened, and we don't need proof. But it turns out we have it anyway.

The jeweler who repaired Ella's necklace did the best he could to restore the original clasp. He took a necklace which was only a week old and left a slight mar on it. It's an imperfection as precious to us, as the necklace itself. It's a reminder of its history. It was purchased in 1971 and repaired in 1966.

It's only been a month since we were at the lake house, but here we are back again for a weekend retreat. The time we spent here brought us more happiness than we've ever dreamed of. We knew we would be returning; we just didn't expect it would be so soon.

Before leaving for the cabin, we got a call from our pal, Anthony. He got an offer for a new position as a photo journalist in California and said we should visit them there as soon as they're settled.

I pull Ella away from the sink but first, I give her some of those sweet little kisses she loves on the side of her neck.

"Come on, come sit outside with me for a while."

As we walk toward the swing, I notice some firefly lights. Imagine that, fireflies in bright sunlight. I give Ella a questioning look.

"Yes, I see them. Are you up for a *practice* adventure?" she asks.

"Hell, yeah. How about Dallas, November 22, 1963?"

"I know Kennedy's your favorite, but we can't go changing history."

"Ah, come on. I just want to know if there really was someone on the grassy knoll, that's all. But yeah," I nod, "we'd probably somehow mess something up."

"Hey, how about London? We can zap ourselves to Abbey Road back to August 8, 1969!" she says, a huge smile on her face.

"Let me guess...you want to be on the cover of the Beatles' *Abby Road* album."

"You got it. I'll just shove the old guy out of the way and stand in his place." She smiles at me broadly.

I give her a wink. "I think you'd look really cute."

She laughs. "And I know just what I can wear." And then she slumps her shoulders, and I hear her sigh.

"What's the matter?"

"Can't do it. Mom and Sebi are getting married next weekend. We never know what might go wrong, wouldn't want to miss that, would we?"

We decide not to sit on the swing, grab lawn chairs instead. Maybe next time.

One thing Ella and I have taken from having been able to visit some of our most precious moments is that time is such a special thing and it passes by so quickly. Cherished moments are over too soon.

Sometimes before we realize just how precious they are. We should all slow down and enjoy life, live our lives to the fullest, and enjoy every special moment we are given. Once that moment's gone, it's the past, and you can't get it back.

Uh—scratch that.

ABOUT THE AUTHOR

Lali Serna Castillo, a native of Brownsville, Texas, "On the Border, By the Sea," resides in the City of Stafford, Texas, with her husband, Ed. This is her debut.